P9-DHB-691

LITTLE,
BROWN

LB

**LARGE
PRINT**

The Perfect Couple

A Novel

Elin Hilderbrand

LB

LITTLE, BROWN AND COMPANY

LARGE PRINT EDITION

Copyright © 2018 by Elin Hilderbrand

Little, Brown and Company
Hachette Book Group
1290 Avenue of the Americas, New York, NY 10104
littlebrown.com

First Edition: June 2018

Little, Brown and Company is a division of Hachette Book Group,
Inc. The Little, Brown name and logo are trademarks of
Hachette Book Group, Inc.

The Hachette Speakers Bureau provides a wide range of authors for
speaking events. To find out more, go to hachettespeakersbureau.com
or call (866) 376-6591.

ISBN 978-0-316-37526-9 (hc) / 978-0-316-52316-5 (large print) /
978-0-316-44938-0 (Canada) / 978-0-316-48571-5 (signed)
LCCN 2018930958

10 9 8 7 6 5 4 3

LSC-C

Printed in the United States of America

For Chuck and Margie Marino
There's no such thing as a perfect couple,
but you come pretty close.
Forever love xo

The Perfect Couple

Saturday, July 7, 2018, 5:53 a.m.

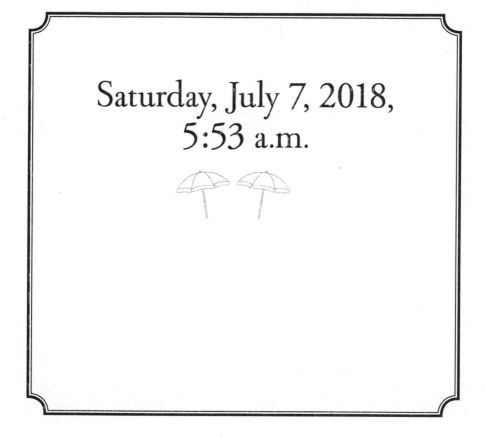

THE CHIEF

A phone call before six on a Saturday morning is never a good thing, although it's not unheard of on a holiday weekend. Too many times to count, Chief Ed Kapenash of the Nantucket Police Department has seen the Fourth of July go sideways. The most common accident is a person blowing off a finger while lighting fireworks. Sometimes things are more serious. One year, they lost a swimmer to the riptide; another year, a young woman did a backflip off the bow of a speedboat and hit the water in a way that left her paralyzed. There are generally enough drunk-and-disorderlies to fill a sightseeing bus, as well as dozens of fistfights, a handful of which are so serious that the police have to get involved.

When the call comes in, Andrea and the kids are fast asleep. Chloe and Finn are sixteen, an age the Chief escaped easily with his own children, he now realizes. Chloe and Finn—who are properly the children of Andrea's cousin Tess and Tess's husband, Greg, who died in a boating accident nine years ago—are proving to be more of a challenge. Finn has a girlfriend named Lola Budd, and their young love is turning the household upside down. Finn's twin sister, Chloe, has a summer job working for Siobhan Crispin at Island Fare, Nantucket's busiest catering company.

The Chief and Andrea have divided their concerns about the twins neatly down the middle. Andrea worries about Finn getting Lola Budd pregnant (though the Chief, awkwardly, presented Finn with a giant box of condoms and a rather stern directive: *Use these. Every single time*). The Chief worries about Chloe getting into drugs and alcohol. The Chief has seen again and again the way the food-and-beverage industry leads its unsuspecting employees into temptation. The island of Nantucket has over a hundred liquor licenses; other, similar-size towns in Massachusetts have an average of twelve. As a summertime resort, the island has a culture of celebration, frivolity, excess. It's the Chief's job to give the annual substance-abuse talk the week before the high-school prom; this year, both Finn and Chloe had been in attendance, and afterward, neither of them would so much as look at him.

He often feels he's too old for the enormous

responsibility of raising teenagers. And impressing them is most certainly beyond him.

The Chief takes his phone out onto the back deck, which looks west over protected wetlands; his conversations here are private, overheard only by the redwing blackbirds and the field mice. The house has a great view of sunsets but not, unfortunately, of the water.

The call is from Sergeant Dickson, one of the best in the department.

"Ed," he says. "We have a floater."

The Chief closes his eyes. Dickson had been the one to tell the Chief that Tess and Greg were dead. Sergeant Dickson has no problem delivering disturbing news; in fact, he seems to relish it.

"Go ahead," the Chief says.

"Caucasian female by the name of Merritt Monaco. Twenty-nine years old, from New York City, here on Nantucket for a wedding. She was found floating facedown just off the shore in front of three-three-three Monomoy Road, where the wedding is being held. The cause of death appears to be drowning. Roger Pelton called it in. You know Roger, the guy who does the expensive weddings?"

"I do," the Chief says. The Chief is in Rotary Club with Roger Pelton.

"Roger told me it's his MO to check on each wedding site first thing in the morning," Dickson says. "When he got here, he said he heard screaming. Turns out, the bride had just pulled the body out of the water. Roger tried CPR but the girl was dead, he said. He seemed to think she'd been dead for a few hours."

"That's for the ME to determine," the Chief says. "Three-three-three Monomoy Road, you said?"

"It's a compound," Dickson says. "Main house, two guest cottages, and a pool house. The name of the property is Summerland."

Summerland. The Chief has seen the sign, though he has never been to the house. That stretch of Monomoy Road is the stratospherically high-rent district. The people who live on that road generally don't have problems that require the police. The houses have sophisticated security systems, and the residents use discretion to keep any issues under wraps.

"Has everyone else been notified?" the Chief asks. "The state police? The ME?"

"Affirmative," Dickson says. "The Greek is on his way to the address now. He was here on island last night, lucky for us. But both Cash and Elsonhurst are on vacay until Monday and I'm at the end of a double, so I don't know who else you want to call in. The other guys are kind of green—"

"I'll worry about that in a minute," the Chief says. "Does the girl have family to notify?"

"I'm not sure," Dickson says. "The bride was so upset that I told the EMTs to take her to the hospital.

She needed a Xanax, and badly. She could barely breathe, much less speak."

"The paper will have to leave this alone until we notify next of kin," the Chief says. Which is one small piece of good news; the last thing the Chief wants is Jordan Randolph from the *Nantucket Standard* sniffing around his crime scene. The Chief can't believe he missed the 911 call on the scanner. Over the years he has developed an uncanny filter where the scanner is concerned; he knows, even in his sleep, what deserves his attention and what he can let pass. But now he has a dead body.

They have to assume foul play by law, although here on Nantucket, violent crime is rare. The Chief has been working on this island for nearly thirty years and in all that time, he has seen only three homicides. One per decade.

Roger Pelton called it in. The Chief has heard Roger's name recently. *Really* recently, at some point in the past couple of days. And a *compound* in Monomoy — that rings a bell too. But why?

He hears a light tap on the window, and through the glass slider, he sees Andrea in her nightshirt, holding up a cup of coffee. Chloe is moving around the kitchen behind her, dressed in her catering uniform of white shirt and black pants.

Chloe is awake already? the Chief thinks. At six

o'clock in the morning? Or did she get home so late last night that she fell asleep in her clothes?

Yes, he thinks. She worked a rehearsal dinner the night before. Then it clicks: Chloe told the Chief that the rehearsal dinner and the wedding were being held in Monomoy and that Roger was the wedding coordinator. It's the same wedding. The Chief shakes his head, even though he knows better than anyone that this is a small island.

"Was the woman you found *staying* at the compound where the wedding is taking place today?" the Chief asks.

"Affirmative," Dickson says. "She was the maid of honor, Chief. I don't think there's going to be any wedding."

Andrea, possibly recognizing the expression on the Chief's face, steps out to the deck, hands Ed his coffee, and disappears inside. Chloe has vanished. She has probably headed upstairs to shower for work, which will now be canceled. News like this travels fast; the Chief expects that Siobhan Crispin will be calling at any moment.

What else did Chloe say about that wedding? One of the families is British, the mother famous somehow—an actress? A theater actress? A playwright? Something.

The Chief takes the first sip of his coffee. "You're still on-site, correct, Dickson? Have you talked to anyone other than the bride and Roger?"

"Yeah, I talked to the groom," Dickson says. "He wanted to go with the bride to the hospital. But first he went inside one of the guest cottages to grab his wallet and his phone and he came right back out to tell me the best man is missing."

"Missing?" the Chief says. "Is it possible we have *two* people dead?"

"I checked the water, down the beach, and out a few hundred yards in both directions with my field glasses," Dickson says. "It was all clear. But at this point, I'd say anything is possible."

"Tell the Greek to wait for me, please," the Chief says. "I'm on my way."

Friday, July 6, 2018, 9:15 a.m.

GREER

Greer Garrison Winbury thrives on tradition, protocol, and decorum but on the occasion of her younger son's wedding, she is happy to toss all three out the window. It's customary for the bride's parents to host and pay for their daughter's nuptials, but if that were the case with Benji and Celeste, the wedding would be taking place in a church at the mall with a reception following at TGI Fridays.

You're a terrific snob, Greer, her husband, Tag, is fond of saying. Greer fears that this is true. But where Benji's wedding was concerned, she *had* to intervene. Look what she'd endured when Thomas married Abigail Freeman: a *Texas* wedding, with all of Mr. Freeman's oil money on grand, grotesque display. There had been three hundred people at the "welcome party" at the Salt Lick BBQ — Greer had hoped to live her whole life without ever patronizing a place called the Salt Lick BBQ — where the suggested dress code was "hill-country casual," and when Greer asked Thomas what that could possibly mean, he'd said, *Wear jeans, Mom.*

Wear *jeans* to her elder son's wedding celebration? Greer had opted for wide-legged ivory trousers and stacked Ferragamo heels. Ivory had turned out to be a poor choice, as the guests of this welcome party had all been expected to eat pork ribs with their fingers. Shrieks of joy had gone up when there had been a surprise appearance by a country singer named George Strait, whom everyone called "the King of Country." Greer still can't imagine how much it must have cost Mr. Freeman to hire the King of Country — and for an event that wasn't even part of the usual nuptial schedule.

As Greer drives the Defender 90 (Tag had it rebuilt and shipped over from England) down to the Hy-Line ferry to pick up Celeste's parents, Bruce and Karen Otis, she sings along to the radio. It's B. J. Thomas's "Hooked on a Feeling."

This weekend, Greer is *effectively* the bride's mother as well as the groom's, for she is 100 percent in charge. She hasn't encountered one iota of resistance from anyone, including Celeste herself; the girl responds to all of Greer's suggestions with the exact same text: Sounds good. (Greer despises texting, but if one wants to communicate with Millennials, one must abandon old-fashioned notions like expecting to speak on the phone.) Greer has to admit, it has been far easier to get her way with the color scheme, the invitations, the flowers, and the caterer than she ever anticipated. It's as if this were her own wedding, thirty-two years later...minus her overbearing mother and grandmother, who insisted on an afternoon reception in the sweltering garden of Swallowcroft, and minus a fiancé who insisted on a stag party the night before the wedding. Tag had gotten home at seven o'clock in the morning smelling of Bushmills and Chanel No. 9. When Greer had started weeping and demanding to know if he'd actually had the gall to sleep with another woman the *night before his wedding,* Greer's mother took her aside and told her that the most important skill required in marriage was picking one's battles.

Make sure they're ones you can win, her mother had said.

Greer has tried to remain vigilant where Tag's fidelity is concerned, although it has been exhausting with a man as charismatic as her husband. Greer has never found hard evidence of any indiscretions, but she has certainly had her suspicions. She has them right up to this very minute about a woman named Featherleigh Dale, who will be arriving on Nantucket from London in a few short hours. If Featherleigh is silly and careless enough to wear the silver-lace ring with the pink, yellow, and blue sapphires—Greer knows exactly what the ring looks like because Jessica Hicks, the jeweler, showed her a picture!—then Greer's hunch will be confirmed.

Greer encounters traffic on Union Street. She should have left more time; she *cannot* be late for the Otises. Greer has yet to meet either of Celeste's parents in person and she would like to make a good impression and not leave them to wander forlornly around Straight Wharf on this, their first trip to the island. Greer had worried about hosting a wedding so close to the Fourth of July, but it was the only weekend that worked over the course of the entire summer and they couldn't put it off until autumn because Karen, Celeste's mother, has stage 4 breast cancer. No one knows how much time she has left.

The song ends, traffic comes to a dead stop, and the sense of foreboding that Greer has successfully held at bay until now fills the car like a foul smell. Usually, Greer feels unsettled about only two things: her husband and her writing, and the writing always sorts itself out in the end (declining book sales aside, although, really, it's Greer's job to *write* the mysteries, not sell them). But now she worries about...well, if she has to pinpoint the exact locus of her dismay she would say it is Celeste. The ease with which Greer has been able to take control of this wedding suddenly seems suspect. As Greer's mother used to say, *Things that seem too good to be true usually are.*

It's as if Celeste doesn't *care* about the wedding. At all. How had Greer ignored this possibility for four months? She had reasoned that Celeste was (wisely) deferring to — or placing extreme confidence in — Greer's impeccable taste. Or that Celeste's only agenda was getting the wedding planned as expediently as possible because of her mother's illness.

But now, other factors come into focus, such as the stutter Celeste developed shortly after the date was set. The stutter began with Celeste repeating certain words or short phrases, but it has become something more serious, even debilitating — Celeste trips over her *r*'s and *m*'s and *p*'s until she grows pink in the face.

Greer asked Benji if the stutter was creating problems for Celeste at work. Celeste is the assistant director at the Bronx Zoo and she is occasionally called upon to give lectures to the zoo's visitors — mostly schoolchildren during the week and foreigners on the weekends — so Celeste has to speak slowly and clearly. Benji replied that Celeste rarely stuttered at work. Mostly just at home and when she was out socially.

This gave Greer pause. Developing a stutter at twenty-eight could be attributed to ... what? It was a *tell* of some kind. Greer had immediately used the detail in the novel she was writing: the murderer develops a stutter as a result of his guilt, which grabs the attention of Miss Dolly Hardaway, the spinster detective who is the protagonist of all twenty-one of Greer's murder mysteries. This is well and fine for Greer, who tends to mine every new encounter and experience in her fiction, but what about in real life, for Celeste? What is going on? Greer has the feeling that the stutter is somehow connected to Celeste's imminent marriage to Benji.

There's no time to think any further because suddenly traffic surges forward and not only does Greer move swiftly into town, she also finds a parking spot right in front of the ferry dock. She still has two minutes to spare. What magnificent luck! Her doubts fade. This wedding, this union of two families on the most festive of summer weekends, is clearly something that's meant to be.

KAREN

Viewed from a distance, Nantucket Island is everything Karen Otis dreamed it would be: tasteful, charming, nautical, classic. The ferry passes inside a stone jetty, and Karen squeezes Bruce's hand to let him know she would like to stand and walk the few feet to the railing now. Bruce places an arm across Karen's back and eases her up out of her seat. He's not a big man but he's strong. He was the Pennsylvania state champion wrestler at 142 pounds in 1984. Karen first set eyes on him sitting in the Easton Area High School pool balcony. She was swimming the butterfly leg for the varsity relay team, which routinely practiced during lunch, and when she climbed out of the water, she spied Bruce, dressed in sweatpants and a hooded sweatshirt, staring at an orange he held in his hands.

"What is that guy doing?" Karen had wondered aloud.

"That's Bruce Otis," Tracy, the backstroker, had said. "He's captain of the wrestling team. They have a meet this afternoon and he's trying to make weight."

Karen had wrapped a towel around her waist and marched up the stairs to introduce herself. She had been well endowed even as a high-school sophomore and was pretty sure the sight of her in her tank suit would take Bruce Otis's mind off the orange and his weight and anything else.

Bruce holds Karen steady and together they approach the railing. People see them coming, take note of the scarf wrapped around Karen's head—she can't bring herself to do wigs—and back up a few steps to make a respectful space.

Karen grips the railing with both hands. Even that is an effort but she wants a good view for their approach. The houses that line the water are all enormous, ten times the size of Karen and Bruce's ranch on Der-hammer Street in Forks Township, Pennsylvania, and these houses all have gray cedar shingles and crisp white trim. Some of the homes have curved decks; some have stacked decks at nifty angles like a Jenga game. Some have lush green lawns that roll right up to stone walls before a thin strip of beach. Every home flies the American flag, and all are impec-cably maintained; there isn't a dumpy or disheveled renegade in the bunch.

Money, Karen thinks. Where does all the money come from? She is seasoned enough to know that money can't buy happiness—and it certainly can't buy health—but it's still intriguing to contemplate just *how much money* the people who own these houses must have. First off, these are *second* homes, so one must account for the first home—a brownstone in Manhattan or a brick mansion in Georgetown, an estate on the Main Line or a horse farm in Virginia—and then factor in the price of waterfront property here on this prestigious island. Next, Karen considers all of the furnishings such houses must contain: the rugs, the sofas, the tables and chairs, the lamps, the pencil-post beds, the nine-thousand-thread-count Belgian sheets, the decorative pillows, the Jacuzzi bathtubs, the scented candles next to the Jacuzzi bathtubs. (Celeste has educated Karen beyond the world of Yankee Candle; there are apparently candles that sell for over *four hundred dollars*. Celeste's future sister-in-law, Abby, gave Celeste such a candle as an engagement present, and when Celeste told Karen that a Jo Malone pine-and-eucalyptus candle sold for $470, Karen hooted. That was nearly as much as Bruce had paid for his first car, a 1969 Chevy Nova!)

Then, of course, there's the staff to pay: landscapers, house cleaners, caretakers, nannies for the children. There are the cars — Range Rovers, Jaguars, BMWs. There must be sailing and tennis lessons, monogrammed seersucker dresses, grosgrain ribbons for the hair, a new pair of Topsiders each season. And what about the food such houses must contain? Bowls of peaches and plums, cartons of strawberries and blueberries, freshly baked bread, quinoa salad, ripe avocados, organic eggs, fat-marbled steaks, and steaming, scarlet lobsters. And butter. Lots and lots of butter.

Karen also factors in all of the dull stuff that no one likes to think about: insurance, taxes, electricity, cable TV, attorneys.

These families must have fifty million dollars each, Karen decides. At least. And how does someone, anyone, make *that much money?* She would ask Bruce but she doesn't want to make him feel self-conscious. Meaning she doesn't want to make him feel any *more* self-conscious; she knows he's already sensitive about money — because they don't have any.

Despite this, Bruce will be the best-dressed man at the wedding, Karen is certain. Bruce works in the suit department at Neiman Marcus in the King of Prussia Mall. He gets a 30 percent discount on clothes plus free alterations. He has managed to keep his wrestler's physique — strong shoulders, tapered waist (no beer belly for him!) — and so he cuts an impressive silhouette. If he were two inches taller, a store vice president once told him, he could work as a model.

Bruce is almost like a woman in the way he loves fine clothes. When he brings home something new (which is fairly often, a fact that used to confuse Karen, as they don't really have the money for new clothes or the money to go anywhere he might wear them), he likes to give Karen a fashion show. She sits on the edge of the bed — lately, she lies *in* the bed — while Bruce gets dressed in the bathroom and then emerges, one hand on hip, and sashays around the room like it's a fashion runway. It cracks Karen up every time. She has come to understand that this is why he buys new suits, shirts, ties, trousers, and socks — to give Karen joy.

And because he likes to look good. Today, for their arrival, he's wearing a pair of pressed black G-Star jeans and a black-and-turquoise paisley Robert Graham shirt with contrasting grasshopper-green cuffs, a pair of zebra-striped socks, and black suede Gucci loafers. It's hot in the sun. Even Karen, who is always cold now thanks to the chemo, is warm. Bruce must be roasting.

A lighthouse swathed in an American flag comes into view, and then Karen sees two church steeples, one a white spire, one a clock tower with a gold dome. The harbor is filled with sailboats of all sizes, power yachts with tiered tuna towers, cigarette boats, cabin cruisers.

"It's like a movie set," Karen says, but her words get carried away on the sea breeze and Bruce doesn't hear her. She can see from the expression on his face that he's as mesmerized as she is. He's probably thinking that they haven't been anywhere this enchanting since their honeymoon thirty-two years earlier. She was eighteen years old then, just out of high school, and after the cost of the wedding clothes and a ceremony at the courthouse, they had $280 left for a weeklong getaway. They bought a case of wine coolers (they're out of fashion now but, oh, how Karen had loved a cold raspberry Bartles and Jaymes back then) and a bunch of snack food—Bugles, Cool Ranch Doritos, Funyuns—and they'd climbed into Bruce's Chevy Nova, popped in his *Bat Out of Hell* eight-track, and taken off for the coast, both of them singing at the top of their lungs.

They had reached the Jersey Shore points early on but neither of them had felt compelled to stop. The shore had been the beach of their youth—class trips, a family vacation to Wildwood every summer—and so they had continued going north to New England.

New England, Karen remembers now, had sounded very exotic.

They ran low on gas in a town called Madison, Connecticut, exit 61 off I-95, that had a leafy main street lined with shops, like something out of a 1950s sitcom. When Karen got out of the car to stretch her legs at the filling station, she had smelled salt in the air.

She said, "I think we're near the water."

They had asked the gas-station attendant what there was to see in Madison, Connecticut, and he directed them to a restaurant called the Lobster Deck, which had an uninterrupted view of the Long Island Sound. Down the street from the Lobster Deck, across from a state park with a beach, was the Sandbar Motel and Lodge; a room cost $105 for the week.

Karen knows she's not worldly. She has never been to Paris, Bermuda, or even the West Coast. She and Bruce used to take Celeste to the Pocono Mountains on vacation. They skied at Camelback in the winter and went to the Great Wolf Lodge water park in the summer. The rest of their money they saved for Celeste to go to college. She had shown an interest in animals at an early age, and both Bruce and Karen had hoped she would become a veterinarian. When Celeste's interests had instead run toward zoology, that had been fine too. She had been offered a partial scholarship at Miami University of Ohio, which had the best zoology department in the country. "Partial scholarship" still left a lot to pay for—some tuition, room, board, books, spending money, bus tickets home—and so there had been precious little left over for travel.

Hence, that one trip to New England remained sacred to both Karen and Bruce. They are even further in the hole now—nearly a hundred thousand dollars in debt, thanks to Karen's medical bills—but there was no way they were going to miss making the trip to Nantucket. On their way home, once Celeste and Benji are safely on their honeymoon in Greece, they will stop in Madison, Connecticut, for what Karen is privately calling the Grand Finale. The Sandbar Motel and Lodge is long gone, so instead, Bruce has booked an oceanfront suite at the Madison Beach Hotel. It's a Hilton property. Bruce told Karen he got it for free by accepting Hilton Honors points offered to him by the store's general manager, Mr. Allen. Karen knows that all of Bruce's co-workers have wondered how to help out their favorite sales associate, Bruce in Suits, whose wife has been diagnosed with terminal cancer, and while this is slightly mortifying, she does appreciate the concern and, especially, Mr. Allen's generous offer to pay for their hotel. Madison, Connecticut, has taken on the paradisiacal qualities of a Shangri-la. Karen wants to eat lobster—with butter, lots and lots of butter—and she wants to watch the honey lozenge of the sun drop into the Long Island Sound. She wants to fall asleep in Bruce's arms as she listens to waves lap the shore, their daughter successfully married.

The Grand Finale.

Last August, Karen learned that she had a tumor on her L3 vertebra. The breast cancer, which she'd believed she'd beaten, had metastasized to her bones. Her oncologist, Dr. Edman, has given her a year to eighteen months. Karen figures she has until at least the end of the summer, which is an enormous blessing, especially when you consider all the people throughout history who have died without warning. Why, Karen could be crossing Northampton Street to the circle in downtown Easton and get hit by a car, making the cancer diagnosis irrelevant.

Celeste had been gutted by the news. She had just gotten engaged to Benji but she said she wanted to postpone the wedding, leave New York, and move back to Easton to take care of Karen. This was the exact opposite of what Karen wanted. Karen encouraged Celeste to move *up* the wedding, rather than postpone it.

Celeste, always obedient, did just that.

When Dr. Edman called last week to say it appeared the cancer had spread to Karen's stomach and liver, Karen and Bruce decided to keep the news from Celeste entirely. When Karen leaves on Monday morning, she will say good-bye to Celeste as if everything is just fine.

All she has to do is make it through the next three days.

Karen can still walk with a cane but Bruce has arranged for a wheelchair to glide her gracefully down the ramp and onto the wharf. Greer Garrison Winbury — or, rather, Greer Garrison; people rarely call her by her married name, according to Celeste — is supposed to be waiting. Neither Karen nor Bruce has met Greer, but Karen has read two of her books: her most recent, *Death in Dubai,* as well as the novel that launched Greer to fame in the early nineties, *The Killer on Khao San Road*. Karen isn't much of a book critic — she has dropped out of three book groups because the novels they choose are so grim and depressing — but she can say that *The Killer on Khao San Road* was fast-paced and entertaining. (Karen had no idea where Khao San Road was; turned out it was in Bangkok, and there were all kinds of elaborate details about that city — the temples, the flower market, the green papaya salad with toasted peanuts —

that made the book just as transporting as watching the travel channel on TV.) *Death in Dubai,* however, was formulaic and predictable. Karen figured out who the killer was on page fourteen: the hairless guy with the tattooed mustache. Karen could have written a more suspenseful novel herself with just *CSI: Miami* as background. Karen wonders if Greer Garrison, the esteemed mystery writer who is always named in the same breath as Sue Grafton and Louise Penny, is coasting now, in her middle age.

Karen has carefully studied Greer's author photo; both of the books Karen read featured the same photo, despite a nearly twenty-five-year span between publication dates. Greer wears a straw picture hat, and there is a lush English garden in the background. Greer is maybe thirty in the photo. She has pale blond hair and flawless pale skin. Greer's eyes are a beautiful deep brown and she has a long, lovely neck. She isn't an overtly beautiful woman, but she conveys class, elegance, regality even, and Karen can see why she never chose to update the picture. Who wants to see age descend on a woman? No one. So it's up to Karen to imagine how Greer might look now, with wrinkles, some tension in the neck, possibly some gray in the part of her hair.

There is a crush of people on the wharf—those disembarking, those picking up houseguests, tourists wandering the shops, hungry couples in search of lunch. Because the cancer has invaded Karen's stomach, she rarely feels hungry, but her appetite is piqued now by the prospect of lobster. Will there be lobster served over the wedding weekend? she had asked Celeste.

Yes, Betty, Celeste had said, and the nickname had made Karen smile. *There will be plenty of lobster.*

"Karen?" a voice calls out. "Bruce?"

Karen searches through the crowd and sees a woman—blond, thin, maniacally smiling, or maybe the smile only looks maniacal because of the facelift—moving toward them with her arms wide open.

Greer Garrison. Yes, there she is. Her hair is the same pale blond, and expensive-looking sunglasses—Tom Ford?—are perched on the top of her head. She's wearing white capri pants and a white linen tunic, which Karen supposes is very chic and summery although she herself always prefers color, a result of having worked in the gift shop at the Crayola factory in Easton for so many years. In Karen's opinion, Greer's look would be more interesting if the tunic were magenta or goldenrod.

Greer swoops down to hug Karen in her wheelchair without confirmation that she is, in fact, Karen Otis, which gives Karen the uncomfortable feeling that she and Bruce stick out so badly that there can be no mistaking them. Or maybe Celeste has shown Greer pictures.

"So wonderful to meet you finally," Greer says. "And on such a happy occasion. I'm thrilled you could make the trip."

Karen realizes that she is prepared to dislike Greer Garrison and take offense at everything she says. *Of course* Karen and Bruce made the trip! Their only daughter, their pride and joy, is getting *married!*

Karen needs to adjust her attitude, and fast. She needs to abandon her petty jealousy, her feelings of inferiority, her embarrassment because she and Bruce aren't wealthy or sophisticated. Mostly, Karen needs to abandon the anger she feels. This anger isn't caused by Greer specifically, by any means. Karen is angry at everyone who isn't sick. Everyone except Bruce. And Celeste, of course.

"Greer," Karen says. "It's so nice to meet *you*. Thank you for having us. Thank you for . . . *everything*."

Bruce steps forward and offers Greer his hand. "Bruce Otis," he says. "It's a pleasure, ma'am."

"Ma'am?" Greer says. She laughs with her head thrown back, her neck — still lovely but indisputably aged — exposed. "Please don't call me that, you make me feel a thousand years old. Call me Greer, and my husband is Tag, like the game. After all, we're going to be family!"

* * *

Family, Karen thinks as Bruce helps her into the backseat of Greer's car, which looks exactly like what people drive in across the savannas of Africa on the Travel Channel. They head up a cobblestoned street. Each cobblestone the car goes over is a punch to the gut for Karen, but she grits her teeth and bears it. Bruce, sensing her pain as if it's his own, reaches a hand between the seats to comfort her. The comment about family might have been a throwaway, but it holds undeniable appeal. Karen and Bruce are low on family. Karen's father died of a heart attack when Karen was pregnant with Celeste; her mother put the house in Tatamy on the market and ended up marrying Gordon, the listing real estate broker. Then, when Celeste was in kindergarten, Karen's mother was diagnosed with a rare myeloma and died six months later. Gordon is still a real estate agent in the area but they hardly ever hear from him. Bruce's younger brother, Bryan, was a state trooper in New Jersey; he was killed in a high-speed chase. After Bryan's funeral, Bruce's parents moved to a retirement community in Bethlehem, where they both died of old age. Karen and Bruce have always clung to each other and Celeste; they are a small, insular cluster of three. Karen somehow never imagined that Celeste would provide them with a whole new family, and certainly not one as esteemed as the Winburys, who not only have a summer estate on Nantucket but also an apartment on Park Avenue in New York City and a flat they keep in London for when Tag takes business trips or Greer misses "home." Karen can't help but feel a secret thrill at the thought of a new family, even though she won't be around to enjoy it.

Greer points out Main Street, a certain restaurant she likes that serves an organic beet salad, a store that sells the red pants that all of the gentlemen will be wearing tomorrow. They've ordered a pair for Bruce, Greer says, tailored precisely to the measurements he sent them (this is news to Karen). Greer points out the boutique where she bought a clutch purse that matches her mother-of-the-groom dress (though the dress itself she bought in New York, of course, she says, and Karen nearly says that of course she bought her mother-of-the-bride dress at Neiman Marcus in the King of Prussia Mall using Bruce's discount but decides this will sound pathetic) and a shop that specializes in nautical antiques where Greer always buys Tag's Father's Day presents.

Bruce says, "Do you have a boat, then?"

Greer laughs like this is a silly question, and maybe it is a silly question. Maybe everyone on this island has a boat; maybe it's a practical necessity, like having a sturdy snow shovel for Easton winters.

"We have three," she says. "A thirty-seven-foot Hinckley picnic boat named *Ella* for puttering over to Tuckernuck, a thirty-two-foot Grady-White that we take to Great Point to fish for stripers, and a thirteen-foot Whaler, which we bought so the kids could get back and forth to Coatue with their girlfriends."

Bruce nods like he approves and Karen wonders if he has any earthly idea what Greer is talking about. Karen certainly doesn't; the woman might as well be speaking Swahili.

How will Karen and Greer be related once the kids are married? Karen wonders. Each will be the mother-in-law of the other's child but no relation to each other, or at least not a relation that has a name. In many instances, she suspects, the mothers of two people getting married dislike each other, or worse. Karen would like to think that she and Greer could get to know each other and find kinship and become as close as sisters, but that would only happen in the fantasy world where Karen doesn't die.

"We also have kayaks, both one-person and two-person," Greer says. "Tag loves the kayaks more than the boats, I think. He may love the kayaks more than the boys!"

Bruce laughs like this is the funniest thing he's ever heard. Karen scowls. Who would joke about something like that? She needs a pain pill. She rummages through her wine-colored Tory Burch hobo bag, which was a present from Bruce when she finished her first chemo protocol, back when they were still filled with hope. She pulls out her bottle of oxycodone. She is very careful to pick out a small round pill and not one of the three pearlescent ovoids, and she throws it back without water. The oxy makes her heart race, but it's the only thing that works against the pain.

Karen wants to admire the scenery but she has to close her eyes. After a while, Greer says, "We'll be there in a jiffy." Her British accent reminds Karen of Julie Andrews in *Mary Poppins*. *Jiff-jiff-jiffy*, Karen thinks. Greer drives around a traffic circle, then puts on her blinker and turns left. With the sudden movement of the car, the oxy kicks in. Karen's pain subsides and a sense of well-being washes over her like a golden wave. It's by far the best part of the oxy, this initial rush when the pain is absorbed like a spill by a sponge. Karen is most certainly on her way to becoming addicted if she isn't already, but Dr. Edman is generous with medication. What does addiction matter at this point?

"Here we are!" Greer announces as she pulls into a white-shell driveway.

SUMMERLAND, a sign says. PRIVATE. Karen peers out the window. There's a row of hydrangea bushes on either side of the driveway, alternately fuchsia and periwinkle, and then they drive under a boxwood arch into what Karen can only think of as some kind of waterfront utopia. There's a main house, stately and grand with crisp white-and-green awnings over the windows. Opposite the main house are two smaller cottages set amid landscaped gardens with gurgling stone fountains and flagstone paths and lavish flower beds. And all of this is only yards away from the water. The harbor is right there, and across the flat blue expanse of the harbor is town. Karen can pick out the church towers she saw from the ferry. The Nantucket skyline.

Karen has a hard time finding air, much less words. This is the most beautiful place she has ever been. It's so beautiful it hurts.

Today is Friday. The rehearsal at St. Paul's Episcopal Church is scheduled for six o'clock and will be followed by a clambake for sixty people that will include a raw bar and live music, a cover band that plays the Beach Boys and Jimmy Buffett. There will be a "small tent" set up on the beach to shelter the band and four rectangular tables of fifteen. And there will be lobster.

The wedding is Saturday at four o'clock, and it will be followed by a sit-down dinner under the "big tent," which has a clear plastic roof so that the guests can see the sky. There will be a dance floor, an eighteen-piece orchestra, and seventeen round tables that seat ten guests each. On Sunday, the Winburys are hosting a brunch at their golf club; this will be followed by a nap, at least for herself, Karen thinks. On Monday morning, Karen and Bruce will leave on the ferry, and Celeste and Benji will fly from Boston to Athens and from there to Santorini.

Stop time, Karen thinks. She doesn't want to get out of the car. She wants to stay right here, with all of those sumptuous plans still in front of her, forever.

Bruce helps Karen down out of the car and hands over her cane, and in the time it takes for this to happen, people pop out of the main house and appear from the cottages as though Bruce and Karen are visiting dignitaries. Well, they *are,* Karen thinks. They are the mother and father of the bride.

She knows they are also something of a curiosity because they are poor and because Karen is sick, and she hopes all of them will be gentle with their appraisals.

"Hello," Karen says to the assembled group. "I'm Karen Otis." She looks for someone she recognizes, but Greer has vanished and Celeste is nowhere to be found. Karen squints into the sun. She has met Benji, Celeste's betrothed, only three times, and all she can remember of him, thanks to chemo brain, is the cowlick that she had to keep herself from smoothing down every ten seconds. There are two young, good-looking men in front of her, and Karen knows that neither of them is Benji. One is in a snappy cornflower-blue polo and Karen smiles at him. This young man steps forward, hand extended.

"I'm Thomas Winbury, Mrs. Otis," he says. "Benji's brother."

Karen shakes Thomas's hand; his grip is nearly enough to turn Karen's bones to powder. "Please, call me Karen."

"And I'm Bruce, Bruce Otis." Bruce shakes Thomas's hand and then the hand of the young man standing next to Thomas. He has very dark hair and crystalline-blue eyes. He's so striking that Karen can hardly keep from staring.

"Shooter Uxley," the young man says. "Benji's best man."

Shooter, yes! Celeste has mentioned Shooter. It isn't a name one forgets, and Celeste had tried to explain why Shooter was the best man instead of Benji's brother, Thomas, but the story was puzzling to Karen, as though Celeste were describing characters on a TV series Karen had never seen.

Bruce then shakes the hands of two young ladies, one with chestnut hair and freckles and one a dangerous-looking brunette who is wearing a form-fitting jersey dress in a color that Karen would call scarlet, like the letter.

"Aren't you hot?" the Scarlet Letter asks Bruce. With a slightly different inflection, it would sound as though the girl were hitting on Bruce, but Karen realizes she's talking about Bruce's outfit, the black jeans, the black-and-turquoise shirt, the loafers, the socks. He looks sharp but he doesn't exactly fit in. Everyone else is in casual summer clothes—the men in shorts and polo shirts, the ladies in bright cotton sundresses. Celeste had told Karen no less than half a dozen times to remind Bruce that the Winburys were preppy. *Preppy,* that was the word Celeste insisted on using, and it sounded quaint to Karen. Didn't that term go out of style decades ago, right along with *Yuppie?* Celeste had said: *Tell MacGyver, blue blazers and no socks.* When Karen had passed on this message, Bruce had laughed, but not happily.

I know how to dress myself, Bruce had said. *That's my job.*

A tall, silver-haired gentleman strides across the lawn and walks down the three stone steps into the driveway. He's dripping wet and wearing a pair of bathing trunks and a neoprene rash guard.

"Welcome!" he calls out. "I'd open my arms to you but let's wait until I dry off for those familiarities."

"Did you capsize again, Tag?" the Scarlet Letter teases.

The gentleman ignores the comment and approaches Karen. When she offers her hand, he kisses it, a gesture that catches her off guard. She's not sure anyone has ever kissed her hand before. There's a first time for everything, she thinks, even for a dying woman. "Madame," he says. His accent is English enough to be charming but not so much that it's obnoxious. "I'm Tag Winbury. Thank you for coming all this way, thank you for indulging my wife in all her planning, and thank you, most of all, for your beautiful, intelligent, and enchanting daughter, our celestial Celeste. We are absolutely enamored of her and tickled pink about this impending union."

"Oh," Karen says. She feels the roses rising to her cheeks, which was how her father always described her blushing. This man is divine! He has managed to set Karen at ease while at the same time making her feel like a queen.

There's a tap on Karen's shoulder and she turns carefully, planting her cane in the shells of the driveway.

"B-B-Betty!"

It's Celeste. She's wearing a white sundress and a pair of barely there sandals; her hair is braided. She has gotten a suntan, and her blue eyes look wide and sad in her face.

Sad? Karen thinks. This should be the happiest day of her life, or the second-happiest. Karen knows

Celeste is worried about *her,* but Karen is determined to forget she's sick — at least for the next three days — and she wants everyone else to do the same.

"Darling!" Karen says, kissing Celeste on the cheek.

"Betty, you're here," Celeste says, without a trace of stutter. "Can you believe it? You're *here.*"

"Yes," Karen says, and she reminds herself that she is the reason that the whole wedding is being held now, during the busiest week of the summer. "I'm here."

Saturday, July 7, 2018, 6:45 a.m.

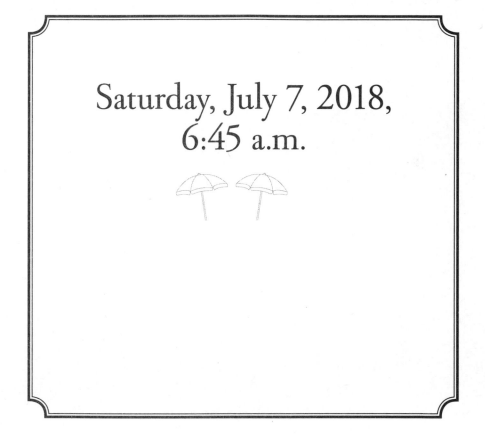

THE CHIEF

He pulls up to 333 Monomoy Road right behind state police detective Nicholas Diamantopoulos, otherwise known as the Greek. Nick's father is Greek and his mother is Cape Verdean; Nick has brown skin, a shaved head, and a jet-black goatee. He's so good-looking that people joke he should quit the job and play a cop on TV—better hours and more money—but Nick is content being a damn good detective and a notorious ladies' man.

Nick and the Chief worked together on the last homicide, a drug-related murder on Cato Lane. Nick spent the first fifteen years of his career in New Bedford, where the streets were dangerous and the criminals hardened, but Nick doesn't subscribe to the tough-guy shtick; he doesn't use any of the strong-arming tactics you see in the movies. When Nick is questioning persons of interest, he is encouraging and empathetic; he sometimes tells stories about his *ya-ya* back in Thessaloníki who wore an ugly black dress and uglier black shoes every day after his grandfather passed. And the results he gets! He says the word *ya-ya* and people confess to everything. The guy's a magician.

"Nicky," the Chief says.

"Chief," Nick says. He nods at the house. "This is sad, huh? The maid of honor."

"Tragic," the Chief says. He's dreading what he's going to find inside. Not only is a twenty-nine-year-old woman *dead,* but the family and guests have to be questioned, and all of the complicated, costly wedding preparations have to be undone without destroying the integrity of the crime scene.

Before the Chief left his house, he went upstairs to find Chloe to see if she had heard the news. She had been in the bathroom. Through the closed door, the Chief had heard the sound of her vomiting.

He'd knocked. "You okay?"

"Yeah," she said. "I'm fine."

Fine, the Chief thought. Meaning she'd spent her postshift hours on the beach drinking Bud Light and doing shots of Fireball.

He had kissed Andrea good-bye in the kitchen and said, "I think Chloe was drinking last night."

Andrea sighed. "I'll talk to her."

Talking to Chloe wasn't going to help, the Chief thought. She needed a new job — shelving books at the children's library or counting plover eggs out on

Smith's Point. Something that would keep her out of trouble, not lead her right to it.

The Chief and Nick walk past the left side of the main house onto the lawn, where an enormous tent has been erected. They find the guys from forensics inside the tent, one bagging, one photographing. Nick heads down to the beach to check out the body; the Chief sees that the girl has been left just shy of the waterline but she'll need to be moved to the hospital morgue as soon as possible on this hot a day. Inside the tent, there is one round table surrounded by four white banquet chairs. In the middle of the table is a nearly empty bottle of Mount Gay Black Barrel rum and four shot glasses, two of them on their sides. There's half a quahog shell that served as an ashtray for someone's cigar. A Romeo y Julieta. Cuban.

One of the forensics guys, Randy, is bagging a pair of silver sandals.

"Where did you find those?" the Chief asks.

"Under that chair," Randy says, pointing. "Connor has a picture of them. Size eight Mystique sandals. I'm no shoe salesman, but I'm guessing they belonged to the deceased. We'll confirm."

Nick returns. "The girl has a nasty gash on her foot," he says. "And I noticed there's a trail of blood in the sand."

"Any blood on the sandals?" the Chief asks Randy.

"No, sir," Randy says.

"Took off her shoes, cut her foot on a shell, maybe," Nick says.

"Well, she didn't die of a cut on her foot," the Chief says. "Unless she swam out too far and couldn't get back in because of the foot?"

"That doesn't sound right," Nick says. "There's also a two-person kayak overturned on the beach, one oar a few yards away lying in the sand. No blood on the kayak."

The Chief takes a breath. The day is still; there's no breeze off the water. It's going to be hot and buggy. They need to get the body out of here, pronto. They need to start their questioning, try to figure out what happened. He remembers what Dickson said about the best man being missing. Hopefully that situation has resolved itself. "Let's go up to the house," he says.

"Should we divide and conquer?" the Greek asks.

"I'll take the men, you take the women," the Chief says. Nick works wonders with the women.

Nick nods. "Deal."

As they're approaching the steps of the front porch, Bob from Old Salt Taxi pulls up in the driveway and a kid in his twenties climbs out. He's wearing Nantucket Reds shorts, a blue oxford, a navy blazer, and loafers; he has a large duffel in one hand and a garment bag in the other. His hair is mussed and he needs a shave.

"Who is this guy?" Nick asks under his breath.

"Late to the party," the Chief says. He waves to Bob as Bob reverses out of the driveway.

The kid gives the Chief and Nick an uneasy smile. "What's going on?" he asks.

Nick says, "You part of the wedding?"

"Best man," the kid says. "Shooter Uxley. Did something happen?"

Nick looks to the Chief. The Chief nods ever so slightly and tries not to let the relief show on his face. One mystery is solved.

"The maid of honor is dead," Nick says.

The bags hit the ground, and the kid — Shooter Uxley; what a name — goes pale. "What?" he says. "Wait . . . *what?*"

Initial questioning, Roger Pelton, Saturday, July 7, 7:00 a.m.

The Chief meets Roger Pelton in the driveway. The two men shake hands, and the Chief grips Roger's arm in a show of friendship and support. Roger has been married to Rita since the Bronze Age, and they have five kids, all grown. Roger has been running his wedding business for over ten years; before that, he was a successful general contractor. Roger Pelton is as solid a human being as God has ever put on this earth. He was in Vietnam too, the Chief remembers, where he received a Purple Heart and a Bronze Star. He's an unlikely candidate to be Nantucket's most in-demand wedding planner, but he has a gift for it that has resulted in a booming business.

Right now, Roger looks *shaken*. His face is pale and sweaty; his shoulders are drooping.

"I'm sorry about this, Roger," the Chief says. "It must have come as a terrible shock."

"I thought I'd seen it all," Roger says. "I've had brides turn around halfway down the aisle; I've had grooms not show up; I've caught couples having sex in church bathrooms. I've had mothers of brides slapping mothers of grooms. I've had fathers who refused to pay my bills and fathers who tipped me five grand. I've had hurricanes, thunderstorms, heat waves, fog, and, once, hail. I've had brides vomit and faint; I even had a groomsman eat a mussel and go into anaphylactic shock. But I've never had anyone die. I met the maid of honor only briefly so I can't give you any information other than that she was Celeste's best friend."

"Celeste?" the Chief says.

"Celeste Otis is the bride," Roger says. "She's pretty and smart, but on this island I see a lot of pretty and smart. More notably, Celeste loves her parents and she's kind and patient with her future in-laws. She's humble. Any idea how rare humility is when you're dealing with Nantucket brides?"

"Rare?" the Chief asks.

"Rare," Roger says. "I hate that this happened on her wedding day. She was a complete mess."

"Let's try to figure out what happened," the Chief says. "I'm starting with you because I know you have work to do." The Chief leads Roger over to a white wrought-iron bench tucked under an arbor that is dripping with New Dawn roses and they both sit down.

"Tell me what you saw when you got here," the Chief says. "From the beginning."

"I pulled in about quarter to six," Roger says. "The rental company was supposed to leave seventeen rounds and a hundred and seventy-five folding chairs. I wanted to double-check the numbers, see how the dance floor settled, make sure there hadn't been any after-hours partying. Standard stuff."

"Understood," the Chief says.

"As soon as I got out of my car, I heard screaming," Roger says. "And I realized right away that it was Celeste. I thought something had happened to her mother." Roger pauses. "Celeste's mother, Karen Otis, is very sick—cancer. Anyway, I could tell just from the kind of scream that someone was dead. It had that *urgency.* So I go charging out to the front of the house and there's poor Celeste trying to pull her friend out of the water by the arms. One look at her, I knew the girl was dead, but I helped Celeste drag her up onto the beach and then I tried to revive her."

"CPR?"

"I tried," Roger says. "I...tried. But she was dead when I found her, Ed. That much I know."

"So why bother with CPR, then?"

"I thought maybe. I had to try *something*. Celeste was begging me to save her. *You have to save her,* she said. *You have to save her!*" Roger drops his head in his hands. "She was dead. There was no bringing her back."

"Then you called 911?"

"I had dropped my phone in the driveway so I used Celeste's phone," Roger says. "The paramedics came in six minutes. They tried CPR as well. Then the police came. Sergeant Dickson. Together, he and I knocked on the front door of the house."

"And who answered? Who did you tell?"

"Greer Garrison, the groom's mother. She and her husband, Tag Winbury, own the house. Greer was already awake. She was holding a cup of coffee."

"She was? You're sure about that?" the Chief says. "She was awake but didn't hear Celeste screaming and didn't notice you pulling a body out of the water in front of her house? With all of those giant windows, she didn't notice? She didn't hear the sirens or see the lights when the paramedics arrived?"

"Apparently not. She had no idea anything was wrong when I knocked."

"When you told her, what did she do?"

"She started to shake," Roger says. "Her coffee spilled. Dickson had to take it from her."

"So it's fair to say she seemed shocked and upset?" the Chief says.

"Oh yes," Roger says. "Mr. Winbury came to see what the ruckus was and I told him as well. He thought we were kidding."

"Kidding," the Chief says.

"Everyone reacts differently, but the first emotion is, of course, shock and disbelief. Celeste was still screaming. She went into one of the guest cottages to wake up Benji—he's the groom—and he tried to calm Celeste down but she was beyond helping. She was...well. Sergeant Dickson told the EMTs to take her to the ER." Roger shakes his head. "I feel for her. It's supposed to be the happiest day of her life and instead...her best friend..."

The Chief flashes back to the day he found out Tess and Greg were dead. He had gone right to the beach to find Andrea. Sometimes, in the dark of night, he can still hear the sound Andrea made when he told her that Tess was gone.

"There is nothing worse than the sudden, unexpected death of a young person," the Chief says.

"Amen," Roger says. "Anyway, while the family gathered inside, I made phone calls — the caterers, the church, the musicians, the Steamship Authority, the photographer, the chauffeur. I called everyone." Roger looks at his watch. "And I hate to say this, but I have two other weddings today."

The Chief nods. "We'll get you out of here. I just wanted to ask if you noticed anything odd or peculiar or suspicious or noteworthy about the bride or the groom or the family or any of the guests. Did anything or anyone strike you?"

"Just one thing," Roger says. "And it's probably nothing."

Probably nothing is usually something, the Chief thinks.

"What's that?" he asks.

"Celeste…" Roger says. "She had her purse and her overnight bag out on the beach. And she was fully dressed. She was wearing her going-away outfit, the one she was supposed to wear on Sunday."

"And you're wondering…"

"I'm wondering why she was wearing it this morning. I'm wondering why she had her purse and her overnight bag. I'm wondering why she was awake at quarter to six in the morning, dressed that way, on the beach."

"We'll ask her," the Chief says. "It does seem odd."

He thinks about what Roger is telling him. "Maybe she and the groom had decided to elope at the last minute?"

"I thought that too, but her parents are here...her mother...something about that doesn't feel right to me. But she's such a good kid, Ed. I'm sure there's a logical explanation. It's probably nothing."

Initial questioning, Abigail Freeman Winbury, Saturday, July 7, 7:15 a.m.

Nick's choices with the women are sparse. The bride, Celeste, has gone to the hospital; the mother of the groom, Greer Garrison, is busy on the phone contacting guests to relay the tragic news; and the mother of the bride, who is quite sick, is still in bed. It's unclear if she has even learned what's happened.

This leaves Abigail Freeman Winbury—Abby—who is the bridesmaid and the wife of the groom's brother.

Abby is short with auburn hair cut bluntly at the shoulders. She has brown eyes and freckles. She is cute, Nick thinks, but not beautiful. When she walks into the formal living room where Nick is doing the questioning—it has glass doors that close, sealing it off from the hallway, the stairs, and the rest of the house—she is holding her breasts up with her hands. Nick blinks. It's okay; he has seen stranger things.

"Hi, Abby, I'm Nick Diamantopoulos, a detective with the Massachusetts State Police. Thank you for talking with me."

Abby lets go of her breasts to shake his hand. "Just so you know, I'm pregnant. Fifteen weeks along. I had an amnio a few days ago, and the baby's fine. It's a boy."

"Oh," Nick says. That, at least, explains why she was holding her breasts. Right? Nick doesn't have children, and he has never been married, but his sister, Helena, has three kids and what Nick remembers from Helena's pregnancies is that a certain amount of personal dignity goes out the window. Helena, who had always been rather private and discreet about her body and its functions, had complained about her aching (and then leaking) breasts as well as the frequency with which she had to pee. "Well, congratulations."

Abby gives Nick a tired but victorious smile. "Thank you," she says. "It'll be the first Winbury heir. That's important, I guess, to British people."

Nick says, "I have some water here, if you'd like any. I'm sure you must be pretty shaken up."

Abby takes a seat on the sofa and Nick sits in a chair opposite her so he can face her. "My stomach has been funny for weeks," she says. "And this news is so terrible. I can't believe it's real. This feels like a movie, you know? Or a dream. Merritt is dead. She's *dead.*" She pours herself a glass of water but doesn't drink. "So do we know . . . is the wedding *canceled?*"

Nick says, "Yes, I believe so." That's what he overheard Greer saying on the phone, he's pretty sure. That they're canceling the wedding.

"Okay," Abby says, but she sounds a little deflated. "I figured. I mean, Merritt is Celeste's best friend, her only friend, really, and she's dead." Abby shakes her head as if to clear it. "Obviously the wedding is canceled. I don't know why I even asked. You must think I'm some kind of monster."

"Not at all," Nick says. "I'm sure it's come as a shock."

"Shock," Abby says. "The wedding is a big deal — very expensive, you know, for Tag and Greer — and Celeste's mother isn't well and I just wasn't sure if . . . if maybe they would just go through with it anyway. But of course not. Of *course* not. Please don't tell anyone I asked."

"I won't," Nick says.

"So . . . what *happened?*" Abby asks. "You're a detective? Do you think someone *killed* Merritt? Like a *murder?*"

"By law, with unattended deaths, we have to rule out foul play," Nick says. "So I'm going to ask you some questions. Easy questions. Just answer as honestly as you can."

"Of course, of course. I just . . . I can't believe this.

I can't believe this is happening. I mean, intellectually my mind knows it's happening, but my heart is resisting. She's *dead*."

Nick says, "Tell me what you know about Merritt."

"I'm not really the best person to ask," Abby says. "I only just met her in May. We had a little bachelorette weekend here and it was the three of us—me, Celeste, and Merritt."

"That's all?" Nick says. "Nobody else?"

"Well, Tag and Greer were here. Greer kind of arranged it, just like she arranged the rest of the wedding. So my in-laws were here, but, like…no other *women*. It's kind of weird? Celeste doesn't have a lot of close female friends. When I got married, I had eleven bridesmaids. Some from St. Stephen's, some from UT. I was president of the Tri Delts, that was my sorority. I could have had thirty bridesmaids. But Celeste had only Merritt, who was a friend she met in New York. Merritt does PR for the zoo where Celeste works."

"Merritt worked in public relations," Nick says. "And Celeste, the bride, works at a *zoo*, you say?"

"Celeste is the assistant director of the Bronx Zoo," Abby says. "She knows a ton about animals, like genus and species and mating rituals and migration patterns."

"Impressive."

"And she's only twenty-eight, which I guess is unusual in that world. Merritt discovered her, in a sense. She chose Celeste as the face of the entire Wildlife Conservation Society. Celeste's picture is in the zoo brochure, and Merritt's big dream was to get Celeste's face on a billboard, but Celeste said no to that. Celeste is pretty conservative. They're a funny match, actually—Celeste and Merritt—like the Odd Couple. *Were* a funny match. Sorry." Abby mists up and waves a hand in front of her face. "I can't let myself get worked up about this because of the baby. I've had four miscarriages..."

"I'm sorry to hear that," Nick says.

"But *poor* Celeste. She must be *devastated*."

Nick leans forward to make eye contact with Abby. "The best way we can help Celeste now is to figure out what happened to her friend. When you say that Celeste and Merritt were like the Odd Couple, what do you mean?"

"Oh, just that they were opposites. Like, complete opposites."

"How so?"

"Well, start with their looks. Celeste is blond and fair, and Merritt had dark hair and olive skin. Celeste goes to bed early and Merritt likes to stay up late. Merritt has a second job—*had*, sorry—a second job as an influencer."

"Influencer?" Nick says.

"On social media?" Abby says. "She has something like eighty thousand Instagram followers who are all just like her—beautiful urban Millennials—and so Merritt gets perks for building brand awareness with her posts. She gets free clothes, free bags, free makeup; she eats at all of these hot new restaurants, goes to velvet-rope clubs, and works out at La Palestra for free, all because she features them on her Instagram account."

"Nice work if you can get it," Nick says.

"I know, right?" Abby says. "Merritt is... *was* a social media *goddess*. But Celeste doesn't even have a *Facebook* account. When I heard that, I couldn't believe it. I thought *everyone* had a Facebook account. I thought people were, like, given one at birth."

"I'm with Celeste," Nick says. He once dated a woman who tried to get him to set up a Facebook profile but the idea of reporting his whereabouts, his activities, and, worst of all, the company he was keeping didn't appeal to him. Nick is a confirmed bachelor; he plays the field. Facebook would be a liability. Speaking of which... "What about boyfriends? Did Merritt have a boyfriend that you know of?"

Abby gives him an uneasy look. One of the reasons Nick is so successful with women is that he has learned to listen not only to what they *are* saying but also to what they're *not* saying. It's a talent taught to him by his mother, his *ya-ya,* and his sister. Abby sustains eye contact long enough that he thinks she's trying to tell him something, but then she shakes her head. "I couldn't say for sure. You'd have to ask Celeste."

"Abby?" Nick says. "Do you know something you're not telling me?"

Abby takes a sip of water, then looks around the room as though she's never been there before. It's not a room that appears to get much use. The walls and trim are impeccably white, as are the half-moon sofa and modern egg-shaped chairs. There are three paintings on the wall, bright rainbow stripes—one diamond, one circle, one hexagon—and there are sculptures that look like Tinkertoys made out of steel and wooden spheres. There's a black grand piano; the top is covered with framed photographs. On a low glass table sits a coffee-table book about Nantucket, which seems redundant to Nick. If you want to see Nantucket, go outside. You're here.

"She came to the wedding alone," Abby says. "Which tells me that either she didn't want to be tied down or she had set her sights on someone who would already be at the wedding."

Ahhh, Nick thinks. Now they're getting somewhere. "Someone like who?"

"That's another way they're opposite!" Abby says. "Benji is Celeste's first real boyfriend. And Merritt... well, she's been with a bunch of people, I'm pretty sure."

"But no one seriously?" Nick asks. He senses Abby

trying to change the subject. "If you ladies went out on the town for a bachelorette party, you must have shared some confidences, right?"

"And also?" Abby says. "Their parents. Celeste is super-close to her parents. Like, *abnormally* close. Well, that might be unfair to say because her mother has cancer. Let me restate: Celeste is very close to her parents, whereas Merritt hasn't talked to her parents in six or seven years, I think she said."

This does succeed in capturing Nick's attention because of the next-of-kin issue. "Do you know where her parents live?"

"No clue," Abby says. "She's from Long Island but not one of the fashionable parts, not the Hamptons or anything. She has a brother, I think she said. Again, you'd have to ask Celeste."

"Let's go back to your previous statement," Nick says. "Do you think maybe Merritt was involved with someone who was attending the wedding and that's why she didn't bring a date?"

"Can I please use the ladies' room?" Abby asks.

"Excuse me?" Nick says. He's pretty sure she's using the bathroom break to wiggle out of answering the question—but then he remembers Helena. "Oh, yes. Certainly."

Saturday, October 22, 2016

CELESTE

Blair Parrish, the head herpetologist at the Bronx Zoo's World of Reptiles, is a hypochondriac. She's "sick" more often than can reasonably be believed. She calls in sick on a *Saturday*—by far the zoo's busiest day—and Celeste assigns Donner from the Aquatic Bird House to cover Blair's ten o'clock snake talk. Donner complains about it (he's an expert on Magellanic penguins and *literally* nothing else), so Celeste assigns Karsang from the Himalayan Highlands to cover Blair's one o'clock snake talk and then she, Celeste, covers the three o'clock snake talk even though handling snakes is her least favorite task at the zoo. Celeste's specialty is primates, but as the assistant zoo director— the youngest in the entire country—it's her job to keep the peace, maintain routine, and lead by example as a team player.

Celeste is experienced enough to know that the three o'clock talk in any area of the zoo can be a mixed bag. Ten o'clock talks are routinely the best; the kids are still fresh, the parents or caregivers bright-eyed and optimistic. One o'clock talks are nearly always a catastrophe; that's the only way Celeste can describe it to Merritt via their work phones without using profanity. At one o'clock the kids are either impatient for lunch or they've just eaten and they are high on sugar and often have sticky hands and faces. Three o'clock talks can go either way. It's usually made up of older children, as younger kids have gone home for their naps by then, and, in general, the older kids are, the better their behavior. However, the three o'clock talk is often populated by people who simply couldn't get their acts together early enough in the day to make the ten o'clock or the one o'clock.

Celeste enters the World of Reptiles at ten minutes to three. She isn't crazy about the smell of the place; it has a musty, lizardy stink that she knows will cling to her hair and clothes, and more than likely, she'll offend people on the bus ride home. As the assistant zoo director, Celeste wears regular business clothes instead of a uniform, but for this talk, she buttons an army-green zoo-issued shirt over her black turtleneck and houndstooth pencil skirt, and because she feels weird wearing her good work shoes (suede kitten heels from Nine West that Merritt helped her pick out) into the World of Reptiles, she switches them out for her running shoes, which she keeps in her work locker for the commute. She looks ridiculous, she realizes, but the kids are coming to see the snakes, not her.

There's already one couple waiting for the snake talk to begin. Genus: *European,* Celeste thinks. Species: *Swedish? Norwegian?* Their natural habitat includes fjords and midnight sun, steam saunas, and lingonberry bushes. They're both tall and hearty and have bushy, straw-colored hair. The man has a prodigious beard; the woman wears rimless spectacles. They both wear Birkenstocks over thick woolen socks. The woman pulls a piece of jerky out of a fanny pack and hands it to the man, and Celeste thinks about reprimanding them. There's no eating in the World of Reptiles, and outside food and drink are forbidden throughout the zoo—but it's the last talk of the day and Celeste doesn't want to be a Debbie Downer.

A few minutes before three o'clock a man and woman walk in with a little girl. She's about seven, Celeste guesses (she has become proficient at pegging children's ages, often down to the month). The little girl has Shirley Temple curls, the kind you want to pull straight just for the sheer joy of watching them bounce back. The couple are giving off static and Celeste gathers from the set of the woman's jaw and from the angry whispers that are flying over the little girl's head that they're arguing. As Celeste reaches into the first tank to retrieve Molly the milk snake, she eavesdrops. The woman wants the man to meet "Laney and Casper" for dinner at Root and Bone tonight, but the man reminds her that he has promised to have dinner at his parents' apartment because his parents are leaving for Barbados on Monday and will then be in London through the holidays so he can't cancel or postpone.

The woman — her hair very blond with tinges of silver but intentional silver, not aged silver, which makes her look like she belongs in a science-fiction movie — says, "You act like a minion around your parents. It's pathetic to watch."

The little girl turns her face up. "Who's a minion, Mommy?"

Science-fiction Mother snaps, "I wasn't addressing you, Miranda. I'm trying to conduct an adult conversation with Benji."

Benji catches Celeste's eye and smiles apologetically. "This nice woman is going to teach us about snakes, Miranda," he says.

Miranda's eyes widen. The mother huffs and Celeste smiles indulgently as if to convey that she knows how tedious trips to the zoo can be. The things parents do for their children! The fighting couple are expensively dressed, lots of suede and cashmere, a nice watch on the man, ballet flats on the woman, and she carries some kind of designer bag. (Merritt would be able to identify not only the designer but also the year; she feels about bags the way that most men feel about

Corvettes.) Genus: *Manhattan,* Celeste thinks. Species: *Upper East Side.* Their natural habitat includes doormen and cabs, private school and Bergdorf's.

It's a typical sighting here at the Bronx Zoo.

Just as Celeste is about to begin — she reviewed Blair's notes over her lunch break — a group of boys in their late teens wander in; they carry the unmistakable scent of marijuana smoke. Celeste raises her eyebrows. "Are you guys here for the snake talk?" she asks. It seems like they might have been lighting up elsewhere in Pelham Park and stumbled into the World of Reptiles by mistake.

"Yeah," the one wearing a fluorescent-orange knit hat says. "You've got an anaconda in here, right?"

"We do, but I don't handle him," Celeste says. "He's way too big."

"I have a big anaconda too," the boy says. "But you can handle it anytime."

Celeste smiles patiently. No wonder Blair is so prone to migraines.

Benji turns on the kid and says, "Hey. Respect the lady, please."

My hero, Celeste thinks. She doesn't want the situation to escalate so she says, "Let's get started. I'm Celeste Otis, the assistant zoo director, but today I'm wearing my World of Reptiles hat. And this is Molly, one of our two milk snakes. Milk snakes aren't venomous or otherwise dangerous to humans; however, they do closely resemble coral snakes, which *are* deadly. This resemblance, known as Batesian mimicry, is one of the ways the milk snake protects itself in the wild."

She moves point by point through Blair's spiel. *All snakes are cold-blooded. Does anyone know what that means?* She smiles at Miranda's mother, but Miranda's mother is in silent-treatment mode, eyes drilling holes into the concrete somewhere over Celeste's shoulder, arms locked across her chest. She keeps sneaking sideways glances at Benji, as if willing him to notice just how angry she is, realize just how unfair it is that he won't go to dinner with Laney and Casper because he committed to his parents. Benji's attention, meanwhile, is fixed on Celeste. He listens as if every word she says is wildly fascinating. *Snakes shed their skins once a year and when they do, their eyes grow cloudy. Snakes smell with their tongues. Snakes don't have ears.*

Benji leans down to Miranda. "Isn't that crazy? Snakes don't have ears."

Miranda giggles.

"Some people think snakes are slimy," Celeste says. "But actually, their skin is dry and cool. Would anyone like to touch Molly?" Celeste holds Molly out to Miranda's mother, who backs up a couple of steps.

"No, thank you," she says.

"Oh, come on, Jules," Benji says. "Be a sport."

"I don't want to touch the snake," Jules says.

"There's no reason to be afraid," Celeste says.

"Snakes have gotten a bad rap since biblical times, but Molly is quite lovely."

"I'm not *afraid*," Jules says. "How dare you suggest such a thing."

"Whoa," the stoner in the orange hat says.

Celeste thinks of apologizing but she doesn't indulge bratty behavior in children and she won't indulge it in their parents either. To prove a point, she holds the snake out to Miranda. "Let's show Mommy how brave you are," she says.

Miranda eagerly reaches out a hand to stroke Molly.

"Look at that," Celeste says. "I think she likes you."

Jules storms out of the World of Reptiles.

Celeste sighs. She has a long-running joke with her boss, Zed, about fund-raising to build a cocktail lounge next to the cafeteria for parents like Jules. It would make all of their jobs a lot easier.

The Swedes must think the talk is over because they follow Jules out.

"Can we see a boa now?" the stoner asks.

Celeste brings out Bernie the boa and she wraps up her talk with a stroll past the poisonous snakes—the puff adder, the rattler, the pit viper, and, a perennial favorite, Carmen the cobra. Celeste taps on the glass, and Carmen rises up like a plume of smoke and unfurls her hood—and everyone takes a step back.

"That concludes our snake talk," Celeste says. "Enjoy the rest of your Saturday."

The stoners tap on the glass of Carmen's tank, trying to get her to strike, while Celeste heads to the utility sink to wash her hands. She finds Benji and Miranda lingering before Molly's tank, and in an attempt to make amends for provoking Jules, Celeste joins them.

"Molly just shed her skin this week," she says. "That's it right there." She points to the gray tube of skin, as delicate as filigree, still mostly intact.

Benji smiles. "Thank you for all this information. I'm sorry Jules stormed out. She's upset about something else."

"No worries," Celeste says. "I'm just filling in for the usual snake expert. My job is mostly administrative these days. It's fun to be hands-on, although I hardly expect real-world problems to vanish when one walks into the World of Reptiles."

"Do you have a card?" Benji asks. "I have a friend who sets up excursions for businessmen traveling to New York from overseas. I want to suggest he bring people here to the zoo."

"Like a field trip for adults?"

"Mostly they like casinos and strip clubs," Benji says. "I think this would be something new and different. Something educational."

"I have cards," Celeste says. "But they're in my office.

You can call the zoo's main number and ask for me. My name is Celeste Otis. Or, if you'd like, you can put my direct line into your phone right now?"

"I'd love that," Benji says. He pulls out his phone. "Go ahead, I'm ready."

Saturday, July 7, 2018, 7:00 a.m.

Initial questioning, Abigail Freeman
Winbury, Saturday, July 7 (continued)

While Abby is in the bathroom, Nick listens for voices from the rest of the house. He hears nothing and sees no one out the glass doors. This room is perfect for questioning; it's almost hermetically sealed off from the rest of the house. Sitting here with the sun streaming in and the hydrangeas visible out the window, you wouldn't know anything was wrong.

Abby comes back in, arms crossed over her chest in what Nick perceives as a defensive attitude. She knows or suspects something about Merritt's romantic life; Nick just needs to get her to spill the beans.

"Where were we?" he asks.

"I'm not sure?" Abby says.

"Why don't you tell me about last night," Nick says.

"Well, the first thing that happened," Abby says, "was that the rehearsal was canceled."

"Canceled?"

"I guess Reverend Derby—that's the Winburys' minister from New York—called to say his flight had been delayed and he wouldn't get to Nantucket until very late. I figured we would go to the church anyway and run through the ceremony with Roger, the wedding planner. But Celeste and Benji decided to cancel it altogether. It was almost as if..."

"As if what?" Nick says.

"As if they knew...they wouldn't be getting married," Abby says.

"What do you mean by that?"

Abby takes a sip of her water and trains her gaze on the front of the Nantucket coffee-table book. The cover is a photograph of the Rainbow Fleet rounding Brant Point Lighthouse during the Opera House Cup. "Nothing," she says.

"Was there any indication that this wedding might not happen?"

"No," Abby says.

"So, no rehearsal, then," Nick says. "But there was still a rehearsal dinner, right?"

"It was a beach picnic here," Abby says. "A clambake. There were raw clams and oysters, which I didn't eat because I'm pregnant and raw shellfish can carry listeria. It's in lunch meat also." Abby takes another sip of water and Nick struggles against his instinct to categorize Abby as painfully self-absorbed and utterly useless to this investigation. "There was chowder, boiled lobster, sausages, potatoes, corn bread. Different kinds of pie for dessert. Oh, and there were cheddar biscuits. I ate about twelve."

"Sounds delicious," Nick says with a tight smile. "The clambake was catered?"

"Catered, yes. By the same people who were supposed to do the wedding reception tonight. Island Fare."

"Was there alcohol served?"

Abby laughs. "This is the Winbury house. These people brush their teeth with vintage Dom Pérignon."

"Were people drinking heavily?"

"The picnic had a signature cocktail," Abby says. "It was a blackberry mojito with big fat ripe blackberries and fresh mint from Bartlett's Farm and lots of rum. People were talking about how delicious they were. They were a gorgeous purple color and it was so hot last night that I'm sure they were hard to resist. And let's see... Greer was drinking champagne; she always drinks champagne at parties. But everyone else was into those mojitos. Oh, and there was a keg of Cisco beer too, so after a while the guys were drinking that."

"Did you notice Merritt drinking?" Nick asks.

"Not specifically," Abby says. "But I'm sure she was. She acts like one of the guys. *Acted;* sorry. She listened to the same music as the guys—by which I mean Tay-K, not Taylor Swift—and she doused her food with hot sauce. She knew every player on the Yankees roster. It was her thing—she wanted to act like a guy but look like a woman." Abby pauses. "I found it a little hard to take, honestly."

"These are exactly the kind of details I'm after," he says, and Abby smiles at the praise. "Tell me what happened during the picnic."

"After we ate, people gave toasts. Celeste's father went first. Mr. Otis's toast was all about Celeste's mom, which seemed strange, but he brought it back around to Celeste and Benji eventually. And then after that, Thomas gave a toast. Thomas, my husband, the groom's brother."

"And he's the best man?"

Abby huffs. "He's *not* the best man. Benji asked Shooter instead. Shooter Uxley."

"Shooter. That's right, that's right. Tell me about Shooter."

"How long do you have?" Abby asks.

"All day," Nick says.

"You know how some people are so charming and magnetic that they can get away with anything?"

"My cousin Phil," Nick says. "Six-foot-two Adonis. My *ya-ya*'s favorite. Everyone's favorite."

"Exactly," Abby says. "Shooter is this wedding's version of your cousin Phil."

Nick smiles. He likes Abby a little better. "So...
after your husband, Thomas, did anyone else make a
toast?"

"No. I thought maybe Tag would speak but he didn't,
for some reason. And Merritt...you know, I don't
remember seeing either Merritt or Tag during the toasts."

Nick makes a note: *MM not present at toasts.*

"Maybe she was in the restroom?" Nick says. "Did
she reappear?"

Abby bites the corner of her lip. "Yes, yes," she says.
"I saw her later. Thomas went over to bum a cigarette
from her."

"Merritt smoked?" Nick says.

Abby shrugs. "When she drank, I guess. Like
everyone else. Except for me now."

"What time did the party end?" Nick asks.

"The band stopped playing at ten. That's a law,
which you probably know because you're in law
enforcement." She winks at him and Nick starts to
feel optimistic. They're building a rapport here and
any second Abby is going to give him what he's looking for. *Come on, Abby!* "I was exhausted, but Thomas
said he wanted to go to town with Benji and his
friends. So then we had a fight."

"A fight?"

"He told me early in our marriage that the way to
keep him happy was to give him freedom. He goes

out with his friends, he takes guy trips, and the rest of the time, he's at work."

Sounds like a real prince, Nick thinks.

"And I told him now that I'm pregnant, he has to change his ways." Abby shrugs. "If he thinks I'm raising this baby alone, he has another think coming."

Nick feels like he's suddenly been thrust into the role of marriage counselor. "Did Thomas end up going out?"

"Yes," Abby says. "But I wasn't happy about it."

"So who went out and who stayed home?" Nick asks.

"I stayed home. Mrs. Otis, Celeste's mother, stayed home. And Greer stayed home. Tag and Mr. Otis had a drink in Tag's study, which is a big deal."

"Oh, yeah?" Nick says. "Why?"

Abby blows her bangs out of her eyes. "No one is allowed to set foot in Tag's study without an invitation. I've never been invited so I'm not sure what's so *magical* about it. I know he keeps really good scotch in there. Anyway, when he invited Mr. Otis for a drink in his study, it meant Tag was . . . accepting him as a part of the family, I guess. And I will point out, not that I care, but Tag never invited *my* father into the study for a drink."

"Did Merritt go into town?" Nick asks.

"I assume she led the charge," Abby says. "No, *wait!*" Abby's voice rises so dramatically that Nick nearly leaps from the chair. "Wait, wait, *wait! I saw*

Celeste and Merritt out in the rose garden after the party broke up! Our bedroom window looks right over the garden and I saw them when I went to pull the shade. Merritt was *crying*. Celeste had her hands on Merritt's shoulders. They were talking. Then they hugged and Celeste walked toward the driveway and Merritt stayed in the garden." Abby looks at Nick in astonishment. "I totally forgot about that until just this instant. If I had remembered, I would have started out by telling you that."

Merritt and the bride in the rose garden. Merritt crying.

"In the scene you're describing, did it look like Merritt was upset and Celeste was comforting her, or did it look like they were arguing?" Nick asks.

"The first," Abby says. "I'm pretty sure Celeste went out with Benji, Thomas, and the others. But I couldn't say for sure about Merritt. I pulled the shade and went to bed."

Really? Nick thinks. Abby didn't seem to miss much, and wouldn't a former University of Texas sorority girl be naturally drawn to drama of this kind? She just described Merritt as "one of the guys," so wouldn't seeing Merritt *crying* make Abby very, very curious? "You didn't peek again?" Nick asks. "To see what happened? To see if Merritt was okay?"

Abby looks him dead in the eye. "I was bone-tired. I went to bed."

This is her reminding him, once again, that she's pregnant. He nods. "From the looks of things under the tent, there was some late-night partying. Is it possible that the people who went out came home and drank some rum?"

"Possible," Abby says.

"Do you have any idea who that might have been?" Nick asks.

Abby's face shuts down. It's as abrupt as a slamming door. "Nope."

She's lying, Nick thinks. This must have been when things got interesting.

"Was Merritt part of the group who had the nightcap?" he asks.

"I honestly have no idea," Abby says. She couldn't be less convincing.

Nick takes a sustaining breath. "When Thomas got back to your room, did you happen to notice what time it was? This is .very, very important. Please think."

"It was late."

"Late like midnight?" Nick says. "Or late like four a.m.?"

"I didn't look at the clock. I didn't know…" Here, Abby tears up. "I didn't know this would *happen!*"

"Please don't get upset," Nick says. "Let me find you some tissues."

"I'm fine," Abby says. And then, almost to herself,

she says, "I can't believe this is real. It's real. Merritt is *dead*."

"Abby, I have to ask: Did you hear anything else in the middle of the night? Did you hear anyone in the water? There was a two-person kayak down by the beach—"

Abby's head snaps up. "A kayak? That would be Tag's."

"You're sure?"

"Yes," Abby says. "Tag has two kayaks and he treats them like they're his babies. They're handmade by some guy in Alaska or wherever kayaks were invented. Tag has a one-person kayak and a two-person kayak and when he invites someone out on the two-person kayak, it's a really big deal, like an even bigger deal than when he invites you into his study to drink his thousand-year-old scotch."

"Since the kayak was out, would you guess Mr. Winbury was the one who used it?"

"Absolutely, yes," Abby says.

"No chance someone might have borrowed it without asking?"

"No chance," Abby says. "Tag keeps the kayaks locked up. I know this because…well, because Thomas and I have tried to use the two-person kayak without permission. We tried to guess the combination—we ran through every birthday, every anniversary, and we could not unlock those kayaks. Frankly, I can't believe a kayak was left out on the beach. That's a sure indication that something went very wrong last night. Tag isn't careless like that."

"Abby, would you say Mr. Winbury is a person with a lot of secrets?"

"*Everyone* in the Winbury family has secrets!" Abby says.

Nick holds his breath. He's afraid to move. *Come on, Abby,* he thinks. *Give me a little bit more.*

"I'm sure Tag has secrets," she says. "But I really like Tag and I admire and respect him and I want that feeling to be mutual. I'm pretty sure both he and Greer think I'm a failure because I haven't managed to give them a grandchild...but they don't know what I'm dealing with. Thomas is...and the pressure..." Abby stops, sniffs. "I'm sorry I'm crying. This can't be good for my baby. May I please be excused?"

Nick sighs. He was so close. But he can't push her, not in her present condition. He'll have to get his answers elsewhere. "Yes, of course. Thank you, Abby." He smiles at her as he lies and says, "You've been very helpful."

Friday, May 18-Saturday, May 19, 2018

TAG

He catches a brief glimpse of the friend on Friday evening when she and Celeste and Abby arrive from the city for the bachelorette weekend that Greer has arranged. Tag sees the friend from the back—long dark hair and a sweet little behind put on display in a tight sequined miniskirt. When she turns, he's treated to her profile. Pretty. Then she pivots at the hip, notices Tag checking her out, waggles her fingers at him, and offers a half smile.

"What's the friend's name?" Tag asks his wife later.

"Merritt Monaco," Greer says. "She's a brunette. Not your type."

Tag gathers his wife up in his arms, and as usual, she places both palms on his chest as if to push him away, but he holds her tight. Tag maintains— untruthfully—that he has no interest in brunettes. "You're my type," he says.

"Yeah, right," she says in an American accent,

which she knows he can't resist. He kisses her neck. He'll introduce himself to the friend later.

The introduction comes the next morning. Tag is in the kitchen reading the weekend *Journal* and enjoying coffee and grapefruit and a poached egg on whole-grain toast after having gone for a five-mile run and then taken a soak in the hot tub. He feels clean and virtuous, nearly relaxed. His wife and future daughter-in-law left a short while ago to meet with the wedding caterers. He has forgotten all about the friend until she comes wandering into the kitchen. She's barefoot, wearing a tiny pair of cotton sleep shorts and a thread-bare T-shirt. No bra. Tag can see the two pellets of her nipples through the material.

"Good morning," he says brightly.

She jumps, startled. Or maybe she's just pretend-ing. She's too pretty to be an innocent. Her hand flies to her chest as she turns to him. Her hair is mussed.

"Good morning," she says, her voice froggy with sleep. Or maybe it's naturally gravelly. She collects herself and offers a hand. "You must be Mr. Win-bury. How are you? I'm Merritt, as in the parkway."

"Call me Tag, please," he says. "As in hash."

This earns him a smile. Oh, the Millennials!

"Thank you for hosting us this weekend," she says. "It's a surprise luxury. Your house is sublime."

"I'm glad you're enjoying it," Tag says. "What did you girls get up to last night?"

"Dinner at Cru," she says. "Great oysters there."

"Agreed," Tag says.

"Then we went to the Afterhouse for caviar," Merritt says.

"Well, well," Tag says. Oysters and caviar. He assumes he was footing the bill.

"Then we went to Proprietors. Then to the Boarding House. Then to the Chicken Box. Then to Steamboat for pizza, since we were all starving. Then we caught an Uber home. Around two, I think? Early night."

Tag laughs. In New York, she's probably out every night until four. If she's anywhere close to Celeste's age, then she's still in her twenties.

"Is there coffee?" she asks.

Tag rises. He's wearing a waffle-knit cotton robe he snagged from the pool house to put on over his wet bathing suit, but now he wishes for regular clothes. The robe feels too feminine; it feels like a dress. "I'll get it for you," he says. "Please, sit and relax. How do you take it?"

"Black," she says.

Girl after his own heart. Tag pours her a cup of coffee. She takes the seat next to his chair and folds her legs up under herself. Cozy. If Greer saw this, she would not be amused, even considering Merritt is a brunette and therefore theoretically not Tag's type. But imagining Greer's reaction turns Tag on. He is most certainly going to hell.

He sits down and considers his half-eaten breakfast. "Can I fix you something to eat?" He is startled by his own offer of hospitality. If this were anyone but a desirable woman, he would go back to his newspaper.

She holds up a hand. "No, thank you."

"So, are there any stories you can share from last night?" he asks.

Merritt tilts her head and gives him a wry smile. "We were perfect angels," she says. "It was rather disappointing."

He laughs.

"Abby threw up on the way home," Merritt says. "Our Uber driver had to pull over on Orange Street."

"She overdid it?" Tag says. "Good for her."

"If you ask me, she's pregnant," Merritt says. "I got that vibe."

"Well," Tag says. "That would be good news." And it would. Thomas and Abby have been trying for a baby ever since they got married four years earlier. Conception isn't a problem. Abby has been pregnant four times that Tag knows of, but each time ended in a miscarriage and one of them necessitated a D and C at Lenox Hill Hospital. However, Tag feels more disloyal discussing Abby's potential pregnancy than he does looking at Merritt's breasts. He changes the subject.

"So what do you do for work, Merritt-as-in-the-Parkway?" he asks.

She takes a deliberate sip of her coffee. "Officially, I handle PR for the Wildlife Conservation Society, which manages all four city zoos and the aquarium. That's how I met Celeste. The Bronx Zoo has the biggest chunk of our budget so I do all of their press releases and whatnot. And Celeste, you know, is a rising star at the zoo. It's not every day you see a woman as young as Celeste named assistant zoo director."

"Right," Tag says. He's very fond of Celeste and thinks her career is magnificent. Greer has been less enthusiastic. *Why does she have to run a zoo?* she said. *Why not a museum or a charitable foundation? Something ladylike?* However, Greer far prefers Celeste to Benji's former girlfriend, Jules. Jules Briar lived on Park Avenue, which was good, but the apartment and the money and the daughter, Miranda, were all from the first husband, Andy Briar, a director at Goldman Sachs, which was bad. Greer wanted Benji to find someone without quite that much baggage—and Celeste offers a clean slate. It's almost as though she spent her first twenty-six years in a convent. Benji is the only serious boyfriend she's ever had.

"And unofficially," Merritt says with a bit of a tease in her voice, snapping Tag back to the present conversation—*Unofficially,* he thinks, *she's a stripper. Or a high-end escort*—"I'm an influencer."

"An influencer?" he says.

"I do work on the side to promote certain brands and events," Merritt says. "So some of my clothes and shoes and bags are by designers I can't afford, but I get them for free as long as I post about them on my social media platforms. I stump for nineteen companies."

"That's impressive," Tag says. He can see how she would succeed as an influencer: She's young, beautiful, cool, sexy. And edgy. She's an interesting match for Celeste, who doesn't have an edgy thing about her.

"What do *you* do for work?" Merritt asks.

Tag laughs; he likes her directness. "I own a hedge fund," he says.

"Note the look of surprise on my face," Merritt says.

"It's terribly boring, I know," he says. "I started my career at Barclays in London but when the boys finished with primary school, we decided it would be best to move to New York." He does *not* mention that the majority of their wealth comes from Greer's family. The Garrisons owned the mills that produced over half the gin in Great Britain. And Greer's book royalties are nothing to sniff at either, although sales are steadily declining and Tag has been tempted to suggest she retire before she becomes a parody of herself. Her fan base is nearly down to no one but the devoted cat ladies.

It's as Tag is thinking about the typical cat lady—tucked away in her Cotswold cottage fixing a cup of tea and preparing to spend a rainy afternoon in an armchair with a tabby spread across her lap as she cracks open the latest exotically located Greer Garrison mystery—that he feels something touch his leg. It's Merritt's foot. She is running her toes up his shin as she sips her coffee and pretends to be gazing out the window at Nantucket Sound. Tag immediately gets an erection. He thinks about lifting up her flimsy T-shirt or, better still, tearing the damn thing in half so he can lick the hard points of her nipples until she groans in his ear. Where can he take her? Maybe if he opens his robe and shows her what she's done to him, she'll get down on her knees in front of him. Right here in the kitchen. Could they be that brazen?

As he starts to reach for the belt of his robe, Abby comes limping into the kitchen, one hand on her stomach and one on the back of her neck as though she's trying to hold herself together. When she sees Tag and Merritt, a startled look crosses her face, then something darker flickers through her expression. *What must this look like?* Tag wonders.

Abby has been raised right. She smiles. "Good morning," she says. "Sorry I slept so late. I am *not* feeling well at all."

"Coffee?" Tag asks.

Merritt stands up. "I'm going to try the outdoor shower," she says.

When Greer and Celeste return, the girls all head out to the pool in their bikinis. Tag would like to join them but he can't possibly do so without seeming like a perverted and pathetic old man. He decides instead to go out in the kayak. He waves as he strolls past the pool, taking one long, appreciative look at Merritt, who is wearing a black bikini with a complicated web of straps across the back. The bikini is possibly meant to reference bondage and inspire any man who looks upon the suit to wish for a pair of sharp scissors to snip the straps and get to the luscious body underneath. However, the suit, with its web, also reminds Tag of a spider. A black widow, he thinks. Merritt is dangerous. He needs to stay away.

Tag paddles out to the Monomoy Creeks, a series of waterways that meander through reeds and eelgrass, around floating islands and sandbars. It's peaceful here. The only sound is the plashing of his paddle against the surface of the water. Up above, an osprey soars, and in the distance, Tag spies sailboats, an approaching ferry, and Commercial Wharf. The sun is unseasonably warm for May. He is tempted to take his shirt off so he can get something vaguely resembling a suntan. He must be bewitched, he thinks, because he hasn't given two thoughts to a suntan since he lifeguarded at Blackpool Sands in the summer of 1981. He's fifty-seven years old, likely more than twice the girl's age. He tries to banish her from his mind and instead focus on everything he already has—a satisfying, if stodgy, career; a beautiful, accomplished wife; and two healthy sons, both of whom are finally starting to get the hang of adulthood. Tag has a five-bedroom prewar apartment on Park Avenue, a flat in London, and this spread on Nantucket. He and Greer first visited Nantucket in the summer of 1997, and with the trust that Greer inherited on her thirty-fifth birthday, they bought the land. It had been quite expensive even then, this remote island of fishermen and free spirits, but Greer had loved it and Tag had loved making Greer happy.

He has grown quite fond of this island, even though his life here now is more fraught. There's always something *happening*—a festival, a benefit, houseguests, a cocktail party, a new restaurant Greer insists they have to try, and, in a few weeks, a wedding for which they will host 170 people. But Tag's favorite way to experience the island is like this, right now—on the water, in his kayak. Nantucket's charm is most easily found offshore. Tag paddles all the way to the Great Harbor Yacht Club, then he turns around and heads for home. He wills himself to be strong enough for what awaits him there.

*   *   *

He has never quite mastered the art of getting out of the kayak and nearly always dunks himself in the process. This gives Greer much joy and himself a much-needed cooling-off so he is half guilty of facilitating the mishap. After he pulls the kayak up on the shore, he towels himself dry and checks his phone. There's a voice mail from his friend Sergio Ramone.

Tag finds Greer arranging flowers on the sunporch.

"Sergio called," he says. "He has two tickets to the Dujac Grand Cru wine-festival dinner tonight. The chef from Nautilus is doing the food and it's at some swanky house out on Quaise Pasture Road. I told him we'd take them. They're ridiculously expensive, but we deserve it."

"I can't go," Greer says.

"What?" Tag says. "Why not? You love Dujac. It's blue-chip terroir. Not Sonoma, not South Africa. These wines will be once-in-a-lifetime. You know how these French vintners are. If you show the proper appreciation, they can't help themselves — they open up the bottles they aren't supposed to, the really, really good stuff, the rare vintages that we'll never have the opportunity to taste again."

"I have to stay home and write tonight," Greer

says. "My deadline is in thirty days and I'm dread-fully behind because of the wedding. Also, I had an idea while Celeste and I were out and I want to get it down before I forget."

"The dinner isn't until seven," he says. "Go write now and you'll be finished by six, in time for a shower and a dressing drink."

"I can't now," Greer says. "I'm busy."

"I'll arrange the flowers," Tag says. "You go write."

"You know it doesn't work like that, darling," she says.

He wants to strangle her. He should never have expected his wife to suddenly display a penchant for spontaneity. He knows it doesn't work like that; he knows Greer can't be prodded to write, that she has to listen to her internal muse, and the muse prefers the nighttime hours, a quiet, dark house, a glass of wine (ordinary wine, a fifteen-dollar bottle of char-donnay, for example, which will have nothing in common with the wine that will be served with this dinner).

"What the hell am I going to do?" Tag says. "I promised Sergio I'd take the tickets off his hands." If it were anyone else, Tag would call and renege, but Sergio is an esteemed criminal-defense attorney and he's also the friend who got Thomas into law school at NYU when there was no prayer of Thomas getting in on his own. And then Sergio angled to get Thomas a job at Skadden, Arps, the law firm where Thomas now works. Thomas, Tag has to admit, isn't the achiever the rest of them are; Tag suspects he'll quit law before he makes partner. But even so, Tag and Greer owe Sergio Ramone a lifelong debt of gratitude. Tag can't back out on these tickets. He can pay the $3,500 apiece and just not go, he supposes, but what a waste that would be. "Please, darling."

Greer stabs a peony into the vase. The peony is deep pink and resembles a human heart unfurling in desperation. Or possibly he's projecting. "Take one of the girls," she says.

Tag scoffs.

"I'm serious," Greer says. "Don't be a martyr for me. I won't like that one bit. Ask one of the girls."

"But isn't this supposed to be a bachelorette weekend?" Tag says.

"They partied last night," Greer says. "Unless I'm mistaken, they're planning on staying home tonight. But I'm sure you can talk one of them into it."

The girls, as Greer calls them, are in the casual dining area, reading magazines, snacking on chips and salsa. Merritt-as-in-the-Parkway, Tag is relieved to see, has covered herself properly, in white jeans and a navy cashmere sweater. Abby is resting her head on her arms on the table.

"Hello, ladies," Tag says. His stomach feels leaden; it's nerves. He knows how this is going to end. Greer too must know how this is going to end. She is the one he will hold responsible. She has suspected him of cheating for the entirety of their marriage, he knows, and now it feels like she is pushing him toward it. "I have an extra ticket to a very fancy wine dinner tonight and my wife feels she needs to stay home and write. Would any of you three like to go with me?"

"God, no." Abby groans.

"No, thank you," Celeste says sweetly. "I'm exhausted."

Merritt raises her face and looks him dead in the eye. His heart skips a beat.

Tag wears a jacket but no tie. Merritt wears a lavender dress with thin straps that crisscross her back and a pair of silver stiletto heels. It's the heels Greer chooses to comment on.

"You'll break your neck in those," she says.

"I'll be fine," Merritt says. "Years of practice."

"Well," Greer says in Tag's ear as she kisses him good-bye, "I believe Quaise Pasture is in for quite a shock."

Once they're in the Land Rover headed out the Polpis Road, Tag worries that Merritt will reach over and put her hand on his leg. Then he worries she won't. He has an erection simply from smelling her perfume and listening to her rummage through her clutch purse in the dark. He can't go inside in this state; he needs to talk himself down. He takes a deep breath. He worries there will be someone he knows at this dinner—and how will he explain who Merritt is? *My future daughter-in-law's best friend.* It sounds sleazy. It *is* sleazy. What will people think? They'll think… well, they'll think the obvious.

But then Tag calls upon one of his favorite sayings: *Perception is reality.* This situation can be translated in more than one way. Tonight, Tag will perceive this outing as innocent and fun and that is what it will become. He relaxes a little.

"Is this your first time on Nantucket?" he asks.

"Not at all," she says. "I've come with friends over the years, in college and then as a so-called adult."

"Where was college?" he asks.

"Trinity," she says. "In glamorous Hartford."

He has friends whose children went to Trinity but he doesn't dare ask if Merritt knows any of them; he's already self-conscious enough about how young she is. Or how old he is.

"Do you have siblings?" Tag asks.

"A brother," she says. "Married with kids and a mortgage."

"And where did you grow up?" Tag asks.

"On Long Island," she says. "Commack."

Tag nods. He and Greer have successfully avoided Long Island, though he does have a client with a house in Oyster Bay whom he visits on occasion and there was one long-ago rainy weekend in Montauk when the boys were small. He has never heard of Commack. "I always wanted a daughter," he says. "But Greer didn't. She's happy with the boys."

"Greer is lovely," Merritt says.

"Isn't she?" he says. "Anyway, now we have a daughter-in-law. Abby. And soon, Celeste."

"Celeste is a treasure," Merritt says. "I met her at a difficult time in my life. She saved me."

This statement seems to warrant a follow-up question, but it's too late. They've arrived. The house is, in fact, grand—it's all lit up from within, overlooking the sound but from a more dramatic vantage point than Tag's house. There are two unfamiliar cars in the driveway.

Tag parks, then smiles at Merritt. This is going to be innocent and fun. "Shall we?" he says.

The evening unfolds easily. There are ten diners, plus the French gentleman from the esteemed Dujac vineyard plus one of the sous-chefs from Nautilus plus two kitchen staff and two waitstaff. Tag doesn't know a soul. The other eight diners are all one group. They tell Tag it's their first time to Nantucket. They live in Texas.

"Where in Texas?" Merritt asks.

Tag steels himself to hear that they're from Austin and then to find out that they are best friends or business partners of Abby's parents, the Freemans.

"San Antonio," they say. "Remember the Alamo."

It quickly becomes obvious that Merritt knows nothing about wine, not even the basics. She doesn't know that cabernet sauvignons are from Bordeaux and that pinot noirs and chardonnays are from Burgundy. She doesn't know what terroir is. She has never heard of pinot franc; she has never heard of the Loire Valley. How can she be an influencer of culture when she doesn't have even a basic vocabulary of wine? What does she drink when she goes out?

"Cocktails," she says. "Gin, bourbon, vodka, tequila. Skinny margaritas are my go-to." She must see him grimace because she adds, "There used to be a place downtown, Pearl and Ash, that made a cocktail called Teenage Jesus, which was my particular favorite. Plus, the name."

Tag can't imagine drinking something called a Teenage Jesus. "What about when you have oysters? When you have caviar? Surely you must drink champagne."

"Prosecco," she says. "But only if someone presses it on me. It gives me a headache."

After his starter glass, a 2013 Chambolle-Musigny, goes down, he decides that Merritt's ignorance is fortuitous. She isn't the jaded, worldly woman he thought she was. He had convinced himself over the past few hours that she was at least thirty but now he fears she's closer to twenty-five. More than thirty years younger than he is.

After his second glass, a 2009 Morey Saint-Denis, he is loose. He will teach Merritt about wine. He will teach her how to roll the wine over her tongue. He will teach her how to identify black-cherry and tobacco notes in pinots, and lemon, mint, and clover in sauvignon blancs. He's excited by this mission, although her palate will be exposed to some of the finest wines in the world tonight, and this worries him. When you start with the best, the future offers only disappointment.

They stumble out of the house well past midnight, hand in hand. At one extremely saturated point during the evening, one of the Texas ladies turned to Merritt and said, "So how long have y'all been married?"

Without hesitation, Merritt said, "We're newly-weds."

"Congratulations!" the woman said. "Second marriage?"

Merritt winked. "How'd you guess?"

So when they leave, they are a couple, married by the incredible wine, the extraordinary food, the camaraderie of complete strangers. It's as if they have stepped out of their lives into another life where everything is new and anything is possible. When Tag opens the passenger door for Merritt, she turns to him and raises her face.

He kisses her once, chastely, on the lips.

"That's all I get?" she says.

Say yes, Tag thinks. *Be strong. Be true to Greer and the boys. Show some integrity, for God's sake.*

But.

Even that faintest touch of her lips sent a surge of electricity through him. Tag is pulsing with desire for her. He won't be able to stop himself from driving Merritt to the beach and making love to her, maybe more than once.

He is, ultimately, only a man.

Saturday, July 7, 2018, 8:30 a.m.

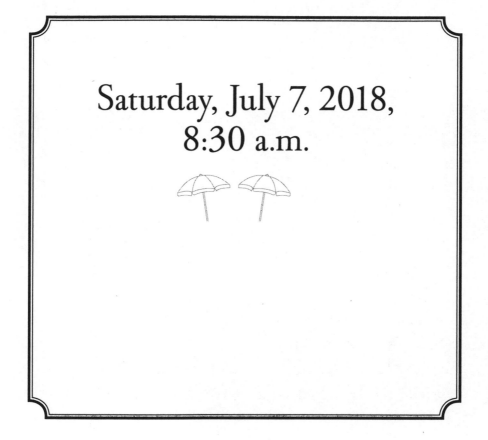

THE CHIEF

After interviewing Roger, the Chief has some choices
for who to talk to next. There's the bride's father, who
is in an upstairs bedroom with the bride's mother;
Greer Garrison has requested that they not be dis-
turbed until the last possible minute because of the
mother's health. And the groom, Benjamin Winbury,
asked permission to go to the hospital to check on
Celeste. He promised to be back in an hour. So, as far
as persons of interest go, that leaves the Chief with
the groom's brother, Thomas; the groom's father,
Thomas Senior, known as Tag; and this Shooter fellow, the best man. The Chief thinks the third option
is the most promising.

Dickson said the best man was missing when he
arrived on the scene, but then the guy turned up in a
cab an hour later. He could have met a woman — or a
man — last night and slept elsewhere. But the per-
plexing thing is that he had his luggage with him. It's

almost as if he'd planned to leave and then changed his mind. There might be a plausible explanation for this, but the Chief can't come up with it himself. He will question Shooter.

The Chief finds Shooter standing behind the police tape at the edge of the beach, staring in the direction of the water. He has shed the blazer, removed his shoes, untucked his shirt.

"Hey there," the Chief says. Shooter turns. His expression is one of fear, maybe, or alarm. The Chief is used to it. In thirty years, no one has been exactly *happy* to see him while he was on duty in the field. "Are you free to answer a few questions?"

"What about?" Shooter says.

"We're interviewing everyone who's part of the wedding. I understand you're the best man?"

"If you're going to ask me what happened to her, I really have no idea," Shooter says.

"I'd just like to get some background," the Chief says. "About the events of last night. Easy stuff."

Shooter nods. "I can handle that, I suppose."

"Great," the Chief says. He leads Shooter across the driveway to the white wrought-iron bench under the rose arbor where he talked to Roger. He sees police tape all around the cottage on the north side of the property, which was where the maid of honor was staying by herself. The Chief is fairly certain that if they can find the girl's phone, they'll have the answers they're looking for. The Chief has learned over the past decade that if you want to know the truth about a person, just look through his or her phone.

Shooter takes a seat and the Chief pulls his notebook out. He has only one question for Shooter. "So . . . where were you last night?"

"Last night?" Shooter says.

Just like that, the Chief knows a lie is coming. "Yes, last night," the Chief says. "The groom told my sergeant that you were missing. Until you pulled up in the cab, we thought maybe you were dead as well. But, thankfully, we were mistaken. Where were you?"

"I'm sorry I caused you to worry," Shooter says. "I was up at the Wauwinet."

"The Wauwinet Inn?" the Chief says.

"The restaurant, actually. Topper's? I'm friendly with the bartender there."

"And what's the bartender's name?"

"Name?" Shooter says. "Oh. Gina."

"The bartender at Topper's is named Gina. And you spent last night with Gina?"

"Yes," Shooter says.

"She lives up there?" the Chief asks. "At the Wauwinet?"

"Yes," Shooter says. "Staff housing."

"Had you *planned* to spend the night with Gina?" the Chief asks. "Because the groom seemed to think you'd spent the night in the cottage."

"I hadn't planned on it, no," Shooter says. "It was just a booty call. It was late, she texted, I went up there."

A booty call. The Chief thinks protectively of Chloe. He feels a hundred years old. "What time was that?"

"I'm really not sure," Shooter says.

"You can check your phone," the Chief says.

Shooter slips his phone out of the pocket of his Nantucket Reds shorts. He pushes some buttons and says, "I must have deleted the text."

"You must have deleted the text," the Chief says. "Tell me why you took your luggage. *All* of your luggage, from the looks of it."

"Right," Shooter says. His tone is cautious, and the Chief can practically see the shadowy interior of his mind where he's groping around for something solid to hold on to. "I took my luggage because I thought I might just stay up at the Wauwinet with Gina."

"But then this morning, quite early, I'd say, you showed back up here. So what happened?"

"I changed my mind," Shooter says.

"You changed your mind," the Chief says. He looks at Shooter Uxley. The kid is sweating, but then again, it's hot, even in the shade. "Would you mind giving me this Gina's cell phone number, please?"

"Her number?" Shooter says. "I'd rather not. I don't want her to get involved in this if we can help it."

"We can't help it," the Chief says. "Because Gina is your alibi."

"My *alibi?*" Shooter says. "Why do I need an *alibi?*"

"We have an unattended death," the Chief says. "And you were missing, then you showed back up. Now, maybe your story holds water. Maybe you did go up to the Wauwinet to hook up with Gina the bartender with all your luggage and maybe you did then decide you didn't like Gina that much or that the staff housing wasn't as nice as the Winburys' guest cottage. That's all feasible. But we have a twenty-nine-year-old woman dead, so I'm going to proceed with due diligence and check out your story. You can either give me the girl's cell phone—which I know you have because you said she texted you late last night—or I'll call the front desk of the Wauwinet and contact her that way."

Shooter gets to his feet. "Call the Wauwinet," he says. "I need to use the bathroom right now. My stomach is funny. I think it was the raw bar from last night."

"Go ahead," the Chief says. He's not stupid. He knows that Shooter will go into the cottage to "use the bathroom," but really he'll text Gina the bartender and ask her to corroborate his story.

The Chief waits until Shooter disappears into the cottage, then he takes out his phone and calls Bob from Old Salt Taxi. Bob, who dropped Shooter off here this morning, has been a friend of the Chief's for twenty-five years.

"Hey, Bob," the Chief says. "It's Ed Kapenash."

"Ed," Bob says. "Sorry I didn't stop to chat this morning. You looked like you were busy. What's going on? Word on the street is there was a murder."

Word on the street. Already? Well, it is a small island. "I can't get into it," the Chief says. "But you remember the kid you dropped off? I need to know where you picked him up. Did you pick him up at the Wauwinet?"

"The *Wauwinet?*" Bob says. "No. That real handsome kid in the red shorts and the blazer? I picked him up down at the Steamship. He had a ticket for the six-thirty slow boat this morning but I guess he missed it. And so he asked me to take him back to Monomoy. He said he was staying there."

"You're *sure* you picked him up at the Steamship dock?" the Chief says. "And not at the Wauwinet?"

"Sure I'm sure," Bob says. "I may not be getting any younger but I have yet to make a twelve-mile mistake. I picked that kid up on Steamboat Wharf. He told me he'd missed the six-thirty."

"Okay, Bob, wonderful, thanks. I'll talk to you." The Chief hangs up and takes a second to think. Shooter had a ticket for the early boat? With the wedding scheduled for this afternoon? Something is going on. And he flat-out lied about the Wauwinet.

Why?

A text comes in on the Chief's phone. It's from the funeral director, Bostic, saying he's on his way to collect the body—which is good news, considering the heat and the fragile state of everyone's nerves. Bostic will get the body ready for transfer to the medical examiner on Cape Cod. The Chief checks the time. If everything goes perfectly, they may have a report on the cause of death by early afternoon.

The Chief waits another few minutes for Shooter to emerge. By now, he must know he's been caught in a lie. The Chief strides across the shell driveway to the cottage that Shooter entered and knocks on the door. "Excuse me?" he says. "Mr. Uxley?"

No answer. He knocks harder. "Sir?"

The Chief tries the knob. The door is locked. He forces the door, which feels extreme, but he wants Shooter Uxley to know he can't hide.

The cottage is empty. The Chief checks the little sitting room, the galley kitchen, the bedroom, and the bathroom—where the window is wide open.

Shooter Uxley is gone.

Friday, July 6, 2018, 4:00 p.m.

KAREN

She wakes up from her nap with the sun striping her bed and for one glorious instant, she feels no pain. She sits up without any help. It's as if Nantucket Island — the quality of the air, the rarefied seaside atmosphere — has cured her. She's going to be fine.

"B-B-Betty?"

Karen turns. Celeste emerges from Karen's bathroom wearing a ruffled sundress the color of a tangerine, a sunset, a monarch butterfly. It's bright and very flattering. Celeste may have the brain and temperament of a scientist, but she has the body of a bathing-suit model. She inherited Karen's breasts, which used to be her best feature, round and firm. But along with the breasts, Celeste may also have inherited the predisposition to cancer. Karen has made Celeste promise that as soon as she and Benji are married and Celeste has comprehensive health insurance, she will go to Sloan Kettering for genetic testing. And if necessary, she will get screened every year. Early detection is key.

"Hello, sweetheart," Karen says. "What are you doing here? Surely you have more important places to be? This is your time to shine."

"I was putting your t-t-toiletries away," Celeste says. "And now I can help you g-g-get ready."

Karen's eyes prick with tears. It is she who should be helping Celeste, she who should be fussing over her daughter, the bride. But there is no denying that if Karen is to get dressed and make herself presentable, she will need help.

"Where's your father?" she asks.

"Swimming," Celeste says.

There's a stabbing pain in Karen's chest. It's jealousy. Bruce is swimming. Karen yearns to be with him, to feel the power of her four limbs. She had once been so strong; she remembers swimming the butterfly leg on her relay team, soaring from the water, arms stretched overhead, legs pumping behind. When she looks back at her life, she sees how much she has taken for granted.

Celeste is by her side. Karen takes a moment to look up at her face. Her eyes are sad, and Karen is concerned about the stutter, although she hasn't mentioned it because she doesn't want to make Celeste self-conscious for fear that the stutter will get worse. She knows that

Benji and Celeste have whittled down their wedding vows so that all Celeste has to say is "I do."

"Is everything okay?" Karen asks.

"Yes, B-B-Betty, of course," Celeste says.

The nickname never fails to give Karen joy, even so many years later. She is Betty, for Betty Crocker, because Karen swears by the tattered, spiral-bound cookbooks she inherited from her own mother. Bruce, meanwhile, is Mac, for MacGyver, because he has a talent for unconventional problem-solving. The man can fix anything and prides himself on not having called a repairman in thirty years of marriage. Celeste gave them the nicknames when she was eleven years old and had outgrown Mommy and Daddy.

Karen strokes Celeste's forearm and Celeste adjusts her smile so that it seems almost real. She's pretending. But why? Is she feeling scared and anxious about Karen's illness? The decline has been significant, Karen knows, even in the two weeks since she last saw Celeste. Karen had dropped thirteen pounds as of a week ago and maybe another ten since then. Her stomach is compromised; she eats a bite or two of food per meal and forces down enough Ensure to keep up her strength. Her hair is nothing but gray fuzz, like one finds on a pussy willow. Her eyes are sunken, and her limbs tremble. It has probably come as a shock to Celeste.

But Karen isn't persuaded that she, Karen, is the reason for Celeste's pensive, faraway mood. It's something else, maybe the stress and pressure of being the center of attention. This wedding is huge; the setting is grandiose. Elaborate, expensive plans have been made, with Celeste and Benji at their center. It would be intimidating for anyone. When Karen married Bruce, there were six people in attendance at the Easton courthouse. She and Bruce celebrated afterward with a bottle of Asti spumante and a pizza from Nicolosi's.

Or maybe the problem isn't the wedding. Maybe it's Benji himself. Karen thinks back on her ill-advised visit to Kathryn Randall, the psychic.

Chaos.

"Darling," Karen says.

Celeste looks at her mother, and their eyes lock. Karen sees the truth in Celeste's clear blue irises: she doesn't want to marry Benji.

Karen needs to reassure Celeste that she's doing the right thing. Benji is a good man. He *adores* Celeste. He keeps her on the exact same pedestal that Karen and Bruce placed her on at the moment of her birth. That's really the wonderful thing about Benji: He loves their daughter the way she deserves to be loved. That...and he has money.

Karen would like to pretend that the money doesn't matter, but it does. For over thirty years,

Karen and Bruce have lived from paycheck to paycheck; 95 percent of their decisions have had to do with money: Should they buy organic fruit so Celeste wouldn't be exposed to a lot of pesticides? (Yes.) Should they drive the extra twenty minutes to Phillipsburg, New Jersey, for cheaper gas? (Yes.) Should they take Celeste to the orthodontist who allegedly had been accused of child molestation but who charged half as much as the reputable orthodontist? (No.) They had enough money to pay their mortgage and send Celeste to college, but any financial surprise — a leak in the roof, a raise in property taxes, a cancer diagnosis — was enough to sink them. Karen doesn't want Celeste to have to live that way. She has a college degree and a good job at the zoo, but Benji can give her everything. And everything is what she deserves.

As Karen opens her mouth to assure her daughter that she *is* doing the right thing, Bruce comes into the room with a navy-and-white-striped beach towel wrapped around his waist. Karen feasts her eyes on her husband — to her, he's every bit as beautiful as he was on the pool balcony so many years ago. His shoulders are defined by rippling muscles; his chest is smooth and broad. They have never had money for gym memberships; Bruce does old-fashioned calisthenics — sit-ups, push-ups, and pull-ups — in their bedroom every morning before work. He has been outside for less than an hour and already his skin has a healthy golden glow. Karen always envied the Mediterranean blood he'd inherited from his mother. He would go outside to mow the lawn and come back a bronzed god.

"Both my girls!" he says. "What a surprise!"

"D-D-Did you get the Reds, Mac?" Celeste asks. "For t-t-tomorrow?"

"Yes," Bruce says. He pulls a pair of pants out of the closet; they are the color of dusty bricks. "I don't see what the big deal is. It's certainly not the style. Is it the color? Mrs. Winbury, Greer, told me they would fade with every washing. It sounds like I'm going to need to spring for the dry cleaner."

"N-N-No, you should wash them," Celeste says. "That's the idea. The m-m-more they f-f-fade, the c-c-cooler they are."

"That makes no sense," Bruce says. "Did you happen to notice the black jeans I had on earlier? Sleek as a panther."

"The Reds are d-d-different, though," Celeste says.

"It's a Nantucket thing, darling," Karen says to Bruce. She thinks she gets it; the older and more worn the pants, the more authentic they are. The sleek-as-a-panther look, shiny and new, doesn't work on Nantucket; the preferred aesthetic is a careless appearance: faded pants, frayed collars, scuffed penny loafers.

Bruce won't understand this but Karen gives him a look that implores him to just get with the program. The last thing they want to do is make a fuss and embarrass Celeste.

Bruce catches Karen's eye and seems to read her mind. "I'll do as you tell me, Bug." He throws on a T-shirt, then takes Celeste's hand and Karen's hand so that they form a human chain. But every chain has a weak link, and in their case, it's Karen. She's leaving them behind. The agony of this is exquisite. There is nothing more terrible, she has decided, than the ferocity with which humans can love.

"I came in to help B-B-Betty get ready," Celeste says. "The p-p-party starts in a little while."

"What about the rehearsal?" Bruce says. "Aren't we all going to the church?"

"Reverend D-D-Derby's flight from New York was d-d-delayed so we decided to scrap the rehearsal," Celeste says.

Karen is relieved. She isn't certain she would have made it through both the rehearsal and the party. Bruce, however, seems miffed.

"How are we supposed to practice our walk?" he says.

"We don't have to p-p-practice," Celeste says. "We link arms, we walk. Slowly. You hand me off to B-B-Benji. You k-k-kiss me."

"I wanted to practice," Bruce says. "Practice doing

it without crying. I figured since today was the first time, I'd cry, but then tomorrow it would be old hat and maybe I wouldn't cry. Maybe. But I wanted to practice."

Celeste shrugs. "We d-d-decided not to d-d-do it."

Bruce nods. "All right. I'll help your mother. You go relax, Bug. Have a glass of wine."

"Find Benji," Karen says. "The two of you could probably use some alone time before all this begins."

"But I want to stay here," Celeste says. "With b-b-both of you."

Bruce helps Karen in and out of the shower.

Celeste helps Karen put on a soft white waffle-knit cotton robe with a light terry-cloth lining—there are two in every guest room, Celeste tells her, laundered after each use by Elida, the Winburys' summer housekeeper—and then Celeste rubs her mother's arms, back, and legs with Greer Garrison's favorite lotion, La Prairie White Caviar Illuminating and Moisturizing Cream, also in every guest room. The lotion is like none Karen has ever used before; it's rich, luscious even. Karen's skin drinks it in.

Bruce helps Karen get dressed. She is wearing a silk kimono over black leggings and a pair of Tory Burch ballet flats from two seasons ago that Bruce plucked off the sale rack for pennies.

"Style," Bruce says. "And comfort."

Karen looks in the mirror. She's swimming in the kimono. She tugs on the belt.

"Lipstick, B-B-Betty," Celeste says. She dabs at Karen's lips with the nub of Karen's old standby, Maybelline's New York Red. It's the only lipstick Karen has ever worn. Or ever will wear.

"I'd say you're ready," Bruce says. "You look stunning."

"I just want to use the toilet real quick," Karen says. This, at least, she can still do without help. She closes the door to the bathroom. She needs an oxycodone. Two, actually, because so much is expected of her. She'll be introduced to dozens of people she doesn't know and wouldn't care about except that some of these people will remain in Celeste's life long after Karen is gone, and Karen is determined that every single one of those people will remember her, Celeste's mother, as a "lovely woman."

Karen can't find her oxy. The pill bottle was in her Vera Bradley cosmetic bag along with her lipstick and a Revlon mascara that was rendered useless when she lost her eyelashes. Where... Karen tries not to panic but those pills are the only thing keeping her going. Without them, she will curl up in bed in a fetal position and howl with pain.

Karen's gaze sweeps the gleaming marble, glass, and mirrored surfaces of the guest bathroom. There's Karen's toothbrush in a silver cup. There's the miraculous body cream. Karen pulls open the little drawers, hoping that maybe Celeste tucked her things away so that she would feel at home.

And yes—in the third drawer, there are her pills. Oh, thank you! It seems like an unusual place to put them, but maybe Celeste didn't want the summer housekeeper to stumble across them and be tempted. Karen thinks about chastising Celeste for pawing through her things. Everyone deserves a modicum of privacy, a secret or two. But mostly, Karen feels an overwhelming relief that is nearly as powerful as the pills themselves. She taps two oxy into her palm, fills the silver cup with water, and swallows.

GREER

She checks her e-mail to review the timetable that Siobhan the caterer sent her and, unfortunately, she sees a new e-mail from Enid Collins, Greer's editor at Livingston and Greville, with the subject line URGENT.

This makes Greer laugh. Enid is seventy-seven years old. She has eleven grandchildren and one great-grandchild and she still marks up Greer's manuscripts with a red pencil. Never once in the twenty-two years that Enid has been editing Greer's novels has she ever used the word *urgent*. Enid believes strongly in letting ideas marinate—for days or weeks or months. There's nothing Enid despises more than a rush.

Greer checks the e-mail even though the definition of *urgent* is transpiring right outside the window of Greer's sitting room: the rental people are setting up chairs, the band is doing a sound check, and sixty people are due to descend on Summerland for the rehearsal dinner, among them Featherleigh Dale.

Dearest Greer, the e-mail begins (Enid composes all of her e-mails as formal letters).

I'm sure you will understand how it pains me to tell you this, since I have long been a champion of your work, your very first champion, if you remember.

Yes, Greer does remember. She was out of her mind with boredom when she was pregnant with Thomas—Tag was at the office day and night back then—and so she'd started writing a murder mystery set in the sixth arrondissement of Paris entitled *Prey in the Saint-Germain-des-Prés*. She had sent it off to Livingston and Greville, the publishing house that brought out the mysteries Greer most enjoyed herself, and, lo and behold, she received a letter of interest from an established editor named Enid Collins who said she would like to publish the book and might

Greer be able to meet and discuss terms of payment and editorial changes? This had launched the Dolly Hardaway murder mystery series, the most successful of which, *The Killer on Khao San Road,* was made into a movie that had somehow attained that elusive thing known as cult status.

But since we have been bought by Turnhaute Publishing Group, my autonomy has been greatly diminished.

Is it really the fault of the corporate Goliath of Turnhaute, fondly known as Turncoat, Greer wonders, or is Enid being pushed out because of her advanced age? Her driver's license will be the next thing taken, Greer supposes.

My editorial director, Mr. Charles O'Brien, also read your manuscript and he has deemed it "unacceptable." He has asked me to let you know you have a fortnight to rewrite it entirely. He suggests you use an alternate exotic locale, one you can describe with more "colorful detail" than what he calls the rather "pale" version of Santorini you present here. I'm sorry to be so blunt and to bear this dreadful news, my darling Greer. But a fortnight makes your new due date July 21, and I felt it best to be direct in light of that looming deadline.

With best wishes,

Enid Collins

Hell and damnation, Greer thinks. Her twenty-first manuscript has been . . . *rejected,* then? Who *is* this Charles O'Brien and what does *he* know? Charlie, old Chuck, an Irishman. Greer can't bring to mind an Irish writer she has ever admired. She has always despised Joyce, pretentious sod, writing in code and asking his readers to follow the twists and turns of his demented mind. She finds Wilde predictable, Swift histrionic, Beckett inscrutable, Stoker overrated, and Yeats dull.

Her cell phone pings. It's Benji. Roger has questions about the seating chart. Where are you?

In my sitting room. Witnessing the end of my career.

What had old Chuck O'Brien said about the book? Pale. He had called Greer's description of Santorini *pale* and suggested Greer use a different exotic locale.

It *has* been over thirty years since Greer set foot on Santorini. She chose it only because back in August when Benji proposed to Celeste, he mentioned he would like to honeymoon there. Greer's own memories of the place were brilliant. She recalled stark limestone cliffs and a red beach, colored by iron deposits; robust, bushy-haired Greek men selling freshly caught fish in woven baskets; she remembered the deep aquamarine of the Aegean Sea, whitewashed churches with cobalt-blue domes, the winding streets of Oia, the seafood restaurants where the water practically lapped onto one's feet and everyone was offered the same wine, a lovely, crisp white that was made on the east side of the island. Greer and Tag had chartered a catamaran, and Tag had sailed them around while Greer sat under a canopy wearing a floppy straw hat and Jackie O. sunglasses. They had swum into the beaches from the boat and paid the cabana boys two drachmas for chaises and an umbrella. Greer had left the island with recipes for garlicky tzatziki, grilled chicken with lemon and fresh oregano, and of course her famous lamb souvlaki.

She had been dismayed to find, upon researching Santorini 2018 via the internet, that Oia is now home to a Jimmy Choo boutique and that the donkey ride from the port up to Fira has been given a one-star rating on TripAdvisor. Greer had adored the donkey ride.

If she is very honest with herself, she will admit that the novel did feel a bit thin on plot, a bit slap-dash, a bit "phoned in," as it were. The key to a good whodunit is a murderer who is hiding in plain sight. Her character with the newly acquired stutter is, per-haps, underdeveloped. She remembers thinking when she handed the novel in, *Well, that wasn't so bad.* She had delivered a seventy-five-thousand-word manu-script on time, despite planning a wedding to rival Prince Harry's, and she hadn't pulled her hair out or been committed to an insane asylum.

Things that seem too good to be true usually are.

Can she rewrite the novel in a fortnight? (No one

but the British—scratch that—no one but *Enid Collins* still uses the term *fortnight*.)

She isn't sure. She'll have to wait and see how the weekend goes.

She clicks out of Enid, clicks out of e-mail entirely. Thinking about the unpleasant reality of her work life has provided a distraction, at least, from the even more unpleasant reality of the present moment. Featherleigh Dale will be arriving in less than an hour. Featherleigh is the rare party guest who sees fit to show up exactly on time. She does this, Greer suspects, so that she can have some private moments with Tag. Tag is ready for every occasion half an hour early and Greer is always half an hour late. It is a cunning and perceptive woman indeed who notes this habit and takes advantage of it, as Featherleigh does.

Greer changes into her party outfit—a sleek ivory silk jumpsuit by Halston, vintage, that looks like something Bianca Jagger might have worn to Studio 54. It's one of the most fabulous pieces Greer owns. She had the trousers temporarily shortened so that she might wear the jumpsuit barefoot in the sand, showing off her toenails, which have been painted pale blue. Her mother-of-the-groom dress for tomorrow is proper—which is to say, matronly—and so tonight, Greer is going to emphasize her youthful, fun, carefree side. (Tag might say she abandoned this side of herself in the nineties and he might be partially correct, but she is reasserting it tonight.) For the first time since primary school, she is going out in public with her hair down, all the way down, straight and loose on both sides of her face. She always wears her hair up or back, normally in a chignon, sometimes in a tight ballerina bun, occasionally braided for casual occasions. When she exercises, which is infrequently, she wears her hair in a ponytail. She never allows herself to wear it like this—like a hippie, or something worse.

But it's sexy. She looks younger.

When she goes into the kitchen, Tag whistles. "You'd better get out of here before my wife sees you. She's quite formidable, with her hairpins and her diamonds."

Greer grins at him. She doesn't do this enough, she realizes. Tag always gets the worst of her: her laser focus, her inflexibility, her condescension, her acerbic tongue. She used to love that she could be herself in front of him, but now it feels like all he gets is the negative, unpleasant, unflattering aspects of Greer Garrison; the sweet, gentle, caring parts of her she saves for others—her sons, certainly, but also virtual strangers, such as her fans, waiters at restaurants, and retail girls in shops. Greer is nicer to Tita at the Nantucket post office than she is to her own husband.

She stands before him, raises her face, lowers her eyelids, purses her lips.

"Darling," he says. "You look gorgeous. No, I take that back. You look *hot*." He kisses her, and his hands cup her behind.

The doorbell rings. *That,* Greer thinks, *will be Featherleigh.*

It isn't a question of *if* Tag has slept with Featherleigh Dale, it's a question of how many times, how recently, and how far things went between them emotionally. Featherleigh Dale is the much younger sister of the late Hamish Dale, who was Tag's closest friend at Oxford. To hear the stories, Featherleigh used to come visit the boys at school when she was merely eight years old and would accompany them first to the pub and then to the Nosebag, where they would reward Featherleigh's patience with cheddar scones and lime posset. They also used her as a lure for young female students who thought it adorable that Hamish and Tag were minding a little sister.

Hamish was killed six years earlier in a gruesome car crash on the M1. Greer and Tag and Thomas and Benji flew to London for the funeral and became reacquainted with Featherleigh, who was then all grown up and living in Sloane Square, working in the fine carpet division of Sotheby's. As far as Greer knows, nothing happened between Tag and Featherleigh at the reception following Hamish's funeral, although certainly cards were exchanged because after that, Featherleigh Dale started to appear at nearly every social event the Winburys attended. She had shown up at a graduation party for Thomas's law-school roommate held at the Carlyle Hotel in New York, and that was when Greer grew suspicious. What were the chances that Featherleigh Dale would be at that party? Featherleigh claimed she had bumped into Thomas at a club downtown a few days earlier and that *he* had invited her. Ha! Preposterous!

The next time they had run into Featherleigh Dale had been when Tag and Greer took Thomas and Abby to Little Dix Bay in Virgin Gorda over the Christmas holidays. Featherleigh had appeared on an enormous yacht belonging to some Saudi Arabian sheikh who was quite definitely gay.

Somehow, Featherleigh had insinuated herself into Greer's life as well. When she left Sotheby's, she started her own business as a personal shopper who matched antiques with private homes in London. Featherleigh was too smart to come to Greer first. Instead, she started finding pieces for Greer's London neighbor Antonia. When Antonia mentioned that she had gotten a hard-to-find Kano School Japanese screen from Featherleigh Dale, Greer had said, *Oh! I know Featherleigh.* And the next thing Greer knew, Featherleigh was calling her about this Morris chair and that Biedermeier walnut commode.

Now Featherleigh is as much a part of Greer's life as she may or may not be of Tag's. There was no question about whether or not to invite her to the wedding. They had to.

And there was no surprise in Featherleigh's response. Despite Greer's fierce wish that Featherleigh would decline, she had responded yes. For one. She would be attending alone.

Will she be wearing the silver-lace ring with the sapphires? Greer wonders. The ring is meant to be worn on the thumb. When Jessica Hicks, the jewelry designer, told Greer this, Greer had thought she'd misunderstood. Who wears a ring on her thumb? Only gypsies, so far as Greer knows. It sounds like a trend — but of course, no one adores a trend more than Featherleigh. She had moved to Sloane Square only because it was where a young Diana Spencer once lived. And what about Featherleigh's penchant for cold-shoulder dresses, which Donna Karan helped make popular in 1993? Greer can too easily picture Featherleigh waltzing right into Greer's home with the ring on her thumb. Greer hopes she can keep her composure while she admires the ring and asks Featherleigh where she got it.

She will then watch Featherleigh Dale squirm.

*　*　*

An hour into the rehearsal dinner (a bit of a misno-mer, as the rehearsal was canceled due to Reverend Derby's travel delay), Greer is enjoying herself immensely. She is floating between the front lawn and the beach in her bare feet with a glass of cham-pagne in her hand that one of the adorable girls who work for the caterer is in charge of keeping filled.

Greer asks the girl her name.

"Chloe," she says. "Chloe MacAvoy."

"Don't be a stranger, Chloe!" Greer says. A steady stream of champagne is the key to Greer staying relaxed.

It's a glorious night. There's a light breeze off the water, and the sky looks like a blue ombré silk scarf as the sun descends, setting the Nantucket skyline aglow. The band is playing songs by James Taylor, Jimmy Buffett, the Beach Boys. Greer tries to man-age her time among all of the guests arriving and the major players—Benji, Celeste, the wedding party, and Mr. and Mrs. Otis. Mrs. Otis—Karen—looks lovely in an embroidered kimono. She leans on her cane for a few minutes talking with Tag's intermina-bly boring colleague from work and then, just as Greer feels she must swoop in and save the poor woman—with so little time left, Karen has none to waste on Peter Walls—Bruce leads Karen over to a chair at the edge of the action. She will sit and receive visitors like a queen. As she should.

Benji is talking with Shooter and the four Alexanders from Hobart—Alex K., Alex B., Alex W., and Zander. Greer is fond of Benji's Hobart friends—all of them have spent long weekends here at Summerland—but no one has captured Greer's heart quite as much as Shooter. Shooter Uxley is the son of a Palm Beach real estate scion and his mistress. Shooter's mother got pregnant with the sole intention of eliciting a marriage proposal, but it never came. The father had five other children by two wives and he was senile enough to let one of his older sons oversee his will, which cut Shooter and his mother out entirely. Shooter had somehow managed to produce the tuition for his last year at St. George's, but after graduation he had been forced to find a job. That he has turned himself into such a success is a testament to his intelligence, his charm, and his perseverance.

Greer sips her champagne and wanders to the raw bar, where Tag is sucking down oyster after oyster, dripping shellfish liquor onto his bespoke pink shirt, tailored for him at Henry Poole. Despite how much Tag loves New York, he trusts only Savile Row tailors, and yet he seems to think nothing of defiling said shirts in the name of a good bivalve. He would stay here all night if Greer let him.

"You should take a plate of those over to the

Otises," Greer says. "Karen is sitting and Bruce is stationed at her side like the Swiss Guard."

"Do they eat oysters, do you think?" Tag asks.

Good question. Celeste confided that Mrs. Otis is excited about having lobster—there had been some confusion with the term *clambake*—because she, Karen Otis, hasn't eaten lobster since her honeymoon more than thirty years earlier. Greer tried to hide her shock. At the end of every summer on this island, it was all Greer could do not to feel weary of lobster, after having lobster rolls at Cru, the lobster spaghetti from the Boarding House, lobster fritters and tartlets and beignets and avocado-toast-with-lobster at every cocktail party she attends. But, of course, Karen Otis lives a vastly different life. Greer informed Siobhan Crispin, the caterer, that the mother of the bride was to be offered as much lobster as she wanted and that all uneaten lobsters should be cracked and the meat stashed in a bag in the fridge of the main house in case Mrs. Otis craved a midnight snack.

"Just offer, please," Greer says to Tag. "Take some of the shrimp with cocktail sauce and lemons—they'll like that."

"Good idea," Tag says. He leans over to kiss her. "You're very thoughtful."

"And hot," she reminds him.

"Hottest woman here," Tag says. "Not that I've noticed another soul."

"Have you seen Featherleigh?" Greer asks. This will not seem like a loaded question, because in all this time, Greer has never confronted Tag with her suspicions.

"I caught a glimpse," Tag says. "She looks god-awful."

"Does she?" Greer says, although she knows the answer is yes. Greer sought Featherleigh out immediately after dealing with the last-minute party logistics, and although it's ungracious, Greer will say that the twenty pounds (at least) that Featherleigh has gained and Featherleigh's bad haircut and her even worse dye job and her reddened nose are the best things about this wedding weekend so far.

Greer had checked both of Featherleigh's hands — she was not wearing the ring. Greer had found herself almost *deflated* by this; she had been ready for a confrontation. Instead, Greer had no choice but to be civil.

"Featherleigh Dale, you're a sight for sore eyes."

The corners of Featherleigh's mouth had pulled down unattractively. "Thank you for having me," she'd said. She had then proceeded to detail the horror of her travel. No money for a first-class ticket so she was squished in coach. The flight from New York to Nantucket was overbooked, everyone was obnoxious, there was no decent food at the airport, she'd had a Nathan's hot dog and the thing was as shriveled as a mummy's pecker. She finds Nantucket damp, just look at her hair, the place she booked is an *inn*, not a hotel, so there's no room service, no fitness center, no spa, and the pillowcases are decorated with tulle flowers, they're honestly the most hideous things she's ever seen, how she's supposed to lay her head on something like that she has no idea, but the inn was the only place available because she'd waited until the last minute. She wasn't going to come at all because she was so low on funds, but then she hoped the trip would help snap her out of her funk.

"Funk?" Greer asked, wondering if this litany was ever going to end.

"My business went belly-up," Featherleigh said. "And I've been through a devastating breakup" — *Aha!* Greer thinks. *So it's over with Tag?* — "which is why I have this bad dye job and I look like an absolute hippo. It's been all vodka and fish and chips and takeout vindaloo for me. I'm forty-five years old, I'm not married, I have no children, I have no job, I'm under investigation —"

"A devastating breakup?" Greer said, backing up to the only one of Featherleigh's complaints that she cared about. "I didn't realize you were seeing anyone special."

"It was on the down-low," Featherleigh said. Her eyes filled with tears. "He's married. I knew he was married, but I thought..."

"You thought he would leave his wife for you?" Greer asked. She had gathered Featherleigh up in a hug, mostly to put an end to the tears—nothing kills a party like somebody weeping—and said, "Men never leave their wives, Featherleigh. You're old enough to know better. Is it anyone I know?"

Featherleigh had sniffed and shaken her head against Greer's shoulder. Greer eased away, suddenly concerned about mascara on her ivory silk jumpsuit. Would Featherleigh cry about her breakup with Tag to Greer? Was she capable of that kind of insidious deception?

"And why," Greer asked, "are you under investigation?"

"For fraud," Featherleigh admitted glumly.

So clearly she *was* capable of deception. And that would explain the absence of the ring.

"When was this breakup?" Greer had asked. "Recently?"

Featherleigh's bottom lip trembled. "May," she said.

May? Greer thought. She's positive Jessica Hicks said that Tag had bought the ring in June. But Greer supposes she could have been mistaken; she should have asked Jessica to forward the receipt to her e-mail, but Greer had been so stunned, so seized with angst, that she had hurried out of the store without proper follow-up.

After writing twenty-one novels in the persona of Miss Dolly Hardaway, Greer had cultivated the mind-set of a detective. Once her head cleared of all this champagne and excitement, she would go back over the events of May with a fine-tooth comb. See what nits she could pick.

"Go get yourself a drink," Greer had said. "It certainly sounds like you could use one."

Greer's seating chart is brilliant, she thinks, except that the seat of honor, the seat next to Benji, is empty. Where is Celeste? She's sitting with her parents, naturally, playing nanny to both Karen and Bruce. Celeste cracks the claws of her mother's lobster and pulls the snowy meat from it with the slender silver pick, just as Greer taught her. She pries the tail meat free and cuts it into bite-size pieces, then identifies the cups of melted butter. Because this is an Island Fare clambake, every traditional element has been given a sophisticated twist. There are three kinds of melted butter for the lobster: regular, lime, and chili pepper. There are two types of corn bread, one with whole sweet corn kernels and one with pork cracklings. There are also feathery-light buttermilk biscuits made even more savory by the addition of aged English cheddar. Alongside the standard grilled linguica are house-made lamb sausages, another offering to please the Brits. In the center of every table is a pinwheel of Bartlett's Farm hothouse tomatoes drizzled with a thick, tangy blue cheese dressing and sprinkled with chopped green onions and crispy bacon.

Celeste goes through the same lobster routine with her father. Greer notices the tender attention Celeste pays to her parents. It's remarkable. It's envy-inspiring. Greer believes she did an impeccable job parenting her boys but she knows bloody well they would never treat her with this kind of loving, thoughtful care. The bond that Celeste has with her parents is special; anyone can see that. Maybe it's because her mother is dying—but somehow, Greer doesn't think that's the sole reason. Maybe it's because the Otises had Celeste when they were so young. Maybe it's because Celeste is an only child.

Maybe Greer should stop wondering.

Greer splits a biscuit in half. She'll allow herself two bites. She turns to Tag. "Do the boys love me, do you think?"

"Is that an actual question?" Tag asks.

Chloe appears at Greer's shoulder with yet another glass of champagne. Greer should stop drinking because following the question *Do the boys love me?* are a host of other questions. Does Tag love her? Does anyone else love her? Does anyone appreciate just how much hard work this wedding has entailed? It took money, yes, but also a good deal of time—

hundreds of hours, if Greer added it up, on lists, phone calls, logistics. She essentially cannibalized her career because the wedding came first, her novel second—and some bloke named Chuck O'Brien has now called her on it. Can she write the novel all over again, or write a new novel start to finish in a fortnight? Maybe without the wedding as a distraction, yes.

Did Tag have an affair with Featherleigh that ended in May?

No more champagne. Greer has to stop. But the flute is such a pretty shape and the liquid is an irresistible platinum color; the bubbles wink at her seductively and she knows exactly how it will taste: cool and crisp, like an apple just plucked from the branch.

Celeste takes her seat next to Benji and for a moment, Greer relaxes. Everyone is in his or her proper place. "We should probably do the toasts now," Greer says. "Before people get antsy."

"I thought toasts were scheduled for after dinner but before dessert," Tag says. He checks his watch. "I have a quick call with Ernie at nine."

"*What?*" Greer says. "A call with Ernie at nine o'clock *tonight?*"

"It's the Libya deal," Tag says. "It'll be quick but I can't reschedule; Ernie is going to Tripoli in the morning. This deal is big, darling. Big, big." Tag kisses

Greer and stands up, leaving an untouched lobster tail on his plate.

"Make it quick, quick," Greer says, trying to maintain her playful attitude. Her eyes flick across the tent to where Featherleigh is sitting; Greer placed her in social Siberia with Tag's work colleagues, among them the tedious Peter Walls. If Featherleigh follows Tag out, Greer will know there is no call to Ernie.

But Featherleigh stays put; she doesn't even seem to notice Tag leaving the party. Or actually, yes, she does. Her eyes trail him. Her expression holds longing, Greer thinks, except, really, her own judgment can't be trusted after so many glasses of champagne. But Featherleigh doesn't move. Instead, she lavishly butters a piece of corn bread and pops it into her mouth. Greer pushes her own plate away.

Bruce Otis, adhering to Greer's wishes if not the precise timetable, stands up and clinks his spoon against his water glass.

"Ladies and gentlemen, I'm Bruce Otis, father of the bride," he says. "I'd like to make a toast."

A murmur ripples through the crowd; the band stops playing and everyone quiets down. Greer is grateful. She isn't sure how much practice Mr. Otis has at speaking to a group this size but it's always easier when people are well behaved.

"When I met my wife, Karen, I thought I was the

luckiest man alive. Boy, not man, because when I met Karen, I was only seventeen years old. But I knew I loved her. I could see myself growing old with her. Which is exactly what we've gone and done."

There is gentle laughter.

"And I know I speak for Karen when I say that our love for each other was so extraordinary that years went by when neither of us wanted children. We were so happy just being together. I would work all week, and every day at five o'clock the sun came out for me because I got to go home to this beautiful, extraordinary woman. On Saturdays we used to run our errands. We would go to the post office to mail packages or check our box, and the line was always extralong on Saturdays, but you know what? I didn't care. I could wait an hour. I could wait all day . . . because I was with Karen." Bruce's voice starts to crack and Greer can see tears shining in his eyes and she realizes that he's using this toast as a way to pay tribute to his wife. It's brilliant; Karen deserves this and more. She deserves a *cure* or a cutting-edge clinical trial that puts her into remission for ten years, or even five years—at least then she might be able to meet her future grandchildren. Celeste has confided to Greer that she sends a hundred dollars from each of her paychecks to the Breast Cancer Research Foundation without Karen's or Bruce's knowledge. Greer was so moved by this that she sat down at her desk that very evening and wrote the organization a $25,000 check without telling Celeste or Benji or even Tag. The charitable acts that count the most, Greer believes, are those done without anyone knowing. But she had wanted very badly to send a note with the check that said: *Please use this money to cure Karen Otis.*

Bruce clears his throat, regroups, and says, "And then, twenty-eight years ago, we had a baby girl. And man, nothing on this earth—and I mean *nothing*—prepares you for how much you love your kids. Am I right?"

There are some *Hear, hears* from the audience. Greer feels a vague recognition. She loved her children. Loves them. It was different when they were small, of course.

"And Karen and I somehow lucked out and got this beautiful, smart, *nice* little girl. She got a hundred percent on all her spelling tests. She was the one who scooped up a spider and carried it outside instead of squishing it with her shoe, and she was always digging in the backyard looking for snakes or salamanders and then putting them in a shoe box with grass and little dishes of drinking water. She was never ashamed or embarrassed of where she came from or *who* she came from, even though she outgrew us and the rest of Forks Township, Pennsylvania, a long time ago." Bruce raises his glass. "And so to you, Benjamin Winbury, I say from the heart: Take care of our little girl. She is our treasure, our hope, our light, and our warmth. She is our legacy. Here's to the two of you and your life together."

Greer wipes a tear from the corner of her eye with a napkin. She isn't normally sentimental, although anyone would have found that toast stirring.

Thomas stands up next and chimes on his own water glass. It's true perhaps that nothing in this world prepares you for how much you love your children, but Greer has always been a realist where her sons are concerned. She has a firm handle on their strengths and weaknesses. Thomas is the better-looking one; Benji inherited Greer's father's crooked nose, and no barber has ever been able to tame Benji's cowlick. But Benji is smarter and has been either blessed or cursed with a natural gravitas, so he has always seemed like the older brother.

For his toast, Thomas tells the story of when Thomas and Benji, ages eight and six, respectively, got lost at Piccadilly Circus and how Benji was the one who had saved them from abduction or worse. The story goes that Benji, against his brother's severe warnings, had approached a group of punk rockers and asked a girl with a bright pink Mohawk to help them find their mummy.

"He said the girl's hair was pretty," Thomas says. "He believed anyone with such pretty hair was sure to have deep reserves of cleverness and wisdom."

Greer laughs along with everyone else, although the story rubs her the wrong way for two reasons. First off, *she* was the one who had taken the boys to Piccadilly, where she had bumped into a woman named Susan Haynes, who sat on the ladies' auxiliary at Portland Hospital, a group Greer had been keen to join. Greer had become so engrossed in conversation with Susan that she had lost track of the boys. Her own children. When Greer surfaced from the conversation, she looked around and found the two of them had *vanished*.

Greer is also dismayed because this is the *exact same story* that Benji told when he had given the toast at *Thomas's* wedding four years earlier. Greer finds it terribly unimaginative for Thomas to recycle the very same story. Greer would like to give Tag a private look to see if he agrees, but he's...where? Still on the call with Ernie? Greer checks on Featherleigh. She's in her seat, gazing at Thomas with an insipid look on her face.

She's blotto, Greer thinks. She has three empty cups of the blackberry mojito punch in front of her.

As soon as the applause for Thomas's half-baked effort subsides, Greer slips discreetly into the house in search of her husband.

She skirts the kitchen, where the catering staff is plating dessert, an assortment of homemade pies: blueberry, peach, Key lime, banana cream, and chocolate pecan. She heads through the den toward the back stairs but stops when she hears a voice coming from the laundry room.

The laundry room? Greer thinks. She pokes her head in.

There's a girl with her back up against the stacked washer and dryer, her face in her hands, sobbing. It's... it's the *friend,* Celeste's friend, the maid of honor. Greer blanks on the girl's name. It's... Merrill or Madison? No, not quite. *Merritt,* she thinks. Merritt Monaco.

"Merritt!" Greer says. "What's wrong?"

When Merritt turns to see Greer, she gasps in surprise. Then she hurries to wipe away her tears. "Nothing," she says. "It's just... the excitement."

"It's overwhelming, isn't it?" Greer says. She feels a wave of maternal concern for this girl who is neither getting married like Celeste nor pregnant like Abby. But still, the freedom! Greer wants to encourage Merritt to savor her freedom because soon enough, certainly, it will be gone.

"Come, let's get you a drink," Greer says. She beckons Merritt forward, thinking she will lead the girl back out to the party and find Chloe-with-the-champagne. Surely Merritt's sadness is nothing a little Veuve Clicquot can't fix.

"I'm fine," Merritt says, sniffing and trying to collect herself. "I'll be out shortly. I need the ladies' room. I should fix my face. But thank you."

Greer gives the girl a smile. "Very well. I'm on a mission to find my husband anyway. He seems to have disappeared." She turns to leave but not before catching the glint of a silver ring on Merritt's thumb.

So it's true, Greer thinks. *All the fashionable girls are wearing them now.*

Monday, October 24, 2016

CELESTE

Two days after giving Benji her direct line at the zoo, he calls — not to put her in touch with his friend who may or may not want to bring groups of foreign executives to the zoo but to ask her out to dinner. He wants to take her to the Russian Tea Room on Friday night.

"They've redone it since the eighties," he says. "It's supposed to be over the top now. Do you like caviar?"

"Um…" Celeste says. She has never had caviar, not only because it's expensive but also because she has seen sacs of fish eggs floating in aquarium water and… no, thank you.

"Or we could go down to the East Village and eat at Madame Vo's? It's Vietnamese. Would you prefer Vietnamese?"

Celeste nearly hangs up the phone. She chastises herself for giving this guy her number. He's an alien species — or, more likely, she's the alien. He's used to beautiful, sophisticated women like Jules, who probably grew up with caviar packed in her lunchbox. Celeste's rent on East One Hundredth Street is a bit of a stretch, so she rarely goes out to eat. Occasionally, she will meet Merritt for brunch or dinner. Many times, if Merritt is photographed eating at the restaurant or if she posts photos of the food online at #eatingfortheinsta, the meal will be comped. Usually, however, dinner for Celeste is the salad bar at the corner bodega or takeout from the cafeteria at the zoo and, yes, Celeste does know how pathetic that is, but only because Merritt has told her.

"Vietnamese sounds great!" Celeste says, manufacturing as much enthusiasm as she can about a cuisine she knows nothing about.

"Okay, Madame Vo's it is, then," Benji says. "I'll come pick you up?"

"Pick me *up?*" Celeste says. Her block — which is too far north to properly qualify as the Upper East Side, though too far south to be called Harlem — is relatively safe but neither sexy nor fetching. There's a laundromat, the bodega, a pet groomer.

"Or we can meet there?" Benji says. "It's on East Tenth Street."

"I'll meet you there," Celeste says, relieved.

"Eight o'clock?" Benji says.

"Sounds good," Celeste says, and she hangs up the phone to call Merritt.

First, Merritt screams, *You have a date!*

Celeste's face contorts into an expression halfway between a smile and a grimace. She *does* have a date, and it feels good, because normally, when Celeste and Merritt talk, the only person who has exciting news, or news of any kind, is Merritt. Merritt's romantic life is so populated that Celeste has a hard time keeping the men straight. Presently, Merritt is dating Robbie, who's the daytime bartender at the Breslin on Twenty-Ninth Street. He's tall and pale with bulging biceps and an Irish accent. *What's not to love about Robbie?* Celeste wondered after Merritt dragged Celeste down to a Saturday lunch at the Breslin so she could meet him. Why didn't Merritt stay with him?

For one, Merritt said, Robbie was an aspiring actor. He was constantly going on auditions, and Merritt felt it was only a matter of time before he was cast in a TV pilot that got picked up, at which point he'd move to the West Coast. It wasn't a good idea to get too attached to anyone not firmly rooted in New York, Merritt said. However, Celeste knew that Merritt was afraid to commit because of a truly heinous situation she'd found herself in the year before she and Celeste met.

The man's name was Travis Darling. Travis and his wife, Cordelia, owned a PR firm called Bright-street where Merritt had worked right out of college. She had been handpicked for her job as publicity associate from a pool of over a thousand applicants, and both Travis and Cordelia saw Merritt as a rising PR star, the next Lynn Goldsmith. Merritt's life had become completely intertwined with the lives of the Darlings. She accompanied them to dinner at least once a week; she hung out at their brownstone on West Eighty-Third Street; she went skiing with them in Stowe and joined them for beach weekends in Bridgehampton.

Travis had always been Merritt's champion. He asked questions about Merritt's personal life, encouraged her interest in fashion; he remembered her college roommates' names. He sought out her opinion because she was young and had a fresh perspective. He would sometimes rest his hand on her shoulder when he was standing behind her desk, and he forwarded her racy jokes from his personal e-mail. When Merritt was out to dinner with Travis and Cordelia, he would pull out her chair. If they were waiting at the bar to be seated, he would usher her forward with his hand on her back. Merritt noted these things but she didn't protest. After all, Cordelia was *right there.*

But then.

It was summer and Merritt was spending a week-end in the Hamptons with the Darlings. On Saturday afternoon, the three of them were lying on the beach when a call came in from a client, a supermodel who had just had an altercation with a flight attendant. Words had been exchanged and a fellow passenger had leaked the story—which cast the supermodel in a very unflattering light—to the press. It was a public-ity situation that could easily escalate into a publicity nightmare. Cordelia had to go back to the city to deal with the fallout.

I'll go with you, Merritt had said. *You'll need help.*

I have Sage, Cordelia said. Sage Kennedy was a brand-new hire. Merritt had sensed Sage's ambition and professional envy immediately; Sage wanted to be the next Merritt. Sage was too young and broke to spend summer weekends away, but now that would work in her favor. When Merritt insisted she was more than happy to go back to the city, Cordelia said, *You stay here and enjoy. I'll see you Monday.*

Had Merritt been uneasy about staying in the house with Travis alone? Not really. By that point, Merritt had been working for Brightstreet for three years. If Travis were going to make a pass at her, she figured, it would have happened already.

But late that afternoon, as Merritt was rinsing the sand off her feet at the outdoor hose before going into the house, Travis came up behind her and, without a word, untied the string of her bikini top. Merritt had frozen. She was petrified, she told Celeste, but she'd decided to laugh it off as a prank. She grabbed the strings and started to retie them but Travis stopped her. He took both of her hands, pulled her to him, and started kissing the back of her neck. Into her ear he whispered, *I've been waiting so long for this.*

"I was trapped," Merritt told Celeste. "I could have pushed him away but I was afraid I'd lose my job. I was afraid he'd tell Cordelia that I was the one who took off my top. So I let it happen. I let it happen."

The affair lasted seven torturous months. Merritt lived in mortal fear of Cordelia finding out, but Travis assured Merritt there was nothing to worry about. His wife, he said, was frigid and possibly even a lesbian and she wouldn't have cared even if she did find out.

Deep down, she wanted this to happen, Travis said. *One of the reasons she wanted to hire you was that she knew I thought you were hot.*

As it turned out, Travis was gravely mistaken about what Cordelia wanted. Cordelia hired a private investigator, who followed both Merritt and Travis, accessed their phone records and text messages, then presented Cordelia with all the proof she needed, including, somehow, 8-by-10 glossies of Merritt and Travis showering together in Merritt's apartment.

Cordelia had swiftly taken the company from Travis, as well as their investments and their brownstone. She fired Merritt and set out to shred Merritt's reputation professionally and personally—and by then, Cordelia's friends were Merritt's friends. Travis forsook Merritt as well. She called and begged him to tell Cordelia the truth: that he had started the affair and he had given her no choice but to be complicit. Travis had responded to her calls and texts by filing a restraining order against her.

Merritt had been suicidal in the aftermath, she confided to Celeste. On bad days she stared at a bottle of hoarded pills—Valium, Ambien, Xanax. On good days, she looked for jobs in other cities, but it turned out Cordelia's tentacles reached all the way to Chicago, DC, Atlanta. Merritt didn't get so much as a callback. Every once in a while Cordelia would text her, and each time Merritt saw Cordelia's name on her phone's screen, she thought that maybe, just maybe, Travis had come clean and told Cordelia that the affair had been his fault, that he had coerced Merritt, then basically blackmailed her. But the texts were always the exact opposite of apologies. One said: If I thought I could get away with it, I would kill you.

But then, one miraculous day, Merritt received a text from Sage Kennedy, who, Merritt knew, had summarily taken her position in the company. The text said: Cordelia has sold the brownstone on Eighty-Third Street and is relocating Brightstreet to LA. Thought you would want to know.

At first, Merritt didn't believe it. She was wary of Sage Kennedy. But when Merritt checked *Business Insider,* she saw it was true. She wondered if maybe Travis had preyed on Sage Kennedy after Merritt left. She was afraid to ask, though she did text Sage back to thank her for the information. She had, essentially, been set free.

Soon thereafter, Merritt found a job in PR with the Wildlife Conservation Society, and although she took a pay cut, she was grateful for the fresh start. She introduced herself to Celeste in her first weeks of work by saying, "You're the best-looking, most normal person who works at any of our zoos. Please let me use photos of you in the literature."

Celeste had been stupefied by Merritt's blunt honesty. "Thanks," she said. "I think." They had gone to lunch together in the zoo's cafeteria, and over tuna fish sandwiches, a friendship was forged. Merritt credited Celeste with "saving" her, although Celeste saw it as the other way around. Celeste had been bound and determined to move out of Forks Township and make it in New York City on her own, but even she had been confounded by just *how* on her own she actually was. The city was home to ten million people and yet Celeste had a hard time meeting anyone outside of work. She had two sort-of friends on her block: Rocky, who worked at the bodega, and Judy Quigley, who owned the pet-grooming business.

Rocky had taken Celeste on a date to the Peruvian chicken place on Ninety-First Street but then he confessed that although he liked Celeste and thought she was very, very pretty, he had neither the time nor the money for a girlfriend. Mrs. Quigley was a pleasant woman and she and Celeste shared a love of animals but it wasn't like they were ever going to go out for cocktails.

Merritt was the New York City friend of Celeste's dreams. She was fun, sophisticated, and plugged in; she knew *everything* that was happening for Millennials in the city. She told Celeste that her experience with Travis Darling had jaded her, but all Celeste saw was her tender heart. Merritt was remarkably patient, kind, and maternal when it came to Celeste, and she knew that Celeste could handle her pulsing, frenetic world only in small bites.

"I don't know what to do," Celeste says to Merritt now. "Benji came to the zoo with his girlfriend and his girlfriend's *daughter*. He and the girlfriend were arguing and then I noticed him staring at me. Then he asked for my card. *For a friend,* he said, and I believed him. I gave him my direct line. So do you think he broke up with his girlfriend already? He wants to take me to Madame Vo's, which is all the way down on Tenth Street. It's Vietnamese."

"Madame Vo's is on everyone's list because SJP eats there," Merritt says. "But I don't like the way they seat twos. It feels like you're on a date with the couples on either side of you."

"Should I cancel?" Celeste says. "I should probably cancel."

"No!" Merritt says. "Don't you dare cancel! I'm going to help you. I'm going to transform you. We are going to make this Benji fall in love with you in only one date. We are going to make him propose."

"Propose?" Celeste says.

Later, Merritt comes over to Celeste's apartment and she uses Celeste's laptop to Google Benji — Benjamin Garrison Winbury of New York City. In a matter of seconds they discover the following: Benji attended the Westminster School in London, then went to high school at St. George's in Newport, Rhode Island, and college at Hobart. Now he works for Nomura Securities, which further Googling discloses is a Japanese bank with a headquarters in New York. He sits on the board of the Whitney Museum and the Robin Hood Foundation.

"He's twenty-seven years old," Merritt says. "And he sits on two boards. That's impressive."

Celeste's anxiety ramps up. She has met several board members of the conservancy; they're all wealthy and important people.

Merritt scans through images of Benji. "The mother has resting-bitch face. The father is kind of hot, though."

"Merritt, stop," Celeste says, but she peers over Merritt's shoulder at the screen. She expects to see pictures of Benji with Jules and Miranda, but if those pictures existed, they've all been expunged. There is a photo of Benji with friends in a restaurant raising cocktails and one of him posing on the bow of a boat. There's a picture of Benji with a guy who must be his brother at a Yankees game, and in the picture Merritt is referring to, Benji poses with a refined older couple, the mother cool and blond, the father silver-haired and grinning. There's Benji hoisting a tropical drink under a beach umbrella and one of him in a helmet sitting astride a mountain bike.

"Girlfriend is gone, I'd say," Merritt remarks. "Thoroughly scoured from his feed. Let's check Instagram—"

"I don't want to check Instagram," Celeste says. "Help me find something to wear."

Celeste meets Benji outside Madame Vo's at exactly eight o'clock on Friday. Merritt advised Celeste to show up ten minutes late but Celeste is always prompt—it's a compulsion—and Benji is already waiting, which is, she decides, a good sign. Celeste has borrowed a dress from Merritt; it's a rose-gold Hervé Leger bandage dress that Celeste knows retails for well over a thousand dollars. Merritt was given it for free to wear to the opening of a new club, Nuclear Winter, in Alphabet City, and when Merritt is photographed in something as much as she was in this dress that night, she can never wear it again. Celeste is also wearing Merritt's shoes—Jimmy Choo stilettos—and she's carrying Merritt's gold clutch purse. The only things she's missing are Merritt's wit, charm, and confidence. Celeste calls upon advice her parents have been giving her since she was old enough to understand English: *Be yourself.* It's wonderfully old-fashioned and possibly ill advised. Celeste has always been herself, but that hasn't won her any popularity contests. Genus: *Girl Scientist.* Species: *socially awkward.*

"Hi," she says to Benji as she steps out of her Uber.

"Wow," Benji says. "I almost didn't recognize you. You look—wow. I mean, wow." Celeste blushes. Benji is taken aback, maybe even awestruck, and it doesn't seem like an act. Celeste is unsure whether to kiss him or hug him and so she just smiles and he smiles back, looking into her eyes. Then he holds the door to the restaurant open and ushers Celeste inside. "Are you hungry?" he asks.

Benji is nice. Celeste didn't think there were any nice guys living in New York. The men she sees on the subway and on the street all seem to leer at her breasts or swear under their breath if she's taking too long with her MetroCard. The men at the zoo are no prizes. Darius, who took Celeste's job in primates when she got promoted, has confessed that he spends nearly half his paycheck on internet porn. Mawabe, who works with the big cats, is addicted to the video game Manhunt; he offers to teach Celeste to play it every time they have a conversation. The problem with people from the zoo in general is that they relate better to animals than to humans, and that's true for Celeste as well.

When Benji tells Celeste that he works for the Japanese bank Nomura, she pretends this is brand-new information. "You mean to tell me you're just another soulless private-equity guy?" she says, hoping it sounds like she is subjected to dates with such guys every weekend.

He laughs. "No, that would be my father." He then explains that he heads Nomura's strategic-giving department, so it's his job to give money away to meaningful causes.

"Eventually, I'd like to run a large nonprofit. Like the Red Cross or the American Cancer Society."

"My mother has breast cancer," Celeste blurts out. Then she bows her head over her crispy spring rolls.

She can't believe she just said that, not only because it's the world's most depressing topic but because she hasn't discussed her mother's cancer with anyone.

Benji says, "Is she going to be okay?"

Well, that's the question, isn't it? Celeste's mother, Karen Otis, had stage 2 invasive ductal carcinoma that reached her lymph nodes, necessitating eighteen rounds of chemo and thirty rounds of radiation *after* her double mastectomy. She rang the bell at St. Luke's for her final treatment back in July and she isn't supposed to have a follow-up appointment for six months. But she was experiencing back pain so she'd gone to see her doctor this week. He ordered an MRI, one that Karen nearly refused because it was so expensive and Bruce and Karen were already loaded down with medical bills for treatments that weren't covered by Bruce's modest health insurance. However, Bruce insisted they do the test. When he talked to Celeste about it on the phone, he quoted a song by the Zac Brown Band. "'There's no dollar sign on peace of mind,'" he said. "'This I've come to know.'"

Celeste figures they must play this song on the Neiman Marcus Pandora, because she hasn't known her parents to like any song recorded after 1985.

The results of the MRI should be back on Monday.

Celeste raises her eyes to Benji's, his brown to her blue. Brown is a dominant gene. Benji's DNA, she is sure, is composed of only dominant genes. She's not sure what to say. Her mother's cancer is a private matter, and Celeste's entire relationship with her parents is too intense to explain to most people.

"I don't know?" Celeste says. She raises her voice at the end so that she sounds more hopeful than maudlin. She doesn't want Benji feeling sorry for her. This is one reason why Celeste doesn't like talking about Karen's illness. Also, she doesn't want to hear anyone else's inspiring story about a sister-in-law who went through *exactly the same thing* and is now running ultramarathons. Celeste doesn't mean to be ungenerous in her thoughts, but she has come to the chilling conclusion that we are all alone in our bodies. Irrefutably, immutably alone. And hence, no one's story offers hope. Either Karen will survive the cancer or it will metastasize and she will succumb to it. The only people Celeste can tolerate discussing Karen's treatment with are Karen's doctors. Celeste believes in science, in medicine. She has secretly been donating a hundred dollars a week to the Breast Cancer Research Foundation. "She's okay now. For the time being." Celeste is too superstitious to say her mother has beaten it, and she refuses to call her mother a survivor. Yet.

"Thank you for telling me," Benji says.

Celeste nods. He understands her, maybe? He senses the agony lurking behind her metered answers?

He seems perceptive the way so few men—so few *people*—are. Celeste picks up a spring roll and dips it into the vinegary sauce. "These are really good."

"Wait until you taste the *pho*," he says. He takes a sip of his beer. "So, tell me about the zoo," he says, and Celeste relaxes.

Benji insists on taking Celeste home in a taxi, which seems quaint. He asks the driver to wait while he walks Celeste to the door of her apartment building. She feels a huge relief that there will be no quandary about whether to invite Benji up and if she does invite him up about how far to let things go. Merritt believes in sleeping with a guy on the first date, but Celeste feels very much the opposite. She would never, ever.

Ever.

Benji tells her he would like to see her again. The following night, if she's free, he has tickets to see *Hamilton*.

Celeste gasps. Everyone in this city wants to see *Hamilton*.

Benji laughs. "Is that a yes?"

Before she can answer, he's kissing her. Celeste starts out feeling self-conscious about the taxi driver who is waiting, but then she surrenders. *There is nothing in the world that is quite as intoxicating as kissing,* Celeste thinks. She lets herself get lost in Benji's lips, his tongue. He tastes delicious; his mouth is both soft and insistent. His hands are on her face, then her neck, then one hand travels to her hip. Before she can guess what will happen next, he pulls away.

"I'll see you tomorrow night," he says. "I'll call with details in the morning." With that, he goes down the stairs and by the time Celeste's head clears, his taxi has pulled away.

They go to see *Hamilton*. It turns out that Benji's father is one of the original investors and has house seats, which are first-row center of the first balcony. Benji has seen the musical five times but he doesn't tell her this until afterward, when they're sitting at Hudson Malone, dipping jumbo shrimp into cocktail sauce, and Celeste has to admit, she would never have known. He had seemed as enraptured as she was.

Benji says he would like to see her Sunday and Celeste suggests a walk in Central Park. The park is a place she feels comfortable, nearly has a sense of ownership. She runs the reservoir any chance she can get and in the summer lies out on a towel in North Meadow. She loves Poet's Walk and the Conservatory Pond, but her favorite spot is surely a place Benji hasn't experienced before. She meets him south of Bethesda

Fountain where a group of roller skaters congregates on weekends. There's a motley crew of characters—Celeste has come to recognize most of the regulars—who skate in an oval around a boom box that plays classic rock songs.

When Benji arrives, they're skating to "Gimme Three Steps," by Lynyrd Skynyrd.

"I didn't think anyone roller-skated anymore," Benji says. "This is like something out of 1979."

"I come here all the time," Celeste says. "I think I like it so much because this is the music my parents listen to."

"Oh, yeah?" Benji says. "Are they big Skynyrd fans?"

"All classic rock," Celeste says. "They especially love Meat Loaf." As Celeste watches the skaters, she thinks about being a little girl sitting in the backseat of their Toyota Corolla while her parents cranked up the volume on their cassette of *Bat Out of Hell*. They loved all the songs, but their favorite was "Paradise by the Dashboard Light." When the song got to the middle section with Meat Loaf and Mrs. Loud, Karen would sing the woman's part, and Bruce would sing the man's part, and at the end of the song they would belt out the lyrics together with so much gusto that Celeste got swept away. Her parents, in those moments, had seemed the most glamorous couple in the world. Celeste fully believed that if they had shared their car-singing with the wider world, they would be famous.

The roller-skating song changes to "Stumblin' In," by Suzi Quatro and Chris Norman, and Celeste gets light-headed. It's *eerie;* this song is a particular favorite of her parents, and it's not a song that's played on the radio anymore. Celeste is stunned. She turns to Benji, overcome. How can she explain that this song so strongly evokes her parents, it's as if Betty and Mac are standing right there? Benji makes the slightest movement of withdrawal but Celeste can't possibly leave the skaters until this song is over. She sings along softly under her breath and Benji seems to understand. He stays patiently at her side. The next song is "Late in the Evening," by Paul Simon, which is also on Bruce and Karen's comprehensive playlist, but Celeste realizes that enough is enough. She takes Benji's hand and they stroll toward Bethesda Fountain.

After the park, Celeste and Benji sit at the Penrose and drink beer and watch football. When the game is over, Celeste asks Benji if he wants to grab a pizza and go back to her apartment but Benji says he likes to be in bed early on Sundays so that he's fresh and ready for the week ahead. Celeste says she understands and a part of her is relieved because it once again delays the question of what she and Benji will do once they're alone together. But a part of her is disappointed. She really enjoys Benji's company; he's easy to be with, he's funny, he tells stories about growing up in London and his family's immigration to New York City but he never sounds like he's bragging even though it's clear he's a member of the elite. He listens well too. He encourages Celeste to talk by asking good questions and then giving her lots of time to answer.

But she has probably bored him to death. And freaked him out by wanting to listen to old-people music in the park.

"I do have a question before we leave," Celeste says.

Benji covers her hand with his hand.

She can't believe she's being so bold. It's none of her business, but if Benji is giving her the brush-off and she might never see him again, she might as well ask this question.

"Shoot," he says.

"What happened with your girlfriend?" Celeste asks. "And her daughter?"

Benji sighs. "Jules?" he says. "We broke up. I mean, obviously. But it wasn't your fault. Things had been bad for a long time..."

"How long had you dated?" Celeste asks.

"Just over a year," Benji says.

Celeste exhales. Not as long as she had feared. "I guess I'm mostly worried about her daughter," Celeste says. "She seemed so attached to you."

"She's a great kid," Benji says. "But she has a father

and two really involved uncles who live only a few blocks away, and when I broke things off with Jules, I told her I would be available if Miranda ever needed me." He stares at Celeste. "It says a lot that you would ask about Miranda."

His gaze is so intense that Celeste casts her eyes down to the scarred bar. "What about Jules?" Celeste says. "Did she take it okay?"

"Not at all," Benji says. "She threw her shoes at me. She screamed. She smashed her phone and that made her cry. She's in love with her phone."

"So many people are," Celeste says.

"That was part of the problem. She couldn't be present; she was self-absorbed; she wasn't a kind or thoughtful person. She called herself a stay-at-home mom but she never spent time with Miranda. She went to Pilates class, got her nails done, and met her friends for lunch, where they all engaged in competitive non-eating. The only reason we were even at the zoo that day was that I insisted. Jules was hung over from the night before and all she wanted to do was take a nap and a bubble bath before she met her friends Laney and Casper for dinner at some over-rated restaurant where she would order a salad and eat two pieces of lettuce and half a fig. That trip to the zoo put it all in perspective."

"I just wondered," Celeste says. "I wasn't trying to steal you away or break you up."

Benji laughs and slaps money on the bar. "Let me walk you home," he says.

He kisses Celeste good-bye outside her apartment building and the kissing becomes so heated that Celeste wants to ask him to come upstairs. But he pulls away and says, "Thanks for a great weekend. I'll talk to you later."

Celeste watches him take the steps two at a time, wave, then disappear down the dark street.

When she gets upstairs, she sends Merritt a text: I blew it.

How? is Merritt's response. What happened?

Celeste sends a series of question marks. A few seconds later, her phone rings. It's Merritt, but Celeste declines the call because suddenly she is too sad to speak. She should have canceled the date on Friday, she thinks. Because what she has learned over the course of this weekend is that she *is* lonely and life is nicer when there's someone to talk to. To kiss. To bump knees and hold hands with. Celeste was pretty sure from the start that she was an alien species, but it's disheartening to have it proved true.

He'll talk to her later. Yeah, right.

On Monday, as she is in her office reviewing the following summer's special programming — they're getting a gray-shanked douc langur from Vietnam, which makes Celeste think of Madame Vo's with Benji across the table — there's a knock on her door. It's a quarter after two and Celeste suspects it's Blair from the World of Reptiles saying she has to go home because she has a migraine setting in and can Celeste please cover her three o'clock snake talk, which also makes Celeste think about Benji.

"Come in," Celeste says halfheartedly.

It's Bethany, her assistant, holding a vase of long-stemmed pink roses.

"These are for you," Bethany says.

The next day, Celeste's father calls to say that Karen's MRI came back fine.

"Really?" Celeste says. It's not beyond her parents to lie to her about this.

"Really," he says. "Betty is as fit as a fiddle."

On Thursday night, Benji takes Celeste to a movie at the Paris Theater. The movie is French with subtitles. Celeste falls asleep as soon as it starts and wakes up at the end credits, nestled in Benji's arm.

On Friday, Benji takes Celeste to dinner at Le Bernardin, which is nine courses of seafood. About half the courses press at Celeste's boundaries. Sea urchin custard? Kampachi sashimi? She imagines telling her parents that Benji spent nine hundred dollars on a dinner that included sea urchin, kampachi, and sea cucumber, which is not a vegetable but an animal. There is wine with every course and Celeste gets tipsy. That night, she invites him upstairs.

She is nervous. Before Benji, there have been only two other men, one of whom was the TA in her Mechanisms of Animal Behavior class in college.

The next day, Merritt texts: So???????

Celeste deletes the text.

Merritt texts again: Come on, Celeste. How was our Benji in the sack?

Fine, Celeste texts back.

That bad? Merritt says.

Good, Celeste says. Which is true. Benji was very considerate, very aware of Celeste's desires—what felt good, what she liked. Maybe he was too aware. But that hardly seems like something to complain about.

Uh-oh, Merritt says.

There are dinners in SoHo, the Village, and the Meatpacking District. There is takeout Indian food and sushi and Vietnamese, now a favorite, that they eat at Celeste's apartment while watching *The Americans*. There is brunch at Saxon and Parole, where Benji introduces Celeste to the phenomenon of the bloody mary bar. She loads her glass up with a little of everything: celery, carrots, peppers, house-made pickles and pickled onions, bacon, fresh herbs, beef jerky, olives, and spirals of lemon and lime. Then, when her glass is accessorized like an eighty-year-old woman who is wearing every piece of jewelry she owns, she snaps a photo and sends it to Merritt, who responds ten seconds later: *Are you at Saxon and Parole?*

There's a reading at the Ninety-Second Street Y by a writer named Wonder Calloway, who reads a story about a woman Celeste's age who treks to the base camp of Everest with a man she loves but who does not love her in return. The man suffers from altitude sickness and has to turn back. The woman has to decide whether to stop or keep going. Celeste is moved by the story and by the whole idea that litera-ture can be relevant to *her* life and *her* feelings. She never felt that way when reading *anything* in high school. At the end of the reading, Benji buys Celeste a copy of Wonder Calloway's short stories and Wonder autographs it. She smiles at Celeste and asks her name, then writes *To Celeste* in the book. Celeste is thrilled but also a little chagrined. The experiences Benji is showing her, while extraordinary, are messing with her head. She knows she is fine just as she is — she has a college education and a good job — but each date shows her all the ways she has yet to grow.

She reads the short stories on her commute to work and by the end of the week, she's finished and she asks Benji for another book. He gives her *The Night Circus* by Erin Morgenstern. She loves it so much she reads it any chance she can get. She reads *Small Great Things* by Jodi Picoult and *The Nightingale* by Kristin Hannah. Benji gives her a list of books he's loved and together they go to Shakespeare and Company.

There's a new Burmese place on Broome Street that Benji wants to try and Celeste says, "Burmese?" She didn't even realize Burmese food warranted its own restaurant, but she should know by now that Benji seeks out far-flung cuisines — East African, Peruvian, Basque. He compares it to Celeste's love of exotic animals. She can talk all day about the Nubian ibex and he can talk about momos.

The Burmese restaurant has only ten seats, all of them taken, so they get their order to go and Benji says, "Since we're close, we might as well go to my place."

"You live nearby?" Celeste asks. Benji has referred to his apartment only as being downtown — but everyone lives downtown compared to Celeste. She has wondered why she has never been invited to Benji's apartment. After she finished reading *Jane Eyre,* she joked that Benji must be hiding a crazy wife in his apartment. He bristled at this. "It's nothing special," he said. "You won't like it."

If it's yours, I'll like it, Celeste thought, but she hadn't wanted to push. He obviously had his reasons.

Now, Benji leads Celeste into a high-rise luxury building in Tribeca, right next to Stuyvesant High School, and after greeting the doorman and the man behind the front desk, they get into the elevator and Benji presses the button that says 61B.

The sixty-first floor, Celeste thinks. Her building is a six-floor walk-up and she lives on the fifth floor in the rear.

Celeste's ears pop on the way up and Benji is uncharacteristically quiet. The elevator fills with the scent of the Burmese food, but Celeste's appetite is quelled by a sudden case of nerves.

The elevator doors open and Celeste steps *into* an apartment. She's confused for a second.

"So, wait," she says. She turns around. Yes. The elevator has opened up right into Benji's apartment.

Benji takes Celeste's hand. She is fixated on the elevator. An elevator into his apartment. Did she know places like this existed? Yes, she has seen it in the movies. If she lived here, she might be tempted to press the elevator button just so she could experience its arrival *solely for her,* even when she didn't have to go anywhere.

The apartment has been professionally decorated

and it's immaculately clean. There are black leather sofas, deep royal-blue club chairs, a colorful kaleidoscope of a rug, an enormous flat-screen TV, and, on either side of the TV, shelving that is crisscrossed on the diagonal, which is one of the coolest things Celeste has ever seen. She didn't even know diagonal bookshelves existed, but now all she wants in the world, other than an elevator that opens up into her apartment, are diagonal bookshelves and books to put on them.

There's a gourmet kitchen, which is sleek and gleaming except for a wide, rough-hewn wooden bowl filled with fruit: pineapple, mangoes, papayas, limes, kiwis. The fruit in that bowl probably costs as much as everything in Celeste's apartment. She feels a sudden hot shame about the futon she uses as a bed, covered with a quilt her mother bought from an Amish market in Lancaster, and about her Ikea side tables and the lamps she took from her parents' house, the bases of which are mason jars filled with beans. She cringes when she thinks of the vintage zoo posters that she had framed at great expense (they had been ninety dollars apiece and she had blanched) and the rainbow candles her mother made out of melted crayons.

Benji says something about showing her around and she mutely follows him into the bedroom, where there is a floor-to-ceiling window that looks out on uptown. All of Manhattan is rolled out before them, colorful and twinkling—and one of those lights, just one dim bulb a hundred-plus blocks up and to the east, is in Celeste's apartment window.

She presses her hands against the window, then removes them; she doesn't want to leave prints.

"You hate it," Benji says.

"How could you possibly think that?" she asks. "It...it...defies my humble vocabulary."

"My parents pay for it," Benji says. "They offered it to me and I couldn't say no. I mean, I guess I could have said no, but you'd have to be crazy to turn a place like this down."

Part of Celeste agrees, of course, but another part of her stands in righteous opposition. She thinks of Rocky, who rents a studio apartment in Queens; he rides the N/R train into the city at five o'clock each morning to run the bodega. At night, he takes classes at Queens College. He's studying to be a teacher. There's nobility in that, Celeste sees, a nobility and an ethic that's missing when one lives in an apartment that could easily cost seven or eight thousand dollars a month, paid for by one's parents.

"This building has a gym," Benji says. "And it has a pool. You can use the pool this summer. You can kiss North Meadow good-bye."

I don't want *to kiss North Meadow good-bye!* Celeste thinks stubbornly. But she knows she's being silly.

"We should appreciate this place while we can," Benji says. "My parents are threatening to buy me a brownstone uptown."

A brownstone uptown, Celeste thinks sardonically. Of course; the next logical step.

"East Seventy-Eighth Street," she murmurs in spite of herself. When she first moved to Manhattan, before she met Merritt, she used to spend her week-ends wandering the Upper East Side, looking in windows, admiring leaded-glass transoms and iron fretwork. The block between Park and Lexington on Seventy-Eighth Street had been her very favorite. She used to gaze at the fronts of the homes and wonder just what lucky people lived there.

People like Benji.

"I'll tell them to look only on East Seventy-Eighth Street," Benji says. "Now let's eat."

Celeste spends all week feeling uneasy about Benji's privilege. She can't exactly claim to be blindsided, she knew it existed, but now that the extent of his wealth and advantage has been fully revealed, her view of him is tinged, ever so slightly, with distaste.

But then Benji informs her that on the last Sunday

of every month, he volunteers at a homeless shelter in the basement of his parents' church on the Upper East Side. He asks Celeste if she would like to come. It entails serving the guests a hot supper, then making up the cots and staying overnight. Benji would be in a room with the men and Celeste with the women.

"It's not everyone's cup of tea," he says.

"I'll do it," Celeste says.

At Benji's suggestion, Celeste dresses casually, in sweatpants and a T-shirt. She helps chop vegetables for soup, and during the meal, she pours coffee. All of the guests want sugar in their coffee, lots of sugar; the pockets of Celeste's pants bulge with packets. One of the male guests starts calling her Sugar Girl. Benji hears him and says, "Hey there, Malcolm, slow your roll. She's *my* Sugar Girl." This makes everyone laugh. Benji has an easy rapport with the guests and knows many of them by name—Malcolm, Slick, Henrietta, Anya, Linus. Celeste tries to be respectful, to pretend she's working at a restaurant for paying guests, but she can't help wondering what circumstances life threw at these people that they ended up here. With one stroke of bad luck, she supposes, it could be her. Or her parents.

After dinner, Celeste makes up fourteen cots with sheets and blankets. She doles out one flat pillow per guest. Benji had told her that the guests go to bed

early—even though TV is allowed until ten—
because being homeless is cold and exhausting. Most
of the women lie down right away. Celeste has
brought her toiletries in a plastic bag and she goes to
the bathroom to brush her teeth and wash her face.
It's kind of like living in the college dorms, but she
suspects Benji is right: this isn't for everyone. Celeste
can't imagine Merritt here in a million years and his
ex-girlfriend Jules even less so. She feels proud of herself for being a good person, then decides that the
pride means she's not so good after all.

She kisses Benji chastely in the hallway between
the men's dorm and the women's dorm.

"Are you going to be okay?" he asks.

"Yes, of course," she says.

"I wish I could be with you," he says. He kisses her
again.

Celeste crawls onto her cot. The sheets smell like
industrial-strength bleach, and the pillow is no more
effective than a cocktail napkin. She stuffs her winter
coat under her head.

She falls asleep listening to the other women snore.
She misses her mother.

Merritt sends a text in the middle of the following
week: How's everything with the boyfriend?

Boyfriend. The term gives Celeste pause—but there's no denying it. Celeste and Benji like each other. They're a couple, doing couple things. They're boyfriend and girlfriend. They're happy.

And then Celeste meets Shooter.

Saturday, July 7, 2018, 9:30 a.m.

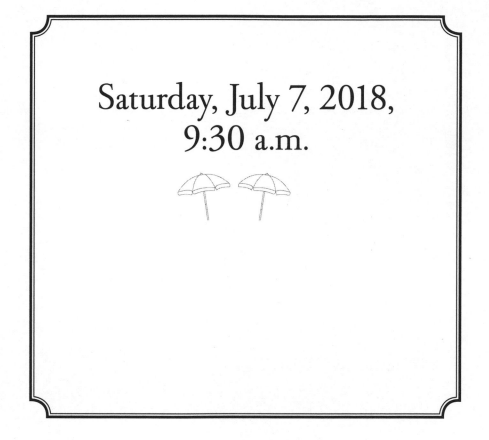

NANTUCKET

Marty Szczerba (Skuh-*zer*-ba) is the head of security at the Nantucket Memorial Airport. It's a town job and comes with full benefits, which nearly makes up for the ball-breaking stress of his job in the summer.

June and July are foggy months. In the early summer on Nantucket, warm, moist air flows over the colder water. The moist air cools to its dew point and a cloud forms at the water's surface. This is fog. Marty wishes the town had a budget allocation for a program in Fog Awareness because cutesy T-shirts and mugs that display the slogan FOG HAPPENS don't seem to be getting the message across. Fog *happens*. It will happen to *you*, Mr. Millionaire from Greenwich, Connecticut, and to *you*, Ms. Billionaire from Silicon Valley. Your flight will be delayed or canceled if the ceiling drops below two hundred feet. You will miss your connection, and your day's plans—board meeting, daughter's graduation from Duke, rendezvous with your lover at the Hotel Le Meurice in Paris—will have to be canceled.

On Saturday, July 7, Marty sits down at his desk for his hot breakfast from Crosswinds, the excellent airport diner—a perk of the job he has greatly appreciated since his wife of thirty-one years, Nancy, died—to look over his choices on Match.com. Finding an age-appropriate woman who wants to live year-round on Nantucket has proven to be something of a challenge. Marty has been on three dates in the past six months, but not one of the women has looked a single thing like her profile picture, which has thrown the integrity of the website into question for Marty. His assistant, Bonita, is a thirty-three-year-old single woman and she keeps telling Marty to use Tinder.

"Swipe right," she always says. "Guaranteed action."

It has become a joke between them; Marty isn't after "action." What he would like is a meaningful relationship, a leading lady for his second act. It's just when he is, for the first time, seriously considering Tinder—*could* he swipe right, just once?—that a phone call comes in from the chief of police. They have found a body floating out in Monomoy and there's a person of interest—the name the Chief gives Marty is Shooter Uxley—on the run.

Marty writes down the name and a description of the guy—late twenties, dark hair, wearing Nantucket Reds shorts, blue oxford shirt, navy blazer, and loafers. Good-looking, the Chief says. Marty laughs because this description fits any of a hundred guys in the airport at any given moment over the summer. He shovels in a bite of scrambled eggs and home fries, clicks out of his dating website, and goes downstairs to talk to the state police.

Lola Budd has shocked every adult in her life by excelling at her job on the ticket desk at Hy-Line Cruises. Lola's aunt Kendra, who has been her legal guardian since her mother overdosed and her father went to jail, told Lola she was too young and *too immature* to handle such a job. Lola Budd has exhibited some uneven behavior both at home and at school, but she convinced her aunt that if she took on a job with a lot of responsibility, she would rise to the challenge. She wants to eventually attend the hospitality school at UMass and she feels a summer job that involves a lot of interfacing with the public will give her an advantage.

She has been at the job for three weeks now and she absolutely loves it. Unlike school, which she believes is a waste of time, this job makes her feel adult, relevant. She is doing something meaningful, facilitating travel between Nantucket and Hyannis, which is to say, between a summer fantasyland and the real world.

Lola especially likes her job on frenetic days like today, the Saturday after the Fourth of July, when the line is 117 people long. This boat, the 9:15, is sold out. Every boat today and all of the boats tomorrow are sold out. To get tickets for you, your wife, and your three kids back to America today, you basically had to make that your New Year's resolution and execute on January second.

The woman who works at the station next to Lola's, a sixty-year-old Nantucket native named Mary Ellen Cahill, has a sign in front of her computer terminal that says: BAD PLANNING ON YOUR PART DOES NOT CONSTITUTE AN EMERGENCY ON MY PART. Although Lola agrees with this sentiment, she finds the most satisfying parts of the job are when she can be a hero, when she can arrange for a last-minute ticket to appear out of thin air, when she can fix a snafu. Mr. and Mrs. Diegnan meant to book the last boat back on Friday, not Thursday, even though the ticket Susan Diegnan was showing clearly said Thursday, which was the day before. *No problem!* Lola would switch the Diegnans to the Friday boat, free of charge. Lola loves calling a name off the waiting list and seeing joy and relief flood someone's face.

This particular day, however, there will be no faces filled with relief, and Lola has nothing to offer but a manufactured expression of sympathy. "I'm sorry, sir. I don't have a boat ticket available until Monday at four oh five. You may want to check with the Steamship Authority. Their car ferries accommodate far more passengers." Today there will be people swearing in front of and *at* Lola. Today there will be people calling the Hy-Line a "Mickey Mouse operation" and a "dog-and-pony show."

A dog-and-pony show? Lola thinks. *What even is that?*

In job training, Lola was taught to accept all comments with calm reserve. The worst thing she can do is react with anger or indignation, thereby engaging the disgruntled customer.

"I have a problem," a puffy-faced pregnant woman says. She's sweating, carrying a toddler, and she has another child, perhaps five years old, clinging to her leg. "I was holding my ferry tickets for two adults and two children, and I set them down for a second and when I picked them back up I had only one adult and two children, which means someone stole one of my ferry tickets."

Lola nods. She has yet to be confronted with accusations of ticket theft, but if it was going to happen, she thinks, then it was going to happen today. On the other side of her counter is a mob of desperate people.

"Have you checked with your husband?" Lola asks. "Is it possible he took his ticket without you realizing it?"

"Of course I checked with my husband!" the woman says. "He doesn't have it. I was in charge of the tickets and he was in charge of handling the luggage, which really means sneaking in one final beer at the Gazebo because he has a crush on the bartender. The one with the..." She gives Lola a good approximation of the eye-roll emoji. "You know how men can be."

One of the things Lola has learned on this job is *how men can be.* Before, Lola knew only how boys could be. She has had a boyfriend for nine months, two weeks, and five days. His name is Finn MacAvoy and Lola loves him like crazy, it's true love forever, et cetera, and she presumes they'll end up getting married. Finn lost both his parents in a sailing accident and so he and Lola are both in the same situation — virtual orphans.

But Lola would be lying if she said she hasn't been amazed by the power she seems to exert over certain men. She has been propositioned by some and blatantly ogled by others. It's common for a pale, chubby, balding married dude to confront Lola and find himself tongue-tied. What had he meant to ask her? He can't recall.

And that's how men can be.

Lola feels bad for the pregnant woman (Aunt Kendra worries about Lola getting pregnant, but this job is effective birth control), but there is nothing she can do.

"I'm sorry," Lola says. "I don't even have one extra seat on this boat. The next seat I do have available is on Monday at four oh five."

"But I had the ticket!" the woman shrieks. "I paid for it! And someone stole it!"

"Unfortunately, we have no way to prove that," Lola says. "You might have dropped it accidentally and someone else might have picked it up. You do have your hands full."

"But my mother is sick!" the woman says. "She's in the hospital with shingles. We have to get off today. It's a medical emergency."

Lola remembers to breathe. It's astonishing the lies people will fabricate when they're desperate. Lola wants to quietly tell this woman that her best bet for getting off the island is to pretend she's going into labor. She will be taken to the mainland in a medical helicopter and her husband can use the one remaining adult ferry ticket.

"I'm sorry," Lola says. "And I'll have to ask you to step aside so I can help the next customer."

The next customer swears she has a reservation under the name Iuffredo but Lola doesn't see it on her computer. "Could it be under a different name?" she asks.

"I have the reservation number somewhere," Ms. Iuffredo says. She rummages through her purse.

The phone rings. Lola looks down at her console. It's the emergency line, one that can't be ignored. Lola picks it up.

"Hello, Hy-Line Cruises. This is Lola Budd speaking. How may I help you?"

There's a split-second pause, then a man's voice. "Lola Budd? Oh, that's right. I forgot you worked there. Lola, this is Chief Kapenash. May I talk to your supervisor, please?"

"Oh, hi, Chief!" Lola says. The Chief is Finn's uncle and legal guardian. He is a very important person on Nantucket. He's the Chief. Of. Police. Lola has the distinct impression that the Chief doesn't like her, doesn't *approve* of her. He probably wishes Finn were dating someone like Meg Lyon, a three-sport athlete with good grades and squeaky-clean behavior. But now the Chief will witness Lola Budd in her new persona as a responsible, competent Hy-Line Cruises employee. "My supervisor isn't here right now. It's just me, Mary Ellen, and Kalik and we have a boat leaving in eight minutes so everyone is really busy. Gracie should be back soon, though. Would you like me to leave her a—"

"Eight minutes?" the Chief says. "Put Mary Ellen on the phone, please."

"She's with a customer," Lola says.

"Put her on the phone, Lola," the Chief says. "This is an emergency."

Marty Szczerba talks to Brenner, the state policeman on duty at the airport, and gets more details about the potential murder. The body they have is a twenty-nine-year-old New York City woman who came to Nantucket to be the maid of honor in her best friend's wedding.

The news lands like a punch to Marty's gut because his very own daughter, Laura Rae, is getting married in September and her maid of honor, Adi Conover, is like a second daughter to Marty. Because Marty's wife, Nancy, is gone, Marty has been the one planning the wedding with Laura Rae. They hired Roger Pelton to help — Marty and Roger go way back, as Roger's daughter Heather and Laura Rae played softball together in high school — and out of curiosity plus some kind of hunch, Marty asks Brenner the state policeman if Roger Pelton was doing the wedding.

"Roger Pelton?" Brenner says. "He's the one who called it in. But I'm pretty sure he's been cleared."

Cleared? Marty thinks. Of course Roger has been *cleared*. He certainly didn't murder anyone! Marty tells Brenner to call over to Blade, the private helicopter service, as well as the private plane hangar ASAP.

There's no way a person of interest would escape Nantucket via a commercial flight. The TSA are too assiduous; they're bulldogs. They don't let peanut butter through, much less a person of interest.

Brenner says he'll handle the private services, and Marty alerts the TSA and the policeman on duty inside security, then he goes back upstairs to his desk to call Roger Pelton.

"I heard about the body," Marty says. "I'm so sorry, Roger."

"I can't...I don't think..." Roger sounds choked up. "I can't describe what it was like, pulling that poor girl out of the water. The bride was the one who found her floating, her best friend, her maid of honor. The bride was...well, she was hysterical and she's such a sweet, sweet kid. Her big day ended before it even began, and in complete tragedy."

"Aw, jeez, Roger," Marty says. He eyes his breakfast, which has now grown cold. He pushes the plate away. "Who's this person of interest on the lam? This Shooter Uxley?"

"On the *lam?*" Roger says. "Shooter?"

"The Chief called a little while ago," Marty says. "They're looking for someone named Shooter Uxley."

"He's the best man," Roger says. "Real gregarious kid, strong handshake. He went out of the way to notice the details. He's in event planning himself, I guess. I have twenty weddings this month alone and I can't remember anyone—but that guy I really liked."

"Well, he's missing," Marty says. "He was about to be questioned by the police and he escaped through a bathroom window."

"That doesn't look good," Roger says. "I guess you never know."

"Ain't that the truth," Marty says. And then he says good-bye, hangs up, and gets back to the job.

When Mary Ellen Cahill gets off the phone with the Chief, she hands Lola a slip of paper that says *Shooter Uxley.*

"He's not in the computer," Mary Ellen says. "So he would have been a walk-in. He's six feet tall, dark hair, wearing a blue blazer."

"That narrows it down," Lola says.

"My guess is he took the Steamship," Mary Ellen says. "I hope he took the Steamship. We're too busy for a murder suspect today."

Lola looks at the name again. Shooter Uxley. She pulls out her phone, which is expressly forbidden on the job, and finds him instantly on Facebook. He's as handsome as Tom Brady. And then Lola figures it out.

"Hold the boat!" she shouts. She tears out from behind the counter and goes charging out of the office and down the dock. George, the steward, is just about to fold up the gangplank.

"Lola." George winks at her. He has a crush on her, she knows, which will work to her advantage.

"I need to get on that boat," she says. "And as soon as I get on, I need you to find a policeman and send him right behind me."

"Whoa!" George says. "You buggin'?"

"Trust me, Georgie. This is an urgent matter. A life-and-death matter. Let me on the boat, then find a policeman."

"Seriously?"

"Seriously," Lola says.

She wants to go charging through the cabin but she maintains her calm. The stolen ticket. The movie-star handsome Shooter Uxley stole a ticket from the pregnant woman and went sauntering onto the boat. Lola scans the faces. She sees old people, sunburned people, men wearing Nantucket Reds; she sees yellow Labs, crying babies, Boston terriers, women who have had a lot of plastic surgery. She sees a kid in a Spider-Man costume. She sees a shirtless guy in a pair of American-flag trunks, passed out and snoring.

Lola Budd feels a hand on her arm. She turns to see a policeman standing with Fred Stiftel, one of the captains.

"Young lady," the policeman says. "What's going on?"

Lola glances around the cabin. Her eye snags on a face in line at the bar. He has his sunglasses on but she recognizes the set of his jaw and the dark, floppy forelock. Blue shirt, navy blazer.

"There he is," Lola says to the policeman. She keeps her voice normal and her eyes trained on the person of interest. "Shooter Uxley. He's right there."

The officer approaches Shooter Uxley, who drops his beer. In the ensuing commotion, he tries to run but it's too crowded, there's nowhere to go, and the policeman easily pins Shooter's arms behind his back and cuffs him. He informs Shooter that he is a person of interest in an ongoing investigation and that he will be detained until the police release him from questioning. Everyone on the boat is watching. There's a low-level hum beneath a general hush.

It's just like on TV! Lola thinks. In this case, the hero is her! Lola Budd!

She can't wait to text Finn and tell him about it. The Chief will *have* to like her now.

Friday, July 6, 2018, 8:30 p.m.

KAREN

Bruce brings her a cup filled with a pale, fizzy liquid garnished with two blackberries.

"What is this?" she asks. "Not the punch? I don't think I can handle the punch."

"Not the punch," Bruce says. "It's a wine cooler, handcrafted by yours truly. More cooler than wine, but I tasted it and I think you'll approve."

Karen takes a sip and is transported back to her youth. Her husband is the most thoughtful man on earth. "Thank you, baby," she says.

He kisses her full on the lips, and even after so many years, something inside of Karen stirs. "Anything for you," he says. "And I do mean anything."

At the table, Karen eats half a lobster tail. Each butter-drenched bite makes her moan with pleasure. Never in her life has anything tasted so divine.

Bruce tries to cajole her into tasting his biscuit. He pulls it apart so she can see the fluffy layers, but she demurs. The lobster was enough, more than enough.

Bruce chimes his spoon against his water glass as he holds it aloft. The tent grows quiet. Karen hopes this goes well. Bruce has had at least three cups of the punch.

Bruce says, "Ladies and gentlemen, I'm Bruce Otis, father of the bride."

His face radiates pride. He loves the title and Karen has to admit, she does too. The last time either of them were people of distinction, she thinks, was when they were in high school. She swam the butterfly leg on the four-hundred-meter relay team, and anyone who isn't impressed by that has never tried to swim a hundred yards of butterfly, much less swim it fast. And Bruce, of course, won the state wrestling title.

Karen gazes down at the table and closes her eyes to listen. *We would go to the post office to mail packages or check our box, and the line was always extra-long on Saturdays, but you know what? I didn't care. I could wait an hour. I could wait all day . . . because I was with Karen.* Karen embeds these words deep within herself. She has been loved in her life, deeply and truly loved. She has been known and understood. Is there anything more she is supposed to want?

But following her gratitude is . . . guilt. She hasn't

told Bruce about the three pearlescent ovoid pills mixed in with her oxy. The pill is an unpronounceable compound that she bought illegally off the internet from a website she stumbled across when she Googled *euthanasia*. She e-mailed with a person named Dr. Tang who used to be an anesthesiologist, licensed in the state of Utah, and now provides terminally ill patients with drugs—for a price—so that people like Karen can end their lives with dignity.

The three pills cost twelve hundred dollars, eleven hundred of which Karen withdrew from her own personal checking account, money she had stashed away from working at the Crayola factory gift shop— her "mad money," as her mother used to call it. The other hundred dollars she stole from Bruce's wallet in five- and ten-dollar increments. She justifies the act because, unlike Bruce, she does not have a penchant for expensive clothes. She has never spent a frivolous dollar in her life, and she certainly isn't now. These pills will put her down instantly, saving both Bruce and Celeste the anguish, mess, and expense of her natural demise.

If she told Bruce, he would understand, she thinks. In thirty-two years of marriage, they have always viewed the world the same way. But what if he *doesn't* understand? Euthanasia is a topic that taps into deeply personal views of dignity and fear but, mostly, spirituality. Karen is afraid of pain, yes, she's afraid of the cancer eating her up from the inside. Bruce is afraid of being left alone, but he might also be afraid for her soul. She has no idea. They haven't been big church people, though they identify loosely as Catholic and celebrate all the holidays. They had Celeste baptized at St. Jane's in Palmer Township, back when Karen's mother and Bruce's parents were still alive. But Karen hasn't set foot in St. Jane's for years and years. Bruce has always seemed to be on the same page as Karen—she doesn't know what she believes in; she just tries to be a good person and hopes for the best. But what if Bruce secretly holds the tenets of the Catholic Church to be absolute and believes that suicide will automatically assign Karen to hell?

Karen hasn't talked to Bruce about life after she's gone because he refuses to acknowledge the inevitable—which, she supposes, is better than him accepting it too readily. As the assembled guests raise their glasses to Celeste and Benji, Bruce gazes down on Karen with an expression so filled with tenderness, with love and awe, that Karen can barely meet his eyes. Her ardor matches his own, but she is a realist. Cancer has made her a realist.

She has, for example, come to terms with the likelihood that Bruce will remarry. She wants him to. It won't be the same, she knows. He will always love her first, last, and best. The new wife will be younger—not as young as Celeste, Karen hopes—and she will add a new vitality to Bruce's life. Maybe the new wife will have a job that provides money for traveling, real traveling—national parks, cruises, bicycle tours of Europe. Maybe Bruce will take up yoga or watercolor painting; maybe he'll learn to speak Italian. Karen can imagine these possibilities without jealousy or anger. That's how she knows it's time for her to go.

After dessert, she and Bruce dance to one song, "Little Surfer Girl." Karen has always loved this song even though she has never been anywhere near a surfboard. She heard her father sing it once, in the car, when she was a little girl and that was all it took. Her father's happiness and his carefree falsetto had been contagious. Bruce knows about this memory and so he croons in Karen's ear. They are dancing—shuffling, really—among the other guests. No one is staring at them, she hopes, or taking photos or marveling that a woman so sick can still dance.

When the song is over, everyone claps. The band, it seems, is calling it a night. The evening is drawing to a close.

Celeste appears out of nowhere. "D-D-Did you have fun, B-B-Betty?"

"So much fun," Karen says. "But I'm exhausted."

She feels Bruce's hand against her back; even the light pressure is excruciating. The oxy is wearing off, leaving her nerve endings to glint like shattered glass. She needs one more oxy before she falls asleep.

"We have a big day tomorrow," Bruce says.

Celeste says, "T-T-Tag is really looking forward to having a drink with you in his st-st-study. A drink and a Cuban cigar. He's been t-t-talking about it all week."

"He has?" Bruce says. "News to me."

"I'll get B-B-Betty up to b-b-bed," Celeste says.

"No, no, darling," Karen says. "You go have fun. It's the night before your wedding. You should go out with your friends."

Celeste gazes across the yard to where Benji and Shooter are filling up cups of beer at the keg. Shooter looks up, then jogs over. Karen is embarrassed at how handsome she finds him. He's as good-looking as the teen idols from her era—Leif Garrett, David Cassidy, Robby Benson.

"Mrs. Otis," he says. "Can I get you anything? I happen to know where the caterers stashed the extra lobster tails."

This makes Karen laugh despite the knives starting to twist in her lower back. How darling of Shooter to remember that Karen likes lobster, even though the days when she might have enjoyed a midnight snack are gone.

"We're going to bed," Karen says. "But thank you. Please take my daughter out on the town."

"I need my b-b-beauty sleep," Celeste says.

"You're beautiful enough as it is," Shooter says. "You couldn't get any more beautiful."

Karen looks at Shooter and notes the expression on his face: tenderness. Celeste inspires it in people, she supposes.

"I couldn't agree more," Karen says.

"The defense rests, then," Bruce says. He kisses Celeste's forehead, then nudges her gently toward Shooter. "Go have fun, darling."

"But Mac, T-T-Tag wants—"

"Your father will go find Tag for a drink," Karen says. "I'm perfectly capable of getting myself to bed."

Shooter takes Celeste's arm but she pulls away to give Karen one more hug and a kiss on each cheek. This is an echo of how Karen kissed Celeste good night when she was growing up. Does Celeste realize this? Yes, she must. Karen would like Celeste to come upstairs, tuck her in, read her something, even if it's just an article from the issue of *Town and Country* on the nightstand, and then lie with her until she falls asleep, just as Karen used to do with Celeste. But she will not be a burden. She will allow—indeed, encourage—Celeste to pursue her new life.

Bruce turns to Karen. "Let me just walk you upstairs."

"I'll be fine," Karen says. "Go find Tag now so you can come up to me sooner. I'd prefer that."

Bruce kisses her on the lips. "Okay. Just one drink, though."

Karen takes her time on her way to her room upstairs. She wants to experience the house at her own pace. She wants to touch the fabrics, sit in the chairs to judge their comfort; she wants to smell the flower arrangements, read the titles of the books. She has never been in a house like this, one where every piece of furniture has been professionally chosen and arranged, where the clocks tick in unison and the paintings and photographs are lit to advantage. The other homes Karen has visited in her lifetime have all been variations of her own—corner cabinets to display the wedding china, sectional sofas, afghans crocheted by maiden aunts.

Karen wanders into the formal living room and stops immediately at a black grand piano. The top of the piano is down flat and it's covered with framed photographs. The frames themselves strike Karen initially—the majority look like real silver and others are burled wood—and then she looks at the photographs. All of them seem to have been taken on Nantucket over the years. In the one that Karen studies first, Benji and Thomas are teenagers. They're standing on the beach in front of this house with Tag and Greer behind them. Tag looks then like Benji does now—young and strong with a wide smile. Greer's expression is inscrutable behind her sunglasses. She wears white capri pants with red pompoms dangling from the hems. *That's a playful touch,* Karen thinks. In her next life, she will own such pants.

When she goes to pick up the next photo, she hears someone cough. Karen is so surprised she nearly throws the photograph over her shoulder. She turns to see a woman curled up in one of the curvy modern chairs, like an egg in a cup. The woman is so still that Karen would guess she's asleep except that her eyes are wide open. She has been here all along, watching Karen.

"I'm sorry," Karen says. "You frightened me. I didn't see you."

The woman blinks. "Who are you, then?" she asks.

"I'm Karen Otis," Karen says. "Celeste's mother. The bride's mother."

"The bride's mother," the woman says. "Yes, that's right. I noticed you earlier. Your husband gave that lovely toast."

"Thank you," Karen says. She suddenly feels very weak. This woman has a British accent; she must be a friend of Tag and Greer's—nearly everyone here is. Karen remembers her vow to shine. "And what's your name?"

"Featherleigh," the woman says. "Featherleigh Dale. I live in London."

"Very nice," Karen says. She should excuse herself for bed but she doesn't want to appear rude to this Featherleigh. Why do the British give their children last names for first names? Winston. Neville. And Greer. When Karen first heard Celeste say the name Greer, Karen had thought it was a man. And this practice is catching on in America, she's noticed. She used to shake her head in wonder at the children who would come through the Crayola factory gift shop. Little girls named Sloane, Sterling, Brearley. Boys named Millhouse, Dearborne, Acton. And what about Celeste's maid of honor, Merritt? *Like the parkway,* Karen heard her say, though Karen has no idea what that means. "I just took a detour on my way to bed. But I should really excuse myself. It was nice to meet you, Featherleigh. I suppose I shall see you tomorrow."

"Wait!" Featherleigh says. "Please, can you stay another couple of minutes? I'm too drunk to get back to my inn right now."

"Would you like me to go find Greer?" Karen asks. She's only asking to be polite. The mere prospect of hunting down Greer is exhausting.

"No!" Featherleigh says. "Not Greer."

Something in her tone catches Karen's attention.

Featherleigh lowers her bare feet to the ground and leans forward. "Can you keep a secret?"

Karen nods involuntarily. She can keep a secret, yes. She is keeping a secret from her husband and her daughter, the secret of the three pearlescent ovoid pills, the secret of her intentions, and that is surely a bigger secret than whatever this Featherleigh wants to disclose.

Featherleigh says, "I've been involved with a married man. But he broke things off with me in May and I can't seem to recover."

"Oh dear," Karen says. What she thinks is *Serves you right!* Karen cannot abide adulterers. She doesn't like to judge but she can say with certainty that if any woman had pursued Bruce and managed to ensnare him in an affair, her life would have been destroyed. She and Bruce are lucky, she knows, in that they're both true blue. This isn't to say that Karen has never felt jealous. Bruce would sometimes talk about the housewives who came into his department looking to buy their husbands a suit, and Karen would wonder what the women looked like and if they flirted with Bruce more than he let on. There had been one period—right after Celeste left for college—when Bruce had come home from work singing unfamiliar country music songs and acting strangely distant, and Karen thought that maybe...maybe he'd met someone else. She finally asked him about it. He very bluntly said that he was just upset about Celeste being away. He was finding it more challenging than he expected. Karen admitted that she was taking it harder than she'd expected too, and they ended up crying together and then making love in the kitchen, which was something that hadn't happened since Celeste was born.

"I think the truth might interest you," Featherleigh says. "Maybe, maybe not."

Karen can't stand to hear it. "Stop," she says. "Please, just stop." Karen holds her hand aloft, as though she can swat the words away. She backs out of the room.

The words swarm her as she climbs the stairs. *I think the truth might interest you. I've been involved with a married man.* Karen badly needs an oxy and her bed. Why, oh why, did that woman choose Karen to confess to? How could Featherleigh's adulterous relationship possibly matter to *Karen?* She knows no one here! Featherleigh was clearly quite drunk, and drunk people, in Karen's experience, love nothing more than to confess. Featherleigh would have told anyone. It serves Karen right for snooping around.

When Karen finally reaches the top of the stairs, she's disoriented. Is her room to the right or the left?

She steadies herself with her cane and thinks, *The right.* When she turns right, it's the last door on the left. But at that instant, the door Karen thinks is hers opens and Merritt "as in the parkway" steps out. Merritt is the same young woman Karen thought of as the Scarlet Letter when she'd first arrived before she realized that it was Merritt, Celeste's maid of honor. Celeste adores Merritt, thinks she hung the moon, and while Karen is thrilled that Celeste has found a real friend, she can't help thinking Merritt is a little fast.

Fast. Now Karen sounds like her own mother, or even her grandmother. Who uses the word *fast* to describe a woman? No one. At least, not in the past forty years. Karen is sure Merritt must be very nice, otherwise Celeste would not be so fond of her. Tonight, Merritt is wearing black.

"I…" Karen says. Now she is really and truly confused. This house has more rooms than a hotel. "I think I've gotten turned around somehow? I thought that was *my* room."

"Oh, it is your room, Mrs. Otis," Merritt says. "I was just looking for Celeste. You don't know where she is, do you?"

"Celeste?" Karen says. "Why, she was outside when last I saw her. She's planning on going out with Benji."

"Okay," Merritt says. She seems to be in a tremendous hurry; she sidles her way past Karen and heads down the stairs. "Thank you, Mrs. Otis. Good night."

"Good night," Karen says. She stands in place, staring at the bedroom door. Looking for Celeste? In Bruce and Karen's room? What on earth for? Why not look for Celeste in *Celeste's* room, which is down the hall on the left? Clearly that Featherleigh woman has written her filthy graffiti on the walls of Karen's mind because all she can think is that she's going to open the bedroom door and find Bruce inside and then she will have to ask why Merritt and Bruce were in the bedroom alone together.

Hadn't Merritt been flirting with Bruce earlier that day? *Aren't you hot?*

Karen turns the knob and swings open the door. The room is dark and empty.

Karen exhales. She props her cane against the nightstand and sits on the bed. She waits for her heart to stop racing.

Saturday, July 7, 2018, 10:20 a.m.

Initial questioning, Greer Garrison Winbury, Saturday, July 7, 10:20 a.m.

After Nick finishes writing notes from his interview with Abby, he pulls on a pair of latex gloves and enters the cottage where Merritt Monaco was staying. He has gotten in ahead of forensics, which is how he prefers it.

"Tell me a story," he whispers. "What happened?"

The cottage has been decorated with a feminine sensibility, in pastels and florals. It's probably meant to evoke an English garden, though to Nick it feels cloying and overwrought; it's like walking into a Crabtree and Evelyn.

The living area appears untouched; Nick doesn't see a thing out of place. He moves into the bedroom, where the air-conditioning has been turned up so high, the room is like a meat locker. Nick has to admit, it feels good, nearly delicious after the oppressive heat outside. The bed is made, and Merritt's suitcase is open on the luggage rack with her shoes underneath. Her bridesmaid dress—ivory silk with black embroidery—hangs alone in the closet. Nick enters the bathroom. Merritt's cosmetics are lined up on the lower glass shelf—she is clearly a fan of Bobbi Brown—and her hairbrush and flat iron are on the upper glass shelf. Toothbrush in the cup.

She was nice and neat, Nick thinks.

A quick check of Merritt's cosmetic bag reveals eyeliners, mascaras, lipsticks, and powder, but nothing more.

Hmmpf, Nick thinks. He's looking for something, but what? He'll know it when he sees it.

On the dresser, Nick finds an open clutch purse that contains a driver's license, a gold American Express card, seventy-seven dollars in cash, and an iPhone X. He studies the license: *Merritt Alison Monaco, 116 Perry Street, New York, New York.* She's a beautiful woman, and young; she just turned twenty-nine. It's such a shame.

"I'm going to do right by you," Nick says. "Let's figure this out."

He picks up the iPhone X and swipes across. To his enormous surprise, the phone opens. *Whaaaaa...* He didn't think there was a Millennial alive who left her phone unsecured. He feels almost cheated. Does this woman have *nothing* to hide?

He scrolls through her texts first. There is nothing new today, and yesterday there's one text from someone named Robbie wishing her a belated "Happy Day of American Independence"; he hopes she's well. The day before that, Merritt sent a text to someone named Jada V., thanking her for the party. Attached is a photo of fireworks over the Statue of Liberty.

The call log is ancient as well—by *ancient,* Nick means nothing within the past twenty-four hours. Friday morning there was a call placed to a 212 number but when Nick calls that number from his own phone, he gets the switchboard for the Wildlife Conservation Society. Merritt had probably been checking in at work.

The scant offerings on Merritt's phone lead Nick back to Abby's comment that Merritt might have set her sights on someone who was already at the wedding. She wouldn't have to call or text anyone if she could talk to him in person.

Nick puts the clutch purse down where he found it and pokes around a little longer. A journal left lying around is too much to hope for, Nick knows, but what about a joint, a condom, a doodle on a scrap of paper with the name of the person she was involved with? She's too attractive for there not to have been *someone.*

He finds nothing.

*   *   *

The mother of the bride is still in her bedroom, and the bride herself still at the hospital. Nick finds Greer Garrison, mother of the groom, on her phone in the kitchen. She has obviously just told someone the awful news and is now accepting condolences.

"Celeste is devastated," she says. "I can't imagine her agony." She pauses. "Well, let's not get too far ahead of ourselves...we're all still in shock and"— here, Greer raises her eyes to Nick— "the police are trying to figure out what happened. I believe I'm the next to be interrogated, and so I really must hang up, I'm afraid. Love to Thebaud." Greer punches off her phone. "Can I help you?" she asks Nick.

She looks fairly put-together, considering the circumstances, Nick thinks. She's dressed in white pants and a beige tank; there is a gold cross on a thin gold chain around her neck. Her hair is sleek; she's wearing lipstick. Her expression is guarded. She knows her task is about to be interrupted and she resents it.

Nick says, "Ms. Garrison, I'm Detective Nick Diamantopoulos with the Massachusetts State Police. I'll need you to put away your phone."

"You're *Greek?*" she says, tilting her head. She's probably trying to reconcile the name with his black skin.

He smiles. "My mother is Cape Verdean and my

father is Greek. My paternal grandparents are from Thessaloníki."

"I'm trying to write a novel set in Greece," she says. "Problem is, I haven't been there in so long, I seem to have lost the flavor of the place."

As much as Nick would love to talk about the Aegean Sea, ouzo, and grilled octopus, he has work to do. "I need to ask you some questions, ma'am."

"I don't think you understand my predicament here, Detective," she says. "This is *my* wedding."

"*Your* wedding?"

"I planned it. I have people to call. All of the guests! People need to know what's happened."

"I understand," Nick says. "But to find out exactly what *did* happen, I require your cooperation. And that means your undivided attention."

"You do realize I have a houseful of people?" Greer says. "You do realize that Celeste's mother has terminal *breast* cancer? And that Celeste has been taken to the hospital? I'm waiting to hear from Benji about how she's doing."

"I'll make this as fast as possible," Nick says. He tries to ignore the phone, although he would like to take it from her. "Would you please come with me to the living room?"

Greer stares at him with reproach. "How dare you order me around *in my own house*."

"I'm very sorry about that, ma'am. Now, please."

He walks down the hall and hopes she follows him. He hears her rustling behind him so he stops at the entrance of the living room and lets her walk in first. He closes the door tightly behind them.

Greer perches on the edge of the sofa, leaning forward as though she might spring to her feet and escape at any moment. Her phone is in her lap, buzzing away.

"Can you please tell me what you remember *after* the rehearsal dinner ended?" Nick says. "Who went where?"

"The young people went out," Greer says. "The old people stayed home. The exception was Abigail, my daughter-in-law. She's pregnant. She stayed home."

"But both the bride and groom went out? Who else?" Nick pulls out his notepad. "Merritt? Did she go out?"

"Do you know what I do for a living, Detective?" Greer asks. "I write murder mysteries. As such, I am intimately familiar with procedure, so I appreciate that you have to ask these questions. But I can tell you exactly what happened to Merritt."

"Can you?" Nick says. "Exactly?"

"Well, not exactly," Greer says. "But the gist is fairly obvious, is it not? The girl drank too much or she took pills and then she decided to go for a swim in her dress and she drowned."

"You'll agree," Nick says, "that as viable as that

explanation might be, it leaves some unanswered questions."

"Such as?"

"I've interviewed one witness who says she's fairly certain that Merritt *didn't* go out. So if she stayed home, where and what was she drinking? Did anyone see her? Did anyone talk to her? I just walked through the cottage where Ms. Monaco was staying. There was no alcohol in the cottage—no bottles, no empties, nothing. And no pills, no prescription bottles. As a fiction writer, you must know that it's difficult, when one is drinking and popping pills, to get rid of all incriminating evidence. Also, Ms. Monaco had quite a nasty cut on her foot. How did that happen? When did that happen?"

"Don't look for drama where there is none," Greer says. "There's a term for that in literature. It's called a *red herring*. The term was coined in the early 1800s by hunters who would throw a kipper down behind their trail to divert the wolves."

Nick almost smiles. He wants to dislike her but there's something about her he admires. He has never met a published author before, and it's true—if she is a seasoned mystery writer, she might be able to help them. "That's good to know," he says. "Thank you."

"I came across Merritt at the end of the rehearsal dinner," Greer says. "She was hiding in the laundry room. She was crying."

"Crying?" Nick says. He remembers that Abby also said Merritt had been crying, out in the rose garden. "Did she tell you what was wrong?"

"She did not," Greer says. "And I didn't press; it wasn't my place. But I think it was clear she was feeling left out. Her best friend was getting married. Celeste was the center of attention and Merritt was at the wedding alone. Maybe she was depressed. I have no idea. But I can say that she was very upset, which only solidifies the argument that she drank too much, maybe took some pills, and went for a swim. Maybe she drowned accidentally or maybe it was intentional."

"Suicide?" Nick says.

"Is that impossible?" Greer asks. "It's not something one likes to think about, of course. But..."

"Let's get back to you," Nick says. "What did *you* do when the party ended? You and Mr. Winbury stayed home, is that right?"

"I don't see why what Tag and I did is relevant," Greer says.

"You're a mystery writer," Nick says. "So you're familiar with the term *alibi?*"

Greer raises an eyebrow at him. "Touché," she says. "Yes. My husband and Mr. Otis, the bride's father, had a drink in Tag's study and then they must have gone outside to smoke a cigar because when Tag came to bed, he smelled like smoke."

"We found a cigar stubbed out on a table under the tent. One cigar. Would you guess that cigar belonged to your husband?"

"I would guess," Greer says, "but I couldn't be sure."

"What kind of cigars does your husband smoke, Ms. Garrison?"

"He smokes Cuban cigars," Greer says, "but more than one kind. Cohiba. Romeo y Julieta. Montecristo. I hardly see how the cigar is relevant to what happened to Ms. Monaco."

"We aren't sure it is relevant," Nick says. "Right now, we're just trying to figure out who was where after the party broke up. It appears a handful of people were out under the tent smoking and drinking, and we're trying to identify who exactly was there. Did Mr. Winbury say where he'd been when he came to bed?"

"I didn't ask where he'd been because I knew where he'd been. Here, on the grounds."

"What time did Mr. Winbury come to bed?"

"I have no earthly idea. I was asleep."

"You were asleep but you noticed that Mr. Winbury smelled like cigar smoke?"

"That's correct," Greer says. "I woke up just enough to know Tag was coming to bed and that he smelled like cigar smoke but not enough to bother checking the time."

"And you didn't wake up again until the morning?"

"That's correct. I woke up on my own at half past five."

"And, Ms. Garrison, what time did you retire? Did you go to bed right after the party was over?"

"No, I did not."

"What did you do after the party? While Mr. Winbury and Mr. Otis were in the study?"

"I sat down at my computer. I was writing. I have a deadline looming."

"I see. And where did you do this writing?"

"On my laptop," Greer says. "In my sitting room."

"And does that desk face a window?"

"Yes, it does."

"Did you notice any activity out the window?"

"I did not."

Nick pauses. Is it likely she didn't see *anything* out the window? No lights? No shadows?

"And what time did you finish writing?" he asks.

"I finished at eleven fifteen," she says.

"You're sure about that?"

"Yes," Greer says. "I made myself stop because I didn't want to be tired today."

"So after you finished writing, you went to bed. Say, eleven thirty?"

"Around then, yes."

Something about Greer Garrison's answers bothers him. They're too neat, too crisp. It's as though she has thought them through in advance. Nick takes a gamble.

"Would you bring me to the computer, please, Ms. Garrison?" he asks.

"I don't see why that's necessary."

"I would like to see it."

"Well, then, I shall go fetch it for you."

"No, you misunderstood me," Nick says. "I would like you to bring me *to* the computer."

"That's an unreasonable request," Greer says.

I've got her, he thinks.

"It's an unreasonable request for you to bring me to the computer but not for you to bring the computer to me? Because there's something you want to delete or hide on the computer?"

"Not at all," Greer says.

"Fine, then bring me to the computer. Please, Ms. Garrison."

She stares at him for a beat, then she rises.

Nick follows Greer down the hall. They step through an arched doorway into an anteroom—there's a niche built into the wall that holds an enormous bouquet of hydrangeas and lilies—and Greer opens a door. There's a sitting room with a sofa, a love seat, antique tables, and a desk that faces out a window. The view out the window is of the side yard —of a fence and the top of the pool house. Through a connecting door, Nick sees the master bedroom. There's a king bed made up with white sheets and a comforter and an assortment of pillows, all of them neatly arranged. A cashmere blanket embroidered with the word *Summerland* is draped on the diagonal across the corner of the bed. Nick blinks. Greer found the time to make her bed so artfully after she found out Merritt was dead—or before? But at that moment, a woman pops out of the master bath holding a bucket and a roll of paper towels. The housekeeper.

"You'll excuse us, please, Elida?" Greer says.

Elida nods and scurries away.

"Does Elida live here?" Nick asks.

"She does not," Greer says. "She works seven to five. Today she came a bit earlier because of the wedding."

Nick follows Greer over to a simple mahogany desk, gleaming as though just polished. On the desk are a laptop, a legal pad, three pens, a dictionary, and a thesaurus. There's a Windsor chair at the desk and Nick takes a seat and turns his attention to the computer. "So this here, *A Slayer in Santorini,* is the piece you were working on last night?"

"Yes," Greer says.

"It says you closed it at twelve twenty-two a.m. But you told me eleven fifteen."

"I stopped writing at eleven fifteen. I closed the document at twelve twenty-two, apparently."

"But you said you went right to bed. You said you went to bed around eleven thirty."

"I did go to bed," Greer says. "But I had difficulty falling asleep, so I had a drink."

"Of water?"

"No, a *drink* drink. I had a glass of champagne."

"So sometime between eleven fifteen and twelve twenty-two a.m. you went to the kitchen for a glass of champagne?"

"Yes."

"And did you notice any activity then?"

Greer pauses. "I did not."

"You didn't see anyone?" Nick says.

"Well, on my way back to my room I saw my daughter-in-law, Abby. She was going to the kitchen for water."

"She was?"

"Yes."

"Why didn't she get water from the bathroom?"

"She wanted ice, is my guess. She's pregnant. And it was a warm night."

"Did you and Abby have a conversation?"

"A brief one."

"What did she say to you?"

"She said she was waiting for Thomas to get home. He had gone out with Benji and the others."

Ah, yes. Nick recalls that Abby was annoyed that Thomas had decided to go out. "Anything else?"

"Not really, no."

"Did you see anyone else?"

"No."

"And after you got your champagne, you returned to your bedroom to sleep?" Nick asks.

"That's right."

Nick pauses to scribble down notes. She lied to him ten minutes ago; there's no reason to believe another word she says.

"Let me switch gears here. We found a two-person kayak overturned on your beach. Do you own such a kayak?"

"It belongs to my husband," Greer says. She cocks her head. "It was left overturned on the beach, you say?"

"Yes. Does that seem odd to you?"

She nods slowly. "A bit."

"And why is that?"

"Tag is fanatical about his kayaks," Greer says. "He doesn't leave them just lying about."

"Is it possible that someone else used the kayak?"

"No, he keeps them locked up. If the two-person kayak was left out then he must have taken someone out on the water. If he were going out alone, he would have taken his one-person kayak."

"Any idea who he might have taken out?"

Greer shakes her head. She looks far less confident

than she did a moment ago, and Nick feels her losing her grip on the explanation she had so neatly written in her mind.

"I suppose you'll have to ask my husband that," she says.

Wednesday, May 30-Tuesday, June 19, 2018

TAG

He takes Merritt's number but makes no plans to see her again. It's a one-and-done, a weekend fling, which is how he likes to keep things with other women. There have been half a dozen or so over the course of his marriage, one- or two-night stands, women he never sees or thinks of again. His behavior has nothing to do with how he feels about Greer. Or maybe it does. Maybe it's an assertion of power, of defiance. Greer entered the marriage with more money and higher social standing. Tag has always felt a touch inferior. The prowling around is how he balances the scales.

When he gets back to New York, two things happen. One is that Sergio Ramone calls. Tag considers letting the call go to voice mail. He fears that Sergio has learned that he took Merritt to the wine dinner and he's calling to express his disapproval. But then Tag reminds himself that taking Merritt to the dinner was done with Greer's blessing.

"Hello," Tag says. "Sergio, how are you?"

It turns out that Sergio is calling for a very different reason. His contact at Skadden, Arps has told Sergio that there's grumbling within the litigation department about Thomas Winbury. He isn't pulling his weight, apparently. He takes long lunches and unscheduled vacation days. He often leaves work at five o'clock when other associates stay until nine or ten at night. At his last review, he was given a warning, but he's shown no improvement. There's talk of letting him go.

Tag sighs. Thomas has always put in just enough work to get by. Abby's family is so wealthy that Tag suspects Thomas *wants* to get fired. He'll work for Mr. Freeman in the oil business. He'll move to Texas, which will break Greer's heart.

"Thanks for the heads-up, Sergio," Tag says. "I'll have a talk with him." He hangs up before Sergio can ask him how the wine dinner was and then he swears at the ceiling.

A few nights later, Thomas and Abby come for dinner at Tag and Greer's apartment. Greer has made a leg of lamb and the apartment is redolent with the smell of roasting meat, garlic, and rosemary, but as soon as Abby enters the apartment, she covers her mouth with her hand and bolts for the bathroom.

Thomas shakes his head. "I guess she's gone and ruined the surprise," he says. "We're pregnant again."

Greer reaches out for Thomas, but they all know to limit their reaction to cautious optimism.

Tag shakes Thomas's hand, then pulls him in for a hug and says, "You'll make one hell of a father." No sooner are the words out of his mouth than Tag doubts their veracity. *Will* Thomas make a hell of a father? He needs to buckle down at work, start setting an example. Tag nearly brings Thomas into his study to tell him as much, but he decides, in the end, to let the occasion be a happy one, or as happy as it can be with a woefully sick Abby. He'll talk to Thomas another time.

That night, Tag can't sleep. He slips from bed and goes into his study. His three home studies — the one in New York, the one in London, and the one on Nantucket — are sanctuaries dedicated to Tag's privacy. No one enters without permission except the cleaning ladies.

Tag takes out his phone and scrolls for Merritt's number.

She answers on the third ring. "Hey, Tag."

Her voice brings it all back. There is noise in the background, voices, music — she's out somewhere. It's two o'clock in the morning on a Wednesday night. Tag should not be pursuing this.

"Hey yourself," he says. "I hope I didn't wake you."

She laughs. "I'm downtown at this speakeasy thing. It looks like a laundromat but there's a secret door, a code word, and voilà, you enter the underworld. Do you want to come join me? I'll tell you how to get in."

"No, thank you," Tag says. "I just called to tell you your instincts were correct. Abby *is* pregnant. She and Thomas told us tonight at dinner."

"Who?" Merritt says.

"Abby. Abby, my daughter-in-law. She was with you during Celeste's bachelorette weekend. You said—"

"Oh, that's right," Merritt says. "Abby. Yeah, I'm not surprised."

Tag feels like a fool. He should hang up. He's going to see Merritt in a few weeks at the wedding and it would be best if their dalliance were a thing of the past. But there is something about this girl. He can't leave it alone.

"Where did you say your apartment is?" he asks. "I think I've forgotten."

Tag sees Merritt the next day after work, and the day after that, and on Saturday he tells Greer he's going to run in Central Park but instead he goes to Merritt's apartment. After sex, they walk down the street to a really good sandwich place and order lunch and sit side by side and talk and laugh—and in the middle of it, Tag realizes that he is losing control of the situation. What is he doing? Anyone might see him here with this girl.

He walks Merritt back to her apartment and she pulls him in by the front of the shirt. She wants him to come inside. And he wants to, oh, does he want to. He agrees, but just for a minute, he says.

She has turned him into a teenager again. His desire is so intense, so relentless, it frightens him. He can't remember wanting anyone or anything as much as he wants this girl. His feelings for Greer seem almost quaint by comparison.

Merritt is twenty-eight years old, nearly twenty-nine. She has a lukewarm relationship with her brother and she doesn't speak to her parents at all. This, Tag can't understand.

"What do you do on Thanksgiving?" he asks. "Christmas?"

She shrugs. "Last year, Thanksgiving was Chinese food and a movie. On Christmas, I flew to Tulum for a yoga retreat."

Tag senses a hole inside of Merritt, an emotional hole, which he knows is very, very dangerous. He needs to end this thing now, while there is still time to recover before the wedding. But the attraction grows stronger. Soon, he thinks only of Merritt—when he's working, when he's exercising, when he and Greer are eating dinner at Rosa Mexicano. Greer is consumed with finishing her novel and planning Benji's wedding. She is so focused on these two projects that she doesn't notice any change in Tag. She doesn't see him, she doesn't hear him, and sex is out of the question. She jokes that they'll have a second honeymoon once Benji and Celeste are on their first honeymoon. But Tag knows that once the wedding is over, Greer will collapse, exhausted, or she'll go into a funk because there's nothing left to look forward to.

He schedules a drinks meeting with clients at the bar at the Whitby Hotel and he asks Merritt to go sit at this bar without letting on that she knows him. She does exactly as he asks, wearing a slinky black dress and five-inch stilettos, and Tag excuses himself from his clients for a moment. He follows Merritt into the ladies' room, where they lock the door and have shockingly hot sex. When Tag walks out, he is so intoxicated he doesn't care who sees him.

Later, he chastises himself for being reckless. He asks himself what he's doing.

She is given tickets to see Billy Joel at Madison Square Garden. Will he go with her?

"I can't," he says. "It's too risky."

"Please," she says. "They're second-row seats."

"That's the problem," he says. "If they were nose-bleed seats, I wouldn't worry about seeing anyone I know."

"Fine, then," she says. "I'll take Robbie."

"Who's Robbie?"

"My on-again, off-again," Merritt says. "He's the daytime bartender at the Breslin."

Tag is addled by news of Robbie's existence, although what did he expect? Naturally, there's a Robbie. He wouldn't be surprised if there were half a dozen Robbies. The thought is so dispiriting that the next day finds Tag at the bar of the Breslin at lunchtime, ordering the rabbit terrine and a scotch egg—at least it's a good place—from a big Irish hunk. Robbie. He has six inches and forty pounds on Tag, plus he's twenty-five years younger. This is who Merritt *should* be dating. Not only is Robbie a bartender, he's an aspiring actor—and idle chitchat reveals that he's just been cast in a pilot. Tag hates Robbie with a bloodred passion; he leaves him an absurdly large tip.

The night of the concert, Tag is agitated. He imagines Robbie putting his shovel-size hands on Merritt's waist and swaying to the music behind her. He's so unsettled by this vision that he tells Greer he isn't hungry for dinner; he might have a sandwich in his study later.

He sends Merritt a text: Let me know when the concert is over. I'll meet you at your place.

Twenty fraught minutes later, he receives a text back: K.

K. Has there ever been a less satisfying response in the short history of texting? Tag thinks not.

Eleven o'clock comes and goes, eleven thirty. Tag succumbs to his hunger and heads to the kitchen for a ham sandwich. He sees a light on in their bedroom. He opens the door to find Greer wearing her tailored blue pajamas. Her hair is in a bun held up with a pencil and her reading glasses are perched on the end of her nose. There's a glass of chardonnay to the right of her laptop. She's in the middle of a scene, he can tell, but she looks up and smiles.

"Shall we go to bed, then?" she asks.

Yes, Tag thinks. *Say yes.* Look how elegant his wife is, how productive, how ingenious. She's absolutely everything he could ever want in a woman.

"I need to keep going," Tag says. "Ernie and I are putting that Libya deal together. It's going to be huge. He'll be at the office first thing in the morning and I have to have the numbers waiting for him."

Greer shuts off her computer. "Well, I'm calling it a night." She raises her face for a kiss. "Don't stay up too late."

"You know I won't," Tag says. "Love you, darling."

* * *

He waits until twelve thirty and when there is still no text from Merritt, he sneaks out of the apartment, hails a taxi, and goes down to Perry Street. He stands outside her building and buzzes her apartment, but there's no answer.

Then he hears her laugh. He looks down the street to spy Merritt and Robbie on approach. They are walking close together but not touching. Tag tries to hurry down the steps of the building before she sees him... but it's too late.

"Tag?" she says.

He's caught. It's nearly one in the morning; there is no way to play this off as casual. He's a worldly, successful man standing in front of a girl's apartment building like some schlub in a rom-com; if Greer could see him now, she would find him so absurd she might even laugh. But the sight of Merritt sends a surge of adrenaline through Tag. He feels enough passion to kick Robbie the lickspittle to the curb despite his size advantage and then carry Merritt up the stairs over his shoulder. She's wearing a white crocheted sundress and dangling earrings and her hair is up. She's as fetching as any woman he's ever seen.

"I need to talk to you," he says.

"Okay," Merritt says. She looks up at Robbie. "Robbie, this is Tag. Tag, Robbie."

Tag extends a hand automatically. Robbie says, "Weren't you in for lunch the other day? At the Breslin?"

Tag shouldn't have left such a big tip. It would have been impossible to forget.

"Were you?" Merritt says. She looks amused. She now understands the power she has over him. He has made such a mess of things, he thinks. He should have just gone to the concert.

Merritt's birthday is June 18. She wants to do something special. She wants to go away with Tag. Tag considers this request. Where would they go? To Paris? Rome? Istanbul? Los Angeles? Rio de Janeiro? He does some research on Istanbul but decides flying overseas is impractical and risky, even if they do so separately. He books a hotel room in New York instead, at the Four Seasons downtown. He worries a bit because before he and Greer moved to New York, they used to stay at the Four Seasons in midtown, and they like to stay at Four Seasons when they travel. But it's a brand he trusts and it's only one night and the hotel is all the way down by the Freedom Tower, which isn't a neighborhood that anyone he knows frequents after five o'clock.

The weekend before Merritt's birthday, Tag and Greer are on Nantucket. Greer has a three-hour meeting with Roger Pelton, the wedding planner. Tag goes for a ride in the kayak, then he drives into town to get lunch — he loves the soft-shell crab sandwich from Straight Wharf Fish — and while he's at it, he decides to buy Merritt a present. He has been trained by Greer to understand that the only acceptable present for a birthday or anniversary is jewelry. He walks into the Jessica Hicks boutique thinking he will get earrings or a choker, but when he describes the young woman he's buying for — he pretends the gift is for his daughter-in-law, Abby, who is pregnant with their first grandchild — Jessica shows him the silver ring with the lace pattern embedded with the multicolored sapphires.

"It's meant to be worn on the thumb," Jessica says.

"The *thumb?*" Tag says.

"Trust me," Jessica says. "It's a thing."

Tag buys the thumb ring and leaves the store feeling a sense of giddy anticipation. The ring is beautiful; Merritt will love it, he's certain.

His happiness is a thing.

On the eighteenth, Tag gets to the hotel early. He has had a bouquet of expensive roses delivered to the room as well as champagne. He sets the box from Jessica Hicks between the flowers and the ice bucket. Everything is as it should be, but he can't relax.

Something about this scenario makes him feel like a run-of-the-mill cheat. He's a stereotype, a middle-aged man sleeping with one of his daughter-in-law's friends because his wife is busy and distracted and he needs to boost his self-esteem.

He waits in the room for Merritt to arrive but she texts to say she's at the salon getting a bikini wax and she'll be late. He's a bit turned off by her frankness. Is it necessary to tell him she's getting *waxed?* It feels inelegant.

He decides to go down to the bar for a drink. A real drink.

As soon as he walks into the bar, he locks eyes with a man, then he realizes with horror that the man is his son Thomas. Before Tag can think better of it, he ducks behind a pole. He waits a few seconds, not breathing, his heart skidding to a near stop as he waits for Thomas to confront him and ask what he's doing there. What should Tag say? Meeting a client for drinks, of course, and then when the client doesn't materialize, Tag can pretend to be annoyed and skip out to make a phone call.

He waits. Nothing happens. Tag saw Thomas, but is it possible that Thomas didn't see Tag or saw him but somehow didn't register the face as that of his father?

Enough time passes that Tag decides to take action. He peers around the column. Thomas is staring into his highball glass. He looks miserable. As much as Tag realizes the urgency of him leaving the bar while he can, he's arrested by his elder son's demeanor. He thinks back to the phone call from Sergio. Thomas is leaving work early; Thomas is taking unscheduled vacations. And now here he is having a drink at a hotel bar at the far tip of Manhattan, which isn't anywhere close to his office. Tag wants to sit down next to Thomas and ask him what's going on.

Maybe he's been fired?

Maybe Abby lost the baby?

If it's either of those, Tag will find out soon enough. He needs to get out of the bar undetected. He turns and hurries out, hoping Thomas won't recognize him from behind. He goes back up to the room for his bag and texts Merritt.

Something came up. Room 1011 is yours for the night. There's champagne and a little gift for you. But I have to take a raincheck. Sorry about that. Happy birthday, Parkway.

Tag takes a taxi back uptown and walks into his apartment to find Greer in her yoga clothes, folded over in child's pose on the living-room rug. She looks up and beams. "You're home!" she says.

And just like that, the spell is broken. Tag is finished fooling around. He is back to being a dutiful husband, a steadfast father, and an expectant grandfather. Merritt calls in tears; she leaves messages, sends texts. She calls him a bastard, she tells him to stick a fork in his eye, only that's not how she phrases it.

She calls Tag's office and speaks to Miss Hillery, Tag's very proper, very British secretary, who is so devoted to Tag that she followed him over from London.

"A Ms. Parkway called?" Miss Hillery says, handing Tag the message slip. "She said it's urgent."

"Thank you, Miss Hillery," Tag says with what he hopes is a carefree smile. He closes the door to his office and collapses at his desk. Merritt calling him at the office is one step away from Merritt calling the apartment or—because Tag knows Celeste might naively give Merritt the number—calling Greer's cell phone.

Well, she's going to get what she wants. Tag calls Merritt back.

"Tag?" she says.

"What on God's green earth are you *doing?*" he asks. "You can't call me here."

"I'm pregnant," she says.

Saturday, July 7, 2018,
12:00 p.m.

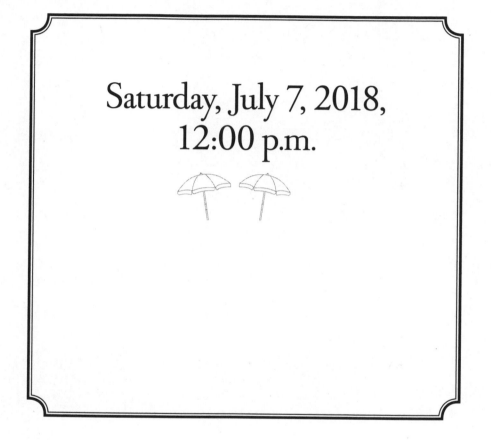

NANTUCKET

By midmorning, the entire island is buzzing with news of the Murdered Maid of Honor. Marty Szczerba calls his daughter, Laura Rae, initially just to hear the sound of her voice and to reassure himself that she is okay, but then he asks about Adi Conover — is *she* okay? — and Laura Rae says, "Yes, Dad, obviously. What's wrong with you?" Marty ends up spilling the whole story, or what he knows of it. Laura Rae tells her fiancé, Ty, who works for Toscana Excavating and who is as tight-lipped as they come. But Ty swings by his mother's house for a second breakfast and he tells her the story. Carla, Ty's mother, volunteers at the Hospital Thrift Shop Saturdays at noon and she proceeds to tell every single person who walks in the door.

Finn MacAvoy gets a text from his girlfriend, Lola Budd, saying I caught a murder suspect! Finn is at Cisco Beach giving surfing lessons to a group of overprivileged eight-year-olds who all want to be John John Florence. Finn casually flings out the content of Lola's text. "My girlfriend caught a murder suspect," he says.

The next thing Finn knows, he is surrounded by the young surfers' mothers, and they're all talking about someone called the Murdered Maid of Honor and they ask Finn if the police had caught the guy and who it was and Finn is sorry he ever opened his mouth.

Finn's twin sister, Chloe MacAvoy, has taken to her bed despite the fact that it's a hot, sunny summer Saturday and work that day has been canceled. Work has been canceled because Merritt Monaco, the maid of honor in the Otis-Winbury wedding, is dead. Roger Pelton found her floating just off the beach earlier that morning.

Siobhan had called to tell Chloe about the death herself instead of having Donna, the waitstaff manager, do it because Siobhan is that kind of owner. She takes responsibility for her employees.

"Chloe," she said. "The wedding has been canceled. Merritt Monaco, the maid of honor, passed away overnight."

"Passed away?"

"She died, Chloe," Siobhan said. "She's dead. She drowned out in front of the house last night."

"But..." Chloe said.

"That's all we know for now," Siobhan said. "The police are working on it."

The police? Chloe thought. She had seen Uncle Ed out on the deck on his phone a short while earlier, but Uncle Ed was always on the phone.

Chloe had hung up with Siobhan and closed her eyes. Chloe had been kept far away from death since she was seven years old, when Uncle Ed and Auntie came to tell her and Finn that their parents were dead. Both of them at once, killed in a sailing accident. Chloe hadn't really gotten it then; she had been too young. What did she know of death at age seven? Not one thing. Her parents' death has gotten much worse for Chloe as she's grown older. Now she knows what she's missing. She has no father to treat her like a princess; she has no mother to rebel against. She does have Uncle Ed and Auntie and they are strong, reliable, capable caregivers... but they aren't her parents. Whenever Chloe thinks about her father playing "Please Come to Boston" on his guitar or her mother painting a rose on Chloe's cheek, she feels unbearably sad.

She texted Blake, a girl who worked with her, Merritt, the maid of honor, is dead.

Blake texted back, I know. I heard there was a lot of blood.

Chloe ran to the bathroom to throw up. After the rehearsal dinner the night before, Chloe had a few beers with Blake and Geraldo. Geraldo is twenty-four years old, from El Salvador, and he always provides Chloe and Blake with postshift alcohol.

Uncle Ed had knocked on the door. "You okay in there?"

"Fine," Chloe said. She wanted to ask Uncle Ed about Merritt but she couldn't handle the conversation right that second. She cursed Geraldo.

Now, back in bed, Chloe revisits the events of the party. Most jobs go the same way. Chloe and her co-workers show up early in their immaculate black pants and crisp white shirts, showered, fresh-faced, ready to serve. Because she is only sixteen, Chloe can't serve alcohol, although this rule gets bent all the time. Nearly the first thing that happened at this rehearsal dinner was that Greer Garrison, the mother of the groom, asked Chloe for a refill of champagne. Chloe told Ian, the bartender, that *he* needed to serve Ms. Garrison but Ian was three-deep and he told Chloe to find Geraldo. But Geraldo wasn't around and Greer Garrison sang out for a refill again with a pointed look at Chloe, so Chloe grabbed the Veuve Clicquot from the cooler and discreetly filled Ms. Garrison's glass.

Chloe didn't notice much else about the actual festivities other than the guests growing drunker and drunker. There was a blackberry mojito punch and the guests were inhaling it. Chloe cleared a bunch of half-empty punch cups with mint leaves and whole fat blackberries trapped among the melting ice; she brought them to the kitchen, where she found Geraldo manning the kitchen trash. He picked up the cup with the most punch and drank it.

"Ew," Chloe said. "Someone else's mouth was on that. Also, if Siobhan sees you doing that, she'll fire you."

"Siobhan just left," Geraldo said. "She has four other events tonight. She won't be back."

"Donna, then," Chloe said, but they both knew Donna wasn't strict at all. If she saw Geraldo drinking, she would do no more than roll her eyes.

"Try it," Geraldo said.

"No," Chloe said.

"Just try it," Geraldo said.

Chloe had never been good at resisting peer pressure. Plus, the drink was a delicious-looking purple color. Chloe drank half a cup without letting her lips touch the rim. The drink was so fruity and minty that she could barely taste the alcohol, but almost instantly she felt lighter, more relaxed.

Saturday, July 7, 2018,
12:30 p.m.

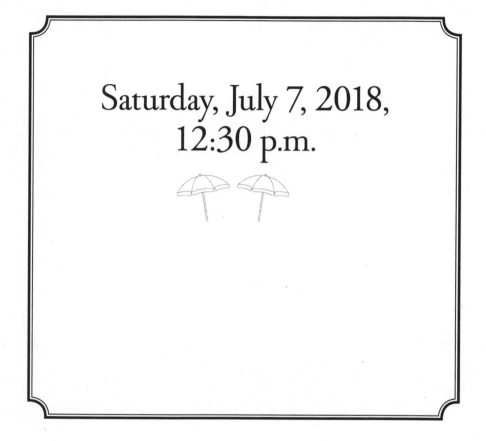

THE CHIEF

He has to drive from Monomoy to the station, where they're holding Shooter Uxley. He has two state policemen back at the scene to make sure nothing is tampered with and no one else flees. He could use two more guys, quite honestly. Nantucket just isn't equipped for a murder during a busy holiday weekend. That is the stark truth.

The Chief inhales through his nose and exhales through his mouth, his takeaway from the stress management course he's required to attend every three years. He'll question Shooter himself and that will likely shed some light on things. He'll hear from the ME about an exact cause of death. If he still hasn't figured out what happened, he has the father, the brother, and the groom himself.

But frankly, the Chief likes the best man for this. Why else would he *run?* Then again, after he'd disappeared last night, why would he come *back?* What is going *on* here?

The Chief talked to Nick briefly before he left the compound. Nick said the mother of the groom, Greer Garrison, the mystery writer, had misled him about her timetable. Intentionally, he thinks.

I didn't like the way our interview went, Nick said. *It had a funny smell.*

The Chief calls home. Andrea answers. "How's it going?"

"Oh, fine," Ed says. Andrea will know he means the exact opposite. He wants to tell Andrea that Finn's girlfriend, Lola Budd, was the one who ended up finding their main suspect. It's a good story and it will hearten Andrea to know that Lola has had a chance to shine, but there isn't time to get into it now.

"How's Chloe?" the Chief asks. "Is her stomach feeling any better?"

"Not sure," Andrea says. "She's locked herself in her room."

"No locked doors," Ed says. This has been a rule since back when his own kids, Kacy and Eric, were growing up.

"You come home and tell her that," Andrea says.

"Because I've tried and she won't budge. She's upset about the girl. The Murdered Maid of Honor, everyone is calling her now."

"Everyone?" Ed asks. "Is it that bad already? People talking? People giving this story a name? We aren't even sure she was murdered. Not sure at all."

"It's a small island, Ed," Andrea says. She pauses, and he realizes she has just lobbed his favorite line right back at him. "Would it be awful if while you were out solving this murder, I went to the beach?"

He's *investigating* a murder, not solving anything. "Go to the beach," he says. "But please be careful."

"You're sweet," Andrea says. "Love you."

He hangs up just as a call comes in from Cape Cod Hospital.

"This is Ed Kapenash," he says.

"Chief, it's Linda." Linda Ferretti, the medical examiner. "Prelims indicate our girl died by drowning around three a.m. The blood work shows someone slipped her a mickey, or maybe she self-medicated. A barbiturate seems to be the culprit. The cut on her foot was the source of all that blood but it was just a surface wound. She has one fingerprint-size bruise on her wrist; my best guess is someone yanked her or pulled on her arm. There are no other signs that she was strangled or smothered and then dumped. She either took pills or was given something. She went out for a swim, passed out, drowned. Could have happened in a bathtub."

"Okay," the Chief says. "What was her blood alcohol content?"

"Low," Linda says. "Point zero-two-five."

"Really?" the Chief says. "You're sure?"

"Surprised me too, at first," she says. "The contents of her stomach were minimal. Either she didn't eat much last night or, what I think is more likely, she vomited up what she did eat."

"What makes you think that?" the Chief asks.

"She was pregnant."

"You're *kidding*," the Chief says.

"Wish I was," Linda says. "Very early stages. My guess is she was six or seven weeks along? She might not even have realized it."

"Wow," the Chief says.

"The plot thickens," Linda says.

The Chief hangs up and his phone rings again. This time it's the Nantucket hospital.

"This is Ed Kapenash," he says.

"Chief, it's Margaret from the ER."

"Hey, Margaret," the Chief says. "What's up?"

"We have the bride from that wedding," Margaret

says. "Kind of strange? She says she wants to talk to the police here at the hospital rather than at the house. Her fiancé came to check on her. They had words, then he stormed out."

"Keep her there, Margaret," the Chief says. "I'll send the Greek the instant he's free."

"The Greek?" Margaret says. "My nurses will be thrilled."

The Chief smiles for the first time that day. "Thanks, Margaret," he says, then he turns into the station.

They are holding Shooter Uxley in the first interview room. When the Chief enters, Shooter is fast asleep with his head on the table. The Chief watches him for a second and listens to him snoring. Whatever anxiety he might be feeling is clearly overridden by exhaustion.

Didn't sleep much last night, buddy? the Chief wonders.

Mr. Uxley has taken off his blazer and untucked his shirt. The Chief looks at his paperwork: Michael Oscar Uxley. New York driver's license, Manhattan address, West Thirty-Ninth Street. Also from New York City, like the deceased. He wonders if Uxley was the father of Ms. Monaco's baby.

The Chief nudges his arm. "Hey there, wake up. Mr. Uxley, sir?"

Shooter groans and raises his head. He seems disoriented for a second, then he straightens up.

The Chief says, "In case you've forgotten, I'm Chief Kapenash, Nantucket Police. You put on some nice moves out there."

Shooter blinks. "I want a lawyer," he says.

Thursday, June 22-Friday, June 23, 2017

CELESTE

She doesn't meet Shooter until she and Benji have been together for nine months. Shooter is Benji's best friend—so why does it take so long? Well, Shooter is busy. He owns and operates a company called A-List, which provides American retreats for foreign businessmen. What this means essentially is that Shooter has made a career—lucrative, Benji says—out of partying. He takes executives from Asian and emerging Eastern European countries and shows these gentlemen (for his clientele is 100 percent male) an old-fashioned American good time. Much of the "work" is centered in Manhattan. The executives are fond of the long-established steak houses—Smith and Wollensky, Gallagher's, Peter Luger's; they like the *Intrepid* and Times Square; they like the clubs, especially the gentlemen's clubs on Twelfth Avenue. Shooter also spends a lot of time in Las Vegas. He is, Benji says with a straight face, a Vegas regular. He divides his time between the Aria Sky Suites and the Mandarin Oriental. Shooter himself plays only craps; in prep school at St. George's, he ran a late-night dice game, and that was the source of his nickname.

"You all gambled in high school?" Celeste asks Benji. She herself has never been to a casino, but if she went, she would steer clear of the craps table. The name alone.

"Shooter made it impossible to resist," Benji says. "I always lost, but it was fun."

When Shooter isn't "working" in Manhattan or Las Vegas, he is at the Kentucky Derby, the Masters, the Super Bowl, the Indy 500, Coachella, or Mardi Gras. He is sunning in South Beach or skiing in Aspen. Wherever you wish you could be on any given weekend, Shooter is there with a group of his executives.

On the weekend of June 23, however, Shooter is coming to Nantucket with Benji and Celeste. Celeste is excited to finally meet him. She's also glad he's coming because this is Celeste's first time to Nantucket, her first time to any summer resort, and it's her first time spending the weekend with Tag and Greer, Benji's parents. Celeste met Tag and Greer on three previous occasions. The first was a dinner at Buvette, then a few weeks later there was Sunday church at St. James's followed by dim sum in Chinatown. The third occasion was a dinner at the Winburys' apartment on Park and Seventieth to celebrate Benji's twenty-eighth birthday.

The Winburys are less intimidating than Celeste expected. Tag is gregarious and charismatic; Greer is high-strung and a bit imperious until her second glass of champagne, when she relaxes into someone quite funny and warm. They are wealthy beyond Celeste's wildest imagination but as she strove to seem cultured and well bred, they strove to seem down-to-earth, and they all met in the middle. Neither of the elder Winburys flinched when Celeste announced that her father sold suits at the mall and her mother worked in the gift shop at a crayon factory. Greer asked several questions about Karen's health that revealed her concern without seeming phony or overbearing. They made Celeste feel comfortable. The Winburys made her feel *acceptable,* which she found a pleasant surprise.

Despite this, staying with them for a long weekend on Nantucket is a daunting prospect and Celeste is glad for Shooter's presence to take some pressure off her.

They are leaving late afternoon on Thursday and returning on Sunday evening. Celeste has taken Friday off work, her first vacation in a year and a half; the last time was when she took a week to care for Karen after her double mastectomy. They are flying from JFK on JetBlue. The flight is only forty minutes long but it's another source of anxiety for Celeste. She has never been on an airplane. Benji couldn't believe it when she told him.

"Never been on a *plane?*"

She tried to explain to him that she grew up sheltered, more sheltered than the most sheltered person he knows. She knows that *sheltered* makes it sound like Bruce and Karen were trying to keep Celeste from the evils of the wider world, but the truth was that Bruce and Karen didn't have the money to explore the world beyond their own neat pocket of it. They didn't have relatives in Duluth or St. Louis to visit, and when Celeste came home from school in sixth grade asking to go to Disney World, Bruce arranged for a Saturday excursion to Six Flags in New Jersey. Over spring break in college, when everyone at Miami of Ohio went to Daytona or the Bahamas, Celeste took the bus home to Easton. There had been no junior year abroad. After college, there had been New York City, her job at the zoo, her life right up until meeting Benji. When would she have boarded a plane?

Celeste is so concerned about arriving at JFK in a timely fashion that she forgoes public transportation and springs for an Uber from the zoo. It's $102. Celeste ignores the tight knot of dread in her gut as she adds this expense to the many others this weekend away has incurred. She needed a whole new summer wardrobe—two bikinis, a cover-up, three sundresses to wear out at night, shorts and flip-flops, and a straw bag. She needed a pedicure and a fresh haircut. She needed sunscreen and a hostess gift for Greer.

"What do you get for a woman who has literally everything?" Celeste asked Merritt.

"Bring her really good olive oil," Merritt said. "It's more interesting than wine."

Celeste bought a forty-two-dollar (gulp) bottle of olive oil at Dean and DeLuca. Transporting the olive oil to Nantucket cost her another twenty-five dollars in checked-bag fees.

Celeste goes through airport security, a soul-shredding experience where she has to stand barefoot among strangers and put her drugstore toiletries on display in a clear plastic bag for others to comment on. The woman behind her points to Celeste's Noxzema and says, "I thought they stopped making that in the eighties."

As Celeste is walking to the gate, she gets a text from Benji. Accident on 55th Street, midtown at a standstill, I may miss the flight. You go, I'll meet you there tomorrow.

Celeste stops and rereads the text. I'll just wait and go with you tomorrow, she texts back. But she imagines undoing all the steps she has just taken only to reiterate them tomorrow. Unchecking her bag,

Ubering back to Manhattan, rebooking her ticket for a Friday.

Just go now, Benji texts. Please. It'll be fine. Shooter will take good care of you.

When Celeste gets to the gate, there is a man in jeans and a white linen shirt who breaks into a grin when he sees her.

"You're as pretty as he said." The man offers his hand. "I'm Shooter Uxley."

"Celeste," she says. "Otis." Celeste shakes Shooter's hand and tries to manage the emotions careening around inside of her. Ten seconds ago she was despondent about having to get to Nantucket and endure an entire night and half the next day without Benji. Now, however, her insides are swooping and dipping like a kite. Shooter is . . . well, the first word she thinks of is *hot,* but she has never described anyone that way and so she switches to *handsome.* Objectively handsome; his handsomeness is a matter of fact, not opinion. He has dark hair with a forelock that falls over one of his blue eyes. Celeste's eyes are also blue, but blue eyes look better on Shooter with his dark hair. But what Celeste is responding to is more than Shooter's looks. It's his gaze, his grin, his energy—they grab her. Is there a better way to describe it? She's in thrall. This, she thinks, is love at first sight.

But no! It can't be! Celeste loves Benji. They have just started saying it. The first time was five days earlier, Sunday evening, as they drove back to the city from a visit with Celeste's parents in Easton. Benji had met Bruce and Karen and seen the modest house on Derhammer Street where Celeste grew up. Celeste had shown Benji her elementary school, her high school, the Palmer pool, downtown Easton, the Peace candle, the Free Bridge, and the Crayola factory. They had supper with Karen and Bruce at Diner 248. Celeste had thought about making a reservation somewhere more refined—Easton had a crop of new restaurants; Masa for Mexican, Third and Ferry for seafood—but Celeste and her parents had always celebrated family milestones at the diner, and to go anywhere else would feel phony. They all ate vegetable barley soup and turkey clubs, and Karen, Bruce, and Celeste split the Fudgy Wudgy for dessert as usual and Benji gamely tried a bite. After supper, they drove back to the house and said their goodbyes at the curb. Bruce and Karen waved until Celeste and Benji turned the corner and Celeste shed a few tears as she always did when she left her parents. Benji said, "Well, now I've seen Easton. Thank you."

Celeste had laughed and wiped tears from the bottom of her eyes. "You're very welcome. It's not Park Avenue or London, of course..."

"It's a sweet little town," Benji said. "It must have been a nice place to grow up."

Celeste flinched at this assessment; something about his tone sounded patronizing. "It was," she said defensively.

Benji reached over to squeeze her knee. "Hey, I'm sorry. That came out wrong. I liked Easton, and your parents are true gems. Real salt of the earth."

They're people, Celeste had thought. Good, honest, hardworking people. She had never understood the phrase *salt of the earth,* but it sounded like something you said about someone you knew was beneath you. To make the moment even more humiliating, Celeste started to cry again and Benji said, "Wow, I'm making things worse. Please don't cry, Celeste. I love you."

Celeste shook her head. "You're just saying that."

"I'm not," Benji said. "I've been wanting to say it for weeks, months even, but I've been afraid because I wasn't sure you felt the same way. But believe me, please, when I say I love you. I love you, Celeste Otis."

She had felt emotionally goosed. He *loved* her. He loved *her.* Celeste didn't know what to say, and yet it was clear Benji was waiting for a response. "I love you too," she said.

"You do?" he asked.

Did she? Celeste thought back to the first time she met Benji, how wonderful he had been with Miranda, how exasperated with glamorous Jules. She thought of the flowers and the books and the restaurants and his mind-boggling apartment and the homeless shelter. She thought about the ease she felt in his presence, as though the world had only good things to offer. She thought about how much his opinion mattered to her. She wanted to be good enough for him.

"Yes," she said. "I do."

If Celeste loves Benji, then what is happening now, with Shooter? Celeste knows her parents' story by heart: Karen came marching up the pool steps and introduced herself to Bruce, who was sweating off water weight and staring at his orange. Karen had stuck out her hand and said, *I admire a man with willpower.* And those, apparently, were the magic words, because they both knew instantly that they would get married and stay together forever.

I wasn't even hungry after that, Bruce said. *I threw my orange away, I made weight, I won my match, but it barely mattered. All I wanted was a date with your mother.*

That's how love works, Karen said.

Does love work only one way? Celeste wonders. She has spent the past nine months carefully, cautiously getting to know Benjamin Winbury and has just decided to call that experience love. But only five days later, she's pretty sure she has made a mistake. Because in meeting Shooter, Celeste has been swallowed whole by the world. *Goner,* she thinks. *I'm a goner.*

No. She is a scientist. She believes in reason. What she's feeling now is as ephemeral as a shooting star. Soon enough, it will fade away.

"The old boy isn't going to make this flight," Shooter says. "He gave me very strict orders to take care of you."

"That won't be necessary," Celeste says. "I can take care of myself."

"Can you?" Shooter says. His eyes flash with blue sparks. Celeste can't look directly at him, then she decides that she's being silly, of course she can look at him, and she does. The bottom drops out of her stomach, *whoosh!* He is so painfully attractive. Maybe she just needs to build up a tolerance. Even the best-looking men in the world—George Clooney, Jon Hamm—might seem run-of-the-mill if you looked at them long enough. "What seat are you in?"

"One-D," she says.

"I'm in twelve-A," Shooter says. "I'm going to ask them to give me Benji's seat."

"I'm not a senior vice president from Prague," Celeste says. "You don't have to babysit me."

"You've been dating my best friend for nine months," Shooter says. "I want to get to know you. Hard to do from eleven rows away, don't you agree?"

"Agreed," Celeste concedes.

They sit side by side in the front row of the plane. Shooter lifts Celeste's carry-on into the overhead compartment, then asks if she would prefer the window or the aisle. She says aisle. She realizes most people who have never flown before might want to sit at the window but Celeste is terrified. Shooter waits for her to sit down and then he sits. He's a gentleman, but then so is Benji. Benji is the ultimate gentleman. Benji stands whenever Celeste leaves the table to go to the ladies' room and he stands when she gets back. He holds doors, he carries a handkerchief, he never interrupts.

Shooter pulls a flask out of his back pocket and hands it to Celeste. She eyes the flask. It's alcohol, she assumes, but what kind? She is far too cautious a person to drink without asking. But in the moment, she doesn't feel like being cautious. She feels like being daring. She accepts the flask and takes a swig: It's tequila. Celeste drinks tequila only when she's with Merritt, although personally she thinks it tastes like dirt. This tequila is smoother than most, but even so it singes her throat. However, an instant later the tension in her neck disappears and her jaw loosens. She takes another slug.

"I carry that because I hate flying," Shooter says.

"You?" Celeste says. "But don't you fly all the time?"

"Nearly every week," he says. "The first time I

flew, I was eight years old. My parents were sending me to summer camp in Vermont." He leans his head back against the seat and stares forward. "Every time I fly I have an atavistic reaction to the memory of that day. The day I realized my parents wanted to get rid of me."

"Were you a very naughty child, then?" she asks. She sounds exactly like Merritt, she realizes.

"Oh, probably," Shooter says.

Celeste hands Shooter back the flask. He smiles sadly and takes a slug.

Later, Celeste will think back on the twenty hours she spent on Nantucket with Shooter alone as the kind of montage they show in movies. Here's a shot of the airplane bouncing and shaking during turbulence and Shooter raising the window shade in time for Celeste to see bolts of lightning on the horizon. Here is Shooter taking Celeste's hand, Celeste imagining her parents' reaction when they are informed that Celeste has died in a plane crash. Here is the plane landing safely on Nantucket, passengers cheering, Shooter and Celeste executing a perfect high-five. Here are Shooter and Celeste climbing into a silver Jeep that Shooter has rented. The sky has cleared, the top of the Jeep is down, and Shooter takes off down the road while Celeste's blond hair blows behind her. Here is Elida, the summer housekeeper, meeting Shooter and Celeste at the front door of the Winbury property, known as Summerland, and informing them that Mr. and Mrs. Winbury have also been detained in New York but that they should make themselves at home; she, Elida, will return in the morning.

Here is Celeste acting nonchalant when she enters the house. It's a palace, a summer palace, like the monarchs of Russia and Austria used to have. The ceilings are soaring, the rooms are open, bright, airy. The entire thing is white — white walls, white wainscoting, whitewashed oak floors, a kitchen tiled in white with pure white Carrara marble countertops — with stunning bursts of color here and there: paintings, pillows, fresh flowers, a wooden bowl filled with lemons and Granny Smith apples. Celeste would say she can't believe how glorious the house is, with its six bedrooms upstairs and master suite downstairs; with its uninterrupted views of the harbor; with its glass-walled wine cellar off the casual "friends'" dining room; with its dark rectangular pool and Balinese-style pool house; with its two guest cottages, tiny and perfect, like cottages borrowed from a fairy tale; with its round rose garden in the middle of a koi pond, a garden that can be accessed only by a footbridge. Shooter gives Celeste the tour — he has been coming to Summerland since he was fourteen years old, over half his life—and hence his attitude is charmingly proprietary. He tells Celeste that he used to have a terrific crush on Greer and had near Oedipal dreams about killing Tag and marrying her.

"Essentially becoming my best friend's stepfather," he says.

Celeste shrieks. "Greer?" Celeste likes Greer, but it's hard to imagine her as the object of teenage lust.

"She was so beautiful," Shooter says. "And she doted on me. She was more my mother than my own mother. I think she would probably write both of her sons out of the will and leave this place to me if I asked her nicely."

Celeste laughs, but she's beginning to believe that Shooter might have the ability to disrupt primogeniture and overturn dynasties.

Here is Shooter pouring Celeste a glass of Greer's wine and opening one of Tag's beers for himself. Celeste feels like they're teenagers throwing a party while their parents are away. Here is Shooter opening a can of cocktail peanuts, then paging through the Nantucket phone book and making a call behind closed doors. Here are Celeste and Shooter clinking wine glass to beer bottle as they sit in Adirondack chairs and watch the sun go down. Here is Shooter going to the front door, paying the delivery boy, and bringing a feast into the kitchen. He has ordered two lobster dinners complete with corn, potatoes, and containers of melted butter.

Celeste says, "I thought it was pizza."

Shooter says, "We're on Nantucket, Sunshine."

Here are Celeste and Shooter after dinner and after several shots of Tag's absurdly fine tequila headed to town in a taxi to the Chicken Box, which is not a fast-food restaurant but rather a dive bar with live music. Here are Celeste and Shooter dancing in the front row to a cover band called Maxxtone who play "Wagon Wheel," followed by "Sweet Caroline." Here are Celeste and Shooter pumping their fists in the air, chanting "Bah-bah-bah!" and "So good! So good! So good!" Here are Celeste and Shooter stumbling out of the Chicken Box and into another taxi that takes them back to the summer palace. It's one thirty in the morning, which is later than Celeste has stayed up since she pulled all-nighters in college, but instead of going to bed, she and Shooter wander out to the beach, strip down to their underwear, and go for a swim.

Here is Celeste saying, "I'm so drunk, I'll probably drown."

"No," Shooter says. "I would never let that happen."

Here is Shooter floating on his back, spouting water out of his mouth. Here is Celeste floating on her back, staring at the stars, thinking that outer space is a mystery but not as much of a mystery as the universe of human emotion.

Here are Celeste and Shooter wandering back inside the house, wrapped in navy-and-white-striped towels that Shooter swiped from the pool house. They linger in the kitchen. Shooter opens the refrigerator. Elida has clearly provisioned for the weekend; the inside of the Winburys' refrigerator looks like something from a magazine shoot. There are half a dozen kinds of cheese, none of which Celeste recognizes, so she picks them up to inspect: Taleggio, Armenian string cheese, Emmentaler. There are sticks of cured sausage and pepperoni. There is a small tub of truffle butter, some artisanal hummus, four containers of olives in an ombré stack, from light purple to black. There are slabs of pâté and jars of chutney that look like they were mailed directly from India. Celeste checks the labels: Harrods. Close enough.

"Okay, can I just say?" Celeste puts a hand on Shooter's bare back and he turns to face her. The two of them are illuminated by the fluorescent light of the fridge and for a second Celeste has the sense that she and Shooter are curious children peering into a previously undiscovered world, like the young protagonists in a C. S. Lewis novel.

"Yes?"

"In my house growing up, if I wanted a snack?

There was a tub of Philadelphia cream cheese. And I spread it on Triscuits. If my mother had been to the Amish farmers' market, there was sometimes pepper jelly to put on top." Celeste knows she must be deeply and profoundly drunk because she never, ever shares details about her life growing up. She feels like a fool.

"You are such a breath of fresh air," Shooter says.

Now Celeste feels even worse. She doesn't want to be a breath of fresh air. She wants to be devastating, alluring, irresistible.

But wait—what about Benji?

It's time to go to bed, she thinks. This is what she always suspected happened when one stayed up too late; reputations were shredded, hopes and dreams destroyed. What had Mac and Betty always told her? *Nothing good happens after midnight.*

"And also?" Celeste says. "If I held the refrigerator door open for this long? I would have been scolded for wasting energy."

"Scolded?" Shooter says.

"Yes, scolded." She tries to frown at him. "I'm going to bed."

"Absolutely not," Shooter says. He regards the contents of the fridge, then grabs the truffle butter. A rummage through the cabinet to the left of the fridge—*he does know where everything is,* Celeste thinks, *just like he owns the place*—produces a long, slender box of... bread sticks. Rosemary bread sticks. "Come sit."

Celeste joins Shooter in the "casual" dining room off the kitchen, where they watch the glass cube of the wine cellar glow like a spaceship. Shooter opens the box of bread sticks and the butter.

"Prepare yourself," he says. "This is going to be memorable. Have you ever had truffle butter?"

"No?" Celeste says. She knows that truffles are mushrooms—pigs dig them out of the ground in France and Italy—but she can't get too excited about mushroom butter. Nothing about it sounds appetizing. Still, she is hungry enough to eat just about anything—the lobster dinner seems like days ago—so she accepts a reed-thin bread stick with a dollop of butter on the end.

She bites off the bottom of the bread stick and the flavor explodes in her mouth. She whimpers with ecstasy.

"Pretty good, huh?" Shooter says.

Celeste closes her eyes, savoring the taste, which is unlike anything she has ever eaten. It's rich, complex, earthy, sexy. She swallows. "I can't believe how... *good*... that is."

Here are Shooter and Celeste eating rosemary bread sticks with truffle butter until the butter is gone and only a few bread-stick stubs rattle around in the box. It was a deceptively simple snack but Celeste will never, ever forget it.

Here are Celeste and Shooter wandering upstairs.

Celeste is sleeping in "Benji's room," which is decorated in white, beige, and taupe, and Shooter is sleeping at the far end of the hallway in "guest room 3," which is done in white, navy, and taupe. Celeste checks the other guest rooms; they're nearly identical and she wonders if people new to the house like herself ever wander into the wrong room accidentally. She gives Shooter a feeble wave.

"I guess I'll call it a night."

"You sure about that?" Shooter says.

Celeste thinks for a second. *Is* she sure about that? They have pressed to the edge of a platonic relationship; there's nothing left they can do while maintaining their innocence other than maybe go down to the game room and play Scrabble.

"I'm sure about that," she says.

"Sunshine," Shooter says.

She looks at him. His eyes hold her hostage; she can't look away. He's asking her without saying anything. They are the only ones here. No one would ever know.

Amid the battle going on in her mind—her fervent desire versus her sense of right and wrong—she thinks of the age-old philosophical question: If a tree falls in the forest and nobody's there to hear it, does it still make a sound? That question, Celeste realizes, isn't about a tree at all. It's about what's happening right here, right now. If she sleeps with Shooter and it remains unknown to anyone but the two of them, did it even really happen?

Yes, she thinks. She would never be the same. And she hopes that Shooter wouldn't be the same either.

"Good night," she says. She kisses him on the cheek and retreats down the hall.

Here are Shooter and Celeste the next morning riding two bikes from the Winburys' fleet of Schwinns into town to the Petticoat Row Bakery, where they get giant iced coffees and two ham and Gruyère croissants, which ooze nutty melted cheese and butter as they pick them apart on a bench on Centre Street. Here is Shooter buying Celeste a bouquet of wildflowers from a farm truck on Main Street, a pointless, extravagant gesture because Tag and Greer's house is set among lush gardens and the house is filled with fresh flowers. Celeste reminds him of this and he says, "Yes, but none of those flowers are from *me*. I want you to look at this bouquet and know just how besotted I am with you."

Besotted, she thinks. It's a peculiar word, old-fashioned and British-sounding. But Benji is the British one, not Shooter. Somewhere in all the sharing of last night, Celeste learned that Shooter is from Palm Beach, Florida. Shooter was shipped off to summer camp at age eight and to boarding school a few years after that. Shooter's father died when Shooter was a junior at St. George's.

"And that was when the wheels fell off the bus," Shooter said. "My father had been married twice before and had other kids and those other Uxleys swooped in and claimed everything. My one brother, Mitch, agreed to pay my final year of tuition at St. George's but I had no discretionary income so I started running a dice game at school. There was no money for college so I moved to DC, where I worked as a bartender. Eventually I found a high-stakes poker game where I met diplomats, lobbyists, and a bunch of foreign businessmen. Which led me to my present venture."

"What happened to your mother?" Celeste asked.

"She died," Shooter said. Then he shook his head and Celeste knew not to ask anything further.

Besotted. What does he mean by that, exactly? There's no time to ponder because he's leading her down the street toward the Bartlett's Farm truck. He buys three hothouse tomatoes and a loaf of Portuguese bread.

"Tomatoes, mayonnaise, good white bread," he says. "My favorite summer sandwich."

Celeste raises a skeptical eyebrow. She was raised on cold cuts—turkey, ham, salami, roast beef. Her parents may have struggled with money but there was always meat piled high on her sandwiches.

Celeste changes her tune, however, when she is sitting poolside in one of her new bikinis and Shooter brings her his favorite sandwich. The bread has been toasted golden brown; the slices of tomato are thick and juicy, seasoned with sea salt and freshly ground pepper, and there is exactly the right amount of mayonnaise to make the sandwich tangy and luscious.

"What do you think?" he asks. "Pretty good, huh?"

She shrugs and takes another bite.

They are lying side by side on chaises in the afternoon sun, the pool cool and dark before them. The pool has a subtle waterfall feature at one end that makes what Celeste thinks of as water music, a lullaby that threatens to put her to sleep in the middle of a very important conversation. She and Shooter are picking the best song by every classic rock performer they can think of.

"Rolling Stones," Shooter says. " 'Ruby Tuesday.' "

" 'Beast of Burden,' " Celeste says.

"Ooooooh," Shooter says. "Good call."

"David Bowie," Celeste says. " 'Changes.' "

"I'm a 'Modern Love' guy," Shooter says.

Celeste shakes her head. "Can't stand it."

"Dire Straits," Shooter says. " 'Romeo and Juliet.' " He reaches his foot over to nudge her leg. "Wake up. Dire Straits."

She likes the song about roller girl. *She's making movies on location, she don't know what it means.* Celeste is sinking behind her closed eyelids. Sinking down. What is the name of that song? She can't... remember.

Celeste wakes up to someone calling her name.

Celeste! Earth to Celeste!

She opens her eyes and looks at the chaise next to hers. Empty. She squints. Across the pool she sees a man in half a suit—pants, shirt, tie. It's Benji. Benji is here. Celeste sits up. She straightens her bikini top.

"Hey there," Celeste says, but the tone of her voice has changed. Her heart isn't in it.

"Hey," Benji says. He moves Shooter's towel aside and sits on Shooter's chaise. "How are you? How has it been?"

"I'm fine," Celeste says. "It's been...fine."

Celeste tries to think of details she can share: lobster dinner, "Sweet Caroline," swimming in her bra and panties under the stars way past her bedtime, truffle butter, a tree falls in the forest?

No.

A bike ride with the morning sun on her face, a bouquet of snapdragons, cosmos, and zinnias, tomato sandwiches?

The name of the song comes to her.

" 'Skateaway,' " she says.

"Excuse me?" Benji says.

Celeste blinks rapidly. Her field of vision is swimming with bright, amorphous blobs, as though she's been staring at the sun.

Friday, July 6, 2018, 11:15 p.m.

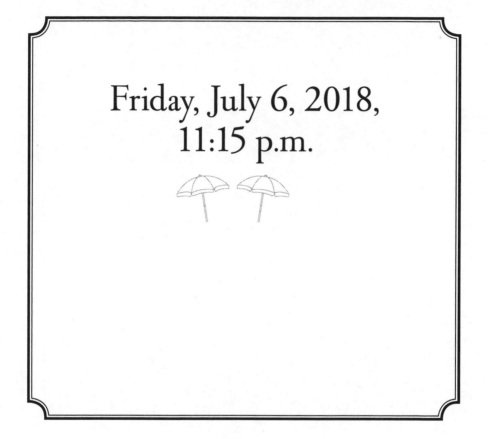

KAREN

She takes an oxy, brushes her teeth, and puts on a nightgown only to take the nightgown off right before she slides into bed. The sheets are Belgian, Celeste said, seven-hundred-thread-count cotton, which is the very best. The bed is dressed in a white down comforter, an ivory cashmere blanket, these white cotton sheets with a scalloped edge, and a mountain of pillows, each as soft as a dollop of whipped cream. Karen places them all around her and sinks in. It's like sleeping on a cloud. Will heaven be like sleeping in one of Summerland's guest beds? She can only hope.

She drifts off, her pain at bay.

She wakes up with a start—*Celeste! Celeste!* She reaches an arm out to feel for Bruce but the other side of the bed is cool and empty. Karen checks the bedside clock: 11:46. Quarter to twelve and Bruce hasn't come to bed yet? Karen feels annoyed at first, then hurt. She realizes her naked body is no longer appealing, but she had thought maybe something would happen tonight. She wants to feel close to Bruce one more time.

She struggles to catch her breath. She was having a dream, a nightmare, about Celeste. Celeste was... somewhere unfamiliar...a hotel with unnumbered floors, different levels, some of which led to dead ends; it was a confusing maze of a place. Celeste kept calling out but Karen couldn't get to her. Celeste had something to tell her, something she needed Karen to know.

Celeste doesn't want to marry Benji, Karen thinks. That is the stark truth.

Involuntarily, the psychic's word comes to her: *Chaos.*

Part of Karen believes Celeste should go through with the wedding anyway. So she isn't madly in love with Benji. Possibly she feels only a fraction of what Karen feels for Bruce, or possibly it's a different emotion altogether. Karen wants to tell Celeste to make the best of her situation, a situation any other young woman would kill to find herself in. Celeste and Benji don't have to be a perfect couple. Really, there is no such thing.

But then Karen stops herself. It is only the most selfish of women who would encourage their daughters to marry people they don't love. What Karen must do—now, she realizes, *now*—is give Celeste permission to back out. There are 170 people descending on Summerland tomorrow for a wedding unlike any other; over a hundred thousand dollars has been spent on these nuptials, perhaps even twice that. But no amount of money or logistics is worth a lifetime of settling. Karen must find Celeste now.

Finding Celeste, however, suddenly seems arduous. Will a phone call suffice? Karen picks up her cell phone and dials Celeste's number. The call goes to voice mail.

This is the universe telling Karen that a phone call will *not* suffice. Celeste turns her phone off when she goes to bed; she must be asleep.

Gingerly, Karen lowers her feet to the floor and stands. She finds her cane and hoists herself up. The oxy is still working; she feels strong and steady with purpose. She wraps herself in the robe and ventures out into the hallway.

If Karen's memory serves, Benji's room, where Celeste is staying alone tonight, is the second door on the left. The hallway has subtle lighting along the baseboard so Karen can see where to plant her cane as she pads down the hall. When she reaches the door, she taps lightly. She doesn't want to wake the whole house up but neither does she want to interrupt anything.

There is no answer. Karen presses her ear to the door. In their house on Derhammer Street, the doors are hollow-core. Here they are true, solid wood, impossible to hear through. Karen eases the door open.

"Celeste?" she says. "Honey?"

The room is silent. Karen gropes for the switch and turns on the light. The bed is made up just as Karen's is—comforter, cashmere blanket, a host of pillows. Celeste hasn't gotten home yet, then. Or maybe she decided to join Merritt in the cottage so they can stay up gossiping and giggling on Celeste's last night as a single woman. But somehow Karen doubts that. Celeste has never been a gossiper or a giggler. She never had close girlfriends growing up, which used to worry Karen, even as she loved being Celeste's closest confidante.

Karen gazes upon the white silk column wedding dress hanging on the back of the closet door. It's a dress from a dream, ideally suited to Celeste's simple tastes and her classic beauty.

But...she won't be wearing it tomorrow. Karen sighs, turns off the light, and closes the door.

As Karen heads back down the dark hallway, she feels a growing irritation. Where *is* everyone? Karen has been left all alone in this house. She wonders if this is what it feels like to be dead.

Stairs are tricky with a cane. Karen decides she feels strong enough to leave her cane behind. She takes the stairs slowly, gripping the rail, and thinks about the leftover lobster tails stashed in the fridge. The idea of them is enticing but she can't make herself feel hungry. The only thing she craves right now is a meaningful conversation with her daughter, and her husband's body next to her in their bed.

Karen hears distant voices and she smells smoke. She tiptoes along, reaching out for the wall when she needs to steady herself. She hears Bruce's voice. When she turns the corner, she can see two figures out on a deck — not the main deck but a horseshoe-shaped deck off to the right, one Karen hasn't noticed before. She wedges herself behind a sofa and peers behind the drapes. Bruce and Tag are sitting on the edge of this deck, smoking cigars and drinking what she thinks must be scotch. She can hear their voices but not what they're saying.

She should either go back to bed or find her daughter. But instead, Karen quietly cranks open the window. In a fine house like this one, the crank is smooth. The window opens silently.

Tag says, "There hasn't been anyone serious before this. Just casual stuff, when I was traveling. A woman in Stockholm, one in Dublin. But this girl was different. And now I'm trapped. She's pregnant and she's keeping the baby. She says."

Bruce shakes his head, throws back a swallow of scotch. He must be very, very drunk after an evening of mojitos, champagne, and now scotch. At home, all Bruce ever drinks is beer—Bud Light or Yuengling. When Bruce speaks, his words are slurred. "So whaddaya go' do, then, my friend?"

"I'm not sure. I need her to listen to reason. But she's stubborn." Tag studies the lit end of his cigar, then looks at Bruce. "So, anyway, now I've told you my war story. How about you? Have you ever stepped out on Mrs. Otis?"

"Naw, man," Bruce says. "Not like that."

Karen takes a deep breath. She should *not* be eavesdropping; this is a conversation between men, and now she has heard Tag confess he has gotten someone pregnant—probably that Featherleigh woman!—and what a mess *that* will turn out to be! Karen feels a little better about the last-minute canceling of the wedding. The Winbury family isn't at all what she thought.

"But I did have a crush on this chick once," Bruce says. "A real intense crush."

Karen is so shocked she nearly cries out. The pain is instant and rude. A crush? A *real intense crush?*

"Oh yeah?" Tag says.

"Yeah, yeah, yeah," Bruce says. *He's drunk,* Karen reminds herself. He hasn't had this much to drink maybe ever. He is probably making up a story to impress Tag Winbury.

"She worked with me at Neiman Marcus," Bruce says. "At first we were all business. In fact, I didn't even like her that much. She was uppity. She came to my store from New York City, from Bergdorf Goodman, where she worked in shoes."

Bergdorf's. Shoes. Yes, Karen vaguely recalls someone... but who was it?

"Oh yeah?" Tag says again.

"Then we became friends. We'd take our dinner break together. She had a different perspective on the world and it was...I don't know...refreshing, I guess, to talk to someone who had been places and done things. This was right after Celeste left for college, and I'm not going to lie, it was like a midlife crisis for both me *and* Karen. Karen hates to shop, *hates* to spend money on frivolous things, but she started going to all these trunk shows, Tupperware parties, something called the Pampered Chef. And I took on more night shifts so that I could be with this other woman."

Karen feels her heart pop, like a tire sliced by a granite curb, like a balloon drifting into a thorny rosebush. There's a concussion in her chest. She can't believe she's hearing this. Now, in her final days, she is learning that the man she has spent her whole life loving once harbored feelings for another woman.

Karen tries to calm herself. A crush is nothing. A crush is harmless. Hasn't Karen herself had crushes on people—the young man who worked in the produce section of Wegman's, for example? She used to give him a little wave and if he waved or smiled back she would float through the store, sometimes so giddy that she would buy treats she shouldn't have—white chocolate Magnum bars, for example.

"Did you two ever..." Tag asks.

"No," Bruce says. "I thought about it, though. It was a confusing time in my life. I can't tell you how much it turned my whole world upside down. I had spent my entire life feeling like one person and then suddenly I felt like someone else."

"Tell me about it," Tag says. "What was her name?"

"Robin," Tag says. "Robin Swain."

Karen does gasp—loudly—but neither Tag nor Bruce hears her. They just puff away on their cigars. Karen feels her insides turn to liquid. She has to sit down. She frantically tries to arrange the drapes back as she found them and she clambers out from behind the sofa. She should go back to her room. She can't have Bruce finding her here. If he knew she had been eavesdropping he would...vaporize.

Robin Swain. No. Please, God, no.

She can't make it back up the stairs. She sits on the

sofa but feels too exposed. She would slide down to the floor but she'll never be able to get back up. She looks around the room in a wild panic. Suddenly, she hates the house, its luxurious furnishings, the ostensible kindness of the Winburys, which now seems like a masked cruelty. Why on earth would Tag ask Bruce *such a heinous question?*

Why would Bruce give such an answer?

Robin Swain.

What did Bruce *mean* by that?

But Karen knows what he meant. And that's why she's reacting this way. She knew there was something unusual about Bruce's friendship with Robin. But of course it was inconceivable, unthinkable. It made no sense.

Karen steadies herself. *Bruce is drunk,* she thinks. He made up a story for Tag, out of machismo. He used Robin Swain's name because it was the first that came to mind. Karen shouldn't put any stock in what she just heard. She should go to bed. She manages to make her way back to the entry hall and climbs the stairs.

Once in her room, she takes an oxy. She takes two. Then she climbs into bed, still in her robe. She's shivering.

An intense crush on Robin Swain. They shared dinners; Bruce worked nights so they could be together. A confusing time in his life. A midlife crisis.

Well, yes, Karen thinks. This *is* confusing.

Robin Swain is a man.

It was September, right after Celeste left for college. Karen and Bruce had rented a U-Haul and driven her all the way across Pennsylvania and nearly all the way across Ohio to Oxford, which was only five miles from the Indiana border. They had helped her move into her dorm room in Hahne Hall, they had met her roommate, Julia, and Julia's parents. Karen and Bruce had attended the opening address by the college president and then they returned with Celeste to her room, both Bruce and Karen at loose ends, unsure of how to say good-bye. Eventually, Celeste decided to go to dinner at the Kona Bistro with Julia and her parents; she had left Karen and Bruce alone in her room. Karen had thought about simply moving in or renting an apartment down the street, and she's sure Bruce did too.

Neither of them had said much on the drive home.

A week or two later, Bruce had come home talking about a new colleague, Robin Swain. He was a man about Bruce's age who had transferred in from the shoe department of Bergdorf's. Robin had grown up in Opelika, Alabama, and had started college at Auburn but hadn't finished. He'd always wanted to go to New York City so he saved his money and bought a bus ticket. He was first hired at Bergdorf's to work in the stockroom.

Initially, Bruce complained about Robin. He might have come from a small town, but working in Manhattan had given him an attitude. He disparaged the King of Prussia store, the mall, the entire Delaware Valley. It was nowhere near as sophisticated as New York City, he said. The area was permanently stuck in 1984, back when the Philadelphia sports teams were good and perms were in fashion and everyone listened to Springsteen. Robin himself listened to country music.

But over the course of a few weeks, Karen noted a shift. Bruce started to talk more favorably about Robin. One of the shirts that Bruce came home to model for Karen was something that Robin had picked out for him. Now that Karen thinks back, *that* was when Bruce's sock fetish started. Robin loved flashy socks, and soon after, Bruce adopted the affectation; he wore rainbow socks, zebra socks, socks printed with the likeness of Elvis. He bought a CD called *When the Sun Goes Down* by Kenny Chesney and started singing the song all the damn time. *Everything gets hotter when the sun goes down.*

One night, Bruce invited Robin home for dinner. This had struck Karen as a bit strange. She and Bruce rarely had guests for dinner, and the town of Collegeville, where Robin was renting an apartment, was over an hour away. It was impractical. If Bruce wanted to have dinner with Robin, he should do so at the mall.

But Bruce had insisted. He had instructed Karen what to cook—her Betty Crocker pot roast with potatoes and carrots, a green salad (*not* iceberg lettuce, he said), and snowflake rolls. He would pick up wine on the way home, he said.

Wine? Karen had thought. They never, ever drank wine with dinner. They drank ice water, and Bruce, occasionally, a beer.

When Bruce and Robin walked in, they had been laughing at something, but they sobered up when they saw Karen. Robin was tall, wearing an expensive-looking blue blazer, a white shirt, navy pants, a brown leather belt with a silver H buckle. He wore light blue socks patterned with white clouds, which Bruce proudly showed off to Karen by lifting Robin's pants at the knee. Robin had a receding hairline, brown eyes, a slight Southern drawl. Had Karen thought *gay* when she saw him? She can't remember. Her overarching emotion at dinner was jealousy. Bruce and Robin talked between themselves—about the merchandise, about the clientele, about their co-workers. With each change of topic, Robin tried to include Karen, but maybe Karen's responses were so frosty that he stopped trying. She hadn't meant to be unkind to Robin but she had felt blindsided by his presence.

Her mind kept returning to the sight of Bruce lifting Robin's pant leg at the knee. The gesture had seemed so familiar, nearly intimate.

She had chalked up her conflicting emotions to the fact that Celeste had left and now it was just Karen and Bruce, and Bruce had gone out and found a friend at work. Which was fine. After all, Karen had friends at the Crayola factory gift shop. She was friends with nearly everyone! But there was no one special, no one she would invite home to dinner, no one she would talk to and laugh with and in so doing make Bruce feel irrelevant.

After dinner, Bruce had suggested Robin help him with the dishes so that Karen could put her feet up. When had Karen *ever* put her feet up? Never, that's when. But she knew how to take a hint. She bade Robin good-bye and Bruce a good night and she had stormed upstairs to lie angrily on the bed and listen to the two men washing and drying the dishes and finishing the wine and then stepping out onto the back porch to talk about heaven knows what.

Karen feels the oxy gripping her by the shoulders, then there is a great release as the pain falls away.

Bruce had an intense crush on Robin. A man. *It was a confusing time,* he said. *Suddenly I felt like someone else,* he said.

To Karen, it's a nuclear confession. Her husband, her state champion wrestler, her hungry wolf in bed had had feelings for another man, feelings he obviously isn't comfortable acknowledging because to Tag, he changed Robin's gender to female.

Robin worked at Neiman Marcus only through the holidays that year. By the time Celeste returned to Oxford after Christmas break, Robin had been transferred to the Neiman Marcus flagship store in Dallas. Had Bruce been upset? Heartbroken, even? If so, he'd hid it well.

Bruce had a secret, an intense crush. He never acted on it; this, Karen believes.

And Karen has a secret of her own: the three pills in the bottle, among the oxy.

Karen issues Bruce a silent pardon—it *had* been a confusing time. And, as Karen had wanted to tell Celeste, there is *no such thing* as a perfect couple.

Karen will tell Celeste this in the morning. She closes her eyes.

Saturday, July 7, 2018,
12:45 p.m.

NANTUCKET

Nick "the Greek" Diamantopoulos is driving from 333 Monomoy Road to the Nantucket Cottage Hospital, where he is finally going to talk to the bride. She wants to be interviewed *at the hospital,* and Nick hopes this means she has real information. He's eager to find out, but when he rolls around the rotary, he catches the scent of Lola Burger through his open window and the smell is too much to resist. One thing about Nantucket, Nick thinks, the food is top-notch. Even the burger joints. Nick pulls into takeout parking and races inside to charm Marva, the hostess, who scores him a medium-rare Lolaburger (aged cheddar, onion compote, foie gras dipping sauce) with a side of fries. Nick leaves Marva a nice big tip and she says, "Don't be a stranger, Greek man. Come back and see me!"

Nick hops back in his car, stuffing fries in his mouth. At the hospital, the Greek is greeted by a trio of nurses—Margaret, Suzanne, and Patty. Nick has been on dates with both Suzanne and Patty—nothing serious, just fun. He smiles at all three and says, "Where am I going and what do I need to know?"

Patty links her arm through his and leads him down the hall to an exam room. "She came in early this morning and we treated her for hysteria slash panic attack, meaning we took her vitals and gave her some Valium to calm her down. She slept for a little while. I wish there were something more we could do. Her best friend drowned out in front of the house? And Celeste found her? On her wedding day?"

"Wedding was canceled," Nick says. "Obviously."

"Obviously."

"The deceased was the maid of honor," Nick says.

"That's what Celeste told me," Patty says. She gives a dry laugh. "Maybe she didn't like the dress."

Nick shakes his head. He can't make a joke at Merritt's expense. He just can't.

"What happened when the groom showed up here?" he asks.

"That was about an hour ago. Seemed like a nice guy. He was worried about Celeste and he expected to take her home. He was in her room for about ten minutes, then he left. And she asked to speak to you."

"Okay, Patty. Thank you. It's okay if I question her in here?"

"Sure," Patty says. "One strange thing? Celeste

came with a bag packed. I'm just not sure what to make of that. When I asked her about it, she started to cry, so I let it be."

"Okay," Nick says. That *is* strange, but there's probably an explanation.

"My shift ends at three," Patty says. "Call me if you want to get together tonight."

The idea is tempting, but he knows he won't relax until he cracks this case. Hopefully the bride has the answer.

"Will do," he says.

He finds Celeste in a hospital gown, lying back on the examining table. When she sees him, she sits up. "Are you the police?"

"State police detective Nick Diamantopoulos," he says. "I'm very sorry about your friend."

Celeste nods. "You're here to take my statement."

"I am," Nick says. "It's a tragedy, what happened to Merritt."

"She's dead?" Celeste says. "Is she . . . I mean, she's dead, right?"

Nick takes a seat in the chair at the foot of the examining table. The fries start to churn in his stomach. "I'm sorry, yes. She's dead."

Celeste bows her head and cries softly. "It's all my fault."

"Excuse me?"

"It's my fault. I knew something bad would happen. I thought it would be my mother but it wasn't—it was Merritt. She's dead!"

"I'm very sorry," Nick says again. "I know you have a lot to deal with right now."

"You *don't* know," Celeste says. "You have no idea."

Nick takes out his notepad. "The best way to help Merritt is to help me figure out what happened to her. She was your best friend, your maid of honor. She confided in you, right?"

Celeste nods.

"And here's the funny thing about weddings," Nick says. "They bring together people who don't know each other. I've interviewed two people already but neither of them really knew Merritt. So you are a key part of this investigation."

Celeste takes a deep breath. "I'm not sure I want to break Merritt's confidence. Other people are involved. Other people I care about."

"I understand," Nick says. His sympathy is genuine, but he is a sapper looking for land mines. "Why don't you just tell me what you know and we'll see if it's relevant."

Celeste stares at him.

"I have someone who witnessed you and Ms. Monaco in the Winburys' rose garden after the party ended," Nick says. "This person said Ms. Monaco was crying and you were comforting her. Do you want to tell me what that was about?"

Celeste blinks. "Someone saw us in the *rose garden?*" she says. "Who?"

"I can't tell you that," Nick says. "What you tell me here is confidential. That's true for everyone."

"I hear you saying that, but..."

"But what?" Nick says. She's scared to tell him what she knows—but why? "My understanding is that Ms. Monaco was estranged from her parents and there's a brother somewhere but no one knows where. So she doesn't have any family here to advocate on her behalf. That leaves me—and you—to find out what happened. Do you understand the magnitude of that responsibility, Celeste?"

"She was...going through a tough breakup," Celeste says. "With a married man. She was very upset about it."

Nick nods. He waits.

"I told her to end it. Back when I found out, which was only a few weeks ago, I told her to end it and she said she would, but she didn't. And then he ended it."

"The married man?"

"Yes," Celeste says. "And that was why she was crying."

Nick writes on his notepad: *Married man.* Then he scans his other notes and he thinks about Merritt's cell phone. She had just gone through a breakup but there were no calls or texts, either coming in or going out. Except for the one from Robbie wishing her a belated "Happy Day of American Independence" and hoping she was doing well.

"Is the married man named Robbie, by any chance?"

Celeste's eyes widen. "How do you know about Robbie?"

"I'm a detective," Nick says. "Is Robbie the married man?"

"No," Celeste says. "Robbie is her…was…I don't know, her friend. A guy friend. A past boyfriend, but not anymore."

"Celeste, was the married man that Merritt was involved with at the party last night?"

The barest movement of the head forward. Almost involuntary, it seems.

"Is that a nod?"

"It's Tag," Celeste whispers. "Tag Winbury, my father-in-law."

Boom, Nick thinks.

Once the name is out, the rest flows more easily, as though a plug has been pulled.

Merritt and Tag hooked up two months ago during Celeste's bachelorette weekend. They saw each other in the city, Celeste isn't sure when or where. As recently as the Fourth of July, Merritt said the relationship was over. It wasn't a big deal, according to her.

"But I talked to her after the rehearsal dinner. She was upset. I encouraged her to come into town with us but she said she wouldn't be any fun. She wanted to stay home and mope, she said. Get it out of her system so she would be good to go today." Celeste pauses. "For the wedding."

"Was the last time you saw Merritt alive in the rose garden?" Nick asks.

"No," Celeste says. "I saw her when we got back from town."

"You did?" Nick says. "Where was she?"

"She was at a table under the tent with Tag," Celeste says. "And Thomas, Benji's brother. Thomas came with us into town. We went to the back bar at Ventuno but when we got to the Boarding House, his wife, Abby, called and told him to come home. When we got back, he was sitting under the tent with Tag and Merritt... and a friend of the Winburys named Featherleigh Dale."

Nick writes down the names: *Merritt, Tag, Thomas, brother, and a person — woman? — named Featherleigh Dale.*

"Do you know Featherleigh Dale?" Nick asks.

"Not really," Celeste says. "I just met her last night. She's from London."

"And was she also staying at the Winbury house?"

"No."

"But she was there last night?"

"Yes," Celeste says.

"What time was it when you saw Merritt under the tent with Tag?"

"We left town when the bars closed, at one," Celeste says. "So maybe one thirty?"

"And when you saw Merritt with Tag," Nick says, "were you concerned?"

"I was preoccupied..." Celeste says.

"That stands to reason," Nick says. "After all, you were supposed to get married today."

"It's no excuse." Celeste bows her head. "I was preoccupied and I didn't persuade Merritt to come to bed. If I had done that, she would be alive. This is my fault."

Nick needs to keep his bride focused. "Celeste, what were Tag and Merritt and Thomas and...Featherleigh doing under the tent? Drinking? Smoking?"

"Drinking shots," Celeste says. "Of some special rum Tag gets in Barbados. Tag had a cigar. They looked happy. Merritt looked *happy*, or happier, anyway. They tried to get me to join them but Benji and Shooter had gone to bed and I wanted to get some sleep..."

"Understandable," Nick says. "You were getting married the next day."

Again, Celeste shakes her head. It's the mention of the wedding that seems to set her back, so Nick decides not to do it again.

"As I was saying good night to everyone, Abby called down from an upstairs window," Celeste says. "She wanted Thomas to come to bed. And I did hesitate a bit then because I thought it would be bad for Tag and Merritt to be alone together. Honestly, I thought they might rekindle their..." She stops, pinkens. "I thought they might hook up."

Nick nods. "Okay."

"But Featherleigh was there and she showed no intention of leaving. She made a comment that it was morning in London and she had just gotten her second wind." Celeste swallows. "I kissed Merritt good night and I squeezed her hand and looked her in the eye and I said, *Are you okay, my friend?* And she said, *Hey, your stutter is gone.* Because I had a stutter for a few months, actually. Anyway, I figured she was sober enough to notice that, she would be fine. So I went up to bed."

"Did you hear anything outside after that?" Nick asks. "Did you hear anyone in the water? There was a two-person kayak left out on the beach. There was blood in the sand and Merritt had a cut on her foot. Do you know anything about that?"

"Kayak?" Celeste says. She sits up, swings her feet to the floor, and starts to pace. "Did Tag take Merritt out in the kayak? Do you know if that happened?"

"I don't," he says. "I'm working with the Nantucket Police on this. The Chief will question Mr. Winbury about the kayak. The important thing is you didn't *hear* anything?"

"No," Celeste says. "But the house has central air and Benji's bedroom—the room where I was staying—faces the driveway, not the water."

"And this morning...you're the one who found Ms. Monaco, is that correct?"

"Yes," Celeste says.

"You were up early," Nick says. "Why is that?"

Celeste bows her head and starts to shake.

Nick turns to see a yellow paisley duffel bag in the corner of the room. He remembers what Patty said. "And you had a bag packed? I guess I don't understand why you were down at the beach at five thirty in the morning with your bag." Although Nick does understand, or he thinks he does.

When Celeste looks up, tears are streaming down her face. "Is there any way we can be finished for now?"

Nick scans his notepad. This was not your typical wedding. The maid of honor was sleeping with the groom's father. Nick will call the Chief and have him question the father; Nick would likely lose his cool with the guy. He's beginning to have emotions about this case, which is never a good thing.

But then Nick thinks about Greer Garrison. Which of Greer's answers had Nick found suspicious?

All of them, really. She had seemed bloodless, soul-less, unaffected, and . . . unsurprised. And she had intentionally not told Nick about going to the kitchen for a nightcap. Greer writes murder mysteries. *If any-one would be able to plot a murder and get away with it,* Nick thinks, *it would be her.*

Right?

If she knew about this affair, she would be a prime suspect.

But Nick can't leave any stone unturned here. Featherleigh Dale was at the table after both Celeste and Thomas left. Featherleigh might be able to say for sure if Tag took Merritt out in the kayak.

Nick writes on his notepad: *Find Featherleigh Dale!*

The sound of Celeste crying brings Nick back to the present.

"We can be finished," Nick says. "For now." He gets to his feet. The poor kid. It's pretty clear she's going through more than just her best friend dying. "I'll send Patty back in."

Saturday, July 7, 2018,
2:00 p.m.

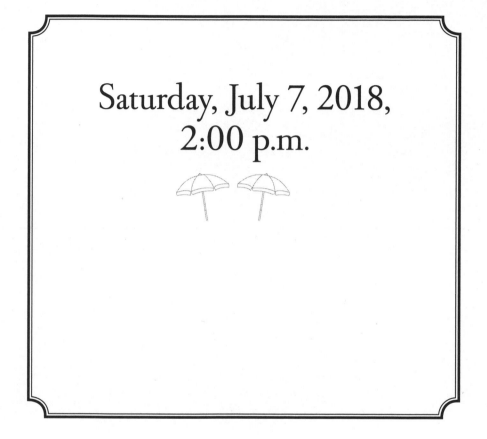

THE CHIEF

Shooter Uxley wants to lawyer up, which is his right, although any cop in America will tell you the same thing: It doesn't look good. Why lawyer up if you have nothing to hide? The Chief tries to point this out to Shooter gently, without making his true motivation known, his true motivation being that they need answers, and fast.

Keira, the Chief's assistant, informs the Chief that before he went off duty, Sergeant Dickson was able to locate and speak to Ms. Monaco's brother, Douglas Monaco, of Garden City, New York, and that Mr. Monaco said he would contact his parents and would, when the time came, make the necessary arrangements for the body.

"How did he sound?" the Chief asks. "Did he have any questions?"

"He was shocked," Keira says. "But he hadn't talked to her since last Christmas and he said his parents hadn't spoken to her in years. They had a falling-out."

"Did he ask you what happened?" the Chief says.

"He didn't," Keira says. "He just thanked me for letting him know and gave me his contact information."

"Good," the Chief says. The last thing he needs now is aggressive, upset family members demanding more intensive police work. And yet the complete opposite of that feels sad, even though it makes his job easier. "You can release the name, age, and the hometown—use New York City—to the press and tell them the matter is under investigation. No further comment."

"Also?" Keira says. "Sue Moran from the chamber of commerce called. She's concerned."

"About what?"

"Weddings on Nantucket generate over fifty million dollars, she said. A Murdered Maid of Honor is extremely bad for business, she said. She wants us to try to keep the wedding angle quiet."

"Fine," the Chief says. "We'll try. But you might want to remind her that it's a small island."

Uxley chooses a local attorney, Valerie Gluckstern. The Chief knows Val well, and while she's not his favorite lawyer on this island, neither is she his least favorite. She started out as a trust and estate attorney and switched to criminal defense six or seven years ago, once there were enough wealthy and connected lawbreakers to keep her in business. Val is willing to relax certain rules because they live thirty miles out to sea and big-city procedure doesn't always apply.

For example, instead of wearing a suit and heels, Val shows up at the station wearing a beach cover-up, a straw hat, and flip-flops.

"I came right from the beach," Val says, and in fact she has sand breading the backs of her legs. "My brother is here with his four kids and his pregnant wife. I wasn't exactly unhappy to be called away." She cocks an eyebrow at the Chief. "Do you ever have houseguests, Ed?"

"Not if I can help it," he says.

"Wise man," Val says. She looks around. "Where's the Greek? I thought he was investigating this case."

That explains Val's prompt arrival more than the houseguests, the Chief thinks. Every woman on this island will jump through hoops of white fire for the Greek.

"He's interviewing a witness at the hospital," the Chief says.

Val nods. "Let me talk to my client."

"He tried to run," the Chief says. "It doesn't look good, Val. You should let him know that."

"Let me talk to my client," Val says again.

*   *   *

While Val is in with Shooter, Ed checks his phone. He sees a text from Nick that says, We need to find a wedding guest named Featherleigh Dale, and the Chief curses under his breath. Here he's liking Shooter Uxley for this and now there's a new person of interest? The Chief calls the Winbury house to speak to Greer.

"We're looking for someone named Featherleigh Dale," he says.

"Yes," Greer says. She sounds unsurprised.

"Do you have any idea where we might find her?" he asks.

"She's staying at an inn," Greer says. "Let me check which one. I have it written down." A moment later she comes back to the phone. "The Sand Dollar Guest House, on Water Street."

"Thank you." The Chief hangs up and dispatches one of his patrolmen to the Sand Dollar to bring this Featherleigh Dale in for questioning.

Nick calls on his way from the hospital to the compound. "Talked to the bride," he says. "She was a gold mine."

"What did she give you?" the Chief asks.

"Our maid of honor wasn't exactly honorable,"

Nick says. "She was sleeping with the groom's father, Tag Winbury."

The Chief closes his eyes. He's so hungry, he's seeing stars—then he remembers that Andrea packed him a lunch: turkey BLT, two ripe, cold plums, a thermos of chilled cucumber-coconut soup. He loves his wife. As soon as he gets off with Nick, he'll eat.

"I talked to Linda Ferretti, the ME," the Chief says. "Victim was seven weeks pregnant."

Nick sucks in his breath and the Chief feels a renewed sense of purpose. This woman's death was no accident. They have a real situation on their hands.

"She was pregnant with Winbury's kid," Nick says. "I wonder who knew. Celeste didn't tell me that. I...I don't think she knew. I wonder if Greer Garrison knew.

"I dispatched Luklo to go pick up Ms. Dale at her inn," the Chief says. "How is she involved?"

"She was sitting under the tent late last night with Merritt, Tag, and Thomas, the groom's brother. The brother, Thomas, went up to bed, leaving Merritt, Tag Winbury, and Featherleigh Dale. She should have something to tell us."

"Yes, we need the Dale woman," the Chief says. "Now that we know what we know. So why am I talking to Shooter Uxley? Why did he run? Where is he in all of this? Why did he, of all people, lawyer up?"

"I guess we'll find out," Nick says. "Who's his attorney?"

"Valerie Gluckstern."

"I like Val," Nick says. "And she likes me."

"Let's hope that works in our favor and we can get the kid to talk," the Chief says. "After I'm finished with Uxley, I'll talk to the father."

"I'll talk to this Dale woman," Nick says. "Once we find her. And, hey, if you need help swaying Val Gluckstern, let me know."

"Thanks, Prince Charming," the Chief says.

Saturday, August 12-Monday, August 21, 2017

CELESTE

She takes a week's vacation from the zoo in August, coordinating with Benji's vacation, and the two of them go to Nantucket.

Merritt says, "You do know how lucky you are, right? Having a rich boyfriend with a huge waterfront home on Nantucket?"

"Right," Celeste says uneasily. She doesn't want anyone — even Merritt — to think she is after Benji for his money. The money makes things nicer and easier. They can go to dinner whenever and wherever they want, they go to concerts and sit in the front row, Benji always treats her to taxis and sends her bouquets of beautiful, exotic flowers, and occasionally she will come home to find he has delivered a box of Pierre Hermé macarons to her doorstep (she had never tasted a macaron before meeting Benji; now, they're one more expensive habit that she's developed). Celeste enjoys these aspects of their relationship — she would be a liar if she denied it — but her favorite things about Benji are that he's kind, thoughtful, solid, steady, and even-keeled.

Despite all this, she had been thinking, right before plans for the vacation were made, of breaking up with him. She likes him but she has been consistently misrepresenting her feelings because she does not love him.

She loves Shooter Uxley.

She has tried to talk herself out of it. How can she love Shooter when she spent only one day with him? After Benji belatedly arrived that weekend in June, Shooter left the island, claiming a work emergency. That Sunday afternoon, once Celeste was back in her own apartment, Shooter had sent her a text that said, I couldn't stay and watch the two of you together.

So, Celeste thought, Shooter had felt it too. He had felt that strong, unmistakable *thing,* that animal attraction. Celeste uses the phrase purposefully because she's a scientist and may understand better than most how human beings are at the mercy of their biology. Celeste thinks of a male lion establishing dominance in a pride or the blue-footed booby showing the female his blue feet by dancing. The natural world is filled with such rituals that can be documented and categorized but ultimately not explained. Celeste can't control her urges or her feelings any better than hyenas or aardvarks; however, she *can* control her behavior. She has no intention of leaving Benji for his best friend. But she knows it's not fair to stay with him when she doesn't love him.

She needs to break it off.

She will break it off, she decides, after they get back from Nantucket.

Saturday, Sunday, Monday: Celeste and Benji lie by the pool, swim in the harbor, eat the finger sandwiches and cubes of melon that Elida brings them on a tray for lunch. In the late afternoon, they go to 167 Raw to buy fresh tuna and swordfish steaks, then they go to Bartlett's Farm for corn, summer squash, greens for salad, a homemade peach pie. In the mornings, they wander the shops in town. At Milly and Grace, Celeste tries on four dresses, and Benji, unable to decide which he likes best on her, buys her all four. That night, Benji takes Celeste out to Sconset to eat at a candlelit table in the garden of the Chanticleer. At the center of the garden stands a carousel horse, and Celeste finds herself staring at the horse throughout dinner.

This week, Shooter is in Saratoga Springs, New York, with a group of tech executives from Belarus; they have gone to see the races. Celeste knows this because Benji keeps her constantly informed about Shooter's whereabouts; Benji shows her every picture Shooter sends him, like a proud uncle. Sometimes he says, jokingly, "I'm boring, but here's my exciting friend." Celeste smiles mildly; she glances at the photos but can't bring herself to focus on Shooter's face. What good would it do? She never responded to Shooter's text. She can't have a secret line of communication with him; she knows where that would lead.

Celeste tears her eyes away from the carousel horse and thoughts of Saratoga and wills herself to be happy. She likes Benji. She cares about Benji.

As she watches Benji sip his wine, she imagines Shooter at the betting window, track pencil behind his ear. She imagines him in the grandstand or the elevated suite with fancy free hors d'oeuvres and scantily clad cocktail waitresses, where only the most important people in the world are allowed to sit. She imagines Shooter's horse pulling ahead on the outside. Shooter has picked the winner again. He high-fives the Belarusians.

"Do you want dessert?" Benji asks. "Celeste?"

Tuesday and Wednesday: Celeste is tan. Celeste is relaxed. Celeste is growing more comfortable with

Benji's parents. One morning, she runs five miles with Tag. The following afternoon she goes to a photography exhibit on Old South Wharf with Greer, and afterward, Celeste suggests they get an Italian ice at the little shop next to the gallery.

"My treat," Celeste says. The ices cost only ten dollars but Celeste leaves the cute red-haired teenager behind the counter a five-dollar tip. Tag and Greer are so generous that it makes Celeste want to be generous on her own scale.

They sit on a bench on the wharf to enjoy their ices in the sun and Greer says, "So, how are things going with you and Benji?"

Celeste isn't sure what Greer is asking. "Everything is fine," she says.

"Tag and I are heading back to the city tomorrow," Greer says. "My friend Elizabeth Calabash's son is getting married at the Plaza."

"Oh," Celeste says. She savors the taste of her passionfruit ice and thinks of how, before she met Benji, she would have stuck to something safe like lemon or raspberry. "That's nice."

"I think Benji would like some alone time with you," Greer says. "Nothing quashes romance like having one's parents around."

"I enjoy your company," Celeste says. It's true. With the elder Winburys in residence, there is a family atmosphere at the house. There are times it feels like she and Benji are siblings. Celeste's greatest dream is that her parents might someday see Nantucket. She tries to describe it in her phone calls, but she can't do it justice, and there are things she knows they won't understand — dining at nine o'clock at night in a garden with a carousel horse, paying seventeen hundred dollars for a photograph, or even passionfruit Italian ice.

Thursday and Friday: Tag and Greer leave late on Thursday. Benji apologizes to Celeste, but he has committed to playing in the member-guest golf tournament at the Nantucket Golf Club, which will eat up most of Friday.

"No problem," Celeste says. She has a new book — *Mrs. Fletcher* by Tom Perrotta — and she looks forward to the time alone. It's not supposed to be this way, she knows.

"I've arranged for a surprise," Benji says. He kisses Celeste. "Shooter is coming."

Celeste blinks and pulls back. "What?" she says. "I thought he was in Saratoga."

"He was," Benji says. "But he has a couple of days free so I asked him to come."

Celeste has no idea what kind of expression crosses her face. Is it one of alarm? Fear? Panic?

"I thought you liked Shooter," Benji says.

"Oh, I do," Celeste says. "I do."

*   *   *

At seven o'clock on Friday morning, Benji pulls away in Tag's Land Rover with his golf clubs in the back. Celeste stands on the front porch and waves until he's gone. Then she steps inside to the entrance hall and studies herself in one of Greer's antique mirrors. She is blond and blue-eyed, pretty but not beautiful, or maybe beautiful but not extraordinary. Is there something she's not seeing? Something inside of her? She likes animals, the environment, the natural world. This has always set her apart, made her less desirable rather than more so. When she was growing up, she was always reading the encyclopedia or *National Geographic,* and when she wasn't doing that, she was collecting snakes and salamanders in shoe boxes and trying to re-create their natural habitat. She wasn't interested in boy bands or wearing friendship bracelets or roller-blading or shopping for CDs and hair clips at the mall, just as now she doesn't care about gender politics or social media or bingeing on Netflix or going to barre class or who wore what to the Met Ball. She is atypical. She is weird.

Shooter is coming. She's not sure what to do. Proceed as normal? She changes into her bathing suit, grabs her new book, and goes out to the pool.

When she wakes up with the book splayed open on her chest, she finds Shooter sitting on the next chaise with his elbow on his knee, his chin in his hand, staring at her.

No, she's dreaming. She closes her eyes.

"Sunshine."

Opens her eyes.

"Hi," he says. He grins. "Benji called to say you needed looking after."

"I don't," she snaps. She refuses to flirt with him. She refuses to be *complicit* in this. It's as though Benji is *trying* to lose her, handing her off to Shooter once again. "You should have stayed in Saratoga."

"You're sexy when you're stern," Shooter says. "And I was happy to come, I wanted to come. All I've wanted since I left the last time was to see you again."

"Shooter," she says.

"You must think I'm a real bastard," he says. "Going after my best friend's girl. People write songs about this very scenario, Celeste—Rick Springfield, the Cars. And do you know why? Because it happens. It happens all the time."

"But why *me?*" Celeste says. It's amazing enough that she won the devotion of Benjamin Winbury, but to have Shooter's attention too seems so inconceivable that she wonders if it's a trick or a joke. Men like Benji and Shooter should be chasing after women like Merritt. Merritt is an influencer; she has power, clout, and she knows everyone. She is connected, savvy, witty, a social genius. Celeste, meanwhile, writes e-mails to other zoo administrators about improving the orangutan habitat.

"Because you're real," Shooter says. "You're so normal and down-to-earth that you're exotic. There is no pretense with you, Celeste. Any idea how rare that is these days? And I had such a good time with you here. I haven't enjoyed a woman's company that much ever before in my life. It's like you cast a spell on me. When Benji asked me to come, I didn't think twice."

"Benji is my boyfriend," Celeste says. "Nothing is going to happen between you and me."

Shooter gives her a laser stare with his sapphire-blue eyes. "Hearing you say that makes me like you even more. Benji is the better choice."

Benji is *the better choice!* Celeste thinks. She wonders if Shooter is motivated by envy. He wants what Benji has—his parents, his pedigree, and now his girlfriend. Probably that's it. Celeste turns her eyes back to her book, hoping Mrs. Fletcher can save her.

"Put your shorts and flip-flops on," Shooter says. "I'm taking you somewhere."

"Where?" Celeste says.

"I'll meet you out front," he says.

Shooter has rented a silver Jeep. He tells Celeste he asked for the exact same one they had before, and when Celeste sits in the passenger seat, she does indeed feel a strong sense of familiarity, like this is their car, like they belong in it.

Shooter drives out to the Surfside Beach Shack. "I was wrong about the tomato sandwich," he says. He climbs out of the Jeep and returns a few moments later with a cardboard box that holds two sandwiches wrapped in foil and two drinks. "These are the best sandwiches on the island, possibly the world." They proceed all the way to the end of Madaket Road, cross a small wooden bridge, and enter what looks like a seaside village from another era. The houses are teensy-tiny beach shacks with funky architectural details: a suspended deck that joins two roof-lines, a slant-roofed tower, a row of round porthole windows. These are nothing like the elegant castles out in Monomoy. These are like beach cottages for elves, and they all have funny names: Duck Inn, It'll Do, Breaking Away.

"They're so small," Celeste says. "How do people actually live in them?"

"The best living is done outside," Shooter says. "And look at the location — they're right on the water."

Celeste nearly points out that the Winburys' house is right on the water, but she understands the inherent charm of these homes. There are brightly striped towels draped over railings and hibachi grills on the decks; the "front yards" are sand and a tangle of *Rosa rugosa* bushes. How idyllic life would be out here. You spent all day at the beach, rinsed off under the outdoor shower, grilled a striped bass that you had caught yourself surf-casting a hundred yards away. At night, your neighbors wandered over to share an ice-cold beer or a gin and tonic while you all gazed up at the stars and listened to the pounding surf. Rainy days would mean cards, board games, or a good paperback mystery read in a comfortable old chair.

Shooter crouches down to let some of the air out of the Jeep's tires; Celeste watches him from her perch in the passenger seat. She studies the back of his neck, the shape of his ears. When he works on the back tires she trains her eyes on him in her side-view mirror. He looks up, catches her, blows her a kiss. She wants to scowl, but instead, she smiles.

Celeste and Shooter drive up over the dunes. The stark natural beauty of Smith's Point is staggering. There's a long stretch of pristine beach in front of them with the ocean to the left and dunes carpeted in eelgrass to the right. Beyond those dunes is the flat blue surface of Nantucket Sound.

Shooter is taking it slow — five miles an hour — so he can easily reach over to the glove compartment, grazing Celeste's knee with the back of his hand as he does so. He pulls out a guide to eastern shorebirds.

"For my zoologist," he says.

Celeste wants to correct him — she isn't *his* anything — but she becomes instantly enthralled by the guidebook. She has always loved ornithology, although it requires more patience than she has been naturally gifted with to pursue as a specialty. Still, she loves to visit the World of Birds and talk to Vern, their resident ornithologist. Vern has sighted over seven thousand of the world's ten thousand bird species, a life list that puts him in a very elite category of bird-watcher. Vern's best stories often aren't about the birds themselves but rather about the travels he has undertaken in order to see them. When he was only eighteen, he hitchhiked from Oxford, Mississippi, to the Monteverde Cloud Forest in Costa Rica to see the resplendent quetzal. He has been to Gambia to see the African gray hornbill and to Antarctica to see the Adélie penguin.

Right away, Celeste points out the sandpiper and the American oystercatcher with its signature orange beak. Shooter laughs and says, "You delight me." He drives out to the tip of Smith's Point — Celeste sees the much smaller island of Tuckernuck across a narrow channel — and then he curves around to the far side of the point. He sets up a camp — a chair for each of them, an umbrella for shade, towels, and a small table, where he lays out their lunch. He shucks off his polo shirt. Celeste tries not to notice the muscles of his back.

"Watch this," he says. He wades out into the water a few feet and then he must drop off a ledge or a shelf because suddenly he is in up to his chest. He lifts his hands in the air, and the water whooshes him down the shore. "Yee-haw!" he cries out. About forty yards down, he climbs out of the water and jogs back to Celeste. "It's a natural water slide," he says. "You have to try it."

Celeste can't resist. Her parents took her to Great Wolf Lodge every summer of her growing up; she has never met a water slide she didn't love. She wades in, her feet feeling for the edge of the shelf. Then she jumps in and the current carries her down the coastline.

It's exhilarating! It's hilarious! Celeste hasn't laughed or enjoyed herself this much since she was a child with her father, going down Coyote Canyon.

"How did you know this was here?" she asks Shooter, breathless.

Shooter says, "It's my business to know the secrets of every universe."

"I want to go again," Celeste says.

The film montage starts once more: Here are Celeste and Shooter riding the current down the beach again and again and again, whooping like rodeo cowboys. Celeste can't get enough; the water is swift, powerful, alive. Shooter gives up first, and finally Celeste declares she is going only one more time. Here are Shooter and Celeste eating their sandwiches — a crab, shrimp, and scallop "burger," topped with avocado, bacon, lettuce, tomato, and a creamy dill and smoked-pepper aioli. And to drink they have fresh water-melon limcades. It's the most delicious lunch Celeste has ever eaten. Is this hyperbole? She doesn't think so, though she realizes the sandwich and the drink are only part of it. The swimming is also part of it, the sand, the view…and Shooter. Celeste is so exhausted after eating that she spreads out a towel and lies facedown. Shooter follows suit, and when Celeste wakes up, his leg is touching hers. Celeste doesn't want to move, but move she must.

At five o'clock, when they drive off the beach, Celeste's skin is tight from the sun, and her blond hair is stiff with salt. She figures she must look a fright, but when she catches a glimpse of herself in the side-view mir-ror, what she sees is a young woman who is happy. She has never, in her life, been *this* happy.

"Hey, Sunshine?" Shooter says.

"Please don't," she says. She doesn't want him to say anything that's going to ruin it. She doesn't want him to make any declarations. She doesn't want him to try to name what is happening. They both know what's happening.

Shooter laughs. "I was just going to ask if you

wanted to stop at Millie's on the way home? Get a margarita?"

"Yes," she says.

As soon as Shooter pulls into the parking lot at Millie's, his phone starts to ping, and so does Celeste's. Shooter cocks an eyebrow at her. "Check our phones?" he asks. "Or ignore them?"

Ignore them, Celeste thinks. But out of habit, she glances at her display. There are three texts from Benji.

I'm back.

Where are you guys?

Hello?

Celeste feels like she's suspended in midair. What should she do? She wants to go into Millie's with Shooter, order a margarita, maybe knock legs with him under the bar.

But that kind of misbehavior is beyond her.

"We need to go," she says.

Back at Summerland, Benji is on the deck, wearing a coat and tie. He has a bottle of vintage Veuve Clicquot chilling in an ice bucket. He stares pointedly at Shooter.

"You're late," he says.

"Late?" Celeste says. "Were you expecting us earlier? I thought you were golfing."

Shooter says, "Sorry, man, I lost track of time."

Something passes between Benji and Shooter. Celeste is afraid to ask what's going on.

"Should I shower?" Celeste says.

"Yes," Benji says. He kisses her. "Wear the new pink dress. We're going out."

Celeste goes upstairs to shower and change. She puts on a green dress instead of the pink, a small but important defiance. She hates when Benji tries to control her; she knows he thinks he's the Professor Henry Higgins to her Eliza Doolittle. But he's not. She's an intelligent adult; she can pick her own dress.

She is suddenly in an incredibly foul humor. She doesn't even want to go to dinner.

She peers down at the deck from her bedroom window. The champagne remains in the ice bucket—but Benji and Shooter are gone.

There is a whisper of a noise and Celeste turns to see a slip of paper slide under the bedroom door. She freezes. She hears footsteps retreating. After a few moments pass, she tiptoes over to pick up the paper. It says: *In case you have any doubts, I'm in love with you.* The handwriting is unfamiliar. It's not Benji's.

Celeste clutches the note to her chest and sits on the bed. This is either the most wonderful or the most horrible thing ever to happen to her.

"Celeste!"

Benji is calling up the stairs for her. Celeste crumples the note. What should she do with it? She reads it one more time, then she flushes it down the toilet.

"Coming!" she says.

Shooter has changed into Nantucket Reds, a white shirt, a double-breasted blue blazer, and a captain's hat that Celeste had noticed hanging on a hook in the Winburys' mudroom but that she assumed was just a prop of sorts.

"Nice hat!" Celeste says. Shooter doesn't crack a smile.

Benji leads Celeste out to the end of the Winburys' dock, where a boat is waiting. It's *Ella,* the Winburys' Hinckley picnic boat. It's so sleek and beautiful with its gleaming wood and pristine navy-and-white cushioned benches that Celeste is afraid to climb aboard. Shooter gets on first and offers his hand to Celeste. She wants to squeeze his hand to let him know she got his note and she feels the same way — but she is afraid of Benji noticing.

She and Benji settle in the back while Shooter takes the wheel. Benji opens the champagne, fills two waiting flutes, and hands one to Celeste.

"Cheers," he says.

"Cheers," Celeste says. She clinks glasses with Benji and forces herself to make eye contact with him. Every second is a struggle to keep her gaze off

Shooter in the captain's chair. "Is Shooter not having any?"

"Shooter is not having any," Benji says. "He's our skipper tonight."

"Where are we going?" Celeste asks.

"You'll see," Benji says.

Celeste leans back in her seat but she can't relax. Shooter is at the wheel in that ridiculous hat; it's almost as if Benji has set out to humiliate him. But maybe she's overreacting. Maybe Shooter offered to drive the boat; maybe he likes it. It is a stunner of an evening, the air clear and mild, the water of the harbor a mirror that reflects the rich golden light of the sun behind them. Other boaters wave as they pass. One gentleman calls out, "Beautiful," and Benji calls back, "Isn't she?" and kisses Celeste.

Celeste says, "I'm sure he was talking about the boat."

"The boat, you, me, this incredible night," Benji says.

Right, Celeste thinks. From a distance, they must seem like the most fortunate, privileged couple in the world. No one would ever guess Celeste's private torment.

She sips her champagne. Benji wraps his arm around her and pulls her in close. "I missed you," he says.

"How was golf?" she asks. He doesn't answer, which is just as well.

They dock at the Wauwinet Inn. Shooter is surprisingly skilled with the ropes and knots, making Celeste wonder at his other hidden talents. Playing the harmonica? Shooting a bow and arrow? Skiing moguls? He secures the boat and then helps Celeste up onto the dock. Benji climbs up behind Celeste and checks his watch. "We'll be back at nine o'clock," he tells Shooter.

"Wait a minute," Celeste says. Her heart feels like it's being squeezed. She turns to Shooter. "Aren't you coming to dinner?"

Shooter smiles but his blue eyes are as flat as eyes in a painting. "I'll be here when you're finished," he says.

Celeste wobbles in her wedge heels. She's unsteady in heels on a good day, never mind on a dock under the present circumstances. Benji takes her arm and leads her down the dock to the hotel.

When they are out of earshot, Celeste says, "I don't get it. Why isn't Shooter coming to dinner?"

"Because I want to have a romantic dinner with my girlfriend," Benji says. For the first time since she has known him, he sounds petulant, like one of the cranky children who are at the zoo past their nap time. This show of unexpected attitude provokes Celeste.

"So, what, you just *hired* him to drive the boat? He's our *friend,* Benji. He's not your servant."

Benji says, "I should have realized you would find this scenario unjust. But when I told Shooter my plans to bring you up here, he offered. He's going to grab dinner in the bar."

"By himself?" Celeste says.

"It's Shooter," Benji says. "I'm sure he'll make some friends."

Dinner at Topper's is an extraordinary experience, with attention given to every detail. Drinks are brought on a tiered cocktail tray; Benji's gin and tonic is mixed at the table with a glass swizzle stick. The bread basket features warm, fragrant rosemary focaccia, homemade bacon-and-sage rolls, and twisted cheddar-garlic bread sticks that look like the branches of a tree in an enchanted forest. Under other circumstances, Celeste would be committing all this to memory so she could describe it for her parents later, but she is preoccupied with the one sentence written on the note that was slipped under her door. *In case you have any doubts, I'm in love with you.*

Their appetizers arrive under silver domes. The

server lifts both domes at once with a theatrical flourish. The food is artwork—vegetables are cut to resemble jewels; sauces are painted across plates. Benji ordered a wine that is apparently so rare and amazing, it made the sommelier stammer.

Celeste doesn't care. Shooter's absence is more powerful than Benji's presence. She does a desultory job on her appetizer—summer vegetables with stracciatella cheese—then excuses herself for the ladies' room.

On her way, she walks past a window that opens onto an intimate enclave that has five seats at a mahogany bar, a television showing the Red Sox game, and a handful of tables with high-backed rattan chairs. The bar has a clubby, colonial British feel that is a little cozier and more casual than the dining room.

Shooter is sitting at the bar alone, drinking a martini.

Celeste stares at Shooter's back and does a gut check. Talk to him or leave him be? *Talk to him!* She will tell him she feels the same way, and then later they can make a plan to be together without hurting Benji. But before Celeste sets foot in the bar, a woman appears. She's wearing black pants, a black apron, a white shirt open at the collar. *Oh, she's the bartender,* Celeste thinks with relief. She's quite attractive, with short, dark, bobbed hair, cat's-eye glasses, and dark red lipstick. She approaches Shooter and he gives her a hug, then pulls her into his lap and starts tickling her. She shrieks with laughter—through the closed door, Celeste can just barely hear it—and just as Celeste's emotions are curdling into hurt and rage, the bartender stands up, straightens her apron, and gets back to work.

Celeste slams into the ladies' room, startling a woman applying her lipstick at the sink.

When Celeste returns to the table, Benji stands up. *He is a gentleman,* she thinks. And she will never have to worry about him.

Between dinner and dessert—they have ordered the soufflé, which takes extra time to prepare—Benji pulls something out of his coat pocket. It's a small box. Celeste stares at the box almost without seeing it.

She realizes she knew this was coming.

"I didn't go golfing today," Benji says. "I flew back to the city to pick up a little something." He opens the box to reveal the most insanely beautiful diamond ring Celeste has ever seen.

She bobs her head at the ring once, as if being formally introduced to it.

"Will you marry me, Celeste?" Benji asks.

Celeste's eyes fill with tears. Not only did *she* know this was coming but Shooter did too. And yet he *still* took her to Smith's Point, *still* showed her how to ride the current, *still* bought her a birding book, *still* called her Sunshine, and *still* made her feel like she was, in fact, the brightest light in the sky. And then he slipped that note under her door.

In case you have any doubts.

He didn't mean in case Celeste had any doubts about him. He meant in case Celeste had any doubts about marrying Benji.

I'm in love with you.

Shooter is a gambler. He's throwing the dice to see if he can win. It's a game to him, she tells herself. His feelings aren't real.

With her napkin, she blots the tears that drip down her cheeks. She can't look at Benji because if she does, he'll see they are tears of confusion, but right now he must be assuming—or hoping—that they are tears of overwhelmed joy.

The whole thing is a mess, a giant, emotionally tangled mess, and Celeste has half a mind to stand up and walk out on both men. She will get herself home, back to Easton, back to her parents.

Celeste thinks of Shooter pulling the sexy, bespectacled bartender into his lap, his wicked grin, his fingers tickling the other woman's ribs. Celeste would have a miserable life with Shooter. Her feelings for him are too strong; they would be her undoing. A better, wiser choice is to marry Benji. Celeste will continue to be who she has always been: The center of someone else's universe. Beloved.

"Yes," Celeste whispers. "Yes, I will marry you."

When Benji and Celeste arrive back at the boat, Shooter is waiting. He has the gleam of a martini or three in his eyes. His hair is mussed; there is a smudge of the bartender's red lipstick on his cheek.

In case you have any doubts, I'm in love with you.

"So how'd it *go?*" Shooter asks with corny enthusiasm. *It might have been more like five martinis,* Celeste thinks. Shooter's words are slurred. Benji will have to drive the boat home.

Celeste holds out her left hand. "We're engaged."

Shooter locks eyes with her. *You lost,* she thinks, gloating for a second. But then she corrects herself. They both lost.

"Well," he says. "Congratulations."

Benji insists that Celeste call her parents on the boat ride home, but strangely, they don't answer. It's even stranger when Benji tells her that he spoke to both Bruce and Karen earlier in the week, told them his intentions, asked for their blessing. They were over the moon, he says.

Celeste leaves a message on the answering machine

asking them to call her back. She doesn't hear from them at all on Saturday. When she calls again on Sunday morning, her father answers, but something is wrong. Her father is crying.

"Daddy?" Celeste says. She holds out hope for one second that he's weeping sentimentally over news of the engagement.

"It's your mother," he says.

Saturday, July 7, 2018,
1:12 p.m.

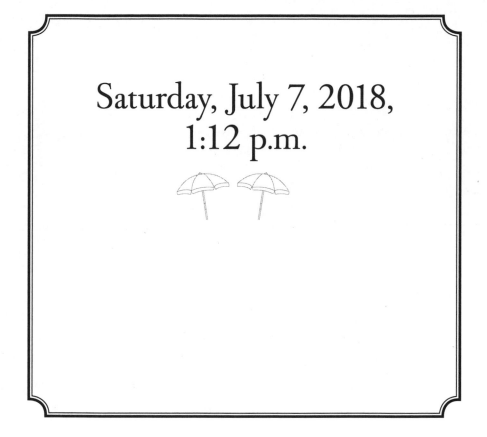

NANTUCKET

As the day unfolds, news about the Murdered Maid of Honor spreads across the island. Because nobody knows what happened, everything and anything becomes a possibility.

A group of New York Millennial women having lunch and cocktails at Cru are told the news by their server, Ryan.

"As if being maid of honor isn't hard enough," says Zoe Stanton, a store manager at Opening Ceremony.

"Maid of honor," a PR associate named Sage Kennedy murmurs. A bell goes off in Sage's head. "What was the woman's name?"

"Not yet released," says Lauren Doherty, a physical therapist at the Hospital for Special Surgery.

Sage pulls her phone out despite her resolution not to use it at meals (unless she's dining alone). She is pretty sure she follows someone on Instagram who was serving as a maid of honor at a wedding on Nantucket this weekend.

She gasps. It's Merritt. Merritt Monaco.

Sage gets a chill that starts at her feet and travels up her spine to the base of her brain. Once upon a time, Sage and Merritt worked together at a PR firm called Brightstreet, owned by Travis and Cordelia Darling. Merritt had an extremely ill-advised affair with Travis Darling and when Cordelia found out— well, Sage had never seen anyone so hell-bent on exacting revenge. She'd *cringed* as she listened to Cordelia bad-mouth Merritt to absolutely every single one of their clients, calling her *disgusting* names. Cordelia even contacted Merritt's parents. Her *parents,* as though Cordelia were the high-school principal and Merritt had been caught setting a fire in the cafeteria. With Merritt's dismissal, Sage's own position in the company improved; she was, essentially, given all of Merritt's responsibilities. Another girl might have delighted in the career-ending poor decisions of the person directly above her—but Sage just felt bad. She suspected that the affair had been Travis Darling's fault. He was creepy.

Sage had wanted to contact Merritt after the smoke cleared, but she was afraid of going behind Cordelia's back. When Cordelia announced that she was moving the business to Los Angeles, Sage took the sparkling reference and robust severance package and immediately found another job. She texted Merritt with news of Cordelia's departure, and Merritt had responded: Thanks for letting me know.

They hadn't become friends, by any means, but Sage kept a cyber-eye on Merritt. She followed her on Instagram under an account with a made-up name — which was strange, she realized, but less complicated than following, liking, and commenting as her real self. She found herself cheering Merritt on as she got a new job at the Wildlife Conservation Society and started stumping for Parker and Young, Fabulous, and Broke, as well as nearly every hot restaurant and club that opened south of Fourteenth Street.

There had been recent posts about Merritt's upcoming maid-of-honor duty this weekend on Nantucket. Earlier this week, Merritt had posted a photo of herself modeling her bridesmaid dress — it was antique-ivory silk with black embroidery on the bodice, meant to look like classic scrimshaw, which Sage thought was such a *cool idea* — with the caption: *Tonight I am Nantucket-bound. #MOH #weddingoftheyear #BFF.*

Had someone murdered *Merritt?*

Sage stared down at her lobster roll and her full glass of Rock Angel rosé, her appetite for lunch gone. Who would want to kill Merritt?

Cordelia, she thinks. She sips her rosé for fortitude and wonders if it's remotely possible that Cordelia came to Nantucket, somehow infiltrated the wedding festivities — maybe dressing up as one of the catering crew — and got to Merritt that way. Absurd? Only happens in the movies? Normally, Sage would think that, but she will forever be haunted by the vitriol she had seen emanating from Cordelia Darling in the days following her discovery of the affair.

Cordelia is in Los Angeles, Sage tells herself. There is no reason for her to celebrate the Fourth of July week on Nantucket; the West Coast has its own beaches.

Sage puts her phone away and smiles at her friends. It might not even be Merritt, she thinks. She follows Lauren's gaze out the open sides of the restaurant. The vista is nothing short of spectacular: sparkling blue harbor, sailboats, seagulls, the bluffs of Shawkemo in the distance. How could anything bad ever happen here?

The Murdered Maid of Honor is all anyone is talking about across town at the Greydon House on Broad Street. Heather Clymer, who is staying with her husband, Steve, in room 2, has just gotten back from the Hospital Thrift Shop, where she heard the whole story from one of the volunteers. Heather brought the story back to the Greydon House, where it spread like a virus: the maid of honor in a big, fancy wedding

out in Monomoy was found early that morning floating in the harbor, and both local and state authorities
suspect foul play.

Laney and Casper Morris are standing by the
hotel's front desk and are just about to head down the
street to the Nantucket Whaling Museum when they
hear the news. Laney digs her fingernails into Casper's
forearm.

"Ouch," Casper says. He's already a bit irritated
with Laney for making him go to the Whaling
Museum on such a gorgeous, sunny day, the final day
of their vacation. They should be headed to the beach!
The Whaling Museum isn't going anywhere; they
can tour it when they're old.

"A big, fancy wedding out in Monomoy?" Laney
says. She pulls Casper back into their elegantly
appointed room, where Casper collapses on the bed,
grateful for the delay in their day's agenda. "The maid
of honor was found floating. She's dead. You know
whose wedding that is, right? Out in Monomoy?"

"Benji's?" Casper guesses. He knows this is the
right answer; it's basically all Laney has been talking
about this week because Laney's best friend is Jules
Briar, Benji's ex-girlfriend. Casper isn't a big fan of
Jules and he knows the friendship wears on Laney as
well, but she and Jules have known each other since
first grade at Spence and some habits are hard to
break. Jules somehow discovered that Benji was

getting married this weekend on Nantucket, and when Jules learned that Laney and Casper would be on the island as well, she implored Laney to keep an eye out and report back. Jules is insanely jealous of Benji's fiancée, *whom he had met when Benji and Jules took Miranda to the zoo!*

Laney had done exactly as Jules asked. Last night, when they were standing in line at the Juice Bar, Laney had seen Shooter Uxley, Benji's best friend, outside of Steamboat Pizza. He was with a blond woman. Laney took a picture of Shooter and the blonde and texted it to Jules.

Jules responded immediately. That's her! That's zoo woman! Benji's fiancée!

They texted back and forth about why the fiancée—Celeste Otis, her name was; Jules had done the requisite stalking—was getting pizza with Shooter instead of Benji. Then they texted about how much they missed Shooter. He had been so much fun.

Now Laney says, "The maid of honor was killed. Poor Benji!"

"Maybe Benji did it," Casper says, and then he laughs because Benjamin Winbury is one of the nicest guys to ever walk the planet, so nice that Casper used to give him a hard time for making the rest of the male population look bad. And, too, Casper has had his own murderous thoughts about some of

Laney's friends; the subject of their present conversation ranks at the top of the list.

"If it were the bride who had died," Laney says, "I would have suspected Jules."

"Damn straight," Casper says.

Laney sighs. "It's sobering, you know. Thinking someone our age could die just like that."

Casper reaches out to his wife. "Hey," he says. "Don't let it get to you. We don't know what happened."

"Life is so short." Laney smiles at Casper. "Forget the Whaling Museum," she says. "Let's go to the beach."

Benjamin Winbury is sequestered in his father's study with his father and his brother.

Intellectually, Benji understands that Merritt is dead, that she drowned out front, but he can't quite come to terms with this new reality. His mind won't switch over to *Merritt is dead*. He is stalled, stuck, in *Merritt is alive and the wedding will go ahead as scheduled at four o'clock*. His tuxedo is hanging up in the closet, and in the breast pocket of the jacket are the rings, which Benji was going to hand over to Shooter along with Shooter's best-man gift, a pair of monogrammed cuff links. He still has things to check off on his to-do list, such as setting up a boat trip and a spa day for Celeste once they get to Santorini, but now his procrastination doesn't matter. The wedding has been canceled.

Of course the wedding has been canceled. There was no question of going forward with a wedding when Celeste's best friend was found dead.

Benji is experiencing a host of very confusing emotions. He is upset, shocked, and horrified just like everyone else. And yet also mixed in there are anger and resentment. It's his *wedding day!* His parents have gone to enormous effort and expense to make this wedding unforgettable and now it's *all for naught.* But aside from the predictable shallow complaint that the happiest day of Benji's life has turned out to be tragic and chaotic, there is a deeper sadness that he won't be entering into a lifelong commitment with the woman he loves beyond all comprehension.

He has been influenced enough by Celeste that he now occasionally thinks in wildlife metaphors. Celeste is like a rare butterfly that Benji was somehow able to capture. That comparison is, no doubt, inappropriate on many different levels, but that's how he thinks of her in his private mind where no one can judge him, that she's like an exotic bird or butterfly. If he takes that imagery further, then marrying her is akin to putting her in a cage or pinning her to a board. She was supposed to be *his.*

What Merritt's death has brought to light, however, is that Celeste belongs only to herself.

She was the one who found Merritt. With Roger's help, Celeste pulled Merritt's body from the water. She was hysterical, beyond talking to, beyond consoling. She couldn't breathe, and Roger and the paramedics had wisely decided to take Celeste to the hospital where they could get her calmed down.

Benji waited two hours before he went to see her in order to give her time and space to process what had happened, but when he arrived to pick her up, their conversation had not gone the way he expected it to.

She had been in bed, woozy from the Valium, her eyelids fluttering open when he walked in the room. He sat at her bedside, took her hand, and said, *I'm so sorry.*

She shook her head and said, *It's my fault.*

For reasons he could not explain, this answer had unleashed a mighty fury within him. He thought Celeste was blaming herself for having an oceanfront wedding, for asking Merritt to be her maid of honor, for bringing her here to Nantucket. And Benji's response to this came flying out: *She was lucky to be here, lucky she had a friend like you, she didn't deserve you, wasn't worthy of you, Celeste. And furthermore, she probably did this to herself! You told me once that she stockpiled pills and considered suicide, so what's to say that's not what this is? She orchestrated this to ruin our big day!*

Celeste had closed her eyes and Benji thought the sedative had reclaimed her but then she spoke. *I can't believe you just said that. You blame Merritt. You think this is* her *fault. Because you've never liked her. You thought she was a bad influence. But she was my* friend, *Benji. She was the friend I'd been looking for* my entire life. *She accepted me, she loved me, she took care of me. If I hadn't met Merritt when I did, I might have left New York. I might have gone back to Easton and worked at the zoo in Trexlertown. I might never have met you. You blame Merritt because you can't imagine a scenario where maybe someone in your house, someone in your family, made a very, very grave mistake. You think your family is beyond reproach. But you're wrong.*

What are you talking about? Benji asked.

You'll find out soon enough, Celeste said. *But right now I'd like you to leave. I want to talk to the police. Alone.*

What? Benji said. *What about your parents? Do they even know? They were still in their room when I left.*

I've called my father, Celeste said. *Now, please, go.*

Benji had been incredulous, but he could see by the set of her jaw that she was serious.

Benji stood to go. He knew there was no point broaching the topic of getting married in Greece or rescheduling the wedding for August. Merritt's death had changed things. He'd lost Celeste.

*   *   *

Now he's left to pace Tag's study, asking the same question over and over again of his father and brother.

"What *happened?*" Benji had gone to bed after they all got back from town last night. But Thomas and Tag stayed up. "Right?" Benji asks. *"Right?"*

"Right," Tag says. "It was Thomas, myself, Merritt, and Featherleigh."

"What were you guys doing?" Benji asks.

Thomas shrugs. "Drinking."

"Drinking what?" Benji asks. "Scotch?"

"Rum," Tag says. "I just wanted to finish my cigar, enjoy the evening. I was sitting in peace with your brother until Merritt and Featherleigh joined us."

"Where did they come from?" Benji asks.

"They'd clearly met at the party and hit it off," Tag says. "They came out of the house chatting like soul sisters. Like Thelma and Louise."

"Abby called me up to bed shortly after those two sat down with us," Thomas says. He holds up his palms. "I literally have *nothing* to do with this. I barely knew Merritt. But she had that look. You know the look? She was trouble."

"Amen," Tag whispers.

"Did Merritt seem really drunk?" Benji asks. "Did it seem like she was on something?"

"You need to relax, bro," Thomas says. "The police will sort this out."

The police, Benji thinks. That's why the three of them are holed up in his father's study; they're waiting to be questioned by the police. The study smells like tobacco and peat and it's filled with antiques—sextants, barometers, prints of long-ago British naval victories. Most men find Tag's study intriguing; Benji finds it obnoxious. Although, under the circumstances, it makes a serviceable bunker, and Benji could use a drink.

"Pour me a Glenmorangie?" he asks his father.

"Before you talk to the police?" Tag asks. "Is that wise?"

"Nantucket Police, intimidating bunch," Thomas says. "I'll pour it." He heads over to the bar. "If they suspected Benji, they would have questioned him first."

"Suspected *me?*" Benji says. This isn't something that has crossed his mind. "Why would they suspect me?" At that moment, there's a knock on the study door, and Benji's heart somersaults in fear. *Do* the police suspect him?

Tag strides across the room to open the door. His father looks respectable in a white polo shirt and a pair of dark madras shorts, but Benji and Thomas are still in the gym shorts and T-shirts they slept in.

It's Reverend Derby at the door. All three Winbury men exhale a sigh of relief. The reverend embraces Tag.

"I came to see if I can help," the reverend says.

Benji can't handle any talk of God right now. He isn't in the mood to hear that this was part of God's plan, nor does he want to debate the question of whether it was a suicide and what that might mean for Merritt's soul.

"What's going on out there?" Tag asks Reverend Derby. "Is there any news?"

"No one has said anything directly to me," the reverend says. "But I overheard someone saying that the medical examiner found a sedative in the young woman's bloodstream. She must have gone swimming for some reason and then just passed out."

A sedative, Benji thinks. *Bingo.* Merritt took an Ambien and went into that well-documented twilight state where her brain was shutting down though her body was still awake. She went out for a late-night swim and she drowned.

Reverend Derby claps Benji on the shoulder. "How are you holding up, young man?"

Benji shrugs. He sees no point in lying to Reverend Derby. He is like part of the family, as close as an uncle. Most of Benji's memories of him are secular. Reverend Derby comes each year to the Winburys' anglicized Thanksgiving; he goes with Tag to Yankee games; he has spent many weekends here on

Nantucket; he attended Thomas's and Benji's graduations from high school, college, grad school. Having Reverend Derby around always lent the family a certain moral authority, although none of the four Winburys is particularly religious. Or Benji isn't. He understands he can't speak for anyone else's interior life, but his life has been so blessed—up to this point—that he has had no *need* for religion.

"I'm mostly concerned for Celeste," he says. "This has blindsided her."

Reverend Derby looks at him with his watery blue eyes but knows better than to speak. He lifts his hand from Benji's shoulder. "I'm going to give you your privacy. Just know I'm here if you need me."

Tag shakes Reverend Derby's hand as he shows him the door.

Thomas says, "Scotch."

Benji and Thomas are each a drink and a half in when there's another knock at the door. Again, Tag stands to answer. Again, Benji's heart reacts like a pit bull straining on a chain.

It's Benji's mother.

"May I come in?" she asks Tag. Her voice is arch. Benji knows she doesn't like the way Tag guards the privacy of his study. It makes her suspicious, she says.

Tag holds the door open and extends a hand. Greer

walks in. She, too, is dressed appropriately, in a pair of white pants and a linen tank the color of whole-wheat bread. Her hair is up in a chignon and she is wearing lipstick. Celeste would be offended, Benji suspects, that Greer saw fit to put on lipstick this morning, but Greer is a certain kind of British woman who wouldn't want the strangers in the house—the police, the forensics experts, the detective—to see her without makeup, no matter the circumstances.

"Mom?" he says. He believes in his mother's ability to somehow make this situation bearable.

"Oh, Benny," she says. She uses his long-abandoned childhood nickname. It hits the right note; he knows she loves him. She squeezes him so tightly he can feel her bones and her beating heart. When she pulls away, she looks right at him and he can feel her trying to shore him up. If anyone's hopes and dreams have been razed as much as his by the wedding going up in smoke, it's Greer's. And yet she seems to be processing the turn of events with mournful dignity, exactly as she should.

"Have you talked to the Otises?" he asks. "Celeste said she called her father."

"They haven't emerged from their room," Greer says. "I had Elida deliver a tray with lunch, but I'm sure they're too upset to eat much." She eyes the tumblers of scotch on the coffee table. "Have you boys eaten anything?"

"No," Benji says.

"I could eat," Thomas says.

Greer looks at him sharply. "Well. There are sandwiches in the kitchen."

"What's going on, exactly?" Tag asks. "We're still waiting to speak to the detectives."

"I had my interview with the fellow from the state police," Greer says. "I daresay, he has it in for me—"

"For *you?*" Benji says.

Greer waves a hand. "I'm not sure what they're thinking. The Nantucket Chief just called to ask what inn Featherleigh is staying at."

"Featherleigh?" Thomas says. "What the hell does *she* have to do with anything?"

"Well," Tag says, "she *was* the last person to see Merritt."

"Was she?" Greer asks.

"She was?" Thomas says.

Tag turns away from all of them and goes to pour his own scotch at the bar cart. "I believe so," he says, looking into his glass before drinking. "Yes."

"Wasn't Featherleigh with you?" Greer asks. She sounds more interested than accusatory. "Didn't you take her out for a ride in the kayak?"

"Featherleigh?" Thomas says. "Why would Dad take Featherleigh out for a ride in the kayak? She's hardly the seafaring type."

"I didn't take Featherleigh out in the kayak," Tag says.

"You didn't?" Greer says.

"I didn't," Tag says.

"You took *someone* out for a kayak," Greer says. "The kayak, the two-person kayak, was left overturned on the beach. With only one oar. And we all know nobody else used it."

Benji sinks into one of the leather club chairs and throws back what's left of his scotch. He doesn't like where this is headed. Here is his nuclear family, his parents and his older brother. They are the Winburys, a very fortunate group, not only because of their money, position, and advantages, but also because, by the standards of today, they are "normal." A happy, normal family; a family, he would have said, without secrets or drama.

But now he's not so sure.

He speaks to the room. "Who did you take out in the kayak, Dad?" He thinks back to what Celeste said, that someone in his family had made a very, very grave mistake.

Benji stands up. "Dad?"

Tag is facing the bar cart. He has one hand on his glass and one hand wrapped around the neck of the Glenmorangie. Greer is watching him. Thomas is watching him. They're all waiting for an answer.

His voice is barely a whisper but his words and tone are clear.

"Merritt," he says. "I took Merritt out in the kayak."

KAREN

Karen wakes up with a start. The sunlight is pouring through the windows, bright and lemony. She was supposed to be up at eight thirty to help Celeste get ready, but she can tell it's much later than that. She reaches over to check her phone. It's half past noon.

Karen shrieks and sits up in bed. Bizarrely, there's no pain. No pain? Her last oxy was late last night, but still, that was twelve hours ago. On a normal day, her nerve endings are screaming after seven or eight hours.

"Bruce?" she calls out. His side of the bed is empty but — she reaches out a hand — still warm.

She hears him retching. He's in the bathroom. The blackberry mojitos and the scotch must have caught up with him. The toilet flushes, the water runs, and then Bruce comes into the bedroom. He looks smaller, she thinks. And ten years older.

He comes to sit next to her on the edge of the bed.

"Karen," he says. "The wedding has been canceled."

"Canceled?" she says. Somehow, she already knew this, but how? She tries to piece together the events of the night before. Celeste had wanted to stay home but Bruce and Karen had encouraged her to go out. They wanted her to enjoy herself.

Celeste!

Karen had had a bad dream—she was trying to find Celeste but couldn't get to her. And then came the revelation: Celeste didn't want to marry Benji. Karen had tiptoed down to Celeste's room; it had been empty. She had gone downstairs. She had overheard the strange, awful conversation between Bruce and Tag.

Robin Swain.

Karen shakes her head. Last night, the confession about Robin Swain had seemed so devastating, but this morning, her shock and horror have vanished, just like her pain. Human beings experience all kinds of crazy and unexpected emotions while they are alive. Robin Swain was nothing more than a tiny blip on the screen of their distant past.

"Celeste doesn't want to marry Benji," Karen says.

"No, Karen," Bruce says. "That's not it."

But that is *it,* Karen thinks. She has never once said this, but she does believe she is naturally closer and more in tune with Celeste than Bruce is. Celeste is Bruce's little girl, no doubt about that, but he doesn't understand Celeste's mind like Karen does.

"Merritt died, Karen," Bruce says. "Celeste's friend Merritt. The maid of honor. She died last night."

Karen feels like her head is going to topple right off her neck and onto the floor. *"What?"* she says.

"They found her floating in the harbor this morning," Bruce says. "She drowned."

"She *drowned?*" Karen says. "She drowned last *night?*"

"Apparently so," Bruce says. "I was with Tag and then I came to bed. You were asleep when I came in. That was pretty late, but it must have happened afterward."

"Oh no," Karen says. She is aghast, really and truly aghast. Merritt was so young, so beautiful and confident. "How...what..."

"She drank or took drugs, I guess," Bruce says. "And then she went swimming. I mean, what other explanation is there?"

"Where's Celeste?" Karen asks.

"The paramedics took her to the hospital," Bruce says. His eyes fill with tears. "Celeste was the one who found her."

"No! No, no, no!" Their poor, sweet daughter! Karen fears Celeste doesn't have the strength to deal with this. She is too fragile, too gentle and kind. This had been true even in adolescence, *especially* in adolescence. Other people's daughters had been drinking and smoking, secretly going on the pill or being fitted for diaphragms. Celeste had stayed home with Bruce and Karen watching *Friday Night Lights.* That had been their favorite show, so much so that Tim Riggins and Tami Taylor felt like friends of the family, and, often, Bruce, Karen, and Celeste would look at one another over their morning cereal and say, "Clear eyes, full hearts, can't lose." Celeste volunteered at the Lehigh Valley Zoo in Trexlertown on the weekends. Bruce would drop her off and Karen would pick her up. Karen would nearly always find Celeste with the lemurs or the otters, either feeding them or scolding them like naughty children. Karen used to have to yank her out of there. On Saturday nights, they would go to Diner 248 and then to the movies. Celeste would often see kids from school in groups or on dates and she would wave and smile, but she never seemed embarrassed to be seen with her parents. She was always even-keeled and content, as though she simply preferred to be with Bruce and Karen. Mac and Betty.

"And so now the wedding has been canceled," Karen says.

"Yes," Bruce says. "And the police are conducting an investigation."

"Does the girl have family?" Karen asks.

"Not much, I guess," Bruce says. "She hasn't spoken to her parents in seven years."

Seven years? Karen thinks. She's nearly as upset

about that as she is about Merritt's passing. And yet, Karen could tell from the girl's demeanor that no one had been looking out for her, not even from afar.

So now there will be no wedding. Karen understood this last night, but she had thought the reason would be different. She thought Celeste would call it off.

And then Karen's visit to the psychic comes flooding back in vivid detail.

The psychic's studio was in downtown Easton, half a block from the Crayola factory; Karen used to pass it all the time on her way to and from work. She had looked at the sign with only mild curiosity. KATHRYN RANDALL, PSYCHIC: INTUITIVE READINGS, ANGEL WHISPERER. Kathryn Randall was such a pretty name, such a normal, field-of-daisies name; this had been part of what triggered Karen's interest. Her name wasn't Veda or Krystal or Starshower. It was Kathryn Randall.

Karen visited Kathryn Randall two days after she received news of her metastases. She wasn't looking for Kathryn to predict *her* future—she would live for weeks, months, a year, and then she would die—but she had to know what life held for Celeste.

Kathryn's "studio" was just a normal living room. Karen sat on a gray tweed sofa and stared at Kathryn's diploma from the University of Wisconsin. She handed Kathryn a photograph of Celeste and said, "I need to know if you have any intuitive thoughts about my daughter."

Kathryn Randall was in her mid-thirties, as pretty as her name, with long light brown hair, flawless skin, a calming smile. She looked like a kindergarten teacher. Kathryn had studied the photograph for a long time, long enough for Karen to grow uncomfortable. She was thrown by the conventional surroundings. She had expected silk curtains, candles, maybe even a crystal ball, something that suggested a connection to the supernatural world.

Kathryn Randall closed her eyes, and she started to talk in a slow, hypnotic voice. Celeste was an old soul, she said. She had been to the earth before, more than once, which accounted for her serenity. She didn't ever feel the need to impress. She was comfortable with who she was.

Kathryn stopped suddenly and opened her eyes. "Does that sound right?"

"It does," Karen said, growing excited. "It really does."

Kathryn nodded. "She'll be happy. Eventually."

"Eventually?" Karen said.

A concerned look passed across Kathryn's face, like a breeze rippling the surface of a pond. "Her romantic life . . ." Kathryn said.

"Yes?" Karen said.

"I see chaos."

"Chaos?" Karen said. Here she had thought Celeste's love life was rock solid. She was engaged to Benjamin Winbury. It was a real-life fairy tale.

Kathryn offered a weak smile. "You were right to come to me," she said. "But there's nothing either one of us can do about it."

Karen had paid the thirty-dollar fee and left. Chaos. *Chaos?*

After that, Karen had avoided walking by Kathryn Randall's studio. She started parking in the lot on Ferry Street, even though it was farther away.

Now, Karen's mind starts to grind. Kathryn Randall was correct about chaos. The wedding has been canceled. Merritt is dead. She drank or took pills, Bruce said, then drowned.

Pills, Karen thinks, and she suddenly feels as nauseated as she did after her first round of chemo. Karen had caught Merritt coming out of this very bedroom last night. Merritt had said she was looking for Celeste, but that sounded like a fabrication. She hadn't been looking for Celeste; she had been looking for pills. Had she gotten as far as the third drawer in the bathroom? Had she found the bottle of oxy and the three pearlescent ovoids mixed in? Had she been curious about those pills and taken one to see what happened?

The notion is too appalling for tears. It is a dense, dark, soul-destroying thought: Not only is Merritt dead but it's Karen's fault.

She needs to check her pills.

She can't check her pills.

If she checks her pills and finds one or more of the pearlescent ovoids missing, what will she tell Bruce? Celeste? The police?

Her thoughts are a soundless scream.

She can't continue another second not knowing. Karen gets to her feet. Her pain is still at bay, which is impossible, she knows. She hasn't taken an oxy in nearly twelve hours, so something else is at work in her body. The shock.

Bruce falls back on the bed, his eyes open. He is there but not there, which is just as well. Karen closes the bathroom door, locks it. She sits on the toilet and slides open the third drawer. She takes out the bottle of pills.

She clutches the bottle in her fist.

Then she lays out a clean white washcloth and empties all of the pills onto it. She stares at the pile, smooths them out.

One, two...three pearlescent ovoids, present and accounted for. And then, for good measure, she counts the oxy. All there.

The rush of relief Karen feels nearly knocks her unconscious. She sways; splotches appear in her vision.

Karen staggers back to lie down on the white bed. The shape of her body is still imprinted in the sheets and blankets, like a snow angel. She fits herself back in like a piece of a puzzle and closes her eyes.

Saturday, July 7, 2018, 2:47 p.m.

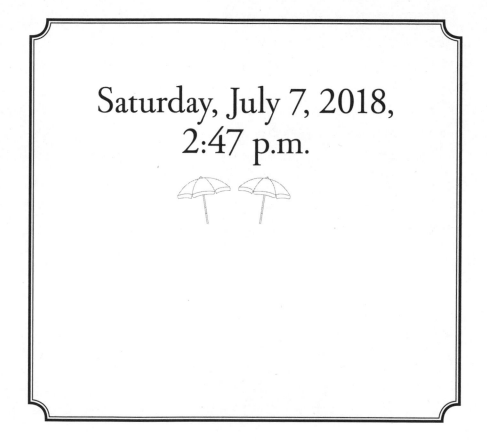

THE CHIEF

He's prepared to give Valerie Gluckstern one hour with Shooter Uxley, but after only twenty minutes, she tells the Chief that her client is ready to answer questions.

In the interview room, the Chief sits down across the table from Shooter and Val. The Chief feels infinitely better since eating his lunch but he needs to come up with something here because Barney from forensics called to say they found nothing in the shot glasses, on the cigar, or in the bottle of rum.

"Are you sure?" the Chief asked. "There has to be *something* in one of the glasses."

And Barney, who did not like having his expertise questioned, had sworn at the Chief and hung up.

"My thinking has changed substantially from this morning," the Chief says. He knows Nick likes to ease into things, build a rapport, and allow information to flow organically, but the Chief isn't feeling it.

A girl is dead, this guy made a run for it, and the Chief wants answers. Now.

"Mr. Uxley is prepared to answer all your questions, as I said," Val says. "He has nothing to hide."

The Chief stares at the kid. He's too damn good-looking to pity, although he seems pretty shaken up.

"Tell me where you were coming from this morning," the Chief says.

Shooter spreads his fingers out on the table in front of him and stares at them as he speaks. "The Steamship," he says.

"What were you doing at the Steamship?" the Chief asks.

"I was trying to leave the island," Shooter says.

"But you missed the boat?" the Chief says.

"I didn't miss the boat," Shooter says. "I just changed my mind."

"You changed your mind," the Chief says. "You'd better start explaining yourself, son." The Chief looks at Val. "Your client lied about being at the Wauwinet. He lied about his alibi. Then he tried to board the Hy-Line with a stolen ticket. Now I'm hearing that he was at the Steamship this morning to board the six-thirty boat, presumably without anyone's knowledge, since the groom told Sergeant Dickson he was missing. The ME put the time of death on the girl between two forty-five and three forty-five. She was dead, and then he decided to flee. On the basis of these facts alone, I have probable cause to hold you for murder one."

"You do not," Val says.

The Chief turns to Shooter. "You'd better cough up one hell of a believable story."

Shooter taps his fingers one by one, starting with his left pinkie, proceeding all the way to his right pinkie, and then going back again.

Val puts a hand on his forearm. "Tell the Chief what you told me," she says. "It's okay."

"I left the Winbury compound early this morning," Shooter says. "I walked all the way to the rotary and caught a cab down to the Steamship. I was going to the Steamship because..." He hesitates, looks at Val. She nods. "Because I was running away with the bride."

Running away with the bride, the Chief thinks. *This was one hell of a wedding.*

"I'm in love with Celeste and she said she was in love with me," Shooter says. "Last night a bunch of us went out after the party and Celeste and I peeled off to get some pizza and I asked her to run away with me." He pauses, looks down at the table, takes a deep, shaky breath, then continues. "I told her that I would take care of her, that I would love her forever. All she had to do was meet me at the Steamship at six o'clock this morning. We were going to hop on the six-thirty slow boat to Hyannis, rent a car, drive to Boston, fly to Las Vegas, and get married ourselves."

Val says, "Mr. Uxley waited at the Steamship for Miss Otis until six thirty-five." She turns to Shooter. "Is that accurate?"

"When I saw the ferry pulling out, when I heard the foghorn, I knew she wasn't coming," Shooter says. "I had figured there was a fifty-fifty chance she'd be there. When she didn't show, I thought she'd decided to marry Benji. So I took a taxi back to the house. Because I was the best man. And there was going to be a wedding after all."

"That's when I saw you?" the Chief asks.

"And you told me Merritt was dead." He shakes his head. "You know, Celeste was afraid to follow through with our plan because she thought something bad would happen if we did it." He swallows. "I'm sure she's blaming herself."

"Why didn't you tell me this in the first place?" the Chief asks. "Instead of coming clean, you lied to me, then you ran off. You understand the light that puts you in? Why should I believe a word you say?"

"I was rattled," Shooter says. "I thought I was coming back to a wedding and instead, you tell me that Merritt is *dead?* I couldn't add our drama on top of that. Celeste would have had to corroborate my story, and I wanted to protect her from that. And I didn't want the Winburys to know. I was agitated and confused and I figured it would be easier to just say I'd been with Gina. I didn't think you'd actually check it out. Then, once I knew I'd been caught in a lie, I figured my only course of action was to bolt." Shooter looks at the Chief. "I realize I handled this poorly. But I didn't kill Merritt."

"Did Merritt know the two of you were running away?" the Chief asks. "Do you think Celeste confided in her?"

"We agreed not to tell anyone," Shooter says. "We were going to make a clean break for it, get off the island, then tell everyone later. Celeste wasn't even going to say anything to her parents. So, no, I do not think she confided in Merritt."

The interview room is quiet for a second. The Chief is combing back through the story. Does it make sense? Does it have any holes? Nick is a strong believer in intuition when it comes to questioning. The story may make sense, but do you believe the guy?

Yes, the Chief thinks. He recalls Roger saying that when Celeste found the body, she had a bag packed. She was headed to meet Shooter and she…what? Caught a glimpse of something in the water as she was leaving? It wasn't impossible.

She had a bag packed. For that reason, and that

reason alone, the Chief is going to choose to believe Mr. Uxley.

He stands up and nods at Val. "You two are free to go," he says. He has to move on — and quickly — to Tag Winbury and the Dale woman, whoever *she* is.

August 2017

CELESTE

Her mother's cancer has metastasized to her bones. There are tumors on her spine. The cancer isn't curable. They can, however, do another course of chemo, which will buy her a year to eighteen months.

Benji's response to the news is to pull Celeste closer and hold her tighter. They are now engaged, and this has inspired him to become the spokesperson for *we*. He wants Karen to get a second opinion at Mount Sinai. His parents know "influential people" who sit on the board of directors. They'll be able to get Karen an appointment with the "best doctors, the very best doctors."

Celeste resents Benji's involvement. She and her parents are an insular unit: Mac, Betty, and Bug. *They* are the *we*. It feels like Benji is horning in with his connections and his optimism. In Benji's world, every problem has a solution, thanks to who the Winburys know and how much money they have.

Celeste says, "My parents can't *afford* to get a second opinion at Mount Sinai. My father's insurance was maxed out long ago."

"I'll pay for it," Benji says.

"I don't *want* you to pay for it!" Celeste says. "My mother has a doctor she likes and trusts. Dr. Edman at St. Luke's—which is a real hospital, by the way, not just some clinic in a strip mall."

"Okay, I get it," Benji says, though Celeste knows exactly what he's thinking. He's thinking that St. Luke's isn't as good as Mount Sinai. How could it possibly be as good when it isn't in New York City and Tag and Greer don't know anyone who sits on the board? "I'm only trying to help."

"Thank you," Celeste says as sincerely as she can. "I'm very upset and I want to handle this my own way."

Because Celeste is just back from her Nantucket vacation, she can't take any more time off; it's the end of summer and the zoo is simply too busy. But in the middle of her first week back, Celeste rents a Zipcar and drives out to see her parents after work. When Celeste reaches the house on Derhammer Street, she finds her mother sitting at the kitchen table with a coloring book for adults and a deluxe set of sixty-four pencils. Celeste walks in, and she holds up the page she's been working on. It's a mandala.

"Not bad, huh?" Karen says. She has colored the mandala in shades of green, blue, and purple.

"Pretty," Celeste says, but her voice is shaky and her eyes well up. Karen has worked at the Crayola factory gift shop for over a decade. Some people sniff at what they see as a menial job selling boxes of crayons, but Karen has always taken pride in it. *I bring color into children's lives,* she says.

Karen stands up and lets Celeste hug her. "I'm going to win this battle," she says.

"You're not supposed to call it a battle," Celeste says. "I read that somewhere. It's a violent word and some survivors find it offensive."

Karen scoffs. "Offensive?" she says. "So what am I supposed to call it?"

"A journey," Celeste says.

"Bullshit," Karen says. Celeste blinks in surprise; her mother never swears. "It's a battle."

They go for a quick dinner at Diner 248 and make a point of ordering the Fudgy Wudgy, though Celeste and Bruce manage only one bite apiece and Karen doesn't have any. Karen makes a big fuss over Celeste's diamond ring: It's the most beautiful ring she has ever laid eyes on. It's the biggest diamond she has ever seen. *A full four carats! And set in platinum!*

Celeste says, "I'm thinking of postponing the

wedding. I'm thinking of quitting my job and moving home until you get better."

"Nonsense," Karen says. Her voice is sharp and loud, and people at nearby tables turn their heads. The three Otises sit in silence for a second; they aren't people who draw attention to themselves.

Celeste knows better than to say anything further. Her mother has spent Celeste's entire life claiming that no mortal man would ever be good enough for Celeste, but that's because she didn't have the imagination to dream up someone like Benjamin Winbury, a real-life Prince Charming. Celeste's future will be blessed. She will never have to worry about money the way that Bruce and Karen did.

Celeste looks at Mac and Betty sitting across from her in the booth the way they always do, her father's arm draped across her mother's shoulders, her mother's hand resting on her father's thigh. Celeste envies them. She doesn't want money; she wants what they have. She wants love.

In case you have any doubts…

"If anything," Karen says in a lower voice, "I was thinking you might get married sooner. Maybe in the spring or early summer."

…I'm in love with you.

Sooner? Celeste thinks.

She nods. "Okay," she whispers.

* * *

Shooter has disappeared back into his own life—steak houses, downtown clubs, the U.S. Open with clients, Vegas with clients to draft fantasy-football teams. Benji shows Celeste the pictures but she barely gives them a glance. She can't think about Shooter; she can't *not* think about Shooter. Part of her suspects her desire for Shooter is what caused Karen's cancer to spread. Celeste knows life doesn't work like that but she still gets the nagging sense that the two things are connected. If she stays with Benji, if she marries Benji, Karen will get better. If they get married in the spring or early summer, Karen will live forever.

Celeste drops five pounds, then ten. Merritt expresses envy and tells Celeste how wonderful she looks.

Celeste is irritable at work. She finally loses her temper with Blair the hypochondriac. One more missed day and Blair will be fired, Celeste says. Blair threatens a lawsuit. She has *legitimate reasons* for calling in sick. Celeste, in a rare fit of rage, tells Blair she needs to stop with the *bullshit,* and the next thing Celeste knows, she's getting called into Zed's office for a lecture on professional attitude, appropriate workplace language, blah-blah-blah.

Greer summons Benji and Celeste to the Winbury apartment for dinner. She has made something called a cassoulet. Celeste is her dutiful self and replies that it sounds good, but in fact, Celeste is annoyed. She has no idea what cassoulet is. She hates constantly being confronted with these erudite dishes—can't Greer just make meat loaf or sloppy joes like Betty?—and it turns out that cassoulet has duck, pork skin, and, worst of all, *beans* in it. Celeste manages two bites. Her lack of appetite goes largely unnoticed, however, because Greer's real motivation isn't to feed Celeste and Benji but rather to let them know that she would like to plan their wedding. They can have the entire thing at Summerland on Nantucket the weekend after the Fourth of July.

Benji reaches for Celeste's hand under the table. "Would that be okay with you?" he asks.

"We don't want you to feel railroaded," Tag says. "My wife can be a bit forceful."

"I'm just trying to help," Greer says. "I want to offer my support and our resources. I hate to think of you having to plan a wedding while your mother is so sick."

Celeste nods like a marionette. "Sounds good," she says.

At first, Celeste stutters only when she's talking about the wedding. She has a problem with the word *caterer;* it's a stuttery word all by itself. Then *reverend,* then *church*. People pretend not to notice but the stutter grows gradually worse. Benji finally asks about it and Celeste bursts into tears. She can't c-c-control it, she says. Soon, all hard consonants give her trouble.

But not at work.

Not on the phone with Merritt.

Not alone in her apartment when she's reading in bed. She can read entire passages from her book aloud and not trip up once.

Celeste holds out hope that a big, elaborate wedding on Nantucket will prove to be a logistical impossibility— it's too last-minute, every venue must already be booked—and so either the wedding will be postponed indefinitely or they can plan something smaller in Easton, something more like her parents' wedding, a ceremony at the courthouse, a reception at the diner.

But apparently, Greer's influence and her pocketbook are mighty enough to make miracles happen. Greer enlists Siobhan at Island Fare, arranges for Reverend Derby to do the service at St. Paul's Episcopal, finds a band and an orchestra, and hires Roger Pelton, Nantucket's premier wedding coordinator— not that Greer can't handle it all herself, but she does have a novel to write and it would be silly to have a resource like Roger on the island and not use him.

The wedding is set for July 7.

* * *

Greer asks Celeste what she would like to do about bridesmaids.

"Oh," Celeste says. This obviously isn't something she can ask Greer to handle. "I'll have my friend Merritt Monaco." Merritt will be a good maid of honor; she knows all the rules and traditions, although Celeste shudders when she thinks about the bachelorette party Merritt might plan. Celeste will have to talk to her about that.

She notices Greer is still looking at her expectantly.

"And who else?" Greer asks.

Who *else?* Her mother? Nobody ever asks her mother to be a bridesmaid; Celeste knows that much. She doesn't have a sister or any cousins. There are no suitable choices at work—Blair is now not speaking to Celeste; Bethany is her *assistant,* so that's too weird; and the rest of the staff are men. There is Celeste's roommate from college, Julia, but Celeste's relationship with Julia was utilitarian rather than friendly. They were both scientists, both neat and respectful, but they parted ways after college. There is Celeste's one social friend from college, Violet Sonada, but Violet took a job at the Ueno Zoo in Tokyo. Is there anyone from high school? Cynthia from down the street had been Celeste's closest friend but she dropped out of Penn State with a nervous condition and Celeste hasn't talked to her since. Merritt has a bunch of people she knows in the city, but Celeste can barely remember who is who.

She is a social misfit and now Greer will know it.

"Let m-m-me think ab-b-bout it," Celeste says, hoping Greer will assume there are too many young women to choose from and Celeste will need to whittle the list down.

But Greer, of course, sees the humiliating truth. It's because she's a novelist, Celeste supposes. She is perceptive to a fault; it's almost as if she reads minds.

"I shouldn't get involved," Greer says, "but I do think Abby would love to serve as a bridesmaid."

Celeste perks up immediately. Abby! She can ask Abby Winbury, Thomas's wife. She's the right age; she is appropriately girly; she has probably been a bridesmaid twenty times before. Celeste relaxes even as she realizes that the Winburys are providing for her once again.

Celeste tells Benji that she's asking Merritt to be her maid of honor and Abby to be her bridesmaid and Benji gets a crease in his brow.

"Abby?" he says. "Are you sure?"

The nice thing is that Celeste doesn't have to hide anything from Benji. "I c-c-couldn't think of anyone else," she says. "You're marrying the most socially awkward g-g-girl in New York."

Benji kisses her. "And I couldn't be happier about it."

"So what's wrong with Ab-b-by?" Celeste asks.

"Nothing," Benji says. "Did she say yes?"

"I was p-p-planning on e-mailing tomorrow f-from work," Celeste says.

Benji nods.

"What?" Celeste says. Abby would be filling a glaring gap. And besides, as Thomas's wife, wouldn't Abby be insulted *not* to be asked? It's true, Abby can sometimes be a bit off-putting — she was a sorority girl at the University of Texas and she has retained some shallow cattiness, and she is presently obsessed with getting pregnant — but she is family.

"I get the feeling Thomas and Abby are on the rocks," Benji says.

Celeste gasps. "What?"

"Thomas is always taking trips alone," Benji says. "And going out with his friends after work. Not to mention his obsession with the gym."

"Oh," Celeste says. She knows Benji is right. They have met Thomas and Abby for dinner a few times and Thomas is always the last to arrive, often straight from the gym, still in his sweaty workout clothes. Abby won't even let him kiss her unless he's showered, she says. He has to shower before sex, and sex is kept to a schedule since they are trying to conceive.

But why try so hard for a baby if you're not planning on staying together?

"I'm not asking Thomas to be my best man," Benji says.

"W-W-What?" Celeste says. This shocks her even more than the news of Thomas and Abby's supposed marital discord. "But he's your b-b-brother."

"Something is going on with him," Benji says. "And I want to distance myself from it. I'm having Shooter serve as my best man."

"Shooter?" Celeste says.

"I've already asked him," Benji says. "He was so happy. He teared up."

He teared up, Celeste thinks. *So happy.* "What are you g-g-going to tell T-T-Thomas?"

"I'll tell Thomas he can be an usher," Benji says. "Maybe."

Saturday, July 7, 2018,
3:30 p.m.

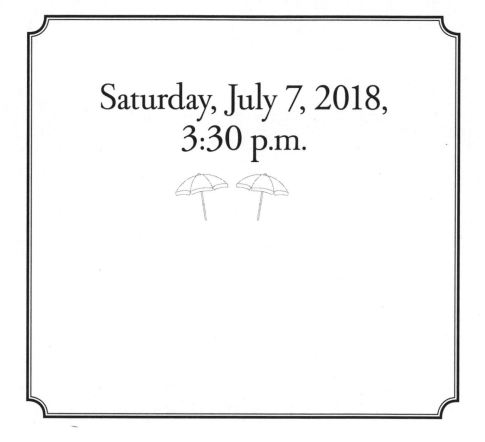

GREER

At half past three, when all of the guests have been called and all of the friends and relatives back in England have been notified about the tragedy and all of the wedding preparations have been summarily undone—except for those that are part of the "crime scene"—Greer takes a moment to peek out the window at the second cottage, the one where Merritt was staying. It's wrapped in police tape like a tawdry present, although the forensics men have left and no one is there to stop Greer from entering. She would love to go in and poke around, but she fears the Winburys are in enough trouble as it is; she can't afford to cause any more.

Tag took Merritt out in the kayak.

Merritt, not Featherleigh.

Greer needs to speak to Tag alone but he said he had to make a phone call, probably to Sergio Ramone, who is not only a friend but a brilliant criminal-defense attorney. Greer isn't sure even Sergio can get Tag out of this mess. He took the girl out on the kayak and she shows up in the morning dead. Drowned in the harbor. Greer retreats to the master suite and perches on the sofa at the end of the bed, waiting for Tag, although she expects him to be led from the house in handcuffs the instant the police figure out this affair was going on.

The boys handled the news badly. Benji exploded. "Did you kill her, Dad? Did. You. Kill. Her?"

"No," Tag said. "I took her out on the kayak, yes, I did. But I brought her back to shore safely."

He sounded like he was telling the truth. His inflection and tone were full of calm conviction, but Greer now knows he's been lying to her for a long time—maybe for the entirety of their marriage—so how would she know for sure?

Thomas hadn't said anything at all. Possibly he, like Greer, had been too stunned to speak.

The ring that Greer thought Tag had bought for Featherleigh he'd bought for Merritt. Greer had seen the ring on Merritt's thumb—she had *seen* it!—but she had one thing so firmly lodged in her brain that there hadn't been room for any other possibilities.

The ring had been Tag's only misstep. Greer had gone in to see Jessica Hicks, the jeweler, about wedding bands. Greer thought it would be a nice touch for Benji and Celeste to have rings fashioned by a

Nantucket jeweler. The instant Greer entered the shop, Jessica's brows had shot up. She said, *Did your daughter-in-law not like the ring, then?*

Daughter-in-law? Greer had said.

The one who's pregnant? Jessica said. *Did she not like the ring?*

The ring? Greer had said.

Your husband came in… Jessica said.

Oh, right! Greer had said enthusiastically, although a bad feeling had started to seep through her. Tag had said nothing about getting a present for Abby. And Tag wasn't known for thoughtful gestures where the kids were concerned; he left that to Greer.

He told me about it but we've been so busy he hasn't had a chance to show it to me, Greer said. *And he wouldn't do a proper job describing it anyway. What did it look like?*

Silver-lace pattern, Jessica said, *embedded with multicolored sapphires. Like this one. It's meant to be worn on the thumb.* Jessica had then shown Greer a ring that sold for six hundred dollars. So it wasn't a fortune, wasn't like a trip to Harry Winston for diamonds, but Greer had been near certain she would never see Abby wearing that ring.

Tag steps into the bedroom, closes the door behind him, and locks it.

"Greer," he says. He holds his hands up as if she might strike him.

She would like to strike him. What has he *done?* The girl dead, the wedding canceled, their marriage, their life...

And yet all Greer can think to say is "I thought you were having an affair with Featherleigh."

Tag's eyes widen. "No," he says.

"No," Greer says. "It was Merritt."

"Yes," he says.

Greer nods. "If you want me to help you, you had better tell me everything. Everything, Tag."

It started the night of the wine dinner, he says. They were both drunk, very drunk, and she came on to him. They slept together; it was unremarkable, regrettable. He thought that would be it but then he bumped into her again in the city, by accident, at a hotel bar, and she invited him to her apartment. He's not sure why but he said yes. And then there was another time or two, but he finally demanded she leave him alone.

"You bought her gifts?" Greer says.

"No."

"Tag."

He sighs. "A trinket. It was her birthday a few weeks ago. That was when I ended it. She wanted to go away together. I said no. She persisted. I booked a room at the Four Seasons downtown..."

The Four Seasons? Every detail pierces her.

"She was late showing up and in the minutes that I was waiting, I came to my senses. I left the hotel and went home to you."

"So how many times did you screw her?" Greer asks. "Sum total."

"More than five, less than ten," Tag says.

Greer feels ill. She can see the allure, she supposes. Merritt was attractive; she was young, free, unfettered. Merritt had the whiff of a rebel about her. Who wouldn't want to shag Merritt? What makes Greer want to vomit on her shoes is the thought of her own self while all of this was going on those six, seven, eight times. What had Greer been doing? Was she writing her perfectly mediocre novel or was she planning their son's wedding? Whatever she was doing, she wasn't paying attention to Tag. She hadn't given Tag a minute's thought.

"And that was it?" Greer says. "Nothing more? You had an affair, you broke it off. She was upset about it. I saw her crying during the rehearsal dinner, in the laundry room, of all places. So when you talk to the police, you'll tell them she was emotionally overwrought and that she threatened suicide if you didn't leave me. You took her out on the kayak to try and talk some sense into her. You delivered her back to shore; you came to bed. She drowned herself."

"Well," Tag says.

"Well what?"

"It's a bit stickier than that," Tag says. He clears his throat. "She was pregnant."

Greer closes her eyes. Pregnant.

"You're going to the gallows," she says.

Tag's face crumples; Greer has landed the poison dart right between his eyes. The girl was pregnant. *Pregnant* with a Winbury bastard child. The thought is hideous, and yet it feels utterly predictable. Thomas Winbury the elder, known to most as Tag, has taken the family down. His poor judgment, his base urges, and his weak character have desecrated the Winbury name. He has committed murder, and he will be caught.

Greer can think ill of Tag all she likes, but in the end, she knows, she will say and do whatever she needs to do to protect him.

There's a knock on the bedroom door.

It's Thomas.

"The chief of police is back," Thomas says. "He'd like to talk to you next, Dad."

Tag looks to Greer. She nods but is afraid to say a word in front of Thomas. Tag should stick to the story they came up with. She tries to convey this with her eyes but Tag hangs his head like a guilty man. Greer would like to go into the questioning with him. Let her talk, let her present the argument. She, after all, is the storyteller.

But that, of course, won't be possible. Tag got into this mess without her; he will have to go it alone.

Greer is exhausted. It's nearly four o'clock, the hour the ceremony was to take place.

She lies down on the bed. She is so tired she could sleep until morning. Maybe she *will* sleep until morning.

Merritt Monaco. She was twenty-nine years old. Pretty, but unoriginal. That was who Tag was screwing.

Disgust courses through Greer's veins. She is hardly naive; she has written scenarios this nefarious and more so. There wasn't one original thing about it—a charming, rich, powerful older man with an indifferent wife seduced or was seduced by a young, beautiful, silly girl. It practically described the history of the entire world—from Henry VIII with Anne Boleyn to an American president with his impressionable intern. But it feels brand-new, doesn't it? Because it is happening to Greer.

Pregnant.

When Tag is charged with murder, the papers will have a field day. Their wealth and the fact that Greer writes murder mysteries will make the story positively irresistible. The *New York Post* will cover it, then the British tabloids. Greer will be cast as an object of pity; her fans will either cringe or rage on her behalf. The thought is horrifying—so many middle-aged women writing indignant Facebook posts or penning sympathetic letters. Thomas's and Benji's lives will be ruined. They'll become social outcasts. Thomas will be fired; Benji will be asked to resign from his charitable boards.

Greer sits up. She can't sleep. She needs a pill.

She goes into the master bathroom and eyes Tag's sink—his razor, his shaving brush, his tortoiseshell comb. She couldn't bear to walk into this bathroom and find Tag's side empty. They have been together too long, endured too much.

Greer opens her medicine cabinet, and as she does so, she gets a peculiar feeling of déjà vu, as though she watched herself go through these exact motions a short time ago—and so a part of her knows that when she looks, her sleeping pills will be missing.

Wait, she thinks. *Wait just a minute!*

The pills were prescribed by her GP, Dr. Crowe. Dr. Crowe is doddering, nearly senile; he has been Greer's "woman doctor" since she moved to Manhattan. The pills are "quite potent," as Crowe likes to remind her, some cousin to the quaaludes everyone was taking in the seventies. "Quite potent" isn't just some humble-brag; the pills knock Greer out immediately and lock her in an obsidian casket for a full eight hours. Greer doesn't keep her sleeping pills in a prescription bottle but rather in a round enamel box decorated with a picture of a young Queen Elizabeth II. Greer received the box as a present from her grandmother on the occasion of her eleventh birthday.

The Queen Elizabeth box always sits in the same spot on the same shelf and Greer knows why it's gone. Or at least she suspects she does.

She closes the medicine cabinet and stares at herself in the mirror. She needs to think this through. But there's no time. She needs to talk to the Chief immediately. She needs to save her husband, that bastard.

Saturday, July 7, 2018,
4:00 p.m.

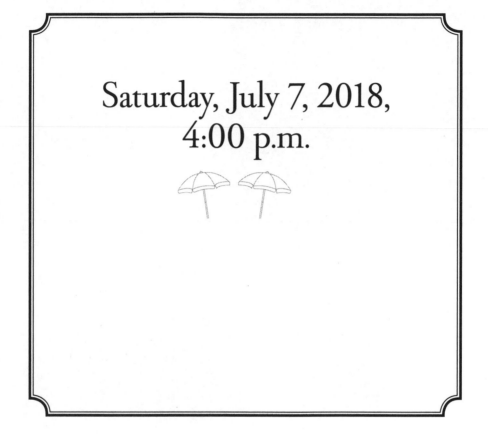

NANTUCKET

Marty Szczerba is sitting at the bar at the Crosswinds restaurant in the Nantucket airport finally eating his lunch. He likes the Reuben, loves the coleslaw; he has gained thirty pounds since Nancy died, which isn't helping in his quest for a new girlfriend. A not-unattractive woman in her early to mid-forties suddenly takes the seat next to his. She points at his sandwich and says, in a posh English accent, "I'm having what this chap's having. And a glass of chardonnay. A large glass."

Marty fumbles with his knife and fork in an attempt to flag down Dawn, the bartender, who is watching Wimbledon on the TV in the corner. "Dawn, this young lady would like to place an order."

While Dawn takes the order for the Reuben, the coleslaw, and the large chardonnay, Marty sneaks a better look at his new neighbor. She is blond, or blondish, in halfway decent shape, with laugh lines around her mouth and fingernails painted cherry red. She is dressed in a strapless army-green jumpsuit type of thing that Marty knows is meant to be stylish. It gives him a good view of her chest and arms. She's a bit puffy, but Marty is hardly sculpted himself.

"I'm Marty Szczerba," he says, holding out his hand.

"Featherleigh," she says. "Featherleigh Dale." She takes his hand and offers a smile, then her chardonnay arrives. She lifts the glass to Marty and says, "I can't wait to get off this island. The past twenty-four hours have not been kind to me."

Marty wishes he had a glass to cheers her with, but he's still on the clock. He, too, has had one hell of a day, beginning and ending with the case of the Murdered Maid of Honor and the runaway person of interest. It turned out the guy they were looking for was caught by a local teenage girl who works for the Hy-Line. Marty is glad the guy isn't still at large but he bristles at being bested by some kid who found him by using Facebook. That's cheating, is it not? Marty would have benefited from a little glory. He has been considering asking out Keira, the chief of police's assistant, but she's in her thirties and goes to barre class every day and is, likely, looking for more of a hero than Marty can currently claim to be.

"So you're just visiting?" Marty says. "Where do you live?" He knows better than to get his hopes up about anyone from off-island; he still has two years left until retirement, although after that, he'll be ready to go. Laura Rae and Ty will be happily married, maybe even starting a family, and Marty will become an annoyance. He hopes this Featherleigh says she lives in Boston. How perfect would that be? He gets two free round-trip tickets to Boston on Cape Air per month. He envisions himself and Featherleigh strolling around the Public Garden hand in hand, stopping in at the Parish Café on Boylston for lunch. They'll have cocktails down at the Seaport. Boston is a great city for people in love. They can ride the swan boats! Have high tea at the Four Seasons! Go to a Sox game! And in two years, when Marty is ready to retire, his relationship with Featherleigh will be established enough to take it to the next level.

"London," she says. "I have a flat in Sloane Square, although I fear it'll belong to the bank by the time I get home."

London, Marty thinks as his dreams deflate. That's too far away. But it wouldn't be a bad place to visit Featherleigh for a casual, no-strings-attached fling. Marty has never been to London, which is something he needs to remedy, especially since his Match.com profile boasts that he loves to travel.

"And what do you do for a living?" Marty asks.

Featherleigh takes a long sip of her wine, then sets her elbow on the bar and rests her head in her hand to regard him. "I sell antiques to rich people," she says. "What do you do, Marty?"

Marty straightens up a little. "I'm head of security here at the airport."

"Well," she says, "that's a very prestigious job, isn't it?" The way she pronounces the word *prestigious* in her English accent sounds so lovely, Marty grins.

"He's the top gun," Dawn chimes in.

Marty silently thanks Dawn for the backup even though he feels somewhat mortified that she's eavesdropping on his first attempt at a pickup since 1976. He bobs his head yes, then wonders if Featherleigh is making fun of him. After all, it's not like he's the head of security at Heathrow. *That would be a hellish nightmare of a job,* Marty thinks. Flights from all over the world converging. How would he ever keep track of the potential threats? And yet somehow those chaps do it, day in and day out.

"In the summer, Nantucket is the second-busiest airport in the state," Marty says. "Only Logan is busier."

"Logan?" Featherleigh says.

"The airport in Boston," he says.

"Ah, right," Featherleigh says. "Well, I'm flying standby to JFK on JetBlue." She checks her phone. "I really hope I get on." She winks at Marty. "You don't have any pull, do you?"

"With the airlines?" Marty says. "No."

This admission sends Featherleigh right into the electronic abyss of her phone. She sips her large glass of chardonnay, then starts scrolling. Marty regards the second half of his Reuben, the cheese now cold and congealed, and his coleslaw, which has grown soupy. Before he loses Featherleigh entirely to the seductive allure of Instagram, he says, "So what was so bad about your stay?"

Featherleigh sets down her phone and Marty feels a childish triumph. "I couldn't begin to explain."

"Try me."

"I came all the way from London for a wedding. Now, mind you, I had no interest in attending the wedding, but this man I've been seeing was going to be there so I said yes."

Marty hears the phrase *man I've been seeing* and what's left of his enthusiasm flags. Even someone not-gorgeous-but-okay-looking like Featherleigh has found someone. *Where are all the half-decent-looking-but-not-attached women?* Marty wonders. *Tell me!*

"And then, for reasons too awful to explain, the wedding was canceled—"

"Wait a minute," Marty says. "Were you going to the wedding out in—" At that moment, Marty's phone starts ringing and a discreet check of his screen shows that it's the chief of police. Marty has to take the call. He holds a finger up to Featherleigh. "Excuse me one moment," he says. He relishes the opportunity to show Featherleigh that he really *is* sort of important. "What can I do for you, Chief?" he says.

"We're looking for someone else now," the Chief says. "And we have good reason to believe she's at the airport, trying to fly standby. Female, early forties, blondish hair, name is Featherleigh Dale."

Marty's mouth falls open and the phone nearly slips from his hand but he manages to compose himself and offer Featherleigh a smile.

"I'm on it, Chief," he says.

TAG

He shakes hands with the chief of police and tries to strike the appropriate tone: mournful yet strong, concerned yet guilt-free. When Greer woke up Tag, jostling his shoulder and saying, "Celeste's friend Merritt, the friend, the maid of honor, Tag, she's dead. She drowned out front. She's dead. The paramedics are here and the police. Celeste found her floating. She's dead. Jesus, Tag, wake *up*. *Do* something," he'd thought he was ensnared in a bad dream. It had taken several long seconds for Tag to realize that Greer was real and that what she was saying was true.

Merritt had drowned. She was dead.

Not possible, he thought. He had dropped her off on the beach after the kayak ride. She had stormed off—upset, yes, but still very much alive.

On solid ground. He'd thought she'd gone to bed.

Tag isn't sure what the police know.

Do they know about the affair?

Do they know about the pregnancy?

They'll find out Merritt was pregnant as soon as they hear from the medical examiner, but will they learn about the affair? Whom did Merritt tell? Did she tell Celeste? Did Celeste tell the police? Tag's first instinct upon hearing the hideous news was to find Celeste and remind her that the future of the Winbury family rested with her discretion. But Celeste had been taken to the emergency room to be treated for anxiety and she hasn't returned to the house— which is, Tag suspects, a bad sign.

Tag leads the Chief to his study. Benji walked out after Tag admitted that it had been Merritt he'd taken on the kayak, and Thomas vamoosed as well. But both of his sons know better than to say a word to the police, Tag is confident of this. Their well-being is contingent on *his* well-being.

Tag says to the Chief, "Can I offer you a drink?"

The Chief lifts a hand. "No, thanks."

Tag settles in the chair behind his desk and offers

the Chief one of the two chairs facing the desk. This makes Tag feel in control of the situation, as if it were Tag who invited the Chief in for a chat and not the other way around. *Perception is reality,* Tag thinks. Why *not* put the Chief in the hot seat?

"What have you got?" Tag asks.

"Excuse me?" the Chief says.

"A young woman is dead," Tag says. "And it happened on my property, or very nearly. Now, maybe it was an accident. Maybe Merritt had too much to drink and drowned. But if you have any evidence that something else is going on, then I deserve to know about it." Tag hardens his gaze. "Don't I?"

"No," the Chief says. "You don't."

Tag opens his mouth to say—to say what? It doesn't matter because the Chief leans forward in his chair and says, "When did you last see Ms. Monaco?"

Tag blinks. His instinct is to lie—of course his instinct is to lie!—because the truth is too incriminating.

"I saw her last night," Tag says.

The Chief nods. "At what time?"

"I couldn't say."

"All right," the Chief says. "Where were you when you last saw her?"

"I was...out back."

"Can you be more specific, please?" the Chief says.

"What were the circumstances surrounding the last time you saw Ms. Monaco?"

Tag takes a moment. He has had all day to consider various answers to this question, but now he's floundering.

If he lies, they'll catch him, he thinks. And he is innocent. Where Merritt's death is concerned, he is innocent.

"We were out back under the tent, drinking," he says. "A group of us. Myself, my son Thomas, a friend of the family named Featherleigh Dale, and Ms. Monaco."

"And how would you describe Ms. Monaco's mood at that time?" the Chief asks.

Tag thinks about this. He had bidden Bruce Otis good night and had planned to go to bed—but Thomas had arrived back from town by himself. Abby had called and insisted Thomas come home; when he'd gone up to check on her, however, she'd been asleep.

"Or she was pretending to be asleep," Thomas said. "It's like she's trying to catch me at something."

"*Catch* you at something?" Tag said. He flashed back to the evening he ended things with Merritt, when he saw Thomas sitting alone at the bar at the Four Seasons. And so instead of going to bed, Tag grabbed a bottle of good rum from the bar in his study. As his favorite auntie, Mary Margaret, used to say, *When you don't know what else to do, get drunk.* Tag would have a heart-to-heart with Thomas; it was long overdue.

"Come on out to the tent with me," Tag said.

Thomas had needed no further enticement. He set up one of the round tables meant for the reception and brought over four folding chairs — thinking, Tag supposed, that the others might join them when they got back from town. Tag had just been pouring the shots when Merritt and Featherleigh appeared out of the shadows. It was almost as though they'd been lying in wait. Tag was spooked to see Merritt but she'd offered him an apologetic smile and Tag thought he'd seen acquiescence in her eyes. She would do as he asked: Take the money, end the pregnancy, walk away. He knew she didn't want a baby.

"Would you ladies care for a nightcap?" Tag asked.

"Answer to my prayers," Featherleigh said.

Merritt hadn't spoken, although she did take a seat next to Tag, and when he set a shot in front of her, she didn't protest.

He had been a little uncomfortable about how chummy Merritt suddenly seemed to be with Featherleigh Dale. What were *they* doing together? And why was Featherleigh still at the house? She was staying at an inn downtown. She had waited until the last minute to book and so she ended up in a real dump, as Greer described it; maybe that was why she was hesitant to leave.

"Merritt seemed to be in fine spirits," Tag says to the Chief. "I mean, I guess. I really didn't know her well."

"Didn't you?" the Chief asks.

Tag's gut twists. Now is the time to ask for an attorney. He had considered calling Sergio Ramone the second he found out Merritt was dead, but in his mind, hiring an attorney is as good as admitting you're guilty. And Tag didn't kill her.

He didn't kill her.

"I had nothing to do with Ms. Monaco's death," he says. "Not one thing."

"Were you having an affair with Merritt Monaco?" the Chief asks.

"I was," Tag says. "But I ended things weeks ago."

"Did Ms. Monaco tell you she was pregnant with your baby?"

"She *said* she was..."

"Okay, then," the Chief says. He leans forward in the chair. "I'm going to guess that when you heard that news, you weren't too happy. I'm going to guess you would have gone to great lengths to keep that news quiet."

Tag sinks into himself. Could he throw himself on the mercy of the Chief, maybe appeal to him man to man? One look at the Chief tells Tag that the guy is honorable. He's wearing a gold wedding band. He has probably been married twenty-five or thirty years and never so much as glanced at another woman.

"I *would* have gone to great lengths to keep that news quiet," Tag admits. "If I were even certain the baby was mine. Merritt was seeing other men. There's an Irish bloke named Robbie who bartends at the Breslin in New York City. It might have been Robbie's baby."

"But she told you it was yours," the Chief says. "Doesn't matter if it was Robbie's. She was threatening *you*. She was threatening to expose your affair. I'm sure that must have been scary for you, especially this weekend, when you were surrounded by family and friends. Your son's getting married; seems pretty unfair for her to choose this time to air your dirty laundry."

Tag hears the phony sympathy in the Chief's voice, even as his words ring true: It *was* unfair.

"I told Merritt that after the wedding I would write her a check. I wanted her to terminate the pregnancy." He holds up his hands. "That's bad, I know. But it's a far cry from killing her."

The Chief stares at him.

"Do you really think I'd be daft enough to drown a woman I was sleeping with, a woman who claimed to be pregnant with my child, and leave her to wash up in front of my house on the morning of my son's wedding? I wasn't that desperate. I was worried, definitely, but I wasn't desperate and I didn't kill anyone."

"You did take Ms. Monaco out for a ride on your kayak, though, correct? The kayak we found on the beach? Your wife and your daughter-in-law both said you're the only person who uses the kayaks."

"Yes," Tag says. "Yes, I did."

"Even though it was the middle of the night," the Chief says. "Did that not seem like a desperate measure to you? Reckless, at the very least?"

"She said she needed to talk to me," Tag says. "Away from everyone, away from the house."

"And what happened while you were out on this kayak ride?"

"I was paddling for an island beach out by Abrams Point but it was dark and I was having a difficult time finding it," Tag says. "And when we were out in open water, in the middle of nowhere, the kayak tilted to the right and I heard a splash. Merritt had jumped off." Tag leans forward. "You have to understand, Merritt was unhinged. She was hormonal, emotional, mentally unstable. She admitted that the only reason she wanted to keep the baby was that it gave her leverage over me. Then she leaped off the boat like a crazy person. I had to paddle back around and haul her up by the wrist."

"By the wrist?" the Chief says.

"Yes," Tag says. "And as soon as she was back up in the kayak, I paddled like hell for home. She got out on the beach and headed off. I thought she was going to bed."

"You didn't tie the kayak up," the Chief says. "You left it overturned on the beach. Which I understand is out of character for you."

"It was unusual," Tag says. "But I worried that if I hung around to tie up the kayak, she would reappear, there would be more drama, she would raise her voice, people would hear us." Tag drops his head into his hands. "I just wanted her to leave me alone."

"Exactly," the Chief says. "You just wanted her to leave you alone." He puts his hands on the desk and leans forward. "The medical examiner found a heavy-duty sedative in Ms. Monaco's system. So let me tell you what I think. I think you were pouring the girl shots and you slipped her a mickey. Then you invited her out for a kayak and you accidentally on purpose capsized and she never made it back to the boat. Or maybe you did as you say, and you pulled her up by the wrist. Maybe you let her pass out on the kayak and then you dumped her off closer to shore so that it looked like she went for a swim and drowned."

"No," Tag says. "That is *not* what happened. I didn't drug her and I didn't dump her anywhere."

"But you do admit you were the one pouring the shots," the Chief says. "Right?"

"Right, but—"

"Did she have anything else to drink?" the Chief asks.

"Water," Tag says. "Water! Featherleigh went to the kitchen at some point..." Now Tag can't recall if it was before or after Thomas went upstairs. Before, he thinks. Thomas can vouch for him. But no...no, it was after. Definitely after. "And Featherleigh brought out a glass of ice water."

"Really," the Chief says. He makes a note on his pad.

"Yes, really," Tag says. This suddenly seems like the detail that will save him. He had been wary when Merritt asked for the water because it seemed to indicate she was concerned about her health—or the health of the baby—and then Tag realized that he hadn't actually witnessed Merritt doing either of the shots he'd poured. He wondered if she'd thrown them over her shoulder. Featherleigh had been only too happy to fetch water for her new best friend, and while she was gone, Merritt told Tag she needed to talk to him alone. "Featherleigh brought Merritt a glass of water. Merritt drank the whole thing."

"She drank the whole thing?" the Chief says. "Nobody else had any?"

"Correct," Tag says. He relaxes back into the chair. Maybe Featherleigh slipped Merritt a mickey, or maybe they popped pills earlier in the night. Featherleigh is a wild card. Tag would have categorized her as harmless but it's not beyond her to have accidentally wreaked this kind of havoc.

"There wasn't a water glass on the scene," the Chief says.

"No?" Tag says. This doesn't make sense. "Well, I'm telling you, Merritt drank a glass of ice water. Featherleigh got it from the kitchen." Tag glowers at the Chief, which feels risky, but he is through being intimidated. He didn't drug Merritt and he didn't kill her. "I think you need to talk to Featherleigh Dale."

"I think you need to stop telling me how to run my investigation," the Chief says. He barely raises his voice but his tone is stern nonetheless. He's a local guy. He must resent men like Tag with their showcase homes and their shaky morals. "I have one more question."

Tag is seeing spots in his peripheral vision, the first sign of a tension headache. "What is it?"

"Ms. Monaco had quite a nasty cut on her foot," the Chief says. "And there were traces of Ms. Monaco's blood in the sand on the beach out front. Do you know anything about this?"

"Nothing," Tag says. "She didn't have a cut on her foot when she was under the tent. You can ask Featherleigh! Ask Thomas! So...she must have cut it when she got back on land. Which is proof I delivered her safely!"

The Chief says, "It's not 'proof' of anything. But thank you for your answers." He stands and Tag stands as well, though his legs are weak and watery.

"I think it's pretty obvious Merritt took some pills because she was upset, and then she wandered back into the water and drowned," Tag says. "You could simply conclude that her death was an accident. It would be easier on everyone—her family, her friends, my son, and Celeste."

"I could conclude it was an accident," the Chief says. "And you're right—it would probably be easier on everyone, including my police department. But it wouldn't necessarily be the truth. And in my job, Mr. Winbury, I seek the truth. Which obviously isn't something you'd understand."

"I resent that," Tag says.

"Oh, well," the Chief says. But then, to Tag's relief, he heads for the door. "I'll let you know if I need anything else."

"So we're finished?" Tag asks.

"For now," the Chief says.

Sunday, June 10, 2018

CELESTE

Benji is away on his bachelor-party weekend. Shooter arranged for complete debauchery: Thursday afternoon they landed in Vegas, where they went to their penthouse suite at Aria and gambled until dawn. Friday brought a double bill of race-car driving and gun club. Saturday they drove to Palm Springs to golf and have a thousand-dollar-a-head steak dinner at Mr. Lyons. And today, Sunday, they are to fly home.

Before he left, Benji tried to apologize in advance. "There will probably be strippers," he said. "Or worse."

"Hookers and b-b-blow," Celeste says, and she kisses him good-bye. "Or p-p-performing lesb-b-bians. I really d-d-don't want to know any d-d-details. Just have f-f-fun."

"Should I be happy that you're not protesting this trip," Benji asks, "or concerned?"

"B-B-Be happy," Celeste says.

* * *

Celeste spent Friday and Saturday night in Easton with her parents. Her mother was finished with treatment; there was nothing they could do now but be grateful for each new day. Karen was feeling pretty good, so the three of them took a walk around the neighborhood and then went for an early dinner at the diner.

Celeste had brought her wedding dress at her father's behest.

He said, "You might want to try it on for your mom."

"B-B-But why?" Celeste said. "You g-g-guys are still c-c-coming, right? To Nant-t-tucket?"

"Just bring it, please," Bruce said.

And so, once her mother was settled at home on Saturday night, Celeste tried on the wedding gown. She put on her white silk shantung kitten heels and her pearl earrings. She didn't bother with hair or makeup but that hardly seemed to matter. Karen beamed; her eyes were shining; she clasped her hands to her heart. "Oh, honey, you're a *vision*."

Thank you, Bruce had mouthed from across the room.

Celeste had twirled and tried to smile.

Now, Sunday morning, Celeste drives back to the city to meet Merritt for lunch at a place called Fish on Bleecker Street.

"I want oysters," Merritt had said to Celeste over the phone. "And I don't want to see anyone I know. I have to talk to you."

When Celeste gets to Fish, Merritt is already there with a bloody mary in front of her. She's breaking peanuts between her thumb and forefinger and throwing the shells on the floor. Fish has the atmosphere of a dive bar, but there are yards of crushed ice upon which rest piles and piles of oysters. The Yankees game is on TV. The bartender wears a T-shirt that says SEX, DRUGS, AND LOBSTER ROLL.

"Hey," Celeste says, taking the stool next to Merritt. She plants a kiss on Merritt's cheek and orders a bloody mary as well. She feels she deserves a little hedonism. She has been performing her daughterly duties while Benji has been on a three-day bender.

"Hey yourself," Merritt says. "Have you heard from Benji?"

"No," Celeste says. "I asked him not to call me." Her mood is suddenly buoyant, her tongue nimble. Her stutter all but disappears when she's alone with Merritt.

"Seriously?" Merritt says.

"Seriously," Celeste says. "I wanted him to enjoy himself and not worry about checking in with the future wife."

"Relationship goals," Merritt says.

Celeste takes a sip of her bloody mary; the alcohol

and spice go right to her head. She considers telling Merritt that the reason she asked Benji not to call was that she didn't want to hear any news about Shooter—what Shooter had planned, what Shooter was doing, what funny thing Shooter said. Celeste is almost to the finish line. The wedding is four weeks away, but still she's afraid she'll get tripped up by her irrational heart. Every day she thinks about calling the wedding off.

Celeste takes another sip of her bloody while Merritt peruses the oyster list on the blackboard. It would be such a relief to confess her feelings to Merritt. That's what best friends are for, right? Technically Celeste is being a bad friend by *not* telling Merritt. And yet Celeste fears naming her feelings. She's afraid if she says the words aloud—*I'm in love with Shooter*—something very bad will happen.

Merritt orders a dozen oysters. She's in a West Coast mood, she says, so six Kumamotos and six Fanny Bays; Celeste has agreed to taste one of each in an attempt to cultivate a taste for the little buggers. Genus: *Crassostrea*. Species: *gigas*.

Merritt takes an exaggerated breath and says, "Please don't judge me."

"I would never," Celeste says. "What's going on?"

Merritt holds out her hand. "I'm so nervous, I'm actually shaking."

"Just tell me," Celeste says. She's used to Merritt's theatrics. They're one of the reasons Celeste loves her.

"I've been seeing someone," Merritt says. "It started a few weeks ago and I thought it was a casual fling, but then the guy called me up and since then it's gotten more serious."

"Okay?" Celeste says. She doesn't understand what the big deal is.

"He's married," Merritt says.

Celeste shakes her head. "I thought you learned your lesson with Travis Darling."

"Travis was a predator," Merritt says. "This guy I really like. The problem is...promise you won't kill me?"

"Kill you?" Celeste says. She can't figure out what Merritt is going to tell her.

"It's your future father-in-law," Merritt says. Her head falls forward but she turns to give Celeste a sidelong glance. "It's Tag."

Celeste is very proud of herself: She doesn't scream. She doesn't hop off her stool, leave the bar, and get back on the subway uptown. Instead, she sucks down the rest of her bloody mary and signals the bartender for another.

It's Tag. Merritt and...Tag.

Celeste has been hanging out with Merritt for too long, she thinks, because she isn't shocked. She can all too easily picture Merritt and Tag together. "Did it start when he took you to the wine dinner?"

"A little before that," Merritt says. "I noticed him checking me out the Friday night of your bachelorette weekend while we were out front waiting for the taxi. And so on Saturday morning, I did an exploratory mission to see if he was actually interested, and he was."

"Have you *slept* with him?" Celeste asks. Tag is an attractive guy, and very alpha, which is how Merritt likes her men. But Celeste can't imagine having *sex* with him. He's older than her father.

"Are you really twenty-eight years old?" Merritt asks. "Of course I slept with him."

"Ugh," Celeste says. "I'm sorry, but—"

"I figured it would be a one-night stand," Merritt says. "He asked for my number but I never thought he'd use it. But then, a week and a half later, he called me at two o'clock in the morning."

"Oh, jeez," Celeste says. Her mind starts traveling the predictable path: *What is Tag thinking? He's such a creep! Such a stereotypical male douchebag!* Up until this very moment, Celeste had liked him. It's heartbreaking to discover he's preying on her friend, a woman the same age as his children. Does he do this all the time? He must! And what about Greer? Celeste would never have guessed she would ever have occasion to feel sorry for Greer Garrison, but she does now. She understands the biological impulse behind Tag's actions: he is still virile, still seeking to spread his seed and propagate the species.

But come on!

"Come on!" Celeste says.

Merritt cringes at the outburst.

"Sorry," Celeste says. She dives into the second bloody mary. "I'm sorry. I won't judge you. But p-p-please, Merritt, you have to end it. Tomorrow. Or better still, t-t-tonight."

"I don't think I can," Merritt says. "I'm in it. He's got me. My birthday is next week and I asked him to take me away. I think he's considering it."

"You're a g-g-grown woman," Celeste says. She winces; her stutter is back. Of course it's back! Celeste went from feeling relaxed to feeling like she just stepped off the Tilt-a-Whirl at the carnival with a stomach full of fried dough. "He hasn't *got* you. You can exercise free will and walk away."

"He's all I think about," Merritt says. "He's in my blood. It's like I'm infected." The oysters arrive and Merritt absentmindedly douses half of them with hot sauce. "Do you have any idea what that feels like?"

In my blood. Infected.

Yes, she thinks. *Shooter.*

"N-N-No," she says.

*   *   *

Against her better judgment, Celeste stays with Merritt at Fish all afternoon. Celeste has a Cobb salad, Merritt a tuna burger with extra wasabi. They order a bottle of Sancerre, and then — because Celeste is very slowly processing the news and Merritt is experiencing some kind of high at finally sharing it — they order a second bottle.

"Sancerre is a sauvignon blanc that comes from the Loire Valley," Merritt says. "Tag taught me that our first night together."

"Great," Celeste says. She is patient as Merritt gradually reveals the particulars of her relationship with Tag. They meet at her apartment. They once went out for sandwiches. Tag paid, pulled her chair out, emptied her trash. Tag is refined, he's mature, he is smart and successful. She knows it's cliché but she is a sucker for his British accent. She wants to eat it, take a bath in it. Tag is jealous of Robbie. He showed up outside Merritt's apartment building in the middle of the night because he was so jealous.

"Does he ever t-t-talk about Greer?" Celeste asks. She pours herself another glass of wine. She is getting drunk. Their food has been cleared and so Celeste attacks the bowl of peanuts.

"Sometimes he mentions her," Merritt says. "But we tend to stay away from the topic of family."

"Wise," Celeste says.

Merritt tells Celeste that, just a few days earlier, Tag asked Merritt to show up at a hotel bar where he was meeting clients for drinks. They had sex in the ladies' room, then Merritt left.

It's like a scene from a movie, Celeste thinks. Except it's real life, her real best friend and her real future father-in-law. She should be *horrified!* But in an uncharacteristic twist, she is almost relieved that Merritt is doing something even worse than she is. She's in love with Benji's best friend. But she has exercised willpower. Willpower, she now understands, is an endangered species. Other people conduct wildly inappropriate affairs.

"I have to get home," Celeste says, checking her phone. "Benji lands in twenty minutes and he's c-c-coming over for dinner."

"You can't tell Benji," Merritt says.

Celeste gives her friend a look. She's not sure what kind of look because her face feels like it's made of Silly Putty. The air in the bar is shimmering. Celeste is *so* drunk.

"Obviously not," she says.

Merritt pays the bill, and Celeste, for once, doesn't protest or offer to pay half, nor does she refuse when Merritt presses thirty dollars in her hand and puts her into a cab headed uptown. It's bribe money, and Celeste deserves it.

Somehow, she makes it up the stairs and into her apartment. She can't imagine sobering up enough to have dinner with Benji, but if she cancels he'll think she's upset about his weekend away.

She *cannot* tell him about Merritt and his father. She can't let anything slip. She has to act as though everything is fine, normal, status quo.

She sends Merritt a text. End it! Now! Please!

Then she falls asleep facedown on her futon.

She wakes up when she hears her apartment's buzzer. The light coming through her sole bedroom window has mellowed. It's late. What time? She checks her bedside clock. Quarter after seven. That will be Benji.

She hurries to the front door and buzzes him in, then she rushes to the bathroom to brush her teeth and splash water on her face. She's still drunk but not as drunk as she was and not yet cotton-mouthed or hung over. She's even a little hungry. *Maybe she and Benji can walk down to the Peruvian chicken place,* she thinks. It's Sunday night, so Benji will sleep at home and Celeste can be in bed by ten. She has two all-school field trips coming to the zoo tomorrow; it's the curse of June.

Celeste is immersed in these mundane thoughts when she opens the door, so what she sees comes as a complete shock.

It's not Benji.

It's Shooter.

"Wait," she says.

"Hey, Sunshine," he says. "Can I come in?"

"Where's B-B-Benji?" she asks, and an arrow of pure red panic shoots through her. "D-D-Did something happen?"

"He took a cab straight home from JFK," Shooter says. "Didn't he call you?"

"I d-d-don't know," Celeste says. She hasn't checked her phone since...since before getting in the taxi to come home.

Shooter nods. "Trust me. He called you and left a message saying he wanted to go home to bed. There wasn't much left of old Benji when we got off the plane."

"Okay," Celeste says. "So what are you d-d-doing here?"

"Can I come in, please?" Shooter asks.

Celeste checks behind Shooter. The stairwell is its usual gray, miserable self. She thinks to feel embarrassed about her apartment — Shooter lives in some corporate condo in Hell's Kitchen, but even that must put her place to shame.

She isn't supposed to care what Shooter thinks.

"Fine," she says. She's doing a good job at sounding nonchalant, even a bit irritated, but her insides are flapping around like the Bronx Zoo's hysterical macaw Kellyanne. Benji has been diminished by his bachelor adventure, and Shooter doesn't look so hot either. His hair is messy and he's wearing a New York Giants T-shirt, a frayed pair of khaki shorts, and flip-flops. He looks younger to Celeste, nearly innocent.

She steps aside to let him in, then she closes the door behind him.

"So how was the bachelor party of the century?" she asks.

Instead of answering, Shooter kisses her, once, and it feels exactly the way Celeste dreamed it would: soft and delicious. She makes a cooing sound, like a dove, and Shooter kisses her again. Their mouths open and his tongue seeks out hers. Her legs start to quiver; she can't believe she is still standing. Shooter takes her head in his hands; his touch is gentle but the electricity, the heat, the desire between them is crazy. Celeste had no idea her body could respond to another person like this. She's on fire.

Shooter's hands travel down Celeste's back to her ass. He pulls her against him. She wants him so badly she could weep. She hates that she was right. She had known if this ever happened, she would become delirious and lose control of her senses.

Don't stop, she thinks. *Don't stop!*

He pulls away. "Celeste," he says. His voice is husky. "I'm in love with you."

I'm in love with you too, she thinks. But she can't say it, and suddenly her good sense kicks in the way it should have a few moments ago. *This is wrong! It's wrong!* She is engaged to Benji! She will not debase that, she will *not* cheat on him. She will not *cheat* on him. She will not be like Merritt or Tag. They may think that the intensity of their desire justifies their actions, but that is morally convenient. Celeste isn't religious but she does have an immutable sense of right and wrong and she also believes—though she would never say this—that if Merritt and Tag continue, something bad will happen. Something very bad.

This will not be the case for Celeste. She can't falter like this or her mother will die. She's sure of it.

"You have to leave," Celeste says.

"Celeste," he says.

"Leave," she says. She opens the door. She feels faint. "Shooter. Please. *Please.*"

He stares at her for a long moment with those hypnotic blue eyes. Celeste clings to the small piece of herself that knows this is the right action, the only possible action.

Shooter doesn't press. He steps out, and Celeste shuts the door behind him.

Saturday, July 7, 2018,
5:15 p.m.

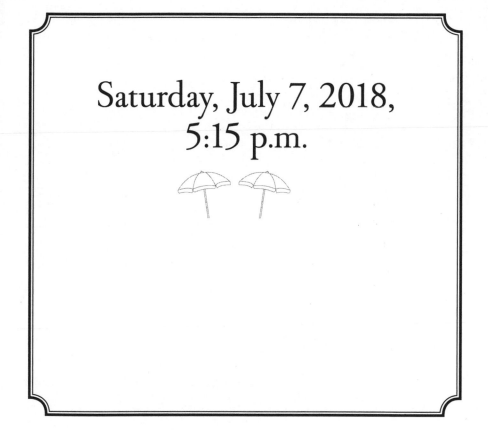

NANTUCKET

Nick has just heard from the Chief: His interview with Featherleigh Dale is suddenly *very important.* Tag Winbury, the father, is still a person of interest but the Chief isn't convinced he did it.

"He admitted he took the girl out in the kayak," the Chief said. "He said she jumped off, on purpose, and he yanked her back up by the *wrist,* which is consistent with the ME's report. He admitted to pouring the shots, so a reasonable explanation is he slipped a mickey into one of the shots, but forensics found nothing in the bottle or the shot glasses. He didn't know about the cut on her foot. He said she must have cut it after they got back to dry land. We need to check with Featherleigh about the cut. And Tag said Merritt drank a glass of water that Featherleigh Dale got from the kitchen."

"Water?" Nick said. "There wasn't a water glass at the scene."

"Exactly," the Chief said. "So maybe he's lying. Or maybe..."

"Someone got rid of the water glass," Nick said. The mother, Greer Garrison, had been in the kitchen at some point, getting champagne. Nick still has a feeling she's hiding something. "If Greer knew about the affair..."

"And the baby..." the Chief said.

"Maybe *she* slipped a pill into the drinking water," Nick said. "And then went back and cleared the glass. Ran it through the dishwasher on the power-scrub cycle. But how would she know Merritt would then go for a swim?"

"Maybe the father and mother are in it together," the Chief said.

"Both of them?" Nick said. "The night before their son's big wedding? A wedding they're paying for?"

"Another thing," the Chief said. "Tag Winbury is a smart guy. If he'd used the kayak ride to drown our girl, he would have made damn sure he locked the kayak up when he got back. Right? To cover his tracks?"

"Are we overthinking this?" Nick asked. "Was it just an accident?"

"Be thorough with Featherleigh," the Chief said.

"You know me," Nick said. "I'm a bloodhound."

*   *   *

Nick is waiting in the interview room when they bring Featherleigh Dale in. He hears her squawking a bit out in the hallway: She's going to miss her flight to JFK. She needs to get back to London. Luklo swings open the door to the interview room and ushers Ms. Dale inside. Nick stands.

He and Featherleigh Dale regard each other.

She says, "Well, you're a tasty morsel, aren't you?"

Luklo smirks and Nick extends a hand. "Ms. Dale, I'm Nick Diamantopoulos, a detective with the Massachusetts State Police. I just have a few questions and as soon as we're through here, assuming we're satisfied with your answers, I'll have Officer Luklo get you back to the airport and on your way."

"If I had known the detective would look like you," Featherleigh says, "then I would definitely have committed a crime."

"If you'll just have a seat," Nick says.

Featherleigh wheels in her roller bag and sets a handbag bursting with *stuff*—a paperback novel, a hairbrush, an open bag of pretzels, which spill all over the floor—on top of the suitcase, then she grabs a smaller clutch purse from within the bag and brings it with her to the table, where she proceeds to put on fire-engine-red lipstick.

Nick waits for her to get settled and thinks, *This woman is too disorganized to kill anyone, even accidentally.* But maybe he's wrong. Featherleigh Dale is in her mid-forties. She's a bit chunky, she has hair halfway between blond and red — it looks like she changed her mind in the middle of a dye job — and she's wearing what looks like a jumpsuit issued by the air force in 1942, minus the sleeves.

"Can I get you anything to drink?" Nick asks.

"Not unless you have a decent chardonnay," she says. "You interrupted my lunch."

Nick takes a seat. "Let's get started, Ms. Dale—"

"Feather," she says. "My friends call me Feather."

"Feather," Nick says, and he nearly smiles. There used to be a transvestite prostitute on Brock Avenue in New Bedford named Feather. He pauses to remind himself that this is serious business and he needs to be thorough. "Let's start with how you know the Winburys."

Featherleigh, now Feather, waves a hand. "Known them forever," she says.

"Meaning?"

"Meaning, let's see... Tag Winbury went to Oxford with my older brother, Hamish, may he rest in peace, so I've known Tag since I was a kid. I reconnected with the family at my brother's funeral, and after that, our paths kept crossing. I own a business finding antiques for people like Greer, people who have more money than God and don't mind plunking down thirty thousand quid for a settee. I found her some salvaged windows from a church in Canterbury. Those went for ten thousand quid *apiece* and I'm pretty sure she's still got them in storage."

"So you have a business relationship with the Winburys, then," Nick says.

"And personal," Feather says. "We're friends."

"Well, yes," Nick says. "You came over from London for the wedding. How well do you know Benji and Celeste?"

"I know Benji a little bit," Feather says. "Celeste not at all. Just met her last night. Her and her friend. Shame what happened."

"What happened?" Nick says.

Feather's eyes widen. "Have you not heard? The bride's friend, Merritt, *drowned*. The maid of honor. I thought that was why you had questions."

"No, right, it is, I do," Nick says. Her disarray is throwing him off his stride. "I meant, what happened last night? You were part of the group that sat out under the tent drinking rum, correct?"

"Mount Gay Black Barrel," Feather says. "Out of Barbados. You know, I've been to the estate where it's made. I love the stuff."

"Who exactly was sitting at the table with you?" Nick asks.

"Tag, Thomas, myself, and Merritt," Feather says. Then she adds gravely, "The deceased."

"So you say you just met Merritt last night," Nick says. "How did that come about?"

"It came about the way those things do at a party," Feather says. "I noticed her right away. She was pretty and stylish and she had natural confidence. I love confidence." Feather beams at Nick. "*You* have natural confidence. I can see it. It's a very attractive trait in a man."

"So you noticed her from afar," Nick says. "Were you properly introduced?"

"Not until later," Feather says. "Much later, in fact—after the party was over."

Nick makes a note and nods. He senses Feather needs only the slightest encouragement to keep talking.

"I was desperately seeking another drink. The young kids went into town—bride, groom, best man, Thomas—but no one thought to invite old Feather, and I just wasn't ready to go back to my inn. I tried to wrangle a bottle of booze out of the catering help but that didn't work, so I went on a hunt."

"A hunt," Nick says.

"I was stealthy," Feather says. "Because I knew if Greer saw me, she would put me right into a taxi."

"Oh, really?"

"Greer doesn't like me, doesn't *approve* of me. She's old money, landed gentry, grew up on a manor called Swallowcroft, went to Wycombe Abbey, all of that.

And she suspects I'm after her hubby. Ha!" Feather hoots. "He's way, *way* too old for me."

Nick needs a verbal leash for this woman so she doesn't go wandering off, although he makes a note: *Greer suspected Feather + Tag???* "Back to how you met Merritt..."

"So I was sneaking around a bit, tiptoeing, dodging behind bushes, harder than it looks because of motion-detector lighting. I figured if I could get to the pool house, I would find alcohol." Feather taps a finger against her temple. "Clever bit of sleuthing on my part there. Anyway, I stumbled across the maid of honor sitting in Greer's rose garden. She was crying."

"Crying?"

"I asked if she was all right. Yes, she said. Then I asked if there was anything I could do. No, she said. I was surprised because I'd pegged her for naturally confident and then there she was, like a little girl on the playground whose friends had all forsaken her. So I asked if she wanted to join in my caper."

"Caper," Nick says.

"Hunting for booze in the pool house," Feather says. "And she said yes and came with me."

"Then what?" Nick says.

"We opened the gate, we selected a couple of chaise longues, I slid the glass doors to the pool house open, and voilà—full bar! I made a couple of Grey Goose and tonics and brought them out. Merritt said she didn't want hers, her stomach was feeling funny, and that was just fine by me. I had them both."

"Did Merritt stay with you?" Nick asks.

"Yes, she stayed. We talked. Turned out we had a lot in common."

"Did you?"

"We were both involved with married men," Feather says. "I mean, *what* are the chances of that?"

Not so slim, Nick wants to say, but he needs to tread carefully here. Feather seems to be genuine but he has been at this long enough to suspect it might be an act.

"Did Merritt say anything about the man she was involved with?" he asks.

"Only that he was married," Feather says. "And was apparently a real bastard. Pursued her, pursued her, pursued her...then dropped her like a hot potato. Won't leave his wife, no way, nohow. And I'll tell you, that all sounded much too familiar."

"But Merritt didn't say who the man was?"

"She didn't tell and neither did I," Feather says. "We were there to commiserate, not confess."

"Did she say if the man she was seeing was *at* the wedding?" Nick asks.

"*At* the...no. She lives in Manhattan. Why would...are you thinking she was seeing a married man at the wedding and he was the one who killed her?"

Nick needs to redirect. "What happened when you left the pool house?"

"We decided to walk back to the main house," Feather says. "And we happened across Tag and Thomas and their bottle of Black Barrel."

"Did they seem surprised to see you two?" Nick asks.

Feather tilts her head. "Did they? I don't remember. Tag asked if we were up for a nightcap. We said yes."

"So you're sitting around under the tent drinking rum and what happens?" Nick asks.

"What do you think happens?" Feather asks. "We get drunk." She pauses. "Drunk*er*."

"Was Merritt drinking?"

"I assume so?" Feather says. "Don't quote me on that because, remember, she had a queasy stomach. After a while, Thomas's wifey called him upstairs and I figured the party was breaking up. But Tag is a night owl and he seemed game to keep going awhile longer and Merritt asked for water. I got it for her, actually."

"You got Merritt a glass of water?" Nick says.

Feather nods.

"Did you put ice in the water?" Nick asks.

Feather's eyes roll skyward, as if the answer to that question is written on the ceiling. "I can't recall. I'm sorry. Is that important?"

"Did anything else happen while you were inside getting the water?" he asks. "Did you see anyone? Do anything?"

Feather nods. "I took a piss."

"You went to the bathroom," Nick says. "Was that before you poured the water? Or after?"

Feather stares at him. "After," she says. "I left the water on the counter. I mean, I didn't bring it into the loo with me."

"But you didn't see anyone else in the kitchen?" Nick asks.

"No."

"Did you hear anyone?"

"No," Feather says. "Fan was on. In very posh houses, you know, they don't listen to one another tinkle."

"No one followed you in from outside?" Nick asks.

"No," Feather says.

"And when you brought Merritt the water, did she drink it?" Nick asks.

"Drank it down like she'd eaten a pound of rock salt."

"Do you remember *clearing* her glass?" Nick asks. "Because the water glass wasn't on the table this morning. But the shot glasses were."

Feather shakes her head. "I've got no memory of clearing the glass or not clearing the glass. If I had to guess, I'd say I left it there, thinking the housekeeper would get it in the morning."

Nick makes a note: *Housekeeper?*

"And how did the party finally break up?" Nick asks.

"We ran through the bottle of rum," Feather says. "Tag said he was going to his study for another. Right after he left, Merritt said she was going to bed. So I was in the tent by myself for a while... then I decided I'd better skedaddle. I didn't want to stay up late drinking with just Tag."

"Why not?"

"It wouldn't look good," Feather says. "If Greer caught us..." Feather pauses. "I'm terrified of that woman."

"Are you?"

"Everyone is terrified of her," Feather says. "She says one thing but you can just tell by looking at her that in her mind she's thinking something else. Novelists are notorious liars, you know."

"Are they?" Nick asks.

"Aren't they?" Feather says. "They lie for a living. They make up stories. So it stands to reason that this tendency runs over into their personal lives."

Nick is intrigued by this answer. "Did you see Greer around at all, even for an instant, after the party? Did you see her in the kitchen pouring herself a glass of champagne?"

"No," Feather says. She gasps. "Why? Do you think Greer had something to do with what happened?"

"You didn't see her?" Nick asks.

Feather shakes her head.

"Did you see Merritt again that night?"

"No," Feather says.

"So the last time you saw Merritt was when she left the tent saying she was going to bed."

"Correct."

"At any point during the night, did Merritt cut her foot?" Nick asks.

"Cut her *foot?*" Feather says. "No."

"Was she wearing shoes when you were doing your stealthy hunting?"

"Yes," Feather says. "Silver sandals. Gorgeous. Merritt said she had gotten them for free from the company and I asked if she could get me a pair for free and she asked what size I wore and I said ten and a half and she said, 'Done.'" Feather's eyes start to water. "She really was a lovely girl."

"Yes," Nick says. "I'm sure she was." He writes: *No cut. Sandals.* He knows there were silver sandals on the scene, under the tent, which Merritt must have left behind when she went for the kayak ride. Nick finally feels like he can see what happened last night . . . except for a few critical details.

"Okay, so when you . . . skedaddled, where did you go? Did you call a taxi and go back to your inn?"

"Mm-hmm," Feather says.

"I'm sorry," Nick says. "I need you to give me a yes-or-no answer."

Feather hesitates.

Okay, then, Nick thinks. *Here it is.* "Feather?"

"Yes," she says. "Yes, I did."

"And what time was that?" Nick asks.

"Couldn't tell you."

"But it was late," he says.

Feather shrugs.

Nick locks eyes with Feather and gives her his best smile. Nick's sister, Helena, calls this smile "the kill," because it usually gets him whatever he's after. And Feather succumbs to it. She cocks an eyebrow.

"Are you single?" she asks. "Because if you are, I could be convinced to stay another night."

"Did you call the taxi right away?" Nick asks. "Or did you stay in the tent? Or did you do something else?"

"Something else?" Feather says.

"The manager of your inn," Nick says, "told our officer that you returned to the hotel at quarter past five this morning. And we have a time of death for Ms. Monaco somewhere between two forty-five and three forty-five. Working backward, then, she likely entered the water between two thirty and three thirty. Now, if you didn't reach your inn until quarter after five..."

"The manager is mistaken," Feather says. "It was earlier than five. Hours earlier."

"But you said only a moment ago that you didn't know what time it was," Nick says.

"Well, I can bloody well tell you it was earlier than five o'clock!" Feather says.

"We can easily check the security cameras," Nick says.

Feather hoots. "*That* place does *not* have security cameras!" she says. "You're trying to *trick* me!"

"They had a break-in last year," Nick says. "Nothing was taken, but Miss Brannigan, who runs the inn, was understandably skittish, so she installed cameras." Nick closes his notebook, grabs his pen, and stands. "I'll send Officer Luklo out to request the camera footage."

He turns, wondering how many steps away he'll get.

Two steps, as it turns out.

"Wait," Feather says. "Just wait."

"Do you want to change your answer?" Nick says.

"Yes," Feather says. "Do you have a cigarette?"

"Quit five years ago," Nick says. "Saved my own life. It's a filthy habit."

"Filthy," Feather agrees. "But sometimes nothing else will do."

"I have to agree with you there," Nick says. He sits

back down. "I do sometimes bum one when I've been drinking bourbon."

"You're human, then," Feather says. She tears up. "And I'm human too."

"That's exactly right," Nick says. "You're human and human beings make mistakes and act in all kinds of ways we shouldn't." He pauses and very slowly opens his notebook. "Now, why don't you tell me what happened. You didn't call a taxi, did you?"

"No," Feather says. "No, I didn't. I went into the house and fell asleep."

Nick drops his pen. "Fell *asleep?*"

"More like passed out," Feather says.

"You expect me to believe that?" Nick says.

"It's the truth," Feather says.

Nick stands up. "You were one of the last people to see Merritt Monaco alive. Unless you can come up with a taxi driver who will vouch for picking you up before two forty-five, I have you at the scene at the time of death. You were also the one who brought Ms. Monaco the water, which was the last thing she consumed before she died. Do you know what kind of trouble that puts you in, Ms. Dale?"

"I stayed at the Winburys' house," Feather says, "because I was waiting for someone."

"Waiting for who?" Nick says. He tries to sort through the major players. Mr. Winbury having an affair with Merritt. Shooter Uxley in love with the bride. Who was Featherleigh Dale waiting for in the middle of the night?

Feather's full-on crying now.

Nick can't decide which way to go. Should he raise his voice and play the bully? *No,* he thinks. That only works on TV. In real life, what works is patience and kindness.

Nick grabs the box of tissues they keep in the interview room for just this sort of occasion. He puts it on the table, plucks out a tissue, hands it to Feather, then eases down into his seat.

"Who were you waiting for, Feather?" he asks, as gently as he can. "Who?"

"Thomas," Feather says.

Thomas? Nick thinks. *Who's Thomas?* Then he remembers: Thomas is Benji's brother.

"Thomas Winbury?" Nick says. "Are you involved with Thomas Winbury...romantically?" *Married man,* he thinks. *Tag...way, way too old...They were there to commiserate, not confess.*

"Was," Feather says. "But then he broke things off in May"—she stops to pluck another tissue out of the box and blow her nose—"when his wife got pregnant. He said he couldn't see me anymore. He told me not to come to the wedding. He said if I came to the wedding, he'd kill me. Those were his exact words."

Nick's thoughts are hopping now. Like father, like son. Thomas was involved with Feather but broke it off when he found out Abby was pregnant. Thomas tells Feather not to come to the wedding. Threatens her. Maybe he thinks she'll tell Abby about the affair.

"Do you think Thomas *meant* it?" Nick says. "People say 'I'm going to kill you' all the time. Too much for my taste. Or do you think...do you think he actually tried to kill you?"

There was nothing in the shot glasses, nothing in the bottle.

The water glass.

"Let's go back," Nick says. "When you went into the kitchen to get water for Merritt, you said everyone was still back at the table, correct?"

Feather pauses. "Yes."

"And there was no one in the kitchen?" he asks. "You're sure you didn't see Greer? I know you're terrified of her but you can tell me the truth."

"No," Feather says. "I did not see Greer."

"And you used the restroom after you poured the water?" Nick says. "How long were you in the bathroom?"

"Couple minutes?" Feather says. "The usual amount of time. But I did try to primp a bit as well."

"So let's say five minutes. Sound fair?"

"Fair."

Plenty of time for Thomas to sneak in and drop a

mickey in the water glass—or for Greer to do the same.

But, Nick thinks, *Merritt wasn't poisoned, just sedated.* Which leads Nick back to the father, Tag Winbury. Tag could have doctored the water before he took Merritt out on the kayak. Then, when she "fell overboard," she would have been more likely to drown.

What about the cut on her foot?

Maybe she cut it on a shell on the ocean floor when she fell off the kayak? But there was blood in the sand. If Feather is telling the truth and Merritt was wearing sandals earlier in the night, then she must have cut her foot after she got back from the kayak ride. Could she have cut her foot on the beach before climbing into the kayak? But there was no blood in the kayak.

Unless Tag had washed it off.

But if he was going to do that, why not tie the kayak back up?

Aaarrgh! Nick feels the answer is *right there*...he just can't see it.

He smiles at Feather again and says, "I'll be back in two shakes."

Nick steps outside the interview room to call the Chief.

"Talk to Thomas, the brother," he says.

KAREN

A knock at the door wakes Karen up. Karen looks over to Bruce and finds him asleep and snoring aggressively.

Another knock. Then a voice: "Betty? Mac?"

It's Celeste. Karen swings her feet to the floor and carefully stands up. She still feels no pain, which is odd.

She opens the door to see her sad, beautiful daughter standing before her, wearing the pale pink dress with the rope detail that she was supposed to travel in tomorrow. She's holding her yellow paisley duffel bag.

"Oh, my poor, poor Bug," Karen says. She gathers Celeste up in her arms. "I am so sorry, sweetheart. So, so sorry about Merritt."

"It's my fault," Celeste says. "She died because of me."

Karen recognizes this response as an opening for a longer conversation. She glances back at Bruce. He's still sawing logs, as they say; she knows she should wake him up — he will want to see Celeste — but she senses that Celeste needs a confidante, and there are some things that men just don't understand.

Karen grabs her cane, steps out into the hallway, and closes the bedroom door behind her. "Where shall we go?"

Celeste leads her to the end of the hall where there is a glassed-in sunporch that is quiet and unoccupied. Karen negotiates the one step down holding on to Celeste's arm. Celeste leads Karen over to a sofa with bright yellow-orange cushions the color of marigolds.

Karen takes a moment to admire the room. The floor is herringboned brick covered with sea-grass area rugs. The perimeter of the room is lined with lush potted plants—philodendron, ferns, spider plants, a row of five identical topiary trees trimmed to look like globe lamps. From the ceiling hang blown-glass spheres swirling with a rainbow of color. Karen becomes mesmerized for a second by the spheres; they look as delicate as soap bubbles.

Celeste follows her gaze and says, "Apparently these were an obsession of Greer's the year she wrote *A Murder in Murano.* Murano is an island near Venice where they make glass. I had to look it up when Benji told me that."

"Oh," Karen says. The room has enormous windows that look down over the round rose garden. "There is no end to the wonders of this house."

"Well," Celeste says, but nothing follows and Karen can't tell if she's agreeing or disagreeing. She sits next to Karen on the cheerful sofa. "I decided last night that I wasn't going to marry Benji."

"I know," Karen says.

"How?" Celeste whispers. "How did you know?"

"I'm your mother," Karen says. She could tell Celeste about the dream with the strange hotel and how, in that dream, Celeste was lost. She could tell Celeste that she woke up so certain marrying Benji was the wrong thing for Celeste to do that she got out of bed and went looking for her, but she had found Bruce and Tag instead and learned something she could have lived the rest of her days without knowing. She could even tell Celeste about her visit to the psychic, Kathryn Randall, who had predicted that Celeste's love life would enter a state of chaos... *But there's nothing either one of us can do about it.*

Instead, Karen lets those three words suffice. She is Celeste's mother.

It's suddenly clear that Karen's remaining time on earth matters. There are so many moments of her life that will be overlooked or forgotten: locking her keys in her car outside of Jabberwocky in downtown Easton, having her credit card declined at Wegman's, peeing behind a tree at Hackett's Park when she was pregnant with Celeste, beating her best time in the two-hundred-meter butterfly in the biggest meet of the year against Parkland when she was a senior, nearly choking on a cherry Life Saver during a game of kickball when she was ten years old, sneaking out to the eighth hole of the Northampton Country Club with Bruce during her prom. Those moments had seemed important to Karen at the time but then they vanished, evaporating to join the gray mist of her past.

However, what Karen says to Celeste here and now will last. Celeste will remember her words for the rest of her life, she is sure of this, and so she has to take care.

"When you met Benji," Karen says, "we were very excited. Your father and I have been so happy together...we wanted you to find someone. We wanted you to have what we have."

Celeste lays her head in Karen's lap, and Karen strokes her hair. "Not everyone is like you," Celeste says. "Not everyone gets that lucky on the first try... or ever."

"Celeste," Karen says. "There are things you don't know..."

"There are things *you* don't know!" Celeste says. "I tried to make myself love Benji. He's a good person. And I understood it was important to you and Mac that I married someone who could take care of me financially—"

"Not just financially," Karen says, although she realizes she and Bruce are probably guilty as charged. "Benji is strong. He comes from a good family—"

"His family," Celeste says, "isn't what it seems."

Karen gazes out the window at the serene expanse of the Nantucket harbor. Maybe Celeste already knows that Tag Winbury's mistress has a baby on the way. It makes either perfect sense or no sense at all that a family as wealthy and esteemed as the Winburys have a second narrative running deep underneath the first, like a dark, murky stream. But who is Karen to judge? Only a few hours ago, she feared *she* had caused Merritt's death.

"So few families are," Karen says. "So few *people* are. We all have flaws we try to hide, darling. Secrets we try to keep. *All* of us, Celeste."

"I made it to the night before the wedding," Celeste says. "Before that, I thought if I acted on my true feelings, something bad would happen. Then I told myself that was silly. My actions don't influence the fate of others. But Merritt died. She *died,* nearly as soon as I made the decision. She was the only real, true friend I've had in my life other than you and Mac, and now she's gone forever. Forever, Mama. And it's my fault. I did this to her."

"No, Celeste—"

"Yes, I did," Celeste says. "One way or the other, I did."

Karen watches the tears stream down her daughter's face. Karen is curious—and more than a little alarmed—that Celeste keeps insisting Merritt's death is her fault. Did Celeste *do* something to her? Did she *not* do something? It can't be a good idea for Celeste to be carrying on about how it's her fault when the house is crawling with police.

"What do you mean by that, darling?" Karen asks. "Do they know what happened?"

"I think she took pills," Celeste says. "I think she did it to herself. She was in a bad relationship, a bad *situation*...and I was emphatic about her breaking it off for good, but she said she couldn't. I found her crying in the rose garden last night."

"You did?"

"She wanted to know why love was so hard for her, why she couldn't get it right. And I hugged her and kissed her and told her it was going to be fine, she just needed to move on. But you know what I should have done? I should have told her that I couldn't get it right either. That love is hard for everybody." Celeste takes a breath. "I should have told her I didn't love Benji. But I couldn't even say the words in my own mind, much less out loud to another person. She was my best friend and I didn't tell her."

"Oh, honey," Karen says.

"Early this morning I went outside to look at the water one last time because I knew I was leaving this view behind for good. And I saw something floating."

"Celeste," Karen whispers.

"It was Merritt," Celeste says.

Karen closes her eyes. They are both quiet. Outside, birds are singing and Karen can hear the gentle lapping of the waves on the Winburys' beach.

Celeste says, "I'm not going to marry Benji. I'm going to take a trip, by myself maybe. Spend some time alone. Try to process what happened."

"I think that's wise, darling," Karen says. "Let's go tell your father."

Bruce is still asleep in bed, though his noisy breathing has quieted. His hair is standing on end, his mouth hangs open, and even from so far away, Karen can smell his night-after whiskey breath. His left hand, the one with the wedding band, is resting on his chest, over his heart. *Their love is real,* Karen thinks. It's strong but flexible; it's unfussy and unvarnished. It has thrived in the modest house on Derhammer Street, in the front seat of their Toyota Corolla, in the routine of their everyday—breakfast, lunch, dinner, bedtime, repeat, repeat, repeat. It has endured long workweeks, head colds, snowfalls and heat waves, meager pay raises and unexpected bills; it endured the deaths of Karen's parents, Bruce's brother, Bruce's parents, and the smaller losses of Celeste's toads, lizards, and snakes (each of which required a burial). It endured through construction on Route 33, a schoolteacher strike when Celeste was in fourth grade, the Philadelphia Eagles losing season after season after season despite Bruce's impassioned ranting at the TV (and finally winning it all this past year when, quite frankly, both Bruce and Karen had stopped caring about football); it endured the sad day the Easley family moved away and took their dogs Black Bean and Red Bean, who at the time were Celeste's best friends, with them. It survived the Pampered Chef parties thrown by women who all secretly thought they were better than Karen, it survived Bruce's bizarre friendship with Robin Swain, and it will survive this tragic weekend.

We would go to the post office to mail packages or check our box, and the line was always extra-long on Saturdays, but you know what? I didn't care. I could wait an hour. I could wait all day... because I was with Karen.

While Celeste gently jostles Bruce's shoulder to wake him up, Karen slips into the bathroom and locks the door behind her. She opens the third drawer, finds the bottle of pills, picks out the three pearlescent ovoids, and flushes them down the toilet.

Karen's pain is gone. She feels stronger than she has in weeks, months even. It makes no sense, and yet it does.

Karen can't go anywhere just yet. She needs to see what will happen next.

GREER

She catches the Chief on his way out of Tag's study.

"There's something I think you should know," she says.

The Chief barely seems to hear her. He's looking at his phone. "If you'll excuse me," he says. He reads his screen, then says, "Your son Thomas is...where? I'll need to talk to him next."

Greer can't believe he's brushing her off. She deliberated about her best course of action: Tell him about the pills or not? Yes, she decided, for a couple of reasons. She will tell him about the pills and they will finally be able to put all this to rest.

"I haven't seen Thomas," Greer says. "But Chief Kapenash, sir, there's something I must tell you."

The Chief finally seems to notice her. They are standing in the hallway; God only knows who's listening. Tag is in his study. He might have his ear pressed up against the door. Greer wonders if she should have discussed her decision with him first. He has always been good at seeing a problem from every possible angle and ensuring that a strategy won't backfire. Many times, when Greer needed help with the plot in one of her mysteries, she would consult Tag and he would nearly always come up with a creative answer. Those were some of Greer's favorite moments in her entire marriage—lying in bed with Tag, her head resting in the crook of his arm as she explained her characters and their motivations while Tag asked provocative questions. He praised her imagination; she gushed over his insightful solutions. Character development required a humanist like Greer, but plotting often benefited from the mind of a mathematician. Greer had felt, in those instances, like part of a team.

Oh, how she hates him! For an instant, she wishes she'd married someone mediocre, uninspiring. *Wealthy* and uninspiring—her third cousin Reggie, for example; posh accent and not an original bone in his body.

"Shall we go into the living room?" Greer asks the Chief. She turns on her heel, not waiting for an answer.

The Chief follows her into the living room and Greer closes the door behind him. She doesn't bother with sitting. If she sits, she thinks, she might lose her nerve.

"I forgot to tell the detective something," she says.

The Chief's expression hardens into all business. He's not a bad-looking man, Greer thinks. He has a gruffness that she finds sort of appealing, nearly sexy. And he's age appropriate. This is what Tag has done; now Greer has to appraise candidates for future romantic interludes. Would the Chief be interested in her?

Never, she decides.

The Greek, maybe, Nick, if he were in the mood for an older woman. Greer flushes, then she notices the Chief looking at her expectantly.

"I didn't forget, exactly," Greer says. She wants to clarify this. "It's something I only just remembered."

The Chief nods almost imperceptibly.

"I went to bed whenever, midnight or so, but I couldn't sleep. I was wound up."

"Wound up," the Chief says.

"Excited about the wedding. I wanted everything to go well," Greer says. "So, as I told the detective, I got up and went to the kitchen to pour a glass of champagne."

"Yes," the Chief says.

"Well, what I forgot to tell the detective — meaning what I didn't remember at *all* until just a little while ago — is that I brought my sleeping pills to the kitchen. My intention was to take a pill with water before I drank my champagne."

"What kind of pills were they?" the Chief asks.

"I'd have to call my physician in New York to be sure," Greer says. "They're quite potent, put me to sleep instantly and knock me out for eight hours straight. Which was why, in the end, I decided *not* to take a pill. I needed to be up early this morning. So I hoped the champagne would do the trick by itself, and that was, in fact, what happened. But when I looked for the pills a few moments ago in my medicine cabinet, where I keep them, they weren't there. And that's when I recalled bringing them to the kitchen. I checked the counter next to the refrigerator plus every shelf, every drawer, every possible hiding place. I asked my housekeeper, Elida. She hasn't seen them."

"Were they in a prescription bottle?" the Chief asks. "Were they marked?"

"No," Greer says. "I have a pillbox. It's an enamel box with a painting of Queen Elizabeth on the top."

"So who would have known that the pills inside were sleeping pills?" the Chief asks.

"The sleeping pills and the pillbox were something of a family joke," Greer says. "My husband obviously knew. And the children."

"Would Ms. Monaco have known they were sleeping pills?" the Chief says.

Greer knows she can't hesitate here, even for a second. "Oh, yes," Greer says. "I offered Merritt a sleeping pill from the box the last time she stayed with us, in May." This answer wouldn't pass a polygraph, she knows. The truth is that Greer had offered Merritt aspirin for the headache she had after the wine dinner but never a sleeping pill. "So I think we can conclude what happened."

"And what's that?" the Chief says.

"Merritt took a sleeping pill," Greer says.

The Chief says nothing. It's infuriating; the man is impossible to read, even for Greer, who can normally see people's agendas and prevailing emotions as though she were looking into a clear stream.

"She helped herself to my pills," Greer says. "Then she went for a swim, maybe thinking she would cool down before slipping into bed. And the pill knocked her out. It was an accident."

The Chief pulls out his pad and pencil. "Describe the pillbox again, please, Ms. Garrison."

He's bought it, she thinks, and relief blows through her like a cool breeze. "It's round, about four centimeters in diameter, cherry red with a portrait of the queen on the top," she says. "The top is hinged. It flips open."

"And how many pills inside?" the Chief asks.

"I couldn't say exactly," Greer says. "Somewhere between fifteen and twenty-five."

"The last time you remember seeing the pillbox, it was in the kitchen," the Chief says. "There's no chance you brought it back to your bedroom?"

"No chance," Greer says. Her nerves return, multiplied, quivering.

"So you know there's no chance you brought the pills back to your bedroom," the Chief says, "and yet you didn't remember bringing the pills into the kitchen when you talked to the detective. I guess I'm questioning how you can be so certain."

"I keep the pills in only one place," Greer says. "And they weren't there. If I had brought the pills back to my room, they would have been where I always keep them."

"No guarantees of that," the Chief says. He clears his throat. "There are a couple of reasons why I don't think Merritt took a pill of her own volition."

Of her own volition, Greer thinks. Oh, dear God. They'll suspect Tag of drugging the girl, of course. Or they'll suspect Greer herself.

"But wait..." Greer says.

The Chief turns away. "Thank you for the information," he says. "Now I'm going to find your son Thomas."

Tuesday, July 3-Friday, July 6, 2018

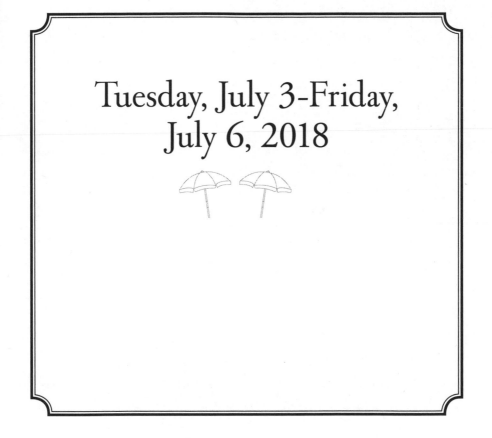

CELESTE

Tuesday at work, she makes a list of things that might take the place of love.

Security, financial
Security, emotional
Apartment

After the honeymoon, Celeste is moving into Benji's apartment in Tribeca. Together they surveyed Celeste's studio to see what would make the trip downtown. Not her futon, not her yard-sale furniture, none of her dishes or pots and pans, not her shower curtain or bathroom rug, not the pair of mason-jar lamps filled with beans. When Celeste said that she wanted to bring the rainbow candles her mother made, Benji said, "Just bring the candle Abby gave you if you want a candle." The candle he was referring to was a Jo Malone pine-and-eucalyptus luxury candle that Abby gave Celeste as an engagement present. Celeste does love the way it smells but once she found out how much it cost, she knew she could never, ever light it.

Celeste immediately decided she would bring her mother's candles despite Benji's obvious opinion that they weren't as good as a department-store candle. Celeste would set them on the mantel!

Benji told Celeste that he contacted a real estate agent at Sotheby's who is searching for a brownstone on East Seventy-Eighth Street, specifically on the block between Park and Lexington. Celeste tries to imagine herself living on that block, owning a home on that block. Would that be as good as love?

Shooter has the condo in Hell's Kitchen. The condo has nothing in it but a mattress and a TV, Benji has told her. Shooter is never there.

Family

Tag, Greer, Thomas, Abby, Abby's future baby, assorted aunts, uncles, and cousins in England.

Shooter has even less family than Celeste. Shooter has no one.

Nantucket

This is, perhaps, the strongest competition for love. Because Celeste has never felt about a place the way she feels about Nantucket. She tries to ignore that her most romantic storybook times there have been with Shooter. She could easily go to the Chicken Box with Benji; she could take Benji out to Smith's Point and show him the natural water slide. On Nantucket, she will always have a beach to walk on, a path to run, a farm to provide heirloom tomatoes and corn on the cob, a boat to putter around the harbor in, cobblestoned streets to stroll in the evenings. Celeste yearns to experience Nantucket at every time of year. She wants to go to the Daffodil Festival in the spring, wear a yellow sweater, make a picnic of cold roast chicken and deviled eggs and asparagus salad, and cheer as the antique-car parade passes by. She wants to go in the fall when the leaves change and the cranberries are harvested and the high-school football team is playing at home. She wants to go at Thanksgiving, swim in the Turkey Plunge, watch the tree-lighting on Friday night, eat scallops just harvested from the sound. She wants to go in the dead of winter during a blizzard when Main Street is blanketed with snow and not a soul is stirring.

Shooter won't be able to give her Nantucket the way that Benji can.

Celeste can't come up with anything else, so she rolls back up to *Security, financial.* Celeste will have health insurance. Celeste will be able to shop for groceries at Zabar's, Fairway, Dean and DeLuca. She will be able to buy expensive salads, bouquets of fresh flowers—every day if she wants! Orchids if she wants!—boxes of macarons, bottles of Veuve Clicquot, *cases* of Veuve Clicquot! She will be able to buy hardcover books the day they come out and get orchestra seats for the theater. They'll be able to take trips—to London, certainly, but also to Paris, Rome, Shanghai, Sydney. They'll be able to go on safari in Africa, maybe even hike to see the silverback gorillas in Uganda, a dream so far-fetched that Celeste has put it in the same category as space travel. She will shop with Merritt at Opening Ceremony, at Topshop, at Intermix. She'll try things on without checking the price tag. It's inconceivable. It doesn't seem real.

How will it work? Celeste asked Benji. *M-M-Money, I m-m-mean. Once we're m-m-married?*

I'll put your name on my accounts, Benji said. *We'll get you an ATM card, a checkbook. Once I turn thirty-five, I'll have access to the trust from my Garrison grandparents, so there will be that money as well.*

Celeste has wondered since then how much money is in the Garrison trust. A million dollars? Five million? Twenty million? What is the amount that takes the place of love?

What about m-my salary? Celeste had asked.

Keep it for yourself, Benji said.

Celeste earns sixty-two thousand dollars a year, but Benji makes that sound like a quarter she found on the sidewalk. She supposes that, to him, it is.

Celeste's assistant, Bethany, walks into her office without knocking and Celeste scrambles to hide the list. What would Bethany think if she saw it? What kind of woman has to make a list of reasons she's happy to be marrying Benjamin Winbury?

"Celeste?" Bethany says. Her expression is uneasy, as though she suspects she interrupted something.

"Mmm?" Celeste says.

"Zed wants to see you in the conference room," Bethany says.

"Conference room?" Celeste says. She was supposed to meet with Zed in his office because tomorrow starts a two-and-a-half-week vacation that includes her wedding and honeymoon and she needs to delegate the work on her desk.

Bethany shrugs. "That's what he said."

The door to the conference room is closed and when Celeste swings the door open she sees a dozen golden balloons and, in the center of the table, a round bakery cake ringed with icing flowers and the words *Congrats, Celeste!* A cheer goes up and Celeste looks around at her zoo colleagues: Donner, Karsang, Darius, Mawabe, Vern, even Blair from reptiles.

Celeste tears up. A shower! Her co-workers have thrown her a bridal shower, complete with balloons, cake, a few bags of chips, and a wrapped present.

Celeste can't believe it. This isn't *that* kind of office and these aren't *those* kind of co-workers. They obviously know Celeste is getting married, and she knows that Blair feels her long-ago migraine was responsible for Celeste and Benji meeting in the first place. Three of Celeste's co-workers are actually making the trip to Nantucket—Bethany, Mawabe, and Vern—but because it's the Fourth of July week, all of the reasonably priced hotels were sold out, so the three of them are arriving Saturday at noon and leaving on the nine-thirty fast boat. Celeste is touched that the three of them are making the trip—to drive from the city and take the boat requires more effort than she thought they'd make—but Celeste is also a bit nervous about their arrival. Benji exacerbated Celeste's concern when he said, "I can't imagine Mawabe and Vern in the same room as my mother."

Although Benji's sentiment echoed Celeste's own feelings, she took umbrage. "Why not?" she said. "It would be g-g-good for your mother to realize people like Mawabe exist. I'm just sorry B-B-Blair isn't coming." She paused. "B-B-Bethany is normal. Sort of."

"Sort of," Benji conceded.

Now, Bethany comes forward holding out the gift. Celeste assumes Bethany selected the gift and everyone else chipped in, but some people—like Darius—probably have yet to pay their share.

"What c-c-could it be?" Celeste asks. She unwraps

the box and lifts off the top to find a simple white apron with *Mrs. Winbury* embroidered in black on the front.

Mrs. Winbury. Celeste's heart sinks.

"I love it," she says.

Her stutter is so debilitating and so unpredictable that she and Benji have had to tailor their wedding vows with Reverend Derby so that all Celeste has to say is "I do."

But even those two words present a challenge.

It's Wednesday, the Fourth of July. Benji and Shooter, Thomas and Abby, and Tag and Greer are already up on Nantucket. But Celeste had to work through Tuesday, and Merritt has a can't-miss fireworks party tonight. Celeste's parents aren't due to arrive until Friday. Celeste decides she will fly to Boston with Merritt on Thursday morning and then Uber to the Cape and take the fast ferry across to Nantucket.

Celeste calls Merritt at three o'clock on Wednesday afternoon. "I c-c-can't do it," she says.

"What?" Merritt says. "What do you mean?"

What *does* she mean? She means she can't marry Benji. She knows she's making a mistake. She's in love with Shooter. It's a physical condition, an affliction. It is, as Merritt said, in her blood. Celeste feels like she's standing on a cliff. If Shooter were here right now by her side, willing to hold her hand and never let go, she would jump.

But he's not. He's on Nantucket, executing the best-man duties with his usual flair.

"I c-c-can't say my vows," Celeste says. "I st-st-st..." She can't force it out. *Stutter* is, ironically, the hardest word.

"I'll be right there," Merritt says.

Merritt stands before Celeste and says, "Do you, Celeste Marie Otis, take Benjamin Garrison Winbury to be your lawfully wedded husband? To have and to hold, to bug and to pester, to scream at and screw, until death do you part?"

Celeste smiles.

"Say it," Merritt says.

"I d-d-do," Celeste says. She winces.

"Pretend it's a different word," Merritt says. "Pretend it's *dew* like on a leaf in the morning or *due* like your rent. I think you're just psyching yourself out."

Dew, like on a leaf in the morning, Celeste thinks.

"I dew," she says.

The corners of Merritt's mouth lift.

"Again," she says.

"I d-d-do," Celeste says. "I mean, I dew."

"Just like that," Merritt says. She glances at her

phone. "I have to go. We'll practice more tomorrow. And Friday."

"Okay," Celeste says. "Merritt—"

Merritt holds up a hand. "You don't have to thank me," she says. "You're my best friend. I'm your maid of honor."

"No," Celeste says. "I mean, yes, thank you. B-B-But what I want to know is, d-d-did you end things with Tag?"

"No," Merritt says. "He ended things with me."

Once Celeste is on Nantucket, she becomes a marionette operated by Greer and Roger Pelton, the wedding planner. Roger is like a kind and supremely capable uncle. He goes over the three-day schedule with Celeste—where she needs to be, what she needs to do, what she will be wearing; the outfits are lined up in the closet. Thursday afternoon, Greer has scheduled Celeste for a massage, a mani-pedi, and an eyelash extension.

"Eyelash extension?" Celeste says. "Is that n-n-necessary?"

"No," Roger says. "I'll call R. J. Miller and cancel that part of the appointment."

"Thank you," Celeste says.

"The most important part of my job," Roger says, "is protecting my brides from their mothers and mothers-in-law."

Celeste loves how Roger refers to her as "my bride." She pretends she's marrying Roger, and this lightens her mood. Temporarily.

Celeste keeps one eye trained on Shooter at all times, like she's a spy or a sniper. Their gazes meet and lock, and Celeste dissolves inside. He's trying to tell her something without speaking — but what? Celeste craves the looks, even though they're ruining her. When Shooter isn't looking at her, when he's joking with Merritt or Abby or Greer, she feels sickeningly jealous.

Celeste's parents arrive. Celeste worries that, like Benji, the Winburys will think Karen and Bruce are "the salt of the earth" and will patronize them, possibly without their even realizing it.

But Greer is fine with Celeste's parents, and Tag is better than fine. Celeste wants to hold a grudge against Tag, but he is so gracious and charming with her parents that she can feel only gratitude toward him. She'll confront her anger and disappointment later, after the wedding.

The rehearsal dinner unfolds exactly as it should. Other people are drinking the blackberry mojito punch. Celeste has one sip of Benji's and decides to stick to white wine. She doesn't have time to keep track of Shooter; she's too busy meeting this person and that person: a friend of Tag and Greer's from London named Featherleigh, a business associate of Tag's named Peter Walls, neighbors from London, neighbors from New York, Benji's lacrosse coach from St. George's, and the four Alexanders—blond and preppy Alexander, Asian Alexander, Jewish Alexander, who is engaged to a black woman named Mimi who is a Broadway dancer, and the Alexander known as Zander, who is married to a man named Kermit.

Celeste feared her parents would be shy and overwhelmed but they are holding their own and Betty looks better than Celeste anticipated. She walks with a cane and Celeste knows she's on a mighty dose of painkillers, but she appears happy, nearly radiant. She is far happier about this wedding than Celeste is.

Celeste makes a deal with God: *I will go through with this if You just please keep my mother alive.*

There are passed hors d'oeuvres, each one more creative and delicious-looking than the next, although Celeste is far too anxious to eat. She sips her wine but it has little effect. Her body is numb. The only thing that matters is Shooter. Where is Shooter? She can't find him. Then he will appear, brushing past her elbow; even the slightest touch lights her up. She has thought back on the kissing in her apartment only a few thousand times since it happened. How did she have the willpower to refuse him? She is in awe of herself.

Her father stands to give a toast. It's about Betty first, and Celeste's eyes well with tears. Then it's about Celeste and Bruce says, *And so to you, Benjamin Winbury, I say from the heart: Take care of our little girl. She is our treasure, our hope, our light, and our warmth. She is our legacy. Here's to the two of you and your life together.* And everyone clinks glasses and drinks.

Thomas stands to speak next, and Celeste leans over to Benji and says, "I thought Shooter was giving the toast."

"He didn't want to," Benji says.

"What?" Celeste says.

"He told me he didn't want to speak tonight," Benji says. "He'll give a toast tomorrow, after we're married."

Tomorrow, Celeste thinks. *After we're married.*

Celeste doesn't want to go out; she has done enough pretending for one night. She wants to go to bed. Honestly, she would like to sleep as she did when she was a child: right between Mac and Betty.

Her mother senses something is wrong. Celeste can tell by the emphatic way Betty insists that Celeste go out to be with her friends, be with Benji.

I'll be with Benji the rest of my life! Celeste thinks. Her time with her mother is dwindling; the sand is running through the hourglass more quickly now, at the end. But Celeste knows her mother will be happier if she goes out.

Besides, Shooter is going. And Merritt—Celeste needs to keep an eye on Merritt. However, when they are all piling into cars, Merritt is missing.

"Wait a minute," Celeste says. She climbs out of the Winburys' Land Rover and runs across the driveway to the second cottage. She pokes her head in but the lights are off; Merritt isn't there.

"Celeste," Benji says. "Come on!"

"I have to find Merritt," she says. She tries to remember the last time she saw Merritt. It was during the dinner, obviously, but Celeste had to meet and mingle with so many people that she didn't get to spend any time with her one true friend. And Merritt didn't give a toast, even though she'd intimated that she might. *Please,* Celeste thinks, *don't let her be with Tag.* But that has to be it. Where else could she be? She is always the one leading the charge when it comes to continuing the fun.

Celeste tears through the house checking each room—the kitchen, the formal dining room, the casual dining room, the powder room, even the glowing cube that is the wine cellar. She goes down the hall and checks the alcove outside Greer and Tag's room but she doesn't have the courage to knock on their bedroom door or on the door to Tag's study. She scurries down to poke her head into the white living room, even though she has never once set foot in there. She sees a figure in one of the chairs and she's so startled, she cries out.

"It's just me," someone with a British accent says. It's that Featherleigh woman. "Are you looking for someone?"

"My friend Merritt?" Celeste says. "Maid of honor? Black dress?"

"If you bring me a bottle of whiskey, I'll tell you where she is."

"Excuse me?" Celeste says. She has been told that Featherleigh is an old friend of the family but Celeste can't imagine Greer abiding this kind of rudeness. "Have you seen Merritt? I'm sorry, I need to find her."

"I'm the one who's sorry, love," Featherleigh says. "I noticed her earlier, quite an attractive girl, but I haven't seen her in hours."

"Okay, thank you," Celeste says, hoping she doesn't now seem rude by rushing out. What is Featherleigh doing in the living room, anyway? Certainly Greer didn't offer to let her *sleep* there?

Celeste sails through the laundry room and out the side door, hurrying toward the pool house. She hears coughing and can just barely make out the shadow of a figure bent over in the rose garden. It's Merritt.

"Merritt!" Celeste says. She crosses the arched

footbridge over the koi pond into the rose garden. Merritt is spitting into the grass. "Are you *sick?*"

Merritt straightens up and wipes her mouth. There are tears running down her face. "The oysters aren't agreeing with me."

Celeste reaches out to embrace her friend. "You poor thing," she says. "Let me walk you back to your cottage. I'm going to tell the rest of them to go to town without me. I didn't want to go anyway."

"No," Merritt says. "No, you go, please, or I'll feel guilty. I just need some air." She tries to smile at Celeste but then she starts crying again. "Only I could mess up a gorgeous night like this."

"Stop it," Celeste says. "Weddings are stressful."

"Especially this one," Merritt says. She holds out her left hand. "You see this ring?" Merritt points to a silver band on her thumb. "He gave me this for my birthday."

"Tag did?" Celeste whispers. She takes hold of Merritt's hand and studies the ring. It's set with tiny multicolored stones. It's very pretty, but Merritt has a lot of cool jewelry, some of it given to her for free by various fashion labels.

"It's a *ring*," Merritt says. "He could have given me anything for my birthday—a book, a scarf, a brace-let. But he gave me a *ring*."

"Yes, well." Celeste is pretty sure Tag meant the

ring to be a token of his fondness, nothing more, but he might have chosen something a little less emotionally charged. Just then, Celeste hears the Land Rover's horn and she knows Benji is losing patience; she has been gone much longer than she intended. "I love you. You know that, right? And when you leave here Sunday, you never have to see Tag Winbury again. I promise I won't make you attend any family functions."

"I wish it were that easy," Merritt says. She takes an exaggerated breath. "There's something I have to tell you."

The car horn sounds again. Celeste feels annoyed at Benji's impatience, but she knows he has a caravan of people waiting on her. "I have to scoot," she says. "Come with us."

"I can't," Merritt says. "I don't feel well. I'm just going to hang around here, maybe go to bed."

"Before midnight?" Celeste says. "That would be a first." She gives Merritt another hug. "Tomorrow we'll find time to talk, I promise. I don't care if a church full of people have to wait."

Merritt gives a small laugh. "Okay."

They are a party of twelve, and town is crowded with holiday revelers. There's a line to get into the Boarding House; the Pearl is at maximum capacity, as is Nautilus. The Club Car piano bar is an option, but

Thomas announces that one *ends* at the Club Car; one never starts there. Asian Alexander's wife is wearing stilettos and doesn't want to risk walking down to Straight Wharf or Cru.

Celeste looks to Benji, waiting for him to make an executive decision. As it is, they are spilling off the corner of India and Federal into the street.

"Let's go to the back bar at Ventuno," he says.

Everyone agrees. It's nearby, it's open-air; they'll go for one drink, then reassess.

Somehow Celeste gets sifted to the back of the group, probably because she's literally dragging her feet. She doesn't see the point of yet another drink. If anything, she needs food. She was so busy worrying about Mac and Betty and getting them set with their lobsters that she hadn't eaten anything.

"I'm starving," she says to herself.

"You and me both."

Celeste turns to see Shooter at her right shoulder.

She looks for Benji. He's up front, talking to Mimi the Broadway dancer.

"He's occupied," Shooter says. "Let's go get pizza." He grabs her hand.

"I can't," Celeste says. She's afraid to look at him, so she stares down at her feet in her jeweled sandals. Her toes are painted a color called Sunshine State of Mind to match her dress tonight. She does leave her hand in his, however, for a few forbidden seconds.

"We'll come right back," Shooter says. He whistles sharply, and Benji spins around. "I'm taking your bride to get a slice. Back in ten."

Benji waves, then turns again to Mimi—and Kermit, who has joined their conversation.

He couldn't care less.

"Okay," Celeste says. "Let's go."

There's a line outside Steamboat Pizza and a steady stream of cars unloading from the late ferry. Celeste feels weirdly exposed and she distances herself half a step from Shooter. She has dreamed of being alone with him but now that it's happening, she's tongue-tied. Across the street she sees a woman with long jet-black hair wearing suede booties with shorts—suede booties in July; even Celeste recognizes that as a no-no—and the woman looks like she's pointing her phone at Celeste and Shooter. Taking a picture? Celeste turns her back. She wants to make a joke about the care and feeding of the bride but she can't manage small talk and, apparently, neither can Shooter.

"Follow me," he says.

He gets out of line, which is fine—Celeste wouldn't have been able to eat anything in front of him anyway—and starts walking down the street toward the ferry dock. Celeste follows, bobbing and weaving, skirting groups of teenagers, dodging couples with strollers, stopping short so an elderly couple can pass.

She doesn't ask Shooter where they're going. She doesn't care. She would follow him anywhere.

They cross the Steamship Authority parking lot, Shooter striding ahead, and then he cuts to the right of the terminal building and turns to check that she's behind him. He waits for her, places a hand on her back, and ushers her to a bench at the edge of the dock. The view is over the working part of the harbor. It's not glamorous, but it's still pretty. Everything on Nantucket is pretty.

They sit side by side, their thighs touching, and then Shooter wraps his arm around Celeste's shoulders. She suddenly feels the effect of the wine she drank earlier. She acts impulsively; she doesn't care who sees. She buries her face in Shooter's chest and inhales the scent of him. He is *all she wants*.

"Run away with me," he says.

She takes a breath to say, *Yeah, right*—but he stops her.

"I'm serious, Celeste. I'm in love with you. I know it's wrong, I know it's unfair, I know all of our friends will hate us, especially my own best friend—hell, my brother, because Benji is by every standard my brother. I don't care. I do care, but I care about you more. I have never felt this way about anyone before.

My feelings for you are tragic; they're Shakespearean— I'm not sure which play, some combination of *Hamlet* and *Romeo and Juliet,* I think. I want you to sneak out of the house and meet me here, right here, at six fifteen tomorrow morning. I'll have two tickets on the six-thirty ferry. The boat gets to Hyannis at eight thirty, which is also our scheduled reveille tomorrow, so by the time people realize we're both gone, we'll be safely on the mainland."

Celeste nods against his chest. She's not agreeing, but she wants to hear more; she wants to imagine this escape. The anxiety that has been squeezing her heart loosens its grip. She gets a clear breath.

"You can say no. I expect you to say no. And if you do say no, I'll show up at the altar tomorrow right next to Benji like I promised. I will give a sweet, meaningful toast with the appropriate amount of humor and at least one line about how Benji doesn't deserve you. I will ask for one dance with you and when that dance is over, I'll give you a peck on the cheek and let you get on with the rest of your life. With him."

Celeste exhales.

"If you come with me, I will buy four tickets to Las Vegas—one for me, one for you, two for your parents. And I will marry you by the end of the day tomorrow. Or we can move more slowly. But I need you to know that I am serious. I'm in love with you.

If you don't feel the same way, I will still go to my grave feeling grateful for every second I have had with you. If nothing else, you proved that the heart of Michael Oscar Uxley is not made of stone."

Michael Oscar Uxley, she thinks. She realizes with shock that she has never asked his real name.

"Yes," she says.

"What?"

She raises her face. She looks into Shooter's blue eyes...but what she sees is her parents in profile from the backseat of their old Toyota. They are turned toward each other, singing along to "Paradise by the Dashboard Light." *Do you love me, will you love me forever?* Celeste is eleven years old, she knows all the words too, but she doesn't dare sing because the two of them sound so...*good* together.

Then she flashes back to before they were Mac and Betty to her, before they were even Mommy and Daddy, back to when they were just ideas: love, security, warmth.

Celeste is young, only one or two years old. They are playing a game called Flying Baby. Bruce has Celeste by one hand and Karen has her by the other. They swing Celeste between them until Bruce calls out, "Flying," and Karen calls out, "Baby!" And they lift Celeste up off the ground. For one delicious moment, she is suspended in midair, weightless.

Finally, she thinks of her parents as teenagers—

her mother in her red tank suit, her father in his sweatpants and hoodie staring at the orange. The moment their eyes meet, the moment their hands touch. That certainty. That recognition. *You. You are the one.*

This is what it feels like.

Nothing, as it turns out, can take the place of love.

"Yes," she says.

Saturday, July 7, 2018, 5:45 p.m.

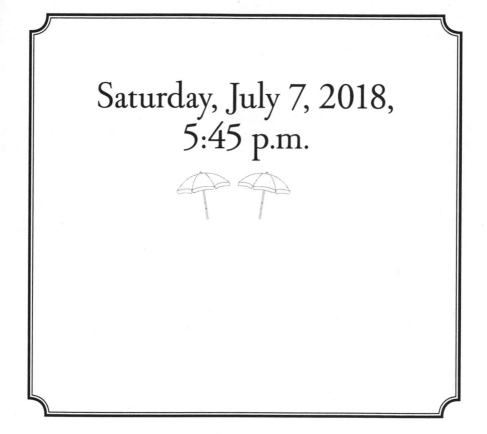

THE CHIEF

He finds Thomas in the kitchen, scarfing down a turkey sandwich. Next to the sandwich plate is a highball glass of scotch, three-quarters full.

"Mr. Winbury?" the Chief says.

"Thomas," he says, wiping his hands hastily on a napkin and then extending one to the Chief. "Mr. Winbury is my father."

"I have a few questions," the Chief says.

"You've talked to just about everyone else," Thomas says. "I don't know that I'd have much to add."

"Please," the Chief says. He's too low on patience to deal with the runaround. "Follow me." He heads down the hall and around the corner to the living room. Thomas has abandoned the sandwich but brought the scotch, and the Chief can't blame him. Thomas takes a seat on the sofa, crosses his ankle over his knee, and sinks back into the cushions like a man without a care in the world, and the Chief closes the door.

"Events of last night?" the Chief asks. "After the party?"

"Back bar at Ventuno, Boarding House. I left after one drink. My wife called to say she wanted me home. Pronto."

"What did you do at home?"

"Went up to see Abby. She was asleep so I went downstairs for a drink."

"Did anyone join you?"

"My father."

"Anyone else?"

"No."

"Are you sure about that?"

Thomas's eyebrows shoot up, but it's acting. He's a man pretending to remember something. The Chief is surprised he doesn't snap his fingers.

"Oh! After a while, Merritt joined us, as well as a friend of my parents' named Featherleigh Dale. She's an antiques dealer from London, here for the wedding."

"Why was Featherleigh Dale at the house so late?" the Chief asks. "Is she staying here?"

"No. I'm not sure why she was still around."

"You're not?"

"I'm not."

The Chief lets the lie sit there for a moment, stinking.

"The four of you sat under the tent drinking rum, is that right?"

"Yes, sir."

"Who was the first to leave the tent? Was it you?"

"It was. My wife called down. I had pushed my luck by then already, so I went up to bed."

"Do you have any idea what time that was?"

"Around two, I think."

"I need you to focus here. Do you remember Featherleigh Dale going into the kitchen for water? A glass of water for Ms. Monaco?"

Thomas shakes his head, but then says, "Yes."

"When Featherleigh went in to get the water, do you recall how long she was gone?"

"Five minutes. Maybe a bit longer."

"Did you have any of the water?"

"No, sir."

"Do you remember anyone else having any of the water? Even a sip?"

"I was there to drink rum, sir," Thomas says. "I don't remember much about the water."

Somewhere in the house, the clock strikes six. The Chief is dying to get home, take off his shoes, crack open a beer, hug his wife, talk to Chloe. This day has lasted five years, but that's the way it is with murder cases. He's sure that, back at the station, his voice mail is filled with messages from insistent reporters. When this is all over, he's going to need another stress-management class.

"Let me switch gears. Does your mother have a pillbox?"

"Excuse me?"

"Does your mother have a box where she keeps her..."

"Her sleeping pills?" Thomas says. "Yes. It's round. It has a picture of Queen Elizabeth on it."

"Would you say this pillbox is well known to members of your family?"

Thomas laughs. "Oh, yes. My mother's pillbox is infamous. It was a gift from her grandmother."

"And would you say that everyone in your family is aware that it holds *sleeping* pills?"

"Yes. And she won't share them. I asked for one once and she told me I couldn't handle it."

"Really," the Chief says. Greer claimed she offered Merritt one of the sleeping pills. So they were "too strong" for her son but she gave one to a houseguest? Does that seem likely?

No, it does not.

"Did you see the pillbox in the kitchen last night?"

"No," Thomas says. "Why? Was it left out?" He sits up straighter. "Do you think Merritt took one of my mother's sleeping pills?"

"You didn't see the pillbox?" the Chief asks. "You didn't *touch* the pills?"

Thomas slaps his knee. "I most certainly did not. But *Merritt* must have seen my mother's pills and taken one—or even two—not realizing how potent they are. And then she went for a swim." He stands up. "I think everyone will be fine with this being called an accidental death. There's no reason to manufacture any more drama. This little inquisition has produced enough anxiety as it is—"

"We're not finished here," the Chief says. He waits while Thomas reluctantly sits back down. "Do you know anything about a cut on Merritt's foot?"

"A cut?" Thomas says. "No. But if she did cut her foot, maybe she went into the water to rinse it."

This isn't something the Chief has considered. She did have quite a nasty gash on her foot. It's possible she rinsed it off in the water to avoid tracking blood into the Winbury house. The only place they'd seen blood was in the sand.

"Also, Merritt had been drinking," Thomas says.

The Chief doesn't respond to this. It's interesting that Thomas is so eager to offer up theories about what happened. The Chief has been at this long enough to know that that is how a guilty person acts.

"What is your relationship with Ms. Dale?" the Chief asks.

"My...I already told you, she's a friend of my parents."

"And that's it? You don't have a personal relationship with her?"

"Not really," Thomas says. "No."

"My colleague with the Massachusetts State Police interviewed Ms. Dale," the Chief says. "She told him that she had been romantically involved with you but that you broke things off in May when your wife got pregnant. Is that true?"

"No!" Thomas says.

"One of you is lying," the Chief says.

"Featherleigh is lying. She's a pathological liar, in fact. She's being investigated for fraud in her antiques business. Did she tell your colleague *that?* She tried to pass off a fake George the Third gilt-wood table to what she thought was a naive client. So, clearly, she lies as a general practice."

"That seems like pretty specialized knowledge to have about your parents' friend," the Chief says.

"My mother told me about it."

"Your mother? So if I ask Greer right now if she told you about Featherleigh's fraud charges and what exactly they were, she'll say yes."

Thomas nods. His expression is confident except for three tense lines high on his forehead.

The Chief stands up. "All right. I'll go talk to your mother."

"Wait," Thomas says. He collapses against the back of the sofa. "We did have a brief fling. Me and . . . Ms. Dale. Featherleigh."

"How brief?" the Chief asks.

Thomas throws up his hands. "Not brief, exactly. But sporadic." He pauses. "Several years."

The Chief sits back down. "So you've been romantically involved with Ms. Dale for several years?"

"On and off," Thomas says. "And like she told you, I ended things in May."

"Did it upset you that Ms. Dale chose to attend the wedding?"

"Of course it upset me," Thomas says. "I want her out of my life. My wife is pregnant, I need to focus on her and on getting my career back on track. This thing with Featherleigh, well, it ran amok. She was blackmailing me."

"Blackmailing you?" the Chief says.

Thomas picks up his scotch and throws half of it back. The Chief feels a mixture of triumph and shame. He has gotten people to break down and talk before and it always feels satisfying on the one hand—like cracking a safe, almost—and vaguely obscene on the other. This guy has been hiding something for *years* and now he's coming clean. So many crimes, and especially murders, are committed by people with dark motivations like Thomas. Thomas likely had no intention of killing anyone; he just wanted to keep the secret of his love affair safe.

"I hooked up with her initially after her older brother, Hamish, died. Hamish was a school friend of my father's. I went to the funeral with my parents—this was before I met Abby—and at the reception afterward, Featherleigh and I got drunk and things happened. After that, I saw her whenever I was in London or she was in New York. Then I met Abby. I told Featherleigh I couldn't see her anymore and she went off the deep end."

"How so?"

"Abby came with my family to Virgin Gorda over the Christmas holiday the first year we were together. Featherleigh must have found out because she showed up on Virgin Gorda with a client of hers from Abu Dhabi who had a gigantic yacht. And then another time, right after I finished law school, Featherleigh made a surprise appearance at my classmate's graduation party. She walked right into Bemelmans Bar at the Carlyle Hotel in New York and told everyone *I'd* invited her there."

"Why didn't you just correct the misperception then?"

"Because...well...there *had* been times that I'd seen Featherleigh since I'd been with Abby. And that's where I messed up. I didn't make a clean break. I didn't keep Featherleigh firmly in my past. The first time I wasn't sure if things were going to work out with Abby and me, so when Feather called and told me she had a suite at the Gramercy Park Hotel, I went. Then, after Abby had her second miscarriage—which was a really bad one—she was weepy and depressed, really difficult to be around. She felt like a failure. I felt like a failure. We started to fight. There wasn't a conversation we could have that didn't lead right back to the pregnancies. Sex was out of the question. It was a tough time. And Featherleigh capitalized on that. She magically appeared in New York and then in *Tampa, Florida,* where I was assisting on a case. She sent me a first-class plane ticket to Paris and then, a few months later, to Marrakech. Then, of course, it turned out she was charging her clients the price of my plane tickets, thinking they wouldn't notice. But of course they did and they dragged Featherleigh to court, which killed her business and depleted her savings and caused her to do something stupid, like try to pass off a fake George the Third gilt-wood table as genuine."

The Chief nods. He has his guy. He can feel it. "The blackmail?" he says.

"The blackmail," Thomas says. He throws back the rest of his scotch and the Chief wishes for the bottle, anything to keep him talking. "It started back in January of this year. I wanted to break things off. And Feather told me if I did, she would tell Abby what we'd been doing. So I had to keep on." Thomas presses his fingers into his eye sockets. "I started failing at work. I was trying to get Abby pregnant and trying to keep Featherleigh from running her mouth. Then, in May, Abby got pregnant and the pregnancy seemed strong and viable and I just made a decision that I wasn't going to let Featherleigh Dale control me any longer. The fraud charges helped because I figured even if she did contact Abby, she would have zero credibility."

"But even so, you must have been upset that Ms. Dale was attending your brother's wedding."

"I asked her not to come," Thomas says. "I pleaded and begged."

"And threatened," the Chief says. "Ms. Dale said that you said if she showed her face on Nantucket, you would kill her. Did you say that?"

Thomas nods. "Yes. Yes, I did."

"Did you drop one of your mother's sleeping pills into the glass of water Featherleigh brought to the table, thinking she would be the one to drink it? Did you think *she* might take a swim and drown or get behind the wheel of a car and have an accident? Did you do that, Thomas? Because after what you've told me, I would understand if you did."

Thomas starts to cry. "I've made such a mess of things."

The Chief breathes all the way out, maybe for the first time since he woke up this morning. "I'll need you to come down to the station and sign a statement. You have the right to an attorney."

Thomas sniffs, shakes his head. "I think you've misunderstood. I've made a mess of things but I didn't drug anyone. I didn't see my mother's pills. I didn't touch the glass of water. And you'll forgive me, but it would take a hell of a lot more than a measly sleeping pill to kill Featherleigh Dale."

"So you..." the Chief says. "You didn't..."

Thomas shakes his head again. "I wanted Featherleigh to disappear. But I didn't put anything in anyone's water. I didn't see or touch my mother's sleeping pills and Featherleigh is still very much a threat to me." Thomas offers the Chief a sad smile. "That is the truth."

The Chief calls Andrea and tells her he's on his way home.

"Did you figure out what happened?" Andrea says.

"Not quite," the Chief says. "We uncovered a bunch of ugly secrets, don't get me wrong, but we can't quite link any of them to the death of the young woman." He thinks of Jordan Randolph at the *Nantucket Standard*. He's going to have questions. Everyone is going to have questions. "How's Chloe?"

"She's upset," Andrea says. "She told me she bonded with the maid of honor at the rehearsal dinner."

"Bonded?" the Chief says. "What does that mean?"

"I tried to get more out of her but she said she wanted to talk to you. I told her you were very busy—"

"No, no, it's fine," the Chief says. He wonders if

the answers he's been looking for are under his own roof. "I'll be there in a few minutes."

The Chief knocks on Chloe's bedroom door.

"Come in," she says.

She's lying on her bed reading a book about turtles. Is that right? *Turtles All the Way Down,* the cover says. The Chief has no idea what that means but he's glad she's reading. Her phone is plugged in on the nightstand and it buzzes and blinks with incoming messages—Instagrams, he supposes, or Snapchats, or whatever has replaced Instagram and Snapchat. Nick would probably know.

"Hey," he says with what remains of his good humor. He closes the door behind him and takes a seat on her bright blue fuzzy chair. The chair reminds the Chief of Grover from *Sesame Street,* but at least it's comfortable. "Auntie said you wanted to talk?"

Chloe nods, sets the book down, sits up. She isn't wearing any makeup, which is unusual. Her face is maturing into beauty, a beauty she inherited from her mother. Tess wasn't much older than Chloe is now when the Chief first met her, Andrea's beloved younger cousin, a cousin as close as a sister.

"There are two things I want to tell you," Chloe says. "About last night."

"Go ahead," the Chief says.

"I was eavesdropping during the party," Chloe says. "I overheard a conversation between the maid of honor and the father of the groom. I think they were...involved. I know they were. She was pregnant with his baby. He wanted her to get rid of it. He said he would write her a check. She said she wanted to keep the baby because it was a link to him. She said she would tell Greer. Greer is his wife."

The Chief nods and tries not to let any emotion show on his face. He's appalled that this particular storyline managed to make its way to Chloe.

"You haven't told anyone that, I hope," the Chief says. "That's volatile information."

"I haven't told a soul," Chloe says softly. "I was waiting for you to get home."

After dealing with one liar after another all day long, the Chief is heartened to know he recognizes the truth when he hears it.

He takes a deep breath. "What's the other thing?"

"The other thing happened when I was clearing," Chloe says. "It was after the dessert, after the toasts, and I had a tray of champagne flutes I was taking back to the kitchen. I wasn't watching where I was going and I tripped and fell and the glasses all broke."

Broken glass, the Chief thinks. "Where did this happen?" he asks.

"At the place where the beach meets the lawn.

Over by the left side of the house if you're standing with your back to the water."

The Chief writes this down.

"The maid of honor helped me clean up," Chloe says. "And she was really cool. She asked my name and where I was from, and when I told her I was from Nantucket, she said I was the luckiest girl in the world." Chloe's voice gets thick and she wipes at her eyes. "I can't believe she's *dead*. She was a person I talked to *last night*."

"Sometimes things happen that way," the Chief says. "There's a good chance she took pills, maybe drank too much—"

"She wasn't drunk," Chloe says. "Not even a little bit. She seemed like the most sober person at the party."

"I just want you to realize, Chloe, that every single decision you make—who your friends are, who you date, whether you decide to smoke or drink—has a consequence. I think that Merritt, ultimately, was the victim of her own poor choices."

Chloe stares at the Chief for a second and he can see she resents his using Merritt's death as a public service announcement—but this is nothing if not a teachable moment. Chloe reaches for her phone and the Chief knows he's lost her. Andrea is better at dealing with Chloe; he always ends up sounding like the gruff uncle who also happens to be the chief of police.

"One other question, Chloe," he says, though he's sure she wants nothing more than to be rid of him. "Did Merritt *cut* herself when she was helping you clean up the glass?"

"Cut herself?" Chloe says. She looks up from her phone. "No. Why?"

"Just wondering," the Chief says. "Are you sure the two of you picked up every bit of glass?"

"It was dark," Chloe says. "We did the best we could. I was worried, actually, that Greer would find a piece of glass we missed and I would get in trouble for it today. But I guess they had bigger things to worry about."

The Chief stands up.

"Wait, can I show you one more thing?" Chloe says. She holds her phone up and scoots to the edge of the bed. The Chief takes a seat next to her. "Merritt is an influencer, so I started following her on Instagram last night when I got home. This was her last post."

The Chief accepts the phone from Chloe and puts on his reading glasses. He has never looked at Instagram before, and he sees it's nothing more than a photograph with a caption. In this instance, the photo is of two young women posing on the bow of the Hy-Line fast ferry. Their hair is windblown, and Nantucket is visible behind them in the background— the harbor, the sailboats, the gray-shingled fisherman cottages of the wharves, the steeples of the Unitarian and Congregational churches. The blond—Celeste, the bride, the Chief realizes—looks nervous; there's a hesitation in her smile. The brunette, Merritt, however, is beaming; she is luminous, giving the moment everything she has. *She's a good actress,* the Chief thinks. There's no hint or clue that she was pregnant with the baby of a married man and that he wanted nothing to do with her. The caption of the photo reads: *Goin' to the chapel…wedding weekend with the BEST FRIEND a woman could ask for. #maidofhonor #bridesmaid #happilyeverafter.*

"Hashtag happily ever after," Chloe says. "That's the part that kills me. Isn't that the saddest thing you've ever seen?"

"Just about," the Chief says, handing the phone back to Chloe. "Just about."

The Chief changes into casual clothes and looks longingly at the cold blue cans of Cisco beer in his fridge—but he can't relax yet. He has arranged to meet Nick back at the station to go over everything one last time.

"Don't worry about dinner," he tells Andrea. "I'll have Keira order us something."

"I hate murder investigations," Andrea says, lifting her face for a kiss. "But I love you."

"And I love you," he says. He gives his wife a kiss, a

second kiss, a third kiss. He thinks about letting Nick wait.

The Chief and Nick meet in an interview room back at the station. Keira, the Chief's assistant, has ordered a kale Caesar and a couple of artisanal pizzas from Station 21 so they can have a little dinner.

Nick takes a lusty bite of the shrimp and pancetta pizza. "This isn't bad," he says. "Normally I stay away from anything called 'artisanal.' I like my food real."

"Chloe said Merritt didn't cut herself when she helped clean up," the Chief says. "But she may have cut herself after the kayak ride. The place Chloe said she dropped the tray is right near the path Merritt would have taken to get back to her cottage."

"That could explain why Merritt went in the water," Nick says. "I mean, you'd rinse a cut at the water's edge, but you wouldn't go all the way in."

"Unless the water felt nice," the Chief says. "It *was* a hot night."

"And I'm guessing the maid of honor didn't care for the heat," Nick says. "The A/C in her bedroom was cranked to ten. It was practically snowing in there."

"But that doesn't tell us who slipped her the sleeping pill," the Chief says.

"She might have taken one herself," Nick says. "After all, we know she was upset."

"Doesn't that seem reckless?" the Chief asks. "Taking a sleeping pill when she's pregnant?"

"The father said she jumped off the kayak way out in the middle of the harbor, right? That's the definition of reckless. Her frame of mind was reckless, sounds like."

The Chief stabs a piece of kale in the round foil container in front of them. "I'm not liking this as an accident. There are two people who wanted Merritt to go away—Tag Winbury and Greer Garrison. And one person who wanted Featherleigh Dale to go away—Thomas Winbury."

"Calling it an accident would be easier on Merritt's family," Nick says. "And the bride."

"We don't work for her family," the Chief says. "We work for the Commonwealth of Massachusetts. And beyond that, we work in the name of justice for the citizens of this great country. Do *you* think it was an accident? Really?"

"No," Nick says. "I like the mother."

The Chief munches a crouton. "Funny. I like the father. Tag Winbury sees his wife's sleeping pills, drops one in Merritt's water glass. He then takes her out in the kayak and eliminates both his problems— no mistress, no baby. What's your angle?"

"Greer finds out about the affair and the baby and *she* drops a sleeping pill in the water, hoping Merritt will drink it and that Tag will take Merritt out in the kayak. Or maybe, *maybe,* Greer is trying to kill her husband. Maybe Greer slips him a mickey hoping he'll go out in the kayak and never return." Nick picks up a piece of the sausage pizza. "Yes, I do realize how far-fetched that sounds."

"It would be different, maybe, if we had that water glass," the Chief says.

Nick cocks his head. "Does it seem odd to you that the water glass was cleared from the table but the shot glasses remained? Someone took *only the water glass* inside. Or someone came out and cleared *only the water glass.*"

The Chief shakes his head and picks up his own piece of pizza. He can't believe that Chloe is the one who dropped the tray of glasses. Shard of glass on the lawn, cut foot, maid of honor goes into the ocean to wash it off, dead maid of honor. It's not Chloe's fault; no one on earth would think that. But if Chloe hadn't dropped the tray, would Merritt still be alive? Yes, if she hadn't taken a sleeping pill or been slipped a sleeping pill and then gone into the water, she *would* be alive. Limping down the aisle of the church, maybe. But alive.

"The fact is, we don't have enough evidence to charge anyone," Nick says.

The Chief knows Nick is right. "Tomorrow we'll call the brother back and tell him we concluded it was an accident. She took a sleeping pill, she went for a nighttime swim, she drowned."

"There were so many secrets in that house," Nick says. "I can't believe one of them didn't cause this."

The Chief raises his cup of coffee. "To the deceased," he says.

Nick touches his cup to the Chief's. "May she rest in peace."

Saturday, July 7, 2018, 6:55 p.m.

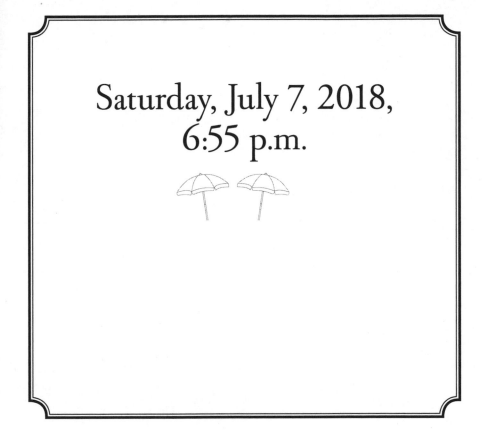

NANTUCKET

The Nantucket Standard — www .ackstandard.net — Saturday, July 7, 2018

Nantucket Police Department Rules Drowning Death Accidental

8:12 p.m.

The Nantucket Police Department, in conjunction with the Massachusetts State Police, has ruled the death of Merritt Alison Monaco, 29, of New York, New York, early this morning, an accident. Ms. Monaco was on Nantucket to serve as an attendant at a wedding on Saturday. She is survived by her parents, Gary and Katherine Monaco, of Commack, New York, as well as a brother, Douglas Monaco, of Garden City, New York. Ms. Monaco was employed by the New York Wildlife Conservation Society and has served as their director of public relations since 2016.

Chief Edward Kapenash of the Nantucket Police Department said, "We have investigated the case and determined Ms. Monaco's death was an accident. We thank the entire Nantucket community for their cooperation and encourage locals and visitors to the island alike to exercise extreme caution in and around the water."

Marty Szczerba gets an alert from the *Inky* on his phone: The maid of honor out in Monomoy apparently drowned accidentally. It sounds suspicious to Marty, and it also feels a bit anticlimactic—after the person of interest trying to escape on the Hy-Line and the dramatic removal of Featherleigh Dale from the Crosswinds restaurant, it turns out the death was *accidental?*

Huh, Marty thinks.

Then Marty realizes this means Featherleigh Dale isn't a murder suspect and thus might be interested in a little romance. Marty can't see himself pursuing anything like a one-night stand, but a drink might be nice.

He decides to call the police station to ask Keira if she knows if Featherleigh was brought back to the airport or taken to stay at an inn overnight.

"Hey, Keira," Marty says when she answers. "This is Marty Szczerba. I have a question for you."

"Hey, Marty," Keira says. Just the sound of her voice reminds Marty that he still harbors a terrific crush on Keira. "I have a question for *you*. When are you ever going to ask me out?"

Marty blinks. The phone grows warm in his hand. *Featherleigh who?* he thinks. "How about tonight?" he says.

Celeste texts Benji to let him know she's taking a taxi back from the hospital.

I'll just come get you! Benji says.

Please don't, Celeste responds. Three dots appear and then a second text comes through. We can talk when I get back.

Benji feels suddenly hot and prickly, uncomfortable in his own skin for the first time in his life. How he longs to shed his identity at this moment. He no longer wants to be a Winbury. Celeste has obviously learned about Merritt and Tag. They were having some kind of affair, some kind of *something*—Benji couldn't bear to press for details—but he has a feeling his father is to blame for Merritt's death.

His own father.

You think your family is beyond reproach, Celeste had said. *But you're wrong.*

*   *   *

Benji meets Celeste out in the driveway but she gives him a hollow look and says, "I need a minute, please, Benji. I have to talk to my parents."

He says, "Your parents aren't the priority right now, Celeste. I'm your fiancé. We were supposed to get *married* today."

She walks right past him and into the house, and it's all Benji can do not to follow behind her like a puppy dog.

Instead, he heads to the kitchen and watches Thomas pile a plate high with sandwiches and potato salad and summer fruit that the caterer had dropped off earlier that afternoon as scheduled—it was supposed to be the pre-wedding lunch—and when Thomas notices Benji staring at him, he says, "What? I'm hungry, and my wife is pregnant and needs food."

Benji says in the calmest voice he can manage, "Is this Dad's fault? Was he *screwing* her?"

"Sounds like it," Thomas says matter-of-factly. He notices the look of disgust that crosses Benji's face. "Oh, don't be such an altar boy, Benny."

Altar boy? Benji thinks. Does it make him an *altar boy* to expect his father to be a man of character and integrity, to not cheat on their mother with someone Benji's age, someone who also happened to be *Celeste's best friend?* "Did you *know* about this?" Benji asks.

"Not really," Thomas says. "But I saw Dad in the bar at the Four Seasons downtown a few weeks ago and he hid from me. I figured *something* was going on." Thomas blinks. "Now I know what that something was."

Benji shudders. The Four Seasons downtown? It was like *that,* like an affair from a novel or a movie? Thomas disappears down the hall with his plate before Benji can ask what *Thomas* had been doing at the Four Seasons downtown.

He doesn't want to know.

Benji loiters at the mail table at the bottom of the stairs until he hears Celeste leaving her parents' room, then he races to the second floor and catches her right before she enters her/his/their bedroom. His bedroom that she was using as a bridal suite that will become their bedroom in this house.

"Celeste."

She turns. "I need to lie down," she says.

"I understand you're tired," he says. He lets her enter the room, follows her, then closes the door behind them.

"Benji," she says.

Her wedding dress is hanging on the closet door; it's as unsettling to him as a headless ghost. "You're not going to marry me," he says. "Are you? Like at all, ever?"

"No," she says. "I'm sorry, Benji, I'm not."

Benji's entire body goes numb. He nods but he feels like his head is being pulled by a string. Celeste! He wants to talk her out of it. He wants to explain that she shouldn't judge him by his family's actions. He's not his father. He's not his brother. He's a good, true person and he will love her forever.

But he stops himself. Every single thing that Benji has comes from his parents—the money, the apartment, the education, the advantages. To denounce his family, to deny his unconditional love for them, would be disingenuous, and Celeste would recognize it as such. He has taken the privilege for granted for twenty-eight years, and now he has to accept the shame.

"What are you going to do?" he asks.

"I'm not sure," she says. "Maybe take a trip. Maybe not."

"I know it seems inconceivable right now," Benji says, "but you will get past this. I don't mean to say you'll ever stop missing Merritt…"

"Benji," Celeste says, and Benji clamps his mouth shut. He sounds like an ass. "My decision doesn't have anything to do with Merritt."

"It doesn't?" he says.

She shakes her head. "It has to do with me."

She doesn't want to marry him.

He would like to say this comes as a complete shock, a wrecking ball out of nowhere—but it doesn't.

"Your stutter is gone," he says.

She smiles, sadly at first, but then with a touch of relief—or triumph. "Yes," she says. "I know."

As Benji is walking back to the first cottage—he needs to hide; he can't bear to see either of his parents—he spies Shooter walking down the driveway.

Shooter. Benji has completely lost track of him, of time, of everything. Shooter looks like he's just survived a shipwreck. He's unshaven, his blue oxford is rumpled and untucked, he has his navy blazer crushed under one arm, and his mouth is hanging open as he stares at his phone.

"You look even worse than I feel," Benji says, trying for the jocular tone they normally use with each other. "Where have you been?"

"Police station," Shooter says. He follows Benji into the first cottage, then goes straight to the fridge and flips the top off a bottle of beer. "Want one?"

"Sure," Benji says.

"Listen, there are some things you need to know," Shooter says.

"Spare me, please," Benji says. "I've heard too much already."

Spare me, please. I've heard too much already.
Shooter lets that comment sink in. He was finally

released from the police station; in the end, they had nothing to hold him on except impeding an active investigation. They issued him a ticket for three hundred dollars, which he paid in cash. Val Gluckstern had offered him a ride back to Summerland, but he said he wanted to walk. He needed to clear his head.

He hadn't been sure how much he would need to explain. Maybe everything. Maybe nothing. He wanted very badly to talk to Celeste but he was afraid. He had spilled the beans to the police, which already felt like a betrayal. He was afraid Celeste would be angry, but he was more afraid she would deny that she had ever intended to run away with him.

As he was walking down the Winburys' white-shell driveway between the rows of hydrangeas and under the boxwood arch, his phone pinged. It was a text from an unfamiliar 212 number. Shooter had clicked on the text more out of habit than anything else.

It was a picture of Shooter and Celeste standing outside Steamboat Pizza. They weren't touching, though they were very close together—too close, probably. Shooter clicked on the photo and zoomed in. Celeste was looking in the vague direction of the camera and Shooter was looking at Celeste, his expression one of naked desire, longing, covetousness.

The photo is chilling, a threat. Did someone else know their plans? Who took it? Who sent it?

Shooter stopped dead in his tracks. He texted back: Who is this?

To which there was no response. Shooter ran through the possibilities. The 212 area code was Manhattan. And whoever this was either had been across the street or knew someone who was.

The implications were obvious, right? Someone was trying to scare him. If the photo was being sent to Shooter, it had probably also been sent to Benji. But Benji knew that Shooter and Celeste had gone to get pizza. It wasn't as if someone had sent a picture of Shooter and Celeste a few minutes later, sitting on the bench by the Steamship terminal. That would have been harder to explain.

Okay, fine. Honestly, Shooter was too tired for games. He proceeded under the boxwood arch and bumped right into Benji.

Spare me, please. I've heard too much already.

"I ran away from the police this morning," Shooter says. "They wanted to question me and I told them I had to use the john and then I slipped out the bathroom window."

"Shut up," Benji says.

"I'm serious."

Benji says, "I hope you told them you didn't want

to talk to the police because of what happened to your mother."

Shooter takes a long pull off his beer. Benji is the only person who knows about Shooter's mother, Cassandra. She became addicted to heroin after Shooter's father died, but she had happened to OD during one of Shooter's rare visits home. He was twenty-one years old, working as a bartender in Georgetown, and he gave Cassandra a fifty-dollar bill. She had spent it on smack. Shooter had woken up in the morning to find his mother dead. And, yes, he had blamed himself. He had basically begged the Dade County police to arrest him, but they had far too much experience with overdoses to blame anyone but the user herself.

"I hopped on the Hy-Line and they caught me, cuffed me, brought me to the police station. I hired a lawyer. She sat with me while I gave my account of last night."

Benji barely reacts. It's as if he expects these kinds of theatrics from Shooter. Either that or he's not really listening. "They found something in Merritt's bloodstream," Benji says. "Pills."

"Really," Shooter says. "How is Celeste taking it?"

Benji shoots up off the sofa. "How is Celeste *taking* it?" he says. "Well, let's see, she was so hysterical that she spent half the day in the emergency room. And yet she seems to have gained a certain clarity. She doesn't want to marry me. At all. Ever."

Shooter is suddenly very alert, despite his profound exhaustion. What is Benji going to say next?

"She says it has nothing to do with what happened to Merritt. It has to do with *her*. She doesn't want to marry me—not next month, not next year, not on a beach in Aruba, not at city hall in Easton, Pennsylvania. She doesn't want to marry me. When was she going to tell me this? Was she going to stand me up at the altar? Oh, and guess what else. Guess what else. Just guess."

Shooter doesn't want to guess, which is okay because Benji isn't waiting for an answer.

"Her stutter is gone! Completely gone! She decides she's not going to marry me and her speech impediment disappears."

Her stutter was gone last night, Shooter thinks. If Benji had paid attention, he would have realized that. When Celeste and Shooter left the bench next to the Steamship terminal, they had gone back to get pizza, and when Shooter asked Celeste what she wanted, she said, "Slice of pepperoni and a root beer, please." Her words had been as clear as the peal of church bells on a summer morning.

"Did she say anything else?" Shooter asks. His plan of running away with Celeste was incredibly cowardly, he sees now. Because this—Benji's reckoning—wasn't anything Shooter wanted to witness.

"Anything *else?*" Benji says. "She didn't need to

say anything else. She destroyed me." He winds up and throws his beer bottle across the room, where it hits the wall and shatters. Benji puts his hands over his face. He makes a choking noise and Shooter realizes he's crying.

Shooter Uxley has envied Benjamin Winbury since the day they met at the St. George's School freshman year, and although Shooter has always longed to have something, anything, that Benji couldn't have, all that comes to mind now are the infinite kindnesses that Benji has shown him: The day after Shooter's mother died, Benji skipped his economics midterm at Hobart and flew down to Miami. During their senior year at St. George's, when Shooter was so destitute that he organized an illegal dice game, it was Benji who had encouraged people to come and gamble. Benji had been a prefect, he could have gotten in trouble, lost his position, faced suspension, but none of that had been as important to him as giving Shooter the opportunity to make enough money to stay at school.

Benji had picked Shooter over his own brother to be his best man.

Benji had always believed in Shooter and continues to believe in him, even as Shooter came *this close* to stealing his bride away.

Celeste has done her part. She has broken things

off. This is how things should go. Let Benji deal with the breakup and let Celeste deal with losing Merritt. After some time passes, Shooter and Celeste can be together. *How much time will that be?* he wonders. He is, by nature, a very impatient person. He wants to start his life with Celeste today.

He decides he will keep the picture of himself with Celeste. It arrived like an anonymous gift from the universe; when Shooter looks at it, he will remember that he finally has something in his life worth waiting for. He will remember that she said yes.

Shooter stands up. He reaches out for Benji, hugs him tight; he absorbs the shudders of Benji's sobs.

He says nothing.

Saturday, July 7, 2018,
8:00 p.m.

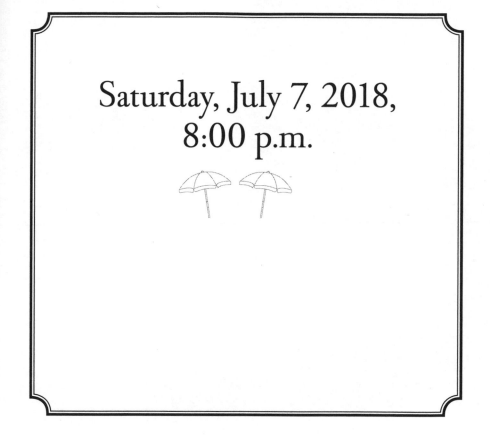

GREER

There's a knock on Greer's bedroom door and she stands.

"Yes?"

Elida, the housekeeper, enters the room. It's way past time for Elida to leave. Even with the wedding, she was supposed to be gone by three so she could attend the ceremony at four. But here she is, quietly and steadfastly doing her job.

"Elida," Greer says, and tears rise in her eyes. What does it say that in her household she can only trust two people: her younger son and her housekeeper?

From behind her back, Elida produces Greer's pillbox.

"What?" Greer says. Her novelist mind immediately wonders if *Elida* had anything to do with Merritt's death. Perhaps Elida learned about the affair and the baby and poisoned the girl out of fealty to Greer.

That would be an unexpected upstairs-downstairs twist. "Where did you find this?"

Elida says, "In Mr. Thomas's room. In the trash."

In Thomas's room, in the trash. In the *trash?* Thomas knows how much Greer cherishes this pill-box. She can't believe he would throw it away. Greer takes the box from Elida. There are still pills inside; she can hear them.

"Thank you, Elida," Greer says. "You can go home."

Elida slips out of the room. Greer returns the pill-box to its rightful place in the medicine cabinet. Then she marches upstairs.

As Greer approaches Thomas's bedroom door, she hears yelling. This is hardly surprising; Greer would very much like to yell herself. She quickly realizes the voices she's hearing belong to Thomas and Abby.

Greer's first thought is that yelling can't be good for the baby, but then she recalls that her greatest rows with Tag were when she was pregnant. Her hormones had turned her into a lunatic with pendulum swings between elation and despair. The worst row—when Greer was bored out of her mind, pregnant with Thomas, and Tag was at work every night until ten and on business trips across Europe every weekend—had actually resulted in Greer picking up a pen and writing her first novel, *Prey in the Saint-Germain-des-Prés.*

Greer sighs. Thoughts of her first novel lead her to thoughts of her twenty-first novel, due in thirteen days. Well, it won't get done now, and no one will blame her. Her husband's pregnant mistress was found dead outside her house on the morning of her son's wedding. Greer gets a pass.

Greer stands just outside the bedroom door, where she can hear distinct words and phrases. She loathes eavesdropping; she's going to insist they pipe down. The last thing anyone else in this house needs to hear is Thomas and Abby's marital squabbling.

But then Greer hears Abby say, "I've known about you and Featherleigh for years, since Virgin Gorda, since Tony Berkus's graduation party at the Carlyle Hotel! Amy Lackey told me she saw you with a trashy-looking woman at L'Entrecôte in Paris on a weekend you told me you were visiting your parents in London. I've read all your texts and e-mails and picked through your credit card bills, including the British Airways Visa Signature card you think I know nothing about!"

Greer stops herself from knocking just in time. Thomas and Featherleigh? *Thomas?* Featherleigh is fifteen years his senior. Surely that can't be right?

"I told you, I broke it off," Thomas says. "I broke it

off for good in May, as soon as we found out about the baby."

Wait! Greer thinks. *Featherleigh told Greer that she had broken up with a married man in May.*

It's a disheartening discovery indeed that Thomas seems to have inherited Tag's questionable morals, setting Abby up to be just like Greer, a generation later.

Thank God Benji is a Garrison, through and through.

"There is no breaking it off for good when it comes to you and Featherleigh," Abby says. "Look at last night! I *saw* you with her under the tent. I saw you! And I knew what was going to happen. You were going to appease me by coming upstairs, and then as soon as I was asleep, you were going to screw her in the pool house!"

"You're crazy," Thomas says. "I came upstairs and Featherleigh *left*, Abby. She left for her inn or her guesthouse. I don't even know where she was staying, that's how little I cared—"

"She did *not* leave!" Abby says. "I sneaked downstairs while you were in the bathroom brushing your teeth and I heard her in the powder room humming 'The Lady in Red.' She wasn't going anywhere. She was lying in wait for you."

At that instant, Greer figures it out.

She hurries back down to her bedroom and finds her cell phone.

She sends a text to both Thomas and Abby. It says: Lower your voices. Everyone can hear you.

Thomas has been having a years-long affair with Featherleigh, and Elida found the pillbox in Thomas's bedroom. In the trash.

Well.

Tag is the plotter, not Greer, but after twenty-one murder mysteries, she has learned a thing or two about motivation. Greer saw Abby last night when she went to the kitchen to pour herself the final glass of Veuve and *left her pills on the counter*. Abby had either snatched the pills up then or noted their existence. Much later, she went down to see if Featherleigh had left. She overheard Featherleigh humming in the powder room and must have decided to put the old girl to sleep... to keep her from fooling around with Thomas.

And who could blame her?

Abby dropped a pill in Featherleigh's drink, only the drink had gone to the wrong person. It had somehow gone to Merritt.

The police have ruled Merritt's death accidental — and an accident it indeed was. Abby may not even realize she's to blame, and Thomas will never put two and two together. The secret resides with Greer, and with Greer it will remain until her death.

The future of the Winbury family depends on it.

Saturday, July 7, 2018, 2:47 a.m.

NANTUCKET

Nantucket Island holds her people's secrets.

When Merritt Monaco and Tag Winbury get back from the kayak ride, Merritt is soaking wet and crying. Tag is a man struggling with both fury and feelings of tenderness. Merritt staggers off down the beach, and Tag kicks over the kayak, bringing up a spray of wet sand. He considers going after Merritt but instead heads up to the house. She can't be reasoned with right now; he'll have to postpone further talks until after the wedding.

Merritt turns her face just enough to see Tag scurry for the safety of his home base. She can't believe how craven and heartless he has turned out to be. Only a few weeks ago, she found him standing outside her apartment building like a lovesick teenager; now, he is someone else entirely.

Merritt wrenches the silver ring off her thumb and throws it into the water, then immediately regrets it. This is another childish gesture on her part. The first was jumping off the kayak when they were hundreds of yards offshore. Merritt was like any other woman who went to desperate measures to gain her lover's attention.

There had been one moment when Merritt had believed she would drown. She was so tired, so lethargic, her limbs were too leaden to swim, and she'd nearly sunk to the harbor floor like a stone.

Tag had grabbed her by the wrist and hauled her back up onto the kayak. He had been even angrier then than he was when they started out.

It was a fling, he said, *for* fun, *for a* release, *for* escape. *Nothing more, Merritt. Nothing more!*

You were obsessed with me, she said, but her words had been garbled and he didn't understand her. If he had understood her, he would have denied it, but Merritt knows he was obsessed, captivated, enraptured. For hours, days, weeks, he thought of nothing but her.

The problem is it didn't last. The obsession, such as it was, vanished as capriciously as it had arrived. Merritt longs to inspire a more substantial feeling, a real feeling—like what Benji and Celeste feel for each other.

Benji and Celeste are the perfect couple. Merritt wants what they have more than she wants anything else in this world.

It's very late, and Merritt can barely keep her eyes open. She could lie down on the beach right now and sleep until morning, but if she does that, she is sure to wake up to Greer standing over her with a disapproving glare.

Merritt stumbles back up toward the flagstone path that leads around the house to the second cottage. She indulges in a fantasy that Tag is waiting inside the cottage for her or that he has left a note or a rose cut from the garden on her pillow. Anything.

Merritt cries out. There is a rude, sharp pain. She lifts her foot and pulls a shard of glass from her soft instep. She's at the edge of the lawn, where the cute young girl dropped the tray of champagne flutes.

There is blood everywhere. Merritt stumbles back into the sand. Now there's sand in the cut. She will have to rinse it and hop back up to the path.

Salt water is supposed to cure everything, but Merritt doesn't expect the sting. She looks down to see a plume of blood rise and she cries fresh tears. That girl, the niece of the Nantucket police chief, had gazed at Merritt with such wide-eyed awe; she had no idea what kind of mess Merritt had made of her life.

She's pregnant. And alone.

It's okay, Merritt thinks. She will raise the child by

herself; she will hardly be the first woman to do so. Maybe she will write a blog: *Millennial Influencer Turned Unwed Mother.* Merritt's eyes drift close. Rousing herself feels like pulling on a rope to get out of a deep, dark hole—but she does it. When she opens her eyes, she sees a glint of silver on the ocean floor a few yards away.

Her ring.

Yes, she thinks. She should get the ring. It's the only present Tag will ever give her. She will save it for her baby. The baby will no doubt be a girl, and long after Merritt has moved on to the next man and the man after that, she will whisper to her daughter, *This is a ring your father gave me. Your real father.*

Merritt wades in and bends down to grab the ring but she kicks it accidentally and she has to wait for the sand to settle before she can find it again. She is unreasonably sleepy, too sleepy to stand, and so she spreads her arms and legs out and she floats. She opens her eyes underwater.

Where is the ring?

There it is. She sees it.

Like love, she thinks, *it is just beyond her reach.*

ACKNOWLEDGMENTS

I want to start by thanking Detective Sergeant Tom Clinger of the Nantucket Police Department for meeting with me to run through procedure. Because of the nature of the novel and its timetable, I had to make changes that would not happen in a real investigation. Rest assured, Tom gave me good information. His mother, Marie, should be quite proud!

Thank you to my brother, the NOAA/NWS meteorologist Douglas Hilderbrand, who explained in detail how fog happens. He also advocates for people being "weather ready"—and after this past year, I'm with him.

Cindy Auris: You get all credit for introducing me to Meat Loaf back in the 1970s. I've been trying to get "Paradise by the Dashboard Light" into a novel for eighteen years and I've finally done it!

My editor, Reagan Arthur, *yet again* edited this book with sheer brilliance. I tell you the woman is always right, and she *is* always right. For any aspiring writers out there who think a novel like this comes easily and on the first try, I am here to tell you it is hard work, mind-bending work, that requires revision after revision after revision. I am fortunate to have an incredibly intelligent, thoughtful, and clear-eyed sensibility like Reagan's to guide me to my final draft.

To my agents, Michael Carlisle and David Forrer of Inkwell Management: I love you both beyond words. You are my people.

To my publicist, Katharine Myers: You are a kind, gentle, and patient woman, the calm eye in the hurricane of my public life, and I want to say, in equal parts, thank you for all you do and I'm sorry for the chaos and the "enormous changes at the last minute" that are my trademark.

To Tayler Kent: Thank you for continuing in the tradition of great nannies for the Cunningham children. I couldn't have written this novel without you doing the things I was too busy to do and doing it with style, a sense of fun, and unwavering competence.

To my friends, the women in my barre class at Go Figure, and the parents I have sat next to in the football stadium, on the basketball court, by the baseball diamond: Thank you for giving me a community worth bragging about. Special thanks to Rebecca Bartlett, Debbie Briggs, Wendy Hudson, Wendy Rouillard, Elizabeth and Beau Almodobar, Chuck and Margie Marino, John and Martha Sargent, Heidi and Fred Holdgate (Fred was a huge help with all details Nantucket airport–related), Evelyn and Matthew MacEachern, Mark and Gwenn Snider and the entire staff at the Nantucket Hotel, Dan and Kristen Holdgate, Melissa and Angus MacVicar, Jana and Nicky Duarte, Linda Holliday and Dr. Sue Decoste, Paul and Ginna Kogler, the Timothy Fields big and small, Manda Riggs, David Rattner and Andrew Law, West Riggs (who helped me choose the Winburys' boats), Helaina Jones, Marty and Holly McGowan, Scott and Logan O'Connor, Liza and Jeff Ottani (parents of my favorite child Kai), Sheila and Kevin Carroll (parents of my other favorite child Liam), Carolyn Durand of Lee Real Estate, who showed me one of her gorgeous properties in Monomoy so I could better describe the Winburys' home. Thank you to Cam Jones for the inside intel on St. George's School, and to Julia Asphar, about Miami of Ohio.

Thank you to my mother, Sally Hilderbrand; to my siblings, especially my stepsister Heather Osteen Thorpe, the very best friend I have in this world; and to Judith and Duane Thurman, who have been second parents to me for more than thirty years.

Acknowledgments

Always, at the end of this page, I thank my children. It is such a bittersweet year for me as my eldest, Maxwell, heads off to college in the fall. I sold my first novel, *The Beach Club,* in the spring of 1999 when I was pregnant with Maxx, and so his life and my career have run parallel. Maxx Cunningham: I am so proud of you and all you've accomplished, but let me tell you, the best is yet to come, and I can't wait to see it. To Dawson: You are my well-adjusted middle child, possibly the most beloved person on the entire island of Nantucket, and, yes, you do take up 90 percent of my parenting energy but I wouldn't change a thing about you (this might be hyperbole... look it up). To Shelby: You are my hero—at age twelve, already a "strong and independent woman"—and I strive every day to be even half the mother that you deserve.

In closing, I want to acknowledge and send love, strength, and clarity to each and every breast cancer survivor who reads this book. Thank you to the hard-working wonder-folks at the Breast Cancer Research Foundation and to my medical oncologist, Dr. Steven Isakoff, who continues to keep me healthy, four years after my initial diagnosis. It's a journey or it's a battle—you pick what you want to call it—but someday soon, we are going to triumph. We are all going to call ourselves survivors.

ABOUT THE AUTHOR

Elin Hilderbrand is a graduate of Johns Hopkins University and the Iowa Writers' Workshop. She has lived on Nantucket for more than twenty-five years and is the mother of three teenagers. *The Perfect Couple* is her twenty-first novel.